The Turn of the Tide

The dinner party, an unexpected guest, Joris Sanderson's past comes back to haunt him, now woven into a thread of lies. It's imperative the mystery of "Amber" is solved. He has too much on his mind. He's hosting the PM's daughter's wedding; the last thing he needs is Harriet's mother broadcasting it to the press. It's a private affair with good reason, the political stakes are high. Favours for favours, he wants Barry Giordano of MI6 out of Harriet's life for good but can the PM oblige? Joris Sanderson is uncomfortable and not without good reason. He's yet to learn of Rapping Hammer's evil scheming, maliciously sucking in his PhD student Ross Farquerhart. He's yet to learn his past has been viciously tumbled out to Harriet, his "beautiful amber butterfly". That damned dinner party, the chaos theory proved but will it prove too much for Harriet? Will she decide to flutter from his life?

My thanks and appreciation to
Richard Franklin
My ever helpful Publisher
and
To all those enthusiastic followers of Harriet
Who make the writing therein so worth while

Foreword

As this book is the fifth in an ongoing series, please allow me to introduce you to the characters central to the story. Of course you may already have met Harriet and Mark Glover in my first novel, 'A Question of Answers' where the scene is set. Harriet and Mark first meet at university, in the supplies store. Behind each other in the queue they discover they share the same surname, 'Glover'. Herein lies the problem. This coincidence serves only to reinforce Mark's need to remain single. Serves only to reinforce Harriet's desire for marriage and one more baby. Frustrated, she finds herself falling for her boss, the head of her school; the charismatic, charming Mr. Sanderson.

And so we have:

Joris Sanderson, born to a wealthy family of merchant bankers, educated Eton, Cambridge, to qualify as a GP, threw it in to end up Head of **Stetmead Street Primary**, a priority area school where he appointed Harriet. A keen sailor, prominent in the fraternity he decided to open **Starboard Marine North West**, a flourishing business extending support to the children and parents of the school in both a social and educational context. With many friends in high places, this old boy network looks after each other and **Terry and Clive Engells**, well to do brothers, are no exception. Terry and Joris are keen sailors, having frequently entered the Fastnet yacht race, whilst Clive, although an accomplished sailor is rather more grounded, handing over the managing of the 'Lantern Box Hotel' in Dorset to his brother, having made the decision to settle in Wirral.

Harriet and **Mark** and their two daughters **Rachael** and **Clare**, both in their early twenties and newly married, living down South.

Harriet's mother **Frances**, intent on impressing all her WI friends with her social standing, lives constantly in fear of Harriet dragging herself and her husband **George** down to a level from which they'll never recover. Frances is a snob and can't deal with the changing mores of everyday life. Harriet struggles to please her. After all her brothers have managed marriage. **James** to posh **Geraldine.** They have a married daughter **Clarissa**. **Paul** married **Susan** whom Harriet envies. She had another baby last summer and as Harriet observes, they already have four children!

From the outset Frances has had no time for Mark since he got Harriet pregnant just as she started university and made no attempt to marry her.

Mark's mum and dad, **Shirley** and **Harold** aren't too sure about Harriet, either. Oh they were delighted when their own daughter frothed her way down the aisle in a cloud of white netting but no, they're more than happy Mark has never made the same commitment to Harriet. They are good, solid down-to-earth people. Not short of money since they've spent a life-time watching it very carefully.

Harriet and Mark had been wanting to move house for a while. Finally a buyer came along and they planned to move from **4 The Willows** to **1 Haystack Close**. With contracts exchanged and heading for completion the sale fell through. Shirley and Harold stepped in, offering to pay Mark's half of the compensation due to Joris Sanderson who was purchasing the house to add to his business property investment portfolio.

Mark is a scientist and prior to his promotion relocating him to Basingstoke, worked on global warming along with **Geoffrey** and **Melissa**, married only briefly. Melissa leant heavily on Mark following her quick divorce. Harriet can't stand Melissa Scott who mislead Mark regarding her pregnancy after their brief affair.

Harriet, now deputy, teaches at **Stetmead Street Primary school**. This school has many disadvantaged children and Harriet works very hard to redress the balance. The children love her, as do the parents. She's acquired a certain authority; a certain influence over them that **Mr. Sanderson**, the Head and **Mr. Whittle** the Area Chief Inspector sometimes find difficult to deal with. Not to mention **Mr. Brown**, the caretaker. He's convinced Harriet has it 'in' for him and he's constantly threatening her with legal action, always consulting **Mr. Potts** the union man much to Mr. Sanderson's fury. The school has a newcomer, a PhD student **Ross Farquerhart** just back from the Galapagos Islands, researching evolution, fossils and now the lost Roman 9th Legion.

Of course Harriet's undoing is Mr. Sanderson. No matter how hard she tries she just can't get this tall, good-looking guy out of her system and she continues to pay a very high price for compromising her professionalism. She needed space to think and so ended up on an escapade in Venice with Tricia. Here they met **Barry Giordano** and his colleague **Andy** both working for MI6 which was to prove disastrous for Harriet. Barry, amongst other things is an artist which proved her undoing. Divorced, he fell for Harriet in a big way and set out to eliminate the competition.

Before her departure, Mr. Sanderson relied heavily on his newly appointed deputy **Lucinda Lawton**, with whom it was rumoured he'd been having an affair much to Harriet's fury. **Joris Sanderson** is frequently absent from school due to him attending to various business interests, the main one being the afore mentioned Starboard Marine North West, a boat chandlers. A skilled yachtsman he saw the need and opened the business just over a year ago. Never still, last Christmas he installed a coffee shop there after buying out an American coffee franchise company. The place is now well frequented by the parents, as intended. The aim being to lift the life chances of both children and parents alike. Courses of all kinds are run there, including many related to sailing.

A much respected member of the sailing club, Mr. Sanderson managed to gain cooperation from **Tarquin Bridgewater** the Commodore. He, together with the majority of club members, willingly agreed to give the school children and their parents the opportunity to learn to sail. It's flourishing. It seems the whole of Stetmead is thriving under the direction of the charismatic, wealthy **Joris Sanderson.**

Not surprisingly, his parents, **Olivia** and **Charles** are very wealthy, too. They have long-standing friends with one daughter, **Belinda Oxfordshire**, who grew up with Joris. She's classically beautiful and completely obsessed with him, as many women are. She's aware of Harriet's feelings for him and stops at nothing to put her down. **Belinda** works in an administrative capacity at Starboard Marine North West.

Harriet and Mark know **Tricia Harrington** and her husband **Bob** through the sailing club. Bob married Tricia knowing she was already pregnant with her son **Adam**. They have their own daughter, **Michelle**. **Tricia** is employed as a personal assistant/cashier under Belinda Oxfordshire at Starboard Marine North West. **Bob** is a civil engineer.

Harriet and Tricia are long time friends, though initially Harriet saw Tricia as a threat. Her unrelenting flirting with Mark constantly irritated her. However they both did have one thing in common, their attraction to Joris Sanderson. Almost opposite characters, yet this attraction served to bond them into a friendship which deepened as Harriet came to understand her better.

Tricia is scatty and alongside Harriet they make a lethal team. Desperate to provide a celebrity to draw the crowds to the opening of the coffee shop at

Starboard Marine North West on Christmas Eve, they landed on a local rock band **"Rapping Hammer and The Ironing Bards"** which, throughout the series has proved disastrous. They are the crudest, filthiest bunch of drug taking low-life around, causing mayhem and disruption the minute they appear.

Rapping (**Wayne**) **Hammer** has a brother, **Guy Hammer** who works in the local garden centre and has taken a fancy to Harriet.

Harriet first came into contact with **Simon Barnes** the "INTERNEWS TV" reporter on her return from Bruges. Because this guy has forged the link with Harriet and Joris Sanderson and his friends in very high places, he's never far away. Needless to say Rapping Hammer has done more than his bit to ensure their appearance on "INTERNEWS TV".

Harriet and Tricia met **Cedric** and **Violet Moss** during their trip to Venice. Violet considers herself to be posh so it's not surprising she was looking to downsize to a nice area and ended up buying the bungalow next door to Harriet's mum and dad. Now able to help their pregnant daughter **Avril** to buy a house, Violet is frustrated and insistent it be Harriet's as it would seem 4 the Willows is the only one Avril really wants.

Harriet met **Molly** and **Percy**, both widowed, on "**The Christiana**" cruise ship. Subsequently married they decided to sell both their properties to buy a house close to Joris Sanderson's in the wealthy location of **Lower Tideside**.

Finally I turn to Harriet's dearest friend, **Pepper**, her cat. Pepper is central to Harriet's well-being, though she has a mind of her own! This little black cat licks and purrs comfort into Harriet when there's no one else to turn to.

Now, before reading **'The Turn of the Tide'**, I hope you've learned enough to make you want to read **'A Question of Answers'** followed by **'Ne Obliviscaris: Do Not Forget'**, **'San Marco the End of the Road'**, and **'Amber'**.

The first book spans ten months, from new year to late autumn. The second continues on through Christmas to the following June. The third covers the next three turbulent weeks in Harriet's life whilst 'Amber' moves the story along to mid September.

However all the books do stand alone as new strands feed into the ongoing story of Harriet, enabling each book to conclude in its own particular way.

Contact via websites:

www.margarethendersonsmith.co.uk

www.aquestionofanswers.com

www.quicksandtimerbookreviews.wordpress.com

www.maryroseanna.wordpress.com

Join me on **Twitter** @Maryroseanna

Follow my boards on **Pinterest** and **Rebelmouse**

You can also find me on these social sites:

About.me and **Linkedin**

Also by Margaret Henderson Smith

A Question of Answers arima publishing 2008 (Kindle edition also available)

Harriet's life is going nowhere! Tired of trying to get her commitophobe partner to marry her, she finds herself falling for her boss, the gorgeous six foot blonde in charge of her school, only to discover she's not the only one! She soon learns he has fingers in other pies and dubious friends in high places.

This is a contemporary novel sparking off the conflicts between the differing worlds of the haves and have nots. Live the highs and lows of Harriet's dilemma as she takes you on a passionate yet humorous journey in pursuit of her dreams.

The Bookbag: review extract
"Margaret Henderson Smith has to perfection Harriet's feeling of being completely enraptured by the man and there were times when my heart ached for her."

"I hope that we'll hear more from Margaret Henderson Smith - and Harriet Glover."

Sue Magee: reviewer

The Writing Pad: review extract
The book is well written and has been well proof read, which makes a pleasant change. It's a promising debut from this new writer and we look forward to seeing more.

David Carter: reviewer

Ne Obliviscaris: Do Not Forget arima publishing 2009

Harriet. Caught between the steady and the charismatic. Wavering. Two very different men. She's trouble. Can't stay out of it. Still digging away. In serious danger of collapsing the fragile corners of her triangular existence into one big hole.

Can Mark really put his fear of marriage behind him? She's only looking for one answer. Unless of course 'that gorgeous hunk of a blonde' in charge of her school gets there first. Him? Unlikely. Different worlds. Too many questions.

A weft pf answers weave their way through the story. In and out. Criss-crossing the threads of rivalry, jealousy, anger, passion and desire. Ride all Harriet's emotions as she takes you on the rest of her journey. Then ask. 'Was she ever in control of her dreams?'

The Bookbag: review extract
"I enjoyed the story, particularly when we got towards what turned out to be a nail-biting finish."
Sue Magee: reviewer:

The Writing Pad: review extract
"The story unfurls with countless twists and turns that will keep you guessing right up to the very last page. Do Not Forget, Ne Obliviscaris, and do not forget to think about acquiring this book when you are next in buying mood.
David Carter: reviewer

A Flight of Fancy! arima publishing 2010

A collection of writings from 'The Big 40 Blog'

The Writing Pad: review extract
'The book is snappily written with short sentences that keep the pages moving along and because of that it's easy to read too and a fun read at that.
  David Carter: reviewer

San Marco the End of the Road arima publishing 2010

Just now Harriet envies the traffic lights outside Starboard Marine North West. Programmed. Devoid of anxiety, turmoil, indecision. Her life? One big hole! How did she manage to dig three men in so soon? She's fighting to get back to amber. But can she? In the face of serious revelations there's no safe place to be. How did she end up in Venice with Tricia? In serious trouble now. Both of them embroiled. Way out of depth.

This story, spiked with humour and the third in the series, tells the next three weeks in Harriet's life. Passionate, painful, tense and intriguing; go with the trail of devastation and fury only Harriet could leave as she tries in desperation to cling to her dreams.

The Bookbag: review extract
"She's adept at the Wodehousian slapstick scene, the quirky turn of events and the ridiculous consequences made to seem almost logical."
  Sue Magee: reviewer

The Writing Pad: review extract
"What on earth is going on?
  Well, mayhem, conspiracy and fun would just about describe it, but that dear reader is for you to discover.
  There are some really funny one liners in this book.....
  Harriet Glover is a character we have grown to cringe with, laugh with, sup with, cry with and sympathise with too."
  David Carter: reviewer Author of 'The Murder Diaries - Seven Times Over' (Kindle edition also available)

Amber arima publishing 2011

Fearing repercussions from the Venice affair, Mr. Sanderson insists Harriet and Tricia attend the school camp, only to suspend them from duty after causing mayhem. On her return, Harriet comes up with a great idea to help solve the parents' debt problems but refusing to heed all warnings, she finds herself up against the new pawnbroker and gets more than she bargains for, dragging Tricia in her wake. Still unable to get Mr. Sanderson out of her mind, she struggles to stay on amber but to Mark's annoyance, her burning desire for him outstrips her reason. That can only mean one thing. Trouble!

The Writing Pad: review extract
"But ultimately is it green for go or are the lights still stuck on amber for Harriet? I couldn't possibly say, but Harriet Glover is a character who has a wicked habit of getting under your skin, making you want to find out more.
David Carter: reviewer Author of 'The Legal & the Illicit'

Smart Read Easy arima publishing 2013

This child centred, simple route to reading for pre-school children has been tried and tested with great success over a number of years by the author, a psychology graduate and qualified teacher. The scheme, a distillation of sight reading and the currently favoured synthetic systematic phonics approach, encourages children to learn to read with Sam, a character they will find fun and very easy to identify with.

This scheme allows children to create their own first reading book which is followed by a series of fifteen short stories gradually extending most frequently used words to include the 45 key words to reading advised by the National Literacy Strategy. With pictures to colour and space for drawing, there is plenty of scope for children to have fun making this book their own.

With no punishing schedules to follow, this all inclusive activity book offers a very flexible approach, ensuring an enjoyable and satisfying reading adventure for both you and your child.

The Bookbag: four star review extract
A gentle and stress-free introduction to reading. Children build their own reading book and they're going to find this fun.
Sue Magee: reviewer

The Turn of the Tide

Margaret Henderson Smith

Published 2015 by arima publishing

www.arimapublishing.com

ISBN 978 1 84549 648 7
© Margaret Henderson Smith 2015

Printed and bound in the United Kingdom

Typeset in Garamond

Swirl is an imprint of arima publishing.

arima publishing
ASK House, Northgate Avenue
Bury St Edmunds, Suffolk IP32 6BB
t: (+44) 01284 700321
www.arimapublishing.com

Chapter 1

'It's him Pepper, it's him! Now just let me see I've got everything. No, I'm going to be needing these, I bet that front bedroom of his is icy cold and draughty at night. Quick let me put them on now.' Harriet found her knee length thermal pants, stretched them over her briefs before slipping herself back into her jeans to rush downstairs.

'No Pepper, in! In you go. I know you hate that basket but it's not going to be for long, twenty minutes at the most and we'll be there.'

She quickly checked her case, struggled to close the zip around the corners as the bulging lid fought with the angry teeth until finally they gripped, meshing themselves closed.

'Gosh I feel nervous, much worse than you sitting in that basket.' She clasped the locks closed expecting to hear Mr. Sanderson's key rattling the door any minute. 'Just my holdall now, Pepper,' she said to the basket, galloping up the stairs only to stop abruptly as the door swung open. She turned to see him smiling as he pushed it to.

'Ah all ready, I see. Here let me give you a hand with that,' insisted Mr. Sanderson, beaming, attacking the stairs two at a time.

'No cat Harriet?' He laughed.

'In her basket all ready and waiting in the kitchen,' she smiled, following him through.

'Look,' she said, flaring the fingers of her left hand to show him the rings and bangle he'd given her. 'I'm wearing them all, they're so very special.' He sighed, she watched his sharp blue eyes twinkle their usual prelude to that engaging smile. This handsome gorgeous man, she could scarcely believe he'd given her such beautiful gifts, could scarcely believe the words "I love you now and forever" he'd translated from the Latin, written on a small piece of paper placed inside the box holding the amber buttercup ring. Then she bent her head, aware of the flush of embarrassment colouring her cheeks. His baby growing inside her, she'd only just admitted it to him. This gorgeous, gorgeous man. Tall, solid, strong, his mop of long blonde hair still uncut since his return from the Galapagos Islands; tousled, falling in waves all the way down to his shoulders, culminating in a running edge of curls, lifting then splitting as he flicked it all away from his face. This man standing there in his white fisherman's knit sweater, from his body the faint smell of sea salt. She watched him roll up his sleeves, noticed the instant spread of blonde hairs on his arms lift to settle fair against his deeply tanned skin. Clasping his hands now behind his head, his sweater rising, her eyes moving swiftly away from the buckle at his waist. She followed his long, muscular legs all the way down to the double row of red stitching sitting along the hem of his navy denim jeans to finally rest her eyes at his feet. Felt his hand lifting her chin. Unable now, to avoid his eyes, quietly she spoke.

'Thank you. How can I ever thank you for all these beautiful things. For all these beautiful words?'

'Don't even try.' He placed his finger on her lips. Drew her so close she could feel her breasts against his body, could feel that part of him at which she'd scarcely dared look pressing hard against her abdomen. Pressing hard into their baby growing inside her. His lips, warm, soft, gentle against hers, then deeper, harder, like a rush of tingling stars, floating her mind away to leave only that driving intensity of desire channelling all her senses into a complexity of need for him she could barely contain. Releasing her gently for a couple of seconds he held her firmly at arms length, this driving desire now permeating every demanding, aching fibre of her body. His expression serious now, his eyes, his mouth, hardening, reflecting every escapade she'd ever created.

'And this time we'll do it my way, shall we? Understand?!'

She looked up at him before resting her head against his chest.

'You mean you're not allowing me to stay on amber, Mr. Sanderson?'

'I mean exactly that Harriet. It's high time I took you in hand. I should have done it long since.'

Chapter 2

'Now Harriet, are you quite sure you've got everything? You're not taking this laundry basket thing, I hope?' Mr. Sanderson laughed.

'Laundry basket? Oh golly no. Oh you mean this? But that's not a laundry basket Mr. Sanderson, that's Pepper's basket. Nearly forgot.'

He narrowed his eyes,

'Not that ludicrous, it's certainly large enough for one Harriet. Can you manage it if I take this lot?'

'Certainly can Mr. Sanderson Come on Pepper, sorry.'

'Apology accepted.'

'Not you, the cat! Wouldn't do to forget you now, would it Pepper? Oh her food. Just let me get that.'

He drew an exaggerated breath.

'Now I think you'll find Mrs. Harris has a stock of that in, having fed Molly's cat for at least the last three weeks. Come on Harriet, sure you wouldn't like to bring your knitting as well?'

'Yes, actually that's a good idea.'

'Not! It'll be bad enough competing with that damned cat!'

'Been kicking around for some time that one.'

'Oh no she hasn't. She's exactly two.'

Mr. Sanderson laughed. 'Not the cat, it's that disreputable thing you trail around like a set of bagpipes. All those lethal points sticking out! Anyhow who's to be the lucky recipient? Or unlucky depending on whether they get stabbed to death whilst trying to come up for air in the struggle to put it on.' He stepped back to better absorb the delights of watching the colour flush her cheeks.

'Well I'm not exactly sure who it's going to be for yet and if you want it, you're certainly not going about it the right way. That's if you do want it, of course?' Harriet feigned a look of hurt as she dashed into the lounge to find it.

'Anyway, Pepper loves playing with the wool, don't you Pepper?' She stuck her fingers into the gaps between the basket's woven reeds, feeling Mr. Sanderson's arm around her as he lifted her holdall from the floor. She smiled, glancing at the amber buttercup petals central to her ring. For the second time in her life she felt an overwhelming sense of wellbeing, exactly the feeling she'd had when they'd escaped from the tunnel into his house, when she'd been helping Mrs. Harris to come to terms with her and Tricia's shocking intrusion from the tunnel that had caused her to faint.

'She OK on the back seat Harriet?'

'Oh yes, that's fine thank you, Mr. Sanderson.'

'I'll pop your luggage in the boot. Here just let me open the door for you.'

Harriet slid into the front seat, hit by the smell of expensive grey leather. Thought about the field of flowers and the magical journey home. She recalled how they'd lain in the wild flower meadow where he'd stopped just short of making love to her. "Save that one for me", he'd said when she'd unintentionally declared how hard she and Mark had been trying for another baby, without success. She could scarcely believe she was sitting in that very same car, now, this minute. Pregnant by this gorgeous hunk of a man. She felt ready, so ready to be his now. It was too soon before. She knew she'd been in shock after being left at the church, after being ditched by Mark. That very same morning she'd discovered she was pregnant, he'd ditched her before he even knew. She recalled Mr. Sanderson taking her in hand wanting to marry her but as the day wore on she knew she couldn't go through with such an immediate change of plan. The thought of marriage to him in just three weeks had frightened her silly, she'd needed to escape but Venice had turned out to be a bad move and the repercussions were even worse. She'd wanted it to work with Mark but in spite of his insistence he'd take on the baby she always had her doubts. Convinced she'd lost both Mark and Mr. Sanderson on all counts she'd quite rightly blamed herself, never dreaming Mr. Sanderson would arrive back from the Galapagos Islands to declare his love and in such a beautiful way. She sat, dazed, drenched in her own disbelief, but determined not to let all this slip away from her again.

She turned to the cat meowing in the basket.

'It won't be long Pepper then you'll be able to find Tim. You'll both have great fun together.'

She swivelled back to Mr. Sanderson's laughter.

'Who the devil's Tim? Not some child you left in that damned tunnel, I hope.'

'No, of course not Mr. Sanderson, I'm talking about Timmy, Molly's cat.'

'Oh I see, so that's its name.' He paused to check the traffic before turning right into the main road. Harriet took a deep breath. She loved the way the steering wheel flicked into a spin through his hands. She loved the way his long legs struggled for space each time he hit the clutch or accelerator. She couldn't take her eyes from following the double seam of red stitching all the way down the side of his leg to his foot. Oh this man, there was nothing about him that didn't send her into a complete spin. He looked across.

'Speaking of Molly, she's asked if we would like to join them for dinner tomorrow evening. I picked up the message when I got back. I rather thought we might turn it into a bit of a dinner party ourselves. Save Molly the bother. Just a small gathering to celebrate your homecoming as it were.'

For a moment he tapped his fingers on the steering wheel.

'I'm sorry Harriet. I should have mentioned it sooner, I don't expect you'll have packed anything suitable. That's if you're happy with that,
of course.'

'Yes, yes, it would be lovely to see Molly and Percy, but you're right. I haven't packed anything like that. Come to think of it I haven't really got anything like that, only my blue bridesmaid dress.'

Mr. Sanderson laughed. 'As beautiful as you look in that I don't think we could call it appropriate. Look let's go into town. There's at least one decent shop we could pop into. Let's get you sorted out shall we? It's not going to take long.' He looked at his watch. 'We should make it before closing time.'

Harriet smiled, nodded her head, felt his hand on hers.

'That would be lovely, thank you Mr. Sanderson.'

'I do have a Christian name you know Harriet.' His hand back on hers now, she looked away. This had always been difficult for her.

'I know. Sorry! It's just that.......'

'I'm still your boss Harriet,' he laughed. 'You are so unbelievably reserved. How did I ever get to make love to you on the sand? Nothing short of a miracle, indeed just like the baby. We can't have it growing up wondering who Mr. Sanderson is, now can we?'

Harriet fidgeted in her seat.

'Now don't go all pink on me again Miss Glover,' he laughed, lifting his hand back to the steering wheel.

'Certainly not Mr. Sanderson. Grown-up people don't do pink. Once my brain gets the message I've grown up now, I'll never go pink again.'

'You won't change Harriet. You'll never properly grow up and I wouldn't want you to. That's not to say a little less of the hole-digging wouldn't go amiss, nor can I say I'm too keen on this penchant you have for gathering adoring young men to your side. I'm not too happy to go along with all this giggling at others' misfortunes either, particularly as you're more often than not, the perpetrator and I certainly can't do with this total disregard you appear to have for the truth. In fact Harriet I can't for the life of me think why I'm taking this bundle of trouble back home with me.'

Unsure, she looked across to see his face break into that most gorgeous of smiles.

'Perhaps it's that "Amo too nunc sweet temper" reason you wrote on that paper?'

He laughed, squeezed her hand tightly.

'Ah, "Amo te nunc et semper", now what does that mean Harriet?'

' "I love you now and forever" Mr. Sanderson, that's what it means.'

'And do you Harriet?'

'I do.' Almost whispered she directed her eyes towards her feet, feeling the full flush of colour to her cheeks. He smiled gently. ' "Tandem", remember that one?'

' "At last", yes that's what it means, "at last".'

'Indeed it does Harriet. My word you've presented me with the hardest challenge of my life. Come on, let's get you that new dress. Ah good, plenty of spaces left. Right in we go.'

The silver Mercedes glided to a halt. Harriet watched every visible gorgeous inch of him walk round the front of the car to let her out. She went to open the back door.

'But Mr. Sanderson the cat's meowing, we can't leave her in here.'

'Oh no Harriet, we won't be more than a few minutes.'

'I can't leave her Mr. Sanderson, she'll be dead in the basket when we get back and if that's the case I'm going back home!'

He scratched his head. 'Crikey Harriet I thought you'd said you'd grown up?'

'And I thought you told me not too?'

'Oh here, let me get the damned thing out. It's staying in the basket mind!'

'But of course it is Mr. Sanderson.'

Chapter 3

'This cat weighs a ton! Crikey I doubt if she'd even fit in my briefcase now.' Mr Sanderson scratched his head wondering just how he'd got away with it. 'Goodness knows how she managed to stow away a second time. Fancy me taking the damned thing all the way to Switzerland and back. Certainly is a load of trouble this one, just like you.'

Harriet checked his face, she needed to see he was still smiling.

'Ah that looks like the back entrance.' He took her hand, marching her through and up the escalators to the third floor following the path from the arrow pointing to "Ladies' Fashion".

'Look Mr. Sanderson, please would you mind sitting down with the basket while I look at the dresses? There's a chair over there, just by the end curtain. I'll be with you in a tick.'

Dazed at the prospect of being thrown into choice, she watched him stride off, then a quick wave as she rummaged her way through the dress racks. With three over her arm she returned to find him making polite conversation with a young assistant.

'Won't be a tick. Is she alright?' Harriet pointed at the cat basket and waited for the nod before disappearing behind the curtain. She missed seeing a neatly tailored woman strutting across, consumed with intense curiosity, rudely brushing the young assistant aside.

'What's in it? It's not the latest in designer baby baskets is it?' Hearing from behind the curtain, Harriet rose to full alert, instantly feeling like some kind of baby snatcher.

'A cat, I hope,' replied Mr. Sanderson, deeply regretting his decision to go to this particular store.

'Do you know, just a couple of months ago someone left a baby here, in the store, in a basket just like that. We found it just inside the rear entrance door parked on the chair under the fire extinguisher. Poor thing, I don't know how it survived with the lid closed like that.' She pointed an accusing finger. 'It looks rather large for a cat basket to me.'

'So are you the store detective or something?' Harriet could hear Mr. Sanderson beginning to get impatient.

'No but I can call her now. We don't want another late night like last time. We've been advised to be vigilant. Would you mind if I looked inside it?'

'I very much would mind you looking inside it,' Mr. Sanderson declared, rising to his full height. 'It's not my cat I'm afraid.'

'In that case it's my duty to call her,' the neatly tailored woman replied.

'Call *who?*' Mr. Sanderson enquired, unable to conceal his irritation whilst trying to deal with the shock of this woman's unexpected appearance.

'The store detective,' she snapped, 'that's the procedure we're instructed to follow.'

Harriet poked her head out from behind the curtain.

'It's OK, open it, I'm sure she could do with some air by now, anyway.'

'Quite unnecessary this Harriet, they have no authority to act in this way,' said Mr. Sanderson reluctantly releasing the catch on the lid.

'No keep hold of her,' screamed Harriet jumping, as it instantly propelled itself to freedom uncoiling like a spring to its feet. 'Oh no she's gone!'

Without a second thought Harriet, clad only in her bra and long-legged thermal knickers dashed out from behind the curtain to chase it, rushing and stumbling between the dress racks all the way through to perfumery.

'Pepper, no, come back here. Pepper stop!'

Aiming for a rotating floor stand the cat leapt up the side, knocking box after box of designer perfume to the floor, before leaping off to squeal under Harriet's feet, between them both managing to bring down the whole stand with the remainder of bottles crashing to the floor. She glanced back to see Mr. Sanderson look over, dangling all three dresses at the till. She looked up to see the neatly tailored woman striding towards her, shaking her head vigorously whilst wagging a menacing finger.

'What the hell do you think you're doing madam? I wanted an early night tonight, if you did but mind.'

Harriet barely heard.

'PEPPER, come here. No Pepper that's not a real mouse,' Harriet panicked. A child instantly screamed as the cat leapt and landed on her very pink pet hamster, only to drop it, leaving the thing rushing mercilessly towards her mother, then a swift change of mind sending the store detective skidding into a forward roll before landing on her back. In a pelt, the cat suddenly changed direction to leap straight into the arms of the laid flat woman, who promptly disentangled herself in favour of capturing Harriet.

'Oh look, terribly sorry but I was trying to get the cat. Where's she gone now? No Pepper. Come back! Don't go in that, it's the lift you stupid thing.'

Harriet rapidly disengaged herself to shoot in after it, scrambling on the floor between an assortment of feet in an attempt to grab it as the doors closed just missing its tail.

'Oh sorry! Lost the cat! Is this thing going up or down? Up, yes of course, silly me!' Silence! She held the cat tightly to her chest grateful for the cover it gave to her white lace bra, then remembered her lack of clothes. Eleven heads turned. Eleven expressionless faces suddenly animated, twitched in disbelief.

'Er do excuse me I was actually trying on dresses when it er, escaped from its basket.' Silence! Grateful to feel the thing judder to a halt she dashed out.

'You streaking love? Might be better without those.' She looked down at her thermals, could feel herself going as red as the fire extinguisher alongside.

'No, no of course not. Where's the stairs?'

The man in the green overall pointed straight ahead. 'Right here, didn't you see me coming up?'

'No, no but thanks.'

Clutching the cat she dashed down to the last stair straight into the arms of the store detective.

'I guessed this is where you'd be. Do you realise your state of dress or should I say undress?'

'Oh gosh, I didn't think twice, I just flew out of the changing room to catch her.'

'I suggest you get dressed and accompany me to the office, you're very lucky I didn't hurt myself falling like that,' she smarted, reluctantly leaning against the door to allow Harriet and the cat through.

'But I'm with Mr. Sanderson. Look he's over there. It looks like he's handing back the dresses I was about to try on. Oh golly, he looks cross. Go and ask him, he'll explain what happened.'

The store detective promptly changed course stabbing her way across the floor in fast, short bursts exploding with desire to speak with Mr. Sanderson. Harriet diverted, striding between the dress racks, determined to catch him first.

'Here, grab this.' She pushed the cat at him then flew to the cubicle. Half in and half out of the curtain, she threw her top and jeans on, grabbed her bag and dashed over to join them.

'It's alright Harriet, I've explained about the over-zealous assistant. Bring that basket over here will you? Let's get this damned cat away before it breaks loose again.'

Harriet turned to the pull on her arm from behind. It was the child's mother, trying to shake off her yowling son from her legs. Her voice was irate and loud.

'Well I suppose you both think it's OK to go now after that flaming cat nearly breaking my neck? Listen to him bawling, just listen. The ruddy thing's stopped working now. Look! Joshua stop crying and try pressing its arse again.' She turned to Harriet. 'It nearly had me for minced meat that thing did.'

'Hmm, er look. This young lady will explain.' Mr Sanderson smiled at the store detective, who was busy slapping at her smart grey suit, making an exaggerated attempt to remove the dust she'd just collected. He reached in his pocket for his wallet. How much, twenty, forty, sixty? Look, take this with our apologies.' Mr. Sanderson pressed the lot into her hand.

'Oh, that'll do nicely thank you.' She turned to the woman in the well-tailored suit. 'Haven't you got a health and safety policy on this floor? That display was ruddy dangerous sticking right out like that. No wonder she sent it all flying. Come on Joshua let's find the manager and report this, unless of course you'd like to compensate me with a couple of those down there.'

The woman in the smartly tailored suit clonked her high heels along the woodblock floor, retrieved two oblong boxes from the scattered pile, then opened them to hold the bottles to the light. Back she clonked to thrust them at the woman.

'It's not my favourite but it'll do,' she declared ungraciously, shaking the perfume to a fizz. 'And I don't want them if I find the bottles cracked,' the woman blurted.

'No, no damage, I assure you,' said the woman in the well-tailored suit. She turned to Harriet. 'Now, if you Madam and you Sir, with her, would quietly depart, I'd be most grateful.' Then all self control evaporated. 'Just sod off all of you, I'm trying to get an early night tonight. I need it working in this dump. I've a date with a fabulous guy this weekend and I intend to look my best.'

Harriet felt the heat from the look she shot at Mr. Sanderson. 'Just sodding well get from under my feet will you and bugger off!'

'I beg your pardon Miss Worsnip, did I hear you correctly? I'm sure I did. Accompany me to the office immediately, will you?'

Harriet looked round to see the door behind the till still swinging. The nameplate, MR. ROGER BOXSOCKS, FLOOR MANAGER matching the white oblong card pinned to his lapel.

'Come on Harriet, grab hold of these. Oh forget it, let's just get the hell out of here! Here just get hold of them will you?'

Harriet blushed, his impatience sending her feet into a bit of a dance.

'That's a bit strong language Mr. Sanderson. Are you sure the lid's properly fastened on that thing?'

'It had better bloody be!'

Harriet scurried behind as he marched ahead, nursing the cat basket to his chest with both hands, the carrier bags resting on the top, secured by his chin. He backed himself against the exit door to let her get past.

'What the hell am I doing taking you two on?' He strode ahead, his words falling to the tarmac as he stood gripping the handle, pulling the car door open to let her in.

'Sorry Mr. Sanderson I really am but I had to chase it or we'd have lost her forever.'

'Yes of course. Of course you did. No, no, I shouldn't have lost my cool. Sorry Harriet, it was that arrogant woman insisting on looking inside. Maybe it would have been better to go along with me on that one, though. The woman had no right to insist.'

'But I wanted to clear our names, I was beginning to feel like we'd done something terribly wrong. If we'd continued to refuse she might have got even more suspicious and we could have ended up being arrested.'

'No I don't think so Harriet.'

He turned the engine on, reversed then squeezed her hand before speeding away.

'No, sorry, I'm the one who needs to apologise. Just a bit of a shock seeing you running around in your underwear. Not that it's something I couldn't get used to, don't get me wrong, but long woolly knickers up to your waist and down to your knees? What are they all about Harriet?'

She went rigid. Never felt more like the fire extinguisher she'd just rushed past.

'No they're not knickers, they're thermals Mr. Sanderson. They're to keep me warm in bed. Your house is very old and big. It's getting colder now, especially in bed on my own and I do want to keep the baby warm.'

'Oh I see, so I take it you're not sleeping with me either, tonight Harriet?'

She caught that gorgeous smile.

'Front bedroom Mr. Sanderson. You promised.'

'Certainly is Harriet. Just checking.' He nodded towards the basket on the rear seat. 'I do recall coming to grief with that thing once before. Too damned possessive your cat, I'm certainly not competing with her for your attentions.' He laughed. Harriet recalled that night on the cruise ship, how it had leapt from nowhere to land on him just at the critical moment. He squeezed her hand again then both silent, each with their thoughts as they moved away from the town towards the country lanes.

Not far to go and climbing. On the far side, the chambray blue sky straddled with pink stripes, like bars of broken rock turning to candyfloss at the edges. The tops of the hills set dark against the early evening splendour. To the west, the sea, exotic, shimmering celestial blue ripples through its silvery haze, the river settling under a blanket of rising mist. The sky a furnace now, pure candyfloss flecked with gold, spreading and changing to the fast sinking sun, intent on chasing away yet another autumnal day as if impatient for winter. Harriet sat back, ablaze with delight. She glanced his profile, his long blonde hair resting at his broad shoulders, his strong straight back pushing against the seat, him tanned and gorgeous. Her mind in perfect equilibrium, all her senses absorbing the sheer magical delight taken from this perfect, exquisite, moment in time.

'Are you alright?'

'Absolutely, thank you.'

'That's good Harriet. Very good. Now which of the three will you be wearing tomorrow evening?'

'Three Mr. Sanderson! You shouldn't have bought all three. Oh that's lovely, so lovely. Thank you so much.'

'Well you'll be needing them. Clive Engells will be back with us tomorrow evening, for some reason best known to himself he's overnighting down the road at the Upper Tideside Hotel. Yes it's far better we do it, I'm sure Molly will understand. What do you think to my inviting Belinda Oxfordshire? I've mentioned it in passing. Needs confirmation of course. You know Clive's pretty cut-up about losing Lucrezia and it might give her something else to focus on other than Mrs. Harrington's husband. If ever there was a mismatch, that's one. Crikey Harriet, did you hear me, you look positively dazed?'

She jumped, pulled herself together.

'Er yes, of course, sorry about that. Yes I have to agree with what you've just said. Actually Bob's a nice guy. A bit of a lad, he's a civil engineer, you know, wellies and hard hats and all that. It's a pity Ross Farquerhart hadn't taken a fancy to her, far more her type I would have thought.'

'Really Harriet she's old enough to be his mother!'

'But that's ageist Mr. Sanderson and very old fashioned thinking. He's a bit on the dozy side but she'd soon put him straight.'

He looked across, puckered his right eyebrow at her.

'Surely you are not referring to my gifted PhD student in such a derogatory way? Indeed his behaviour with you suggests he's anything but dozy.'

Harriet looked down. Didn't wish to be reminded of her total lapse of dignity and common sense allowing Ross Farquerhart to kiss her like that on the cliff top during the school camp.

'Ah silence Harriet. Anyhow where were we? Such a large age gap, hardly a sound basis for marriage, I would say.'

'Well they wouldn't have to get married, that's a bit old-fashioned too. Look at Mark and I, we didn't.'

'Yes Harriet I am looking at Mark and you and it's not exactly been a utopian experience of late, has it?'

'But we were OK until you appointed me, you gave me the job.'

'So it's all my fault now is it?' He ran his fingers through his hair then turned towards her, narrowing his eyes before smiling.

'Yes, you started it.'

'I started it! What exactly did I start Harriet?'

'That first kiss in your office, yes that was it.'

'Ah but I judged your receptivity exactly right, would you not agree?'

She recalled floating back to the classroom, spending the rest of the day with the warmth of his first kiss secured tightly to her lips. She went quiet, knew this was one she couldn't win.

'Yes indeed, silence again! So I'm to take all the blame am I?'

She looked across, saw those dimples in his cheeks elongating as he smiled, wondered why she ever decided to ask for the front bedroom and as for the cat, well there was nothing wrong with Mrs. Harris's broom cupboard. She couldn't wait to arrive. Couldn't wait to peel off her large thermal knickers, either.

Chapter 4

'Harriet how lovely to see you again. I believe you are to be our house guest for a few days,' Mrs. Harris beamed.

'That's right but how are you and Mr. Swift after that terrible ordeal?'

'Oh we're fine thank you now. We've had plenty of time to get over it. Mind you it was a bit of a shocker riding in that helicopter and not knowing where we'd end up. I didn't say so at the time but I fully expected us all to be shot from the sky.'

'That's right Mrs. Harris. Maximise your expectations when Harriet's around, you just can't predict what she'll do next.' He turned, tensing his eyes, sweeping her up into one of those serious, sensual, semi-amused glances.

'Now don't you be getting at Harriet, here. She and her friend have been through such a terrible time. I just thank the dear Lord we were right by the door into the tunnel when they called for help.'

'Me too, Mrs. Harris. It would have been a very different story now,' Harriet agreed.

'Quite, quite! Not a thing for any of us to dwell on. I've stepped up the security since, though I haven't decided quite what to do about that damned tunnel yet.'

'I keep telling him to get it filled in Harriet. I've never liked the thing, not that I've ever been down there. There's something spooky about that part of the house. Do you know Mr. Swift has done everything he can think of to warm that hallway but it's always ice cold.'

'Come, come Mrs. Harris, no point in letting your imagination run riot. We don't want to go frightening the life out of Harriet now, do we, since she's barely through the door?'

Harriet looked around the large square hall. The highly polished woodblock under her feet. Forward of her the expensive flokati rug gracing the beautiful old fireplace. She took a deep breath, looked him straight in the eye.

'Now that is most definitely one thing I do not do. If you have a ghost here please would you be kind enough to take me straight back home Mr. Sanderson?'

'Oh Mrs. Harris, now look what you've done. You shouldn't go frightening our house guest like that.'

'Oh, no, of course not Harriet. Take no notice of me I'm just being silly. Look let me put the kettle on. A nice cup of tea and a piece of ginger cake for Harriet, in front of the fire. How about you Mr. Sanderson?'

'Sounds good Mrs. Harris. Now what time are we dining? Something smells good.'

'It's your favourite Mr. Sanderson, coq au vin bubbling gently away; now would seven-thirty suit?'

He smiled, 'Are you OK with that Harriet?'

'Yes thank you, that's perfect.'

'Now you take Harriet into the lounge and shall I get Mr. Swift to take her luggage upstairs?' Mrs Harris enquired.

'No that's OK, I noticed him working on the far end of the garden as we drove in. It won't take me a couple of ticks.'

He steered Harriet into the lounge. She felt her feet sinking into the deep piled carpet as she looked around. This beautiful, tasteful house. She recalled Christmas day, sitting in this very room, listening to his mother spilling out the family history. Her mother sat between them. She'd been with Mark, his and her family all invited to Lower Tideside for Christmas tea. Couldn't believe how far things had come. Pregnant, carrying his baby now. This was reality. She tried desperately to conjure up those feelings of confidence, those feelings of this being the right place for them both but there was an unwelcome intrusion, suddenly a feeling of something missing strangely pervading her thoughts.

'Nice fire, just the job these cold autumn evenings. Oh do sit down Harriet and relax. We don't bite you know.'

'Oh yes, no of course not. It's me, I just feel a bit nervous that's all.'

Mr. Sanderson strode back to the doorway.

'We'll both have a drop of brandy in that if you would be so kind Mrs. Harris. Now Harriet, what is it? I want you to put all of that behind you and have a good weekend.'

She looked up, irritated with herself. This gorgeous, gorgeous man almost hers for the taking at last. Suddenly she put her hand to her mouth.

'The cat, I'd completely forgotten. It's the cat, I'm worried about the cat Mr. Sanderson. I don't want her to die of suffocation in the back of your car.'

'Crikey, the cat, why on earth didn't you say? I'd better get it now.'

'There Harriet. Let me just pop this down while I bring the small table over.'

Harriet jumped up to smile at Mrs. Harris as she carefully placed the tray on the tea trolley by the door. She watched her lift the small rosewood table, the one he'd taken the two pressed buttercups from to throw away. She looked at the rings on her finger, then the bangle at her wrist. She smiled at the thought of him not wanting to part with them, they were just as precious to her as these very expensive gifts she'd received from him.

'Here, let me help. Just here is it Mrs. Harris, will that be alright?'

'Oh thank you dear, that's just fine,' replied Mrs. Harris, turning to see Mr. Sanderson, loaded, pushing the door open.

'Oh my goodness me, what's this Mr. Sanderson, whatever are you bringing in now?'

'This Mrs. Harris is Harriet's cat. The only way I could get her here!'

'Oh good, a friend for Tim. Do you know that cat trots between here and Molly's now as a matter of course? I love it, friendly little thing it is.'

'Then you might like to try loving this one Mrs. Harris. Personally I have great difficulty and if it doesn't behave it's getting its marching orders!'

'Take no notice of him Harriet, I'm the housekeeper here. Let's just open the lid and say "Hello", what did you say its name is?'

'It's Pepper Mrs. Harris, and the only trouble with her is she's very intelligent and far too sensitive. It gets her into trouble but she'll like you, I know she will.'

Mrs. Harris smiled, lifted the lid then shot back with a loud gasp.

'Where is it, it's empty?'

'Oh no,' panicked Harriet. 'Mr. Sanderson you haven't left the car door open, have you?'

'Indeed I have, not having a third arm Harriet. Quick let's see if the damned thing's still in the car. How the little bugger got out of the basket I don't know!'

'Mr. Sanderson ever since you returned from that exotic place you've been like this. That's a new one for you and if you don't watch your language and get your hair cut I'll be forced to resign.'

Mr. Sanderson laughed but Mrs. Harris was having none of it.

'Here let me come along. It can't have got far,' she protested, visibly shocked.

They flew outside, Mr. Sanderson first in the back, then the front, scrambling under the car seats.

'Ah Mr. Swift. Help us look for this bloody cat will you. It's already caused havoc in the department store now the damned thing's managed to escape from its basket. It can't have got far, I've only just opened the car door.'

'Right you are Mr. Sanderson. Not the best light now. Here let me get a couple of torches.'

'But she might be down on the river bank by now Mr. Sanderson,' worried Harriet.

'Oh crumbs, there's concrete still setting down there. I'm having a mooring built. If she's got her feet stuck in that lot just as it sets off she's had it!'

Harriet could feel the tears welling in her eyes. She couldn't handle the thought of losing both Mark and the cat both at the same time. Now she wished she'd never come as she dashed behind Mr. Sanderson heading for the cliff steps leading to the beach. He flashed the torch around the concrete enclosure.

'No sign of the damned thing here.'

'No she's probably out there somewhere, on her way to Wales. She'll be sinking in the marshland and I'll never see her again.'

She felt Mr. Sanderson's arm around her.

'That's the worse case scenario Harriet, there's a thousand and one other places she could be. Let's stay positive shall we? We actually didn't look under the car now, did we?'

'No Mr. Sanderson, quick, she could well be there. That's one of her favourite places to hide. Don't you remember when I trailed that traffic cone home from school and wondered what the noise was? Remember how you arrived to find me and the cat under the car?'

Mr. Sanderson took a very deep breath. 'Indeed I do Harriet, now let's hope you're right.'

'But how did she get out of the basket when the catch was down?'

'Are we sure the catch was down Harriet? We escaped from the place pretty damned quickly as I recall. I was carrying the thing on both arms. I could well have forgotten to do it.'

'But what if you didn't Mr. Sanderson? What if that ghost Mrs. Harris was talking about, let her out?' Harriet could feel a cold shiver running the length of her back.

'I never heard such ridiculous rubbish Harriet. Now for goodness sake grow up! Look you're getting cold. Go inside by the fire. The tea will be stone cold. Go on bang them in the microwave I'll be with you in a tick.'

Harriet left them, almost fearful to enter the empty house now. She crouched over the fire, warming her hands in the heat of the flames. Then one cup at a time she went to the kitchen and shivered, refusing to look at the passageway alongside, leading to the door at the end of the tunnel.

Chapter 5

'No sign I'm afraid. Still not to give up, especially not on that one.' Mr. Sanderson rubbed his hands together before spreading them again to catch the heat from the logs, each hissing and crackling, stealing the flames from the spent bed of coals beneath. He turned to Mrs. Harris pushing the door open.

'There's the cake. I'll leave you two to it then.' She smiled at Harriet. 'Now you stop worrying. It wouldn't surprise me if she's not somewhere inside here. The front door was open, she could well have shot through while we were all searching. I'll go and have a look around now.'

Harriet instantly felt better. Mrs. Harris wasn't unlike Molly with her warm, comforting nature. Yes, she liked the idea of being so close to them both, so close to Mr. Sanderson. It was not her fault if Mark had finally chosen to go his own way, she sensed from all he'd said this is where he wanted her to be.

'You're very quiet Harriet? A penny for them! I hope they're all happy ones.'

'Oh yes, I was just thinking about Mark actually. I was, still am feeling very happy, well apart from the cat, stupid thing! No, I was just thinking about Mark doing his own thing now. He said you were "a pretty decent sort of chap". I think you helped him a lot Mr. Sanderson when you had that chat together in the Galapagos Islands.'

Mr. Sanderson smiled, brushed the cake crumbs from his fingers before finishing his tea.

'It's like I said Harriet, he's sat comfortable for many years turning a blind eye to your need to be married to him. It's something he hasn't ever been able to face, head on. He tried and failed and he's at least to be applauded for trying. Now how old was he when he first got you pregnant, twenty, twenty-one?'

'Twenty-one, he was in his final year, of course I'd only just started university then.'

'I imagine it's quite a thing doing your finals in the knowledge you're going to become a father before you've barely had chance to live. He took on an enormous responsibility Harriet, he didn't let you down. He set up home, worked his way up to support the three, er four of you. It couldn't have been easy. This phobia of his could be nothing more than a reaction to the pressure he must have felt at that time. I think he's now got the opportunity to spread his wings, he will be sensing a lost freedom returning. He's at a critical age for a man Harriet, he'll be wanting to live free of responsibility for a while. He'll enjoy catching up once he's got over the shock of the separation.'

'Yes, I'm sure you're right. I never really looked at it like that. It will hurt though if he finds someone else. His liaison with Melissa Scott was bad enough.'

'Well you can't have it all ways Harriet, this is something I'm sure you are going to have to accept. He needed his freedom from both of you and you just can't legislate for who he'll meet, what he'll do with his life.'

'Oh, I know,' she said, returning her plate to the table. He stood, gathered them up just as Mrs. Harris returned with the tray.

'Ah thank you Mrs. Harris, no sign of the cat then?'

'No, I've looked everywhere, I do hope she doesn't end up sinking in the shallows.'

Harriet paled, looked at Mr. Sanderson.

'No chance, it's too smart for that. You mark my words it's got itself into a comfortable corner somewhere. It will appear right enough when it wants feeding. Now stop worrying, the pair of you.'

Mrs. Harris smiled, the crockery rattling as she gathered it to the tray. Harriet rushed across to open the door, closing it gently behind her.

'Come and sit down Harriet. Move up, I don't bite you know.'

His arm stretched across the back of the sofa, she seated herself as he drew her closer in.

'There's no need to be shy Harriet, what's the difference between your house and mine? I'd like to think you'll be as relaxed here as you are at home. Now the cat? She can't be that bothered about you, she'd have made damned sure of sticking around, wouldn't you think?'

Couched by his left arm, Harriet snuggled into his white fisherman's knit sweater, laying her hand against his chest. This gorgeous, gorgeous man, she could scarcely believe she was here. The flames wrapping around the logs, leaping, stretching, curling, dancing their warmth into the gentle ambiance of the room.

'I've waited a long time for this Harriet.' He smiled, stroking her hair gently away from her face. She looked up, those intensely blue eyes with that look, just for her. His lips easing into hers, her mind disintegrating with the surging desire for him, running to, spreading from that part of her now desperately opening from the need to draw him in. That part of her he'd opened and entered to make her pregnant on the warm evening sand in Cornwall.

He placed his hand across her abdomen, kissed her forehead.

'I'm amazed you haven't lost this one Harriet, given the exorbitant stress levels you've been subject to. It's ridiculous, quite ridiculous this propensity you have for finding trouble.'

'Well it does have to be there in the first place, Mr. Sanderson. It's not our fault you and the PM dealt with dodgy bodyguards. Tricia had her suspicions straight away about them when you sent her to Switzerland. As soon as she saw the PM's heavies at the opening of Starboard Marine North West she knew it was them and as it turned out her feelings about them proved to be right.'

'What exactly are you saying Harriet?'

She looked up at him, sorry she'd started. Unsure whether to continue.

Then he smiled that smile again.

'Do carry on Harriet.'

'Well I've said it, I've just said it.'

'Said what Harriet? I'm not sure what you're trying to say at all.'

'It wasn't our fault. We couldn't have got involved with them, if you both hadn't been…'

'Indeed, now are you suggesting the PM deliberately went out of his way to surround himself with criminals and I in the full knowledge of that contracted them in respect of this Swiss transaction I needed to make?'

'No, no of course not Mr. Sanderson.' Back-pedalling like mad, Harriet could feel herself metamorphosing into that red fire extinguisher again.

'Mmm, yes indeed, a good place to stop before you start digging yourself into yet another hole. Don't let the PM hear you talking like that, I don't think he's got quite the same measure of you as I have.'

'Now you're cross Mr. Sanderson, how did I manage that?'

He laughed, hugging her closer.

'Oh Harriet, you're going to have to be more like Mrs. Harris, I'm afraid. She can tell when I'm merely joking.'

Harriet took a deep breath, looked up to see him raise his right eyebrow as he lowered the other, wondering if this gorgeous, hunk of a man could ever, in her mind, be anything other than her boss.

'More logs required, just a tick.' She watched the sparks momentarily spitting as the cold wood hit the furnace of settled orange heat beneath, crackling, instantly disturbing the ash laden side coals to coax them back to life.

'Joking aside, you make a fair point Harriet. Of course the PM had his suspicions and in the event I think the pair of you managed to bring it all to a head rather sooner than expected on both occasions. MI6 had, of course, been putting feelers out for some time, but they were in grave danger of losing the trail with you two getting caught up in it all. You could well have sent the lot of them underground.'

'But we didn't, did we? Once we'd got back from Venice they were after us because they thought we were colluding with the authorities. They wanted Tricia's fake designer dress back to destroy the evidence, remember? Actually I think we played a vital part in them being captured.'

'You're not looking for another damehood are you? Not that I can see there to be much joy in a posthumous presentation. The pair of you could so easily have lost your lives. You'll never know what you've put me through Harriet with your evasiveness and compulsion to court both trouble and danger.' Mr. Sanderson, serious now, hugged her tightly to his chest. Suddenly she felt braver, decided to go with the joke.

'No, not! Anyway they don't give damehoods for services rendered to MI6. Tricia and I will just have to take unrewarded, silent satisfaction in risking our lives for crown and country.'

'Am I hearing this correctly?' She gazed into his eyes, crinkling again into laughter, his face rugged, handsome; now her eyes drawn to the slight imperfection in his strong white teeth. The shape of his lips, wide and generous, receptive, poised at the corners, always ready to flicker a response in support of his eyes. This highly intelligent man, seeing all, hearing all, absorbing, thinking, focussing intently on her. She knew. This close to him, the smell of sea salt on his skin exciting her senses. The warmth of his body cosying into hers. His blonde hair shifting and settling in layers to his body shaking with laughter. With all her senses she was breathing, drinking this gorgeous, gorgeous man into her very soul.

She looked down at her ring.

'It's beautiful Mr. Sanderson, just like this one and the bangle. Thank you again.'

'Not necessary Harriet.' He narrowed his eyes, lifted her chin.

'I wonder now, have I finally caught my elusive, beautiful amber butterfly?'

'Well I never thought we'd be sitting here, like this Mr. Sanderson.'

'Let's try it another way shall we?'

Harriet looked down, twisting at the ring on her finger.

'This ubiquitous wretched bag of knitting that keeps threatening to turn into a jumper, who's it for Harriet?'

'Anyone who wants it and really it doesn't sound like it's you.'

'Ah I see! And has anyone expressed interest in it yet?'

'Only the cat Mr. Sanderson.' He laughed as Mrs. Harris first knocked then popped her head round the door.

'It's Mr. Engells on the phone for you Mr. Sanderson, what shall I say?'

'Oh that's alright Mrs. Harris, I'll take it.' He rose, stretched to his full height.

'I'll just tell him you're on the way. Oh and dinner will be ready shortly,'
She finished.

'Jolly good. Look would you be so kind as to show Harriet to her room?' He turned to her.

'Now are you going to slide yourself into one of those dresses for me? They'll need to go back before we find the cat if they don't fit.'

'But I haven't got any tights Mr. Sanderson, I didn't think to put any in.'

'Oh you won't need any, not with those nice long legged thermal knickers to keep you warm Harriet.' He laughed enjoying the pink flush rushing to her cheeks.

'But they're horrible, I really only brought them for bedtime in case it was cold up there.'

'Not cold down here though. Perhaps it would be better to take them off altogether, we don't want anything to spoil the line.' Mrs. Harris cleared her throat.

'Mr. Sanderson, I don't know what's got into you since you came back from those Galpagos Islands.' She turned to Harriet. 'The sooner he gets his hair cut the better, he's behaving just like a hippy. Take no notice of him Harriet.'

'She never does Mrs. Harris, oh and by the way I think you mean the Galapagos Islands, don't you?' He laughed as Mrs. Harris pursed her lips in a fluster.

'Globe in the office Mrs. Harris, should it come up when the PM visits.'

'That's a new one on me Mr. Sanderson. How soon will that be then?'

'Oh a few weeks yet, he'll be bringing his wife and family. Wants them to meet Harriet before his daughter's wedding. Don't worry I'll give you plenty of notice.'

Harriet instantly froze. Decided she'd be well away by then.

Chapter 6

'Splendid meal, thank you Mrs. Harris, Quite splendid. Now Harriet shall we retire to the drawing room for coffee?'

Harriet looked down at her feet, hiding in Mrs. Harris's sixty denier tights, then turned to her.

'Mrs. Harris, thank you so much for such a lovely meal. Gosh, I wish I could cook like you.'

'You'll be wanting to wear her brogues next,' Mr. Sanderson laughed. 'Come on Harriet, let's retire, shall we?'

Mrs. Harris smiled, flicking the tea-towel at him as she began gathering the plates.

'Be with you in a minute. I've moved the coffee table to the French windows, I take it you'll be sitting over there?'

'Ah jolly good Mrs. Harris. Where would we be without you?'

He put his arm around her, Harriet smiled, could see a look of intense satisfaction spreading across her face.

'Follow me Harriet.'

She followed through to a room she'd not seen before. A beautiful expensively furnished room adjacent to the lounge. The carpet almost pearl like in colour, its thick pile catching at her toes as she walked across to take one of the two sumptuously comfortable armchairs placed either side of the doors. She gasped at the view.

'This is so beautiful, oh gosh just look at all those lights twinkling across the river. Look you can see where the roads wind up the sides of the hills almost to the top. I didn't realise you had a room with a view from this side.'

'Not been in here before Harriet? No, no, of course not, you wouldn't have. I've had it only recently refurbished. I'm glad you approve.'

'I can't fault your taste Mr. Sanderson, but these pictures, we're on dry land in here. Meadows, oh no, just look at that one.'

Mr. Sanderson smiled, 'Does it ring any bells Harriet?'

'The field of flowers. It's not *the* field of flowers, is it?'

'Got it in one Harriet. I had it specially commissioned.'

She gazed at the huge watercolour hanging on the opposite wall. The range of delicate pastels, the blues, the pinks, the lilacs, the yellows, depicting a host of differing flowers, dotted with reds and stronger hues of blue and purple; in their variety, the leaves, stems and stalks lifting the eye to the magical blue sky. She took a very deep breath, memories so exquisite as to chase the fear of meeting the PM and his family, clean away. She watched him smile.

'You saved that one for me Harriet. Beautiful, beautiful Harriet, you saved that one for me.'

He poured coffee. 'It's all there, take it as you wish.'

Turning her spoon she ran a little cream down the back, then slowly stirred.

'After dinner mint Harriet?'

'Oh no thank you Mr. Sanderson. I feel as though I've eaten for three, never mind two.'

'You haven't had a scan yet, as far as I understand Harriet. I am correct?'

She nodded.

'But why do you ask?'

'Oh it was just something James said when we were last on the golf course. He's been tracing your ancestors and apparently over the generations there have been four sets of twins on your mother's side.'

'You've got to be joking! It's the first I've heard of it! Oh no, please don't say that!'

'Hardly any need to go into a spiral Harriet. We'll be taking on a nanny, of course. In any case it doesn't mean you're expecting more than one. I would advise you to go along to Dr. Holden and get this scan organised.'

Harriet didn't answer. She looked across to the picture again, couldn't believe he'd decorated a whole room with her at its very heart. She looked at him, his expression serious now. This gorgeous, gorgeous man, this man, a doctor, expecting his baby, in this house with him. She could hardly absorb it all. She allowed her mind to drift to amber, put a stop on time, at this moment she was determined to be free of complications. Yesterday had passed, tomorrow might never arrive. She'd had enough red wine with her meal to saturate the reality of her existence and just at this time she wasn't even going to be worrying about the cat.

'Anyway, I didn't finish telling you about Clive Engells whilst we were dining Harriet. He'll be back here tomorrow. I do apologise for not explaining any of this to you prior to inviting you but it looks like he's got a buyer for his house and needs to get on with looking around. Of course, initially he offered to stay at the Upper Tideside hotel but I felt it would have been churlish to do other than put him up here. I can't quite understand why he should have booked in for last night though. Still, convenient as it happened in view of you being here.'

'Oh right, yes, I suppose so. But no, of course I don't mind him being here Mr. Sanderson. Anyway it's only one night, I'll be back home on Monday.'

He cleared his throat, went to speak then thought better of it.

'Anyway it will be very helpful to chat a few things through regarding the food store at school. He's been absolutely amazing,' Harriet said.

Mr. Sanderson smiled, returned the small cup to its saucer, then swung his right leg across to rest his foot on his knee.

'And so have you Harriet. The feedback I've received whilst away on this has been unbelievable. The value to the parents is immeasurable.'

Harriet smiled, looked out at the night sky to the pale yellow segment of moon coming and going through the mist. The twinkling lights over the water barely discernible now save the occasional glimmer, through the cover of darkness.

'Of course it would have made things rather difficult for tomorrow evening, leaving Clive, had we been dining at Molly's. It's no problem adding another guest if it's here. No, I'll give her a bell now, I think. I'll have a quick word with Mrs. Harris and see if we can't get the caterers in. Molly and Percy must come here and I'll see if Belinda's still up for it. A small dinner party is the answer Harriet.' He scanned her from head to toe.

'And as beautiful as you look in that, we'll pop you back home to get your shoes and tights. Good gracious me Harriet, you aren't wearing those things over those thermal knickers are you?'

He laughed. Harriet went bright red.

'Now has Mrs. Harris sorted you out with your room for tonight?'

'Yes thank you Mr. Sanderson. Actually, if it's alright with you I'm feeling quite tired. It's been quite a day one way or the other.'

'Yes indeed it has.' He glanced at his watch.

'Good gracious me is that the time? We've a busy day tomorrow and I've barely unpacked. I'm in the room just across the landing, straight opposite Harriet should you require anything. Mrs. Harris has her own small apartment at the back of the house so best not to disturb her.'

'Oh no, no, I wouldn't want to do that. No, I'll be fine thank you Mr. Sanderson. Thank you for such a lovely time, and my dresses and these, especially this.' She showed him the amber ring. 'Oh and the buttercups, too.'

'All my pleasure Harriet.'

Suddenly she felt a tiny wave of uncertainty.

'I love being here, I love being with you, but for the moment I can stay on amber, can't I?'

He laughed.

'Of course you can Harriet. At least for tonight, then we'll see.'

He kissed her forehead. 'Sleep well.'

Chapter 7

Harriet shivered as she slipped between the crisp white cotton sheets, wondering why she'd only packed her red silk nightdress. She hadn't worn it since the cruise. It had been too special to her. She'd been wearing it when he'd almost made love to her that night in her cabin. The night when the cat had taken a distinct dislike to him and had almost sabotaged the relationship for good.

She lay, curled like the foetus inside her, trying to shake off the strangeness of the room. Peering from under the duvet she watched the hem of the curtains lift and fall to the draught from the window. Thought about the picture in the wardrobe, wondered what the story behind it was. Wondered why he'd said that was for another time. She felt uneasy, scolding herself as she tried to ward off the fear rising in waves like the onset of a tsunami. Engulfed in the eerie silence, she became fearful for the cat. Suddenly she sat up, straining her ears to a high-pitched wavering sound. Listened harder, thought she could hear it. Shivering she got out of bed, put the light on, grabbed a cardigan and scrambled back into her thermal knickers.

'Pepper, Pepper come out you daft thing. I know you're there.' On her knees now, under the bed. No sign but still catching that same breaking high pitched sound. By the door, a meow. She opened it quickly, still no sign. She turned on the light to peer down the left handed staircase, then shivering from cold and fear she shot across to the other side. The whistling sound louder now, then a faint meow. She thought of the corridor and the door to the tunnel. There was nothing in her would take her down either flight of stairs. Behind her a click. Terrified she turned. Mr. Sanderson standing in the doorway, his dressing gown thrown around him.

'Good heavens Harriet, what on earth are you doing? Good gracious me, you don't sleepwalk do you?'

'Oh Mr. Sanderson you gave me such a fright. I thought I could hear the cat. It sounded like it was out here, but there's a whistling noise Mr. Sanderson, it's that ghost. I'm not going back in there.'

'Oh come here Harriet,' laughing, he took her in both arms.

'You coming in here then?' he shook his head towards his bedroom door left wide open behind him.

'No, you come in mine,' Harriet pleaded. 'I'm too scared to be left on my own.'

He followed her across the landing.

'Harriet you've got your nightdress half-tucked into these huge thermal knickers. And a cardigan! Surely to goodness you don't go to bed like this?'

'No Mr. Sanderson, as you well know. I'm cold, there's a draught from the window, I've been watching those curtains moving.'

'No draughts in this house Harriet. All these well sealed windows have undergone the feather test and came out with flying colours. Are you sure it wasn't the cat on the windowsill?'

'Oh golly, I didn't look there. It could have been.'

He peered under the curtains.

'No not here Harriet, she's probably chewing on a mouse in the broom cupboard.'

'Oh no you haven't got mice as well have you?'

'Of course not Harriet,' he laughed, turning out the light.

'No I want it left on Mr. Sanderson and leave that on too, please.'

'Crikey Harriet, I'm not about to spend the night wrestling this thing. Are you not ready for this?'

'What do you mean?'

'It could be worse I suppose, at least I'm still wearing a tan.'

'No, no, turn it off. I'll put this lamp on instead. Look you put these on, they stretch. Just get in bed, put these on and then take your dressing gown off.'

'You what Harriet you're making me wear those thermal things? This is unbelievable!'

'I'm going home and phoning for a taxi if you don't. I don't like the spooky feel to this house and I'm not in the mood for lying next to a totally naked man. A man I hardly know really.'

'Oh get them off Harriet and pass the damned things over. Are we ever going to get any sleep tonight?'

She turned over, the covers shielding her view, staying that way as she peeled the warm thermal fabric away from her legs, allowing him sufficient time to ensure both his legs were well inside.

'Bloody hell Harriet these legs are far too tight. Our first night in bed together and you're making me wear women's knickers. The damned things have glued themselves to me like Clingfilm. Is this some kind of punishment for suggesting you might be having twins? Are you trying to scupper my manhood once and for all? Sod this Harriet, I'm very sorry but I'm taking them off right now!'

'Stay on that side of the bed then and have that dressing gown at the ready first thing in the morning,' Harriet insisted.

'Harriet you're not talking to that Bast er Bustard boy now, you know! Indeed this is a side of you I didn't know you had. Here have the damned things back. Put them on and do up the buttons on that cardigan while you're at it!'

Harriet wriggled herself back into them.

'Oh blow this Harriet, what are you getting out of bed for now? You're not after that sodding ghost are you?'

'No I am not Mr. Sanderson, I'm just checking to see if the cat's maybe on the windowsill? Oh no, she's not. I know I did hear her meow, though.'

'HARRIET get into bed, *will you?* Now, this minute, before I get out and carry you back myself.'

She flounced onto the duvet, swinging her feet to the floor, struggling to resist the urge to look under the bed.

'But I did hear her Mr. Sanderson, I'm sure I've just heard her meow.'

'Oh crikey, I'm not looking for the damned thing now. If she's here we'll find her in the morning.'

'I'm scared Mr. Sanderson, Tricia thinks this house feels spooky, too.'

'Well Harriet, she's not here right now. I'm here. We could cuddle up, you don't need to look.'

'No, it's quite alright, thank you. I'll be OK.'

'Fine, right then, goodnight Harriet, and do try to get some sleep.'

'Goodnight Mr. Sanderson and don't forget about that dressing gown in the morning.'

Harriet lay still, ears pinned, listening for noises; very quickly Mr. Sanderson, breathing deeply now moving rapidly towards sleep. She turned over towards him as gently as she could then instantly shot up to the sound of that whistling noise again, only much louder now. She shook his arm.

'Can you hear it Mr. Sanderson? Listen, it's spooky. Ooh I'm scared, I'm really scared.'

'Oh sod this Harriet, now you've woken me. Come here!'

She cuddled into his bare chest.

'This bloody thing it's making me itch. Get the damned thing off.'

Harriet rested on her elbows to pull out one arm and then the other, dropping her cardigan to the floor.

'And sod this, I'm not having these thermal things tickling my legs either. Get them off or I go!'

Harriet wriggled out of them, careful not to bring her own pants down in the rush.

'That's better Harriet, now we're both wide awake. What do two people in love do to pass the time?'

'We could talk Mr. Sanderson.'

'Oh no, no, no. You needn't think we're going to lie here talking Harriet.'

She felt his lips on hers. His strong naked body on top of her. Fear giving way to the flood of desire awakening every fibre of her being. He slipped the narrow straps of her silk slip away from her shoulders, ran his fingertips across her breasts, moving from one to the other, his lips, warm and moist kissing each nipple in turn. From his body the faint smell of sea salt, she breathed it luxuriating in the scent. His legs moving back, to hers beginning to part. On top of her again, she knew she'd asked for this, but there was no way she was complaining.

His hand across her waist, gently now and brushing over her stomach, all the time his lips on hers, driving, forcing his kisses into her mouth. His hand moving slowly down.

'Oh crikey Harriet, not more bloody knickers.' He kicked the covers away, sliding his hand underneath the elastic at her hips. Suddenly Harriet squealed to an unexpected brush of fur against her face. Mr. Sanderson jumped up.

'Not that fucking cat again!'

'I don't know, I felt something; no, no Mr. Sanderson you've put the light on.'

'It's trailing that bloody jumper behind it Harriet. Mind yourself on that needle.'

'No, I'm not looking, I'm not ready for it yet!'

'Your not ready for it Harriet? I'm just wondering if I'll ever be!'

Harriet sat up, hugging the cat close to her chest.

'I take it you won't be needing me now you've got that damned thing back?' He tossed the knitting away from his dressing gown resting on the duvet. He'd had enough. He was on his way.

'No, no, please don't go. I know what'll happen, her fur will stand on end any minute now. It won't take her long to pick up the scent of that ghost.'

'Oh no not again. Look Harriet, just do me a favour and go to sleep.'

Still hugging the cat she flew out of bed after him.

'I'm going home tomorrow if you don't come back.'

'Bugger this! Just put the bloody thing down and get back into bed then,' he declared, becoming rapidly depleted of patience.

Instantly she dropped the cat to hide under the covers turning to face the window. Not daring to move she listened for signs of him going to sleep before inching her way backwards towards the centre of the bed.

'Now Pepper just you stay on my side or you're in big trouble,' she whispered.

She lay, nursing the cat to her chest, straining her ears for the ghost until finally being purred into a deep sleep.

Chapter 8

'Oh crikey, am I still dreaming? Harriet get this sodding cat of yours to shift its backside. What time is it anyway? Oh no, it's only six o'clock. It's barely light.'

Harriet didn't budge. He gathered the cat into both hands dumping it, only to see it leap back to curl up at her feet. For a moment he propped himself up on his elbow just to look at her. The light from the bedside lamp catching her face then falling to her partially covered body. Still fast asleep, her long dark eyelashes fringing away the outside world. Her lips full, slightly apart, her skin soft. He gently touched the blonde hair falling over her shoulder from which the narrow strap of her nightdress had slipped. He breathed a very deep sigh at the fullness of her pale breast, barely covered, against the buckling red silk. He dare hardly believe that at last he'd finally caught this infuriating, beautiful, impulsive, funny, almost childlike woman. Just widening the gap with a nudge of his finger to the edge of her nightdress, her rose pink nipple exposed now, gently protruding from the encircling soft pink areola. In the quiet of the morning he absorbed her beauty, knew her breasts were changing. Could scarcely believe inside her, his baby. Recalled making love on the sand. He smiled. All those tiny buttons. Would he ever get to see and touch the fullness of her breasts? Now lying with her, not wishing to move. He smiled again, thought about last night. However was he going to be able to share her with this damned cat? Last night his mouth over this nipple. He looked again, recalled of all the many naked breasts he'd seen as a GP they were never as beautiful as this. Her pale breast round and full, her nipple as a small rose whose outer petals had spread wide and fallen soft into a circling delicate band of pink. Gently he allowed his finger tip to brush against her, creating an unconscious arousal leaving her nipple prominently beautiful. He fought against the driving need to wake her and take her. This beautiful, beautiful woman lying at his side; he knew as yet she wasn't his. He knew she'd flutter away at the slightest whim. He turned his mind to marriage, so painfully aware of his last failed attempt.

The cat stretched, a quick glance at Mr. Sanderson, thought better of it, opting to land on Harriet's face. She woke with a start.

'Oh Pepper, no, off, get down. Oh golly it's you Mr. Sanderson. She didn't wake you did she?'

'Well not this time, she didn't Harriet.' He smiled her that gorgeous smile, removing the tips of his fingers gently away from her breast.

'Oh no how long have I been lying here like this?'

'Only since I chose to edge your nightdress away from this Harriet.'

She felt his lips resting there, just like last night. Then his fingers gently tighten against it, sending wave after wave of sensual desire rushing through her body, sensitising, engulfing, swelling that part of her desperately opening to him.

'Wrong, I know. You'll just have to forgive me.'

With her eyes still half-closed she snuggled closer to him, then suddenly panicked to jump away.

'Oh I forgot you've got nothing on under there!'

Laughing, he moved closer towards her.

'I'll never understand you. It's not as if you haven't seen it all before. Good gracious me you're carrying my baby. How do you think it got there Harriet?'

'But I didn't see it then either. Look, you're just going to have to try to understand Mr. Sanderson. There, I can't even say your Christian name because you are my boss, I'm lying in bed next to my boss completely naked…'

'I wish you were Harriet.' He slid his hand under the seam at the side of her panties then out again to tap the end of her nose. 'Don't you ever take these things off?'

'You know I do Mr. Sanderson. How do you think you made me pregnant?'

'I took those off for you Harriet, as I recall.'

She buried her head in his chest, careful to pin the duvet down between them.

'So we've both got to leave the damned things on until you get round to calling me Joris?'

'That's right Mr. Sanderson, it was exactly the same with Mark.'

'Crikey Harriet, I don't believe I'm hearing this. You mean you leave your knickers on in bed every night? But you've got two daughters, how on earth did he manage? No wonder he wasn't up for marriage!'

'Well I wasn't always like this, actually that's precisely why I started leaving them on. With no sign of marriage I didn't see why I should make it easy for him.'

'Ah I see now Harriet, so it's not all about being your boss and only being able to call me Mr. Sanderson, you'll only take them off for marriage?'

She closed her eyes tightly and stayed like that. she knew what was coming next, the proposal. He lay back, stroked the strands of hair away from her face to look her straight in the eyes.

'Ah but you can't use that one on me Harriet, I wanted you to marry me and you accepted, only to fly away.'

'I was terrified, I just wanted to stay on amber.'

'Indeed, amber is your comfort zone, and may I ask how much was Mark a part of that? Things are not going to be the same for you now he's decided to do his own thing.'

She went very quiet. Mark's phone call had been devastating, too painful to contemplate just now.

'You see Harriet, I know you will need time to come to terms with Mark's decision. You also know I've fallen hook, line and sinker for you regardless of the fact you are expecting my baby. You've driven me to distraction Harriet, it's been like chasing a butterfly with my hands wide open. On this very bed just a few weeks ago I proposed again only to be turned down. Twice Harriet! Now that's hardly going to do much for the male ego. It's enough to make one never want to go near a woman again.'

'But you didn't ask me to marry you after we'd made love on the sand in Cornwall. You knew I was about to marry Mark and then you'd have lost your chance forever.'

'Good gracious me Harriet. How did you think I felt doing the dirty on Mark like that? I wasn't about to snatch his bride as well.'

'No, well, obviously it didn't cross my mind at the time, but it was only after Mark ditched me at the church you proposed. He had to ditch me first.'

'And rightly so Harriet. Regardless of the fact you weren't married, with two grown-up daughters you were bonded in exactly the same way. I would never have dreamed of breaking up your relationship by asking you to marry me.'

'No, no, I didn't mean that. I wasn't wanting that at all. That's where we started with all this. I wanted to stay on amber for most of the time.'

He stretched his arm across her pillow to lie on his back while she drew her knees to her chest in a sideways roll, just looking up at him.

'So you were only flirting with me Harriet? Just dallying with my affections. Digging little holes for yourself here and there, easy to climb out of, leaving enough safe ground to call amber. The trouble is you didn't know when to stop, did you?'

He turned over to gently pin her arms flat against the bed.

'I'm not to be dallied with any more Harriet. Understand? We've more to think about than ourselves now.'

She nestled her head in his neck as he lifted her slip, felt his hand move from breast to breast then down her body to rest where their baby lay.

'You saved this one for me Harriet. My beautiful, beautiful Harriet, you saved this one for me.'

His lips warm and moist on hers, just the sound of the cat purring inside the bag of knitting wool, she allowed her legs to fall apart. Gently he rested his hand between them, careful not to disturb the fabric of her red lace panties. Her mind, splintered, her back arching to the pressure, all desire intensified, running to where his hand lay.

'But last time on the sand, *you* took them off Mr. Sanderson.'

'And if I don't, will you?'

She buried her head further into his chest.

34

'I have my answer Harriet. This isn't easy for me either. It's not now, I believe you'd turn summersaults for me now, it's in the cold light of day you've got to feel comfortable with what we do and I just don't think you are ready.'

He kissed her forehead, then grabbed his dressing gown. She lay back, the need for him conflicting with the sense of relief at his words.

'Eyes tightly closed Harriet.'

Instinctively she obeyed, wondering why, when she'd just felt every inch of his strong, naked, tanned body firmly against every part of hers.

Chapter 9

'Splendid breakfast, thank you Mrs. Harris. Now what do you rate the chances are of getting the caterers in for this evening's meal?'

'Already done Mr. Sanderson, I'll just be needing to confirm the numbers.'

'Quite, er yes. Indeed, thank you. Yes, well done Mrs. Harris, jolly good stuff. Now I'll give Belinda a call straight away. I did inform you Clive Engells is back with us as from tonight, didn't I?'

'Yes you did Mr. Sanderson. As soon as I've seen to these dishes I'll check his room over.'

'Ah thank you Mrs. Harris, you are totally indispensable.'

Harriet nodded, watched her beam. Her eyes almost swallowing themselves as her smile broadened in delight.

'There's no reason why you shouldn't join us Mrs. Harris, give Mr. Hansen a call, and we'll make it a dinner party.'

'Ooh are you certain Mr. Sanderson? I'm sure he'd be very pleased indeed, we would only have been playing bridge down at the club tonight.'

'Call him straight away then Mrs. Harris whilst I get on to Belinda.'

He turned to Harriet, put his arm around her.

'We'll pop you back home as soon as I've done that, you'll be wanting to collect a few more of your things, I take it?'

'Oh yes, please, if that's OK, but what about the cat?'

'She was playing with Molly's cat last time I saw her,' Mrs. Harris volunteered.

'And has Harriet's cat been fed at all?' Mr. Sanderson enquired.

'Yes and don't you worry about her Harriet. She's as right as rain here. I'll keep an eye on them both while you're gone.'

'Ah thank you Mrs. Harris. We shan't be long anyway.'

'Oh Harriet I have noticed something about her though.'

'What's that Mrs. Harris?'

'She won't go down this corridor. Timmy will but yours just stands rigid staring at it with her fur on end.'

Harriet went cold.

'Oh crikey, here we go again. For goodness sake Mrs. Harris don't be telling her that, not after last night.'

'Well it's only the truth Mr. Sanderson.' She turned to Harriet.

'You know I've had my suspicions about that tunnel down there and I'm sure as we're standing here I'm not wrong.'

Harriet covered her mouth with her hand, felt a shiver spread outwards from her spine.

'I told you Mr. Sanderson, you said I was imagining I was hearing things in the night and I know I wasn't.'

'Utter rubbish from the two of you. That damned cat's neurotic. Anti-corridors, anti-tunnels, anti-cabins, anti-baskets, anti-sex. It's bloody selfish, wants all the attention all of the time. I'm up to here with it!' He placed his hand above his head to make the point. A frown crossed Mrs. Harris's face.

'What on earth is he talking about Harriet?'

'I haven't a clue Mrs. Harris.' She looked down for fear of her seeing the flush of guilt rising in her cheeks.

'Get ready Harriet, I'll be with you in a tick. Just let me make this call to Belinda.'

Almost too frightened to go back to her room, she pushed the door open wide to leave it like that. Sunday morning and the sun streaming through the tiny Georgian window panes. Last night's bed already made. Quickly she cleaned her teeth and brushed her hair, then sat on the bed, in the light of day trying to rationalise this lovely feeling of being so at home despite her renewed fear. She decided Mr. Sanderson was right, Pepper, being a very sensitive cat, could even be picking up the fear from the experience she'd had in the tunnel. She knew she'd been very tired last night. It had been quite a day. She rolled over to lie flat on the bed. In her mind, back with him, barely covered lying so very close. Felt sure most men would just have made love to it's natural conclusion. As much as she'd desperately wanted that she loved him for the respect and consideration he'd shown. In her heart she wanted this to work. Decided tunnels are spooky by definition. Decided to put this ridiculous ghost thing to the back of her mind once and for all. Decided she'd let nothing get in the way of being this close to her gorgeous boss.

She jumped as he strode into the room.

'Ah Harriet, Belinda's fine with that. Would you be OK with the Mercedes? It's just that Clive's been on. I've promised I'd go through this school governors' stuff for him before he arrives. We don't want to be having our heads down all evening with it.'

Her stomach flinched to an instant pang of nerves.

'Er, but, are you sure Mr. Sanderson? I've never driven anything like that before?'

'Oh you'll be fine Harriet. Come down, I'll just run you through it. In any case it's probably better you sort yourself out on your own. Happy with the dresses? I must say you looked ravishing last night, apart from the thick brown stockings, I must add.'

He laughed. She watched those dimples elongating to gaze at the slight irregularity in his teeth. This gorgeous hunk of a man actually wanting her to drive his silver Mercedes. She could scarcely believe it.

'Oh but it's school on Monday morning.'

'You'll be needing to gather all that stuff, too.'

'No Mr. Sanderson it's *school* on Monday. Wouldn't it be better if I used my own car?'

'Oh I think the Mercedes will get you there just as well Harriet.' He started laughing. 'I don't think we'll be raising too many eyebrows yet. Not unheard of for a head to give his deputy a lift.'

'Oh right, right, thank you. That's alright then Mr. Sanderson.'

'Oh and kindly take those long woolly knickers you insisted I wear last night, back and don't ever think of doing that again Harriet. I can't say I enjoyed my involuntary transvestite moment one little bit!'

She smiled, he put his arm around her as they walked downstairs. He sat in the car to show her the basics, then got out to watch her drive away, all the time wondering the best way to ensure she'd never slip through his fingers again.

Chapter 10

She drove slowly, crunching her way through the golden gravel towards the automatic gates. Fearful of taking her hand away from the wheel, she waved quickly before turning left into the narrow lane that would take her past Molly's and along the top road then down the steep hill towards Starboard Marine North West. The seat well forward. He'd laughed, teased her about going through the windscreen had it been any closer but at least she felt in better control. Gliding along, her thoughts turned to last night, the very first time she'd shared his bed. The September sun lower now, catching her eyes, she dropped the screen to see it gleaming along the silver bonnet, piercingly bright, she screwed her eyes against its excruciating intensity. Dappling now as the road turned, her eyes catching every intermittent, twinkling spark of light running to her mind already lit bright by this gorgeous hunk of a man. She looked out to the sky. Just the last modest remnants of mists burning away to expose its full, naked splendour. Almost there this morning. His hand resting between her legs. The thought intoxicating her with a rush of pleasure and excitement, mingling to have her mind saturated with this need for him, she could barely wait for tonight. Harriet loved the autumn, it was almost as if, this time it had brought with it this exquisite gift of love, especially for her.

Almost at Starboard Marine North West now, it felt strange approaching the traffic lights from this side. She looked across, thought about Belinda Oxfordshire, of seeing her tonight. Wondered what Tricia would say. Then it suddenly clicked. Yesterday, it seemed like a year ago now, but it was only yesterday she'd played Tricia's message. She was going to dinner with Clive Engells last night. He'd wanted to discuss how far he'd got with getting her "save Venice" tin back from Rapping Hammer. Then a thought.

'That's it, he'd probably take her to The Upper Tideside Hotel. Oh golly but why would he book himself in for the night? Must phone her as soon as I get back.'

She pulled the Mercedes to a halt, noticing the curtain twitch at the corner of the window in the house over the road. Head down she rummaged for her keys feeling strange without Pepper scrambling up her legs. She pushed the door open, lifting the junk mail at her feet before checking if there were any messages. For a couple of seconds she dithered then decided she'd phone Tricia first. 'Three of them and if one's Mummy's I'll be here all morning,' she thought.

'Tricia, oh I am glad you're there. Are you OK? Thanks for your message yesterday, sorry I haven't had chance to get back to you but I've got so much to tell you. Anyway how did you get on? Did you have a nice time last night with Clive?'

'Oh Harriet, he's only just dropped me back. I don't know 'ow, er I mean how, to say this but we went to that hotel down the road from our friend Joris. You know that very posh place where you were goin' to have your wedding reception.'

'Oh yes, The Upper Tideside Hotel Tricia. Was it nice? How did you get on with him?'

'Oh he was lovely Harriet. It must have been a spray tan he had when he met us at the airport because last night he looked a normal colour and I told 'im, er him he looked really handsome and I couldn't make out what was different about him.'

'Oh well, let's hope he works it out. Anyway Tricia how did you get on?'

'Oh I didn't Harriet. It was him who got on me. He had a room booked at the hotel and I have to say we did have quite a bit to drink so we decided to have our coffee in his room.'

'Oh no Tricia, wow, you didn't did you?'

'Well I don't want you to think badly of me but it was just the way the evening went.'

'Of course I don't Tricia, no it's just a surprise that's all. Gosh he's a lawyer and a very charming man. You've done well for yourself there. Do you think you'll be seeing him again?'

'Oh yes I am, tonight as a matter of fact.'

Instantly Harriet covered her mouth with her hand, he was supposed to be attending tonight's dinner party, not to mention Mr. Sanderson's attempt to fix him up with Belinda Oxfordshire.

'Brilliant Tricia, where's he taking you?'

'Oh you'll never believe this Harriet but our friend Joris is havin' a small dinner party and Clive is taking me along as a surprise guest. Well he will be lettin' Mr. Sanderson know but he won't be tellin' him it's me. Oh I wonder if it's goin' to be a little celebration of his marriage? I don't think they could have been on a world cruise, though. She must have already been there on the Galapagos Islands, hiding somewhere. Oh I wonder if Clive would take you too? He might just as well take two surprise guests with him. Would you like to go Harriet, I'm sure Joris wouldn't mind? You know you will have to get used to him being married now.'

'Oh Tricia, I'll already be there! He's not married either. Oh I've got so much to tell you.'

'You're jokin' me Harriet. She was all over him. They had to be gettin' married. Funny Clive never mentioned anythin' about you goin' tonight at all. I'd have been over the moon straight away if I'd known.'

'Well I'm just so pleased Tricia we'll be there together tonight. It couldn't have worked out better. Look, I haven't told you anything yet, have I?'

'No you haven't, and I can't wait to hear, go on then.'

'Mark's been promoted, it was supposed to start in January but they brought it forward, in two weeks he'll be running the Basingstoke Research Centre and basically that's where he wants to be, without me.'

'You what Harriet? I don't believe I'm hearin` this. I thought he was all set to look after you and the baby. What's happened to change his mind?'

'Well I didn't get chance to tell you but Mark did go to the Galapagos Islands, we only just missed him. When I went for that check-up Mr. Sanderson told me he'd had a long chat with him. It seems Mark opened right up, gosh Tricia when I spoke to him on the phone yesterday he was even telling me what a decent bloke Mr. Sanderson is.'

'Oh poor you. It must have been awful for you Harriet. You wanted it to work out with him didn't you and you would have been alright only going as far as Basingstoke.'

'I know Tricia, I was pretty cut-up yesterday afternoon, I'd never felt so alone in the whole of my life.'

'Oh and has somethin` happened to change that? Oh I do hope so.'

'Mr. Sanderson flew back, arrived yesterday morning. I had the cat clutched to me, I was crying all over her when he let himself in.'

'Oh so he still had your key Harriet, that must have given you a bit of a shock.'

'It did, I couldn't believe it. I thought with him getting married that was well and truly the end of it.'

'Flippin` heck Harriet, I'm gob smacked! How come they broke it off?'

'It was never on Tricia. It was all rumours, he knew they'd been flying around since Mark bugged out at the church and he stepped in. Apparently Ross Farquerhart was there researching for his PhD and it had always been somewhere Mr. Sanderson had wanted to go. Anyway he went out to do voluntary work at the hospital and Lucinda Lawton was doing the same at the school. He said she's staying out there hoping to get a permanent post. I didn't know she'd left. Apparently she didn't want a fuss made so no one knew. I got her job Tricia. I'm the new deputy. Of course they're obliged to advertise the post but Mr. Whittle and the governors have already approved my appointment.'

'Congratulations Harriet, I am really pleased for you. You should have been given it the first time round. But what about the baby?'

'Ah thanks Tricia. The baby? Oh he said having to take maternity leave in December is not an issue.'

'Oh no, of course, they're not allowed to discriminate like that. Oh but Harriet talkin` of babies I'm worried sick. With Bob not bein` around I've not been botherin` to take the pill. Well I haven't needed to, I haven't had it properly for ages since Bob seemed to develop a very funny reaction to me. Of course it didn't help me bringin` *er* name up all the time. I can't stand that Belinda Oxfordshire, it's her fault, she's the one who's just driven me into the arms of another man.'

'Oh you didn't go against your better judgement did you? I hope he wasn't taking advantage of you. Are you not alright about it Tricia?'

'Oh I am Harriet, but like I've just said, I didn't take my pill. I told him I had but I hadn't. Did you get any symptoms of being pregnant the day after?'

'Oh gosh Tricia, you've done exactly as I did. I fudged it just like you.'

'Oh no Harriet, please don't say that. Did you get any symptoms the next mornin` Harriet? I need to know.'

'No Tricia, not that I can remember. It never crossed my mind, not until the day before the wedding when I realised I was a day overdue.'

'Oh Harriet I've got to wait two whole weeks to find out.'

'Is it exactly two weeks Tricia?'

'Exactly two, I'm as regular as clockwork. Oh I think I've just done another one of those metathingies Harriet. Now why did you ask me that?'

'No, I wouldn't worry about it Tricia, we're all different.'

'What do you mean we're all different? What are you talkin` about?'

'Well the middle of the month is supposed to be the time when ovulation takes place, the best time for getting pregnant. That's how it happened for me, but honestly I wouldn't worry about it. There are plenty of people desperate to have a baby who do a temperature check and even buy ovulation indicators to make sure they give themselves the best chance of conceiving but still struggle to get pregnant, if they manage it at all. Others get pregnant outside of that time if for any reason their cycle is interrupted so I really wouldn't worry. I'm so sorry Tricia, that's the last thing I wanted to do was make you worry.'

'No, it's not your fault. I was the one who wanted to know in the first place. Oh I do hope that joke I made about Mrs Harris lookin` after our babies while we go off gallivanting isn't goin` to backfire on me. I hardly know him Harriet.'

'Now stop panicking Tricia. We know enough about him to say he's a jolly decent guy. Look how much he's helped out with the food bank at school. And the way he's fighting to get your money back from Rapping Hammer. It's not going to happen just like that, but if against all the odds it has, then I'm sure he's the kind of person that would lavish the whole world on you both.'

'Against all the odds? It must have been the same odds for you and you got caught.'

'Yes, but that's what I mean, we are all different. What happened to me has no bearing on your situation at all.'

'No I suppose you're right Harriet. Ooh we had a fantastic night though. Do you know Harriet I didn't know what I'd been missing out on. I don't know why I've stuck with Bob all these years.'

Harriet suddenly felt a little envious. With too many inhibitions she suddenly wished she was more like Tricia. Couldn't imagine her making Clive Engells hide under the covers. Couldn't believe she'd made Mr. Sanderson put on those long thermal knickers. What on earth must he be thinking of her for doing that? And as for the ghost, well, she decided she was just being ridiculous. Wasn't making a very good job of trying to grow up, at all. 'What on earth am I trying to do? He's probably gone off me already.' She pulled her thoughts back. Swapped them to wonder if she should warn Tricia of Belinda Oxfordshire's invite. In Tricia's shoes Harriet quickly decided she would most definitely want to know herself.

'That's absolutely fantastic Tricia. I couldn't be more pleased for you and don't let anything spoil the moment.'

'No, you're right but what about you Harriet? What did our friend Joris come to say?'

'Oh he was so lovely with me. He flew back especially to pick up the pieces really. Asked me to stay over the weekend with him. He's been just amazing. Oh Tricia I am so glad you will be there tonight. Look, if this was me I would want to be prepared so I'll tell you but please don't let it spoil your evening.'

'Ooh whatever are you going to tell me now?'

'Look of course Mr. Sanderson doesn't know about you and Clive, he was wanting to get Belinda Oxfordshire out of Bob's way so he thought it a good idea to invite her to dinner tonight as well to meet up with Clive.'

'Well I'm very glad you've told me Harriet but he's just a teeny weeny bit too late. Clive told me he'd watched me at the airport walkin` over to his car and somethin` just clicked inside him. he knew he'd fallen in love.'

'Oh wow Tricia that is just so very special. No wonder he wanted you last night. She's not going to stand a chance that Belinda Oxfordshire. It's going to be good fun Tricia!'

'Ooh it is Harriet and I can't wait.'

Chapter 11

Harriet still smiling, replaced the receiver to play the first message.

'It's Mummy Harriet. Just phoning to see if you are still alright. Oh Daddy and I are so relieved you are safe and out of trouble. Only yesterday James was saying what a narrow escape you had. Do promise me you'll be sensible now Harriet and put your mind to sorting out that wedding date with Sir Joris. From what James was saying he gathers Sir Joris has still got a very soft spot for you. It's an ideal time to get this sorted once and for all, especially now that good-for-nothing's still away. Climate change indeed. I don't think he knows what change is Harriet, not being able to bring himself to finally marry my only daughter. No Harriet you'll get nowhere with him he's a real stick-in-the-mud. You get yourself married to Sir Joris while you've still got chance. According to James there's a very pretty young girl taken over as chef at the golf club. I just wanted to warn you Harriet, the way to a man's heart is through his stomach so she'll have a head start on you. You've never been any good at cooking. You get in there Harriet while he's still got that Mrs. Harris. Oh I must go Harriet, Daddy's lost control of the pressure washer and he's just shot it at Violet's hair. She's probably startled him Harriet trying to say hello. Oh no she's soaked. Oh her hair's gone all straight Harriet and she only had it done yesterday. Whatever is he playing at? Look can I tell her you'll pop round tomorrow morning to put a few rollers in it for her? Thanks Harriet. Shall we say about eleven?'

'Oh no Mummy!' Harriet looked at her watch, it was already a quarter to. She dithered wishing she hadn't even played the message. Dashed around gathering her things for school together with her shoes and a pair of tights. 'Can't let Daddy down, Mummy will never let him hear the end of this if I don't go.' Struggling with her bags she banged the front door closed behind her then tried every key on the ring in an attempt to unlock the car boot. 'Oh sod, they're just going to have to go on the floor in the back.'

Behind the wheel now, the silver Mercedes gliding towards the traffic lights outside Starboard Marine North West. This was the familiar approach but oh how different things were now for both her and Tricia. She looked across wondering just where all of this would take them. She shuddered at the thought of them both being held at gunpoint there to be taken hostage. It seemed a long time ago but although the flashbacks had diminished they could still take her by surprise to leave her trembling. She thought about Barry, of how good he and Andy had been. The brief walk they'd had together on the beach in the Galapagos Islands stayed

44

with her. Sat on the outcrop of rocks with the tide swilling their feet he'd left her in no doubt as to his feelings for her. She smiled. She liked him but he had never impacted on her in quite the same way as Mr. Sanderson.

She drove on, glanced left towards Canterbury Drive. Smiled again. No threat! Lucinda Lawton wasn't even there, but even if she were it would have been of no consequence. She wondered how her and Tricia could have got it so wrong. But then as Mr. Sanderson had already said, it was all part and parcel of rumours flying since that cataclysmic morning at the church. She turned into Well Close to park the Mercedes on the drive.

'Oh gosh Mummy will want to know the ins and outs of everything. Just keep it minimal Harriet,' she warned herself.

'Thank goodness you've turned up Harriet. But the car! Isn't that Sir Joris's? He's not sitting in it waiting, is he? Ask him in this minute Harriet. Where is he? I can't see him.'

'That's because he's not in it Mummy. He's just let me borrow it that's all.'

'Oh is that all Harriet? Nothing more than that?'

'Nothing more than that Mummy.'

'Oh and I thought you'd at last acted on my advice. Still it's a start. Now you make the most of this opportunity Harriet. He wouldn't go lending it for nothing. There's something more behind it. Don't go blowing this chance away Harriet. I'm telling you, you're not getting any younger you know. Now Mrs. Moss is waiting. She said for you to go straight round the back. She'll be in the kitchen.'

'Right, thanks. She got all the rollers and things?'

'Oh I would think so Harriet.'

Harriet stood on the doorstep suddenly feeling sick, decided this she couldn't do. She'd dashed from home without giving it a second thought. Instantly she became glued to the spot. Did she really want to get this close to Mrs. Moss? She'd pretty much managed to avoid her since she'd successfully impersonated her on the phone to the travel agent in Venice Mestre, in a posh voice dropping the claim against them for knocking her off her chair. In the confusion it did the trick, Violet Moss never even contested it. She'd had enough of the place to even give it another thought, she was just glad to be home.

'Well go on Harriet, what on earth are you waiting for?' Her mother urged.

'Oh no, I'm sorry, I'm really sorry, I just remembered......' Then a theatrical voice unmistakeably that of Violet Moss made her jump.

'Ah there you are Harriet. Look it's all washed ready. Do come in dear, round the back. I'm in the kitchen.'

Harriet hopped over the low fence to follow her.

'There Harriet, this is so good of you. I've long since given up on trying to do it myself. To tell you the truth I love going to the hairdressers' to keep up with the local news once a week.'

'Gossip more like,' thought Harriet, forcing a smile.

'Yes, good to get out. You should try to persuade Mummy to go with you, I'm sure it would do her good, too. Now how do they do these? Straight from the centre all the way down the back?'

'Oh I don't think so Harriet. She takes them all the way across from here to here, with these on this side going down.'

Harriet, her nerves overheating, made an inward groan. It was bad enough doing her mother's and those curlers knew their way in. This didn't sound in the least bit straightforward.

'A very distinctive car you're driving Harriet. Do you know it's almost identical to the one that arrives here when they've all been playing golf. Ouch!'

'Oh I'm so terribly sorry Mrs. Moss. Did that one roll a little too close?'

'Oh never mind Harriet. I get that at the hairdressers' all the time. I was beginning to think she did it on purpose until Cedric warned me of going paranoid.'

'Oh that's a terrible thing to say Mrs. Moss, of course you're not. It looks easy but it can be very tricky getting the pins to stay in. I do it to Mummy all the time and she's just the same, thinks I'm doing it deliberately when I wouldn't dream of it. It doesn't mean she's going paranoid though.'

'Oh Harriet what a nice, reassuring girl you are. Do call me Violet. You know you can start to get that way. This country's not what it used to be. These young bits of kids they don't know what the meaning of good service is and as for good manners, well they don't seem to know what they are.'

Harriet continued rolling, thankful her complaints were being directed elsewhere.

'Do you know Harriet your dear father was so apologetic when he soaked me yesterday unlike this young streak of misery Avril's got herself tied to.'

'Oh right, yes. They own the fish and chip shop in the Stetmead Row, don't they?'

'Now, however do you know that Harriet?'

'Oh it was by accident really, you know with Avril interested in buying our house. I was in there a few weeks ago and there was a bit of a scene with that pawnbroker guy, you know the one that kidnapped us?'

'Yes, yes Harriet. I didn't know whether I should mention that or not. Terrible, terrible experience for you both. Well you at least, I'm not sure that cocky little madam you call your friend didn't deserve it though.'

Instantly Harriet could feel her stomach drop. 'Surely not Venice,' she thought.

'You know Harriet it upsets your mother badly that you are so well aquainted with her. You know it is distressing when our children wilfully go their own way. Now where was I? Oh yes Avril. He mentioned her then?'

'He didn't know who I was, but it was only when that pawnbroker and his wife left the shop he told me his father was heavily in debt to them. The guy was actually threatening to pull the loans in and close the shop.'

'You what Harriet? Did I hear you correctly? But I've heard nothing of this from Avril. I understood them to be solid, sound business people. You mean she's marrying into a family of debtors? Oh I can't believe all this. CEDRIC, do come here this minute, Harriet wants to fill us in on Frazer Chambers.'

'Oh but I don't Mrs. Moss. I'm terribly sorry but I don't know any more.'

'But you must Harriet. Indeed you must or you wouldn't have known of his association with Avril.'

Harriet could feel herself going bright red, had to steel herself against the urge to drop everything and run.

'What's all this about? Oh hello Harriet, not with that girl then? I thought you two were like the terrible twins, never separate?'

'Oh do leave if off Cedric, Harriet's disclosure is alarming. Do you know Cedric that Frazer Chambers and his family have all but gone bust. Bankrupt Cedric and our Avril's expecting his baby.'

Cedric Moss suddenly screwed up his face, scrutinising Harriet before speaking.

'This is a serious suggestion young lady. Are you sure of your facts?'

Harriet thankful to have finished the crown of her head, fished for some smaller rollers to go round the back.

'If you could just bend forward Mrs. Moss, I'll have this done now in a jiffy.' Cedric Moss could barely restrain from learning more.

'We'd need you to throw some light on this Harriet. You do know Avril is pregnant? We downsized in moving here to be able to get the pair of them on the housing ladder. Fifty fifty with his parents of course. They're in a one-bed apartment at present, no place in which to bring up a young child I can tell you. We're banking on the Chambers to provide the other half of the deposit. Now isn't it your house she's set her heart on?'

Harriet, anxious to leave, delayed her response to wind in a couple more rollers.

'Well I don't know very much actually. I happened to be in the shop when that pawnbroker arrived with his wife. A tussle broke out and he threatened to pull in the loan, Mr. Moss.'

'Yes Harriet, that's what you've already said,' Mrs. Moss interrupted. 'But what did he say about Avril?'

'Oh it was after they'd left. We were both a bit stunned. He just said that would put paid to them getting the house Avril really wants. Well it's a fairly unusual name and obviously I'm very aware of how much Avril wants our house. Mummy never stops telling me.'

'Oh right, I see now Harriet. Oh by the way Violet and I were deeply sorry to learn of the trauma you've been through.'

'Oh she knows all that Cedric, I've already said that. Now what in the name of goodness are we going to do about Avril?'

'Well at least he's been caught Mrs. Moss. I don't know what the legal position is when a fraudster wants to call in debts.'

'No neither do we Harriet but we'll jolly soon find out.'

'There that's the last one Mrs. Moss. I hope it turns out alright for you.'

'Oh thank you so much Harriet. See how different she is Cedric when she's not with that dreadful girl. Now you remember what I've just said and take your mother's advice.'

Harriet looked at her watch. 'Must go, I'll need to pop in to say hello to Daddy as well. Bye!' She gathered her bag, then a quick nod and a wave. With incredible relief she closed the back door behind her, then hopped over the fence to ring her mother's doorbell.

'Oh come in Harriet, I've just made a cup of coffee. All finished? You were quick, you've only been half-an-hour. It takes you much longer than that to do mine.' She planted her hands on her hips, nodding towards the door.

'Oh hello love.'

'You alright Daddy?'

'I am now you've sorted her out. Has she got over her soaking yet, love?'

'Oh yes, I wouldn't worry about it,' Harriet said, wondering whether to declare her faux pas.

'No George, don't worry, she'll be as right as rain now Harriet's done her hair. There'd be nothing stopping you nipping over the fence to do it every week when you've finished mine, do you think Harriet? Save her a bit on the hairdressers' bill.'

'Mummy you've got to be joking. And you keep hold of that pressure washer in future Daddy, I'm not going round there again.'

'Oh dear what ever happened Harriet?'

Chapter 12

Harriet looked at her watch as the automatic gates opened. It was ten minutes to twelve and she felt sure Mr. Sanderson would be wondering about his car. She crunched through the gravel to park next to the caterer's van, got out to see Mr. Sanderson walking towards her.

'You OK Harriet?' He laughed. 'I was beginning to think you'd done a runner with the car!' He put his arm round her for a moment then opened the rear door.

'Ah Mr. Swift would you be so kind as to take all this stuff to Harriet's room? Ah good man, thanks a lot.'

He replaced his arm around her as they walked towards the house. 'Oh come on down here a moment. It was too dark last night to see anything very much. Come on and I'll show you the new quay I'm having built.'

Looking up she smiled at him. His hair blowing slightly back from his shoulders. In profile, this stunning, heart-melting man striding her across the lawn, past the helipad and down the steps. She looked across, the mountains clearly visible on the far side of the river, standing magnificent against the ice blue sky.

'Wow it's fantastic. It's very big,' she declared.

'So is the boat Harriet. I'm wanting to bring Libby back from Falmouth for the winter.'

'Oh wow! "Mare Libertas", she's gorgeous.'

'You liked her then?'

'Absolutely! I love that name. I've always remembered it. "From the sea freedom".'

'Well done Harriet! Fancy bringing her back with me?'

She clenched her fists against her chest rubbing them together in delight.

'Ooh yes please Mr. Sanderson. When are you hoping to do it?'

'As soon as they've finished this. I'd like to bring her in before the weather breaks. Anyhow lunch, I left Mrs. Harris preparing it. How did you get on with the Mercedes then?'

'Oh brilliant, you hardly know you're driving it.'

'Three years old now, we must get round to trading it in. Fancy another or should we look at something different?'

'No, no, it's just got to be another silver Mercedes. Too many memories, I really don't want to see this one go.'

'Well there's no reason why *you* shouldn't keep it Harriet. Give me chance to indulge my whims with the next one. Yes we'll do just that.'

She smiled to whisper an inadequate thank you. Could scarcely believe he'd just said that. Felt his arm around her shoulder as they climbed the steps to head back to the house.

'Oh I've had another call from Clive whilst you were out. Bringing along a surprise guest this evening. What could I say? Mercifully Belinda's unaware of my efforts to pair them off but an odd number's not good is it Harriet? Any suggestions? It's getting to be a bit short notice now, anyhow.'

Harriet looked down for fear of him seeing the red blush overtaking her cheeks. For a moment she swung to and fro wondering whether to come clean then decided against it. It wasn't really anything to do with her. She looked up, relieved to see Mrs. Harris dashing towards them.

'Ah Mrs. Harris. Yes I do apologise for keeping Harriet from lunch. I wanted her to see the new quay, we're on our way. We'll be there in a tick.'

'Yes it is ready Mr. Sanderson but it's not that. No, Belinda Oxfordshire's on the phone wanting to know if she can bring someone along this evening. Shall I say that will be alright?'

'Yes most certainly do Mrs. Harris, if you would be so kind. You'll need to update the caterers though.'

'Right, will do, thank you very much Mr. Sanderson.'

They watched her hurry across the lawn to disappear behind the front door.

'Well, well, it must be something to do with you Harriet. A prayer answered. Now I wonder who she'll bring? Did you say it was on or off with her and Mrs. Harrington's husband? I can never keep up with it all.'

'I'm not actually that sure myself but I wouldn't have thought it likely she'd arrive with Bob.'

'No quite, quite. Actually I think they have a cousin staying at the moment. Lewis I think she said his name was. That'll be it, she'll be bringing him along. It's growing like Topsy Harriet, let me see, how many of us will that be now?'

'Ten, yes that's right, five couples, that makes ten of us.' They looked across to catch Mr. Swift on his way to the greenhouse.

'Oh damn Harriet. I can't leave him out. Do you know it never crossed my mind. Go and see Mrs. Harris will you please before she speaks to the caterers. Tell her there'll be twelve. I'll just go over and have a word with him now. Tell her I'll confirm that.'

'Come on in Harriet and get your lunch. Where's Joris got to now?'

'Oh he's just off to have a word with Mr. Swift, Mrs. Harris. He told me to let you know there'll be twelve of us for dinner now. Oh he wants you to tell the caterers, if you wouldn't mind, please.'

'I'd better do it then. Do you know Harriet they're doing him a favour coming out on a Sunday, they don't need all this messing about.'

Harriet sat herself down at the kitchen table smiling at the two cats with their noses in bowls in the corner. She got up to stroke them, Pepper standing, pushing her head hard against Harriet's hand.

'You're purring Pepper, oh and Timmy, too. Good here isn't it? It's better than being on holiday.'

She washed her hands to return to her seat just as Mr. Sanderson appeared with Mrs. Harris.

'There you are Harriet, just let me serve the soup and you can help yourself to the rest.' The shank of ham sat before them, succulent, roasted to perfection. An assortment of pickles, cheese and pate and the aroma of freshly baked rolls, sitting in the bread basket, beneath the crusts, brown and white bread soft, warm and inviting.

'Mmm this looks gorgeous, thank you Mrs. Harris.'

'I'll second that. Red or white Harriet?'

'Oh red please, thank you Mr. Sanderson.' He smiled, looked up.

'Are you not joining us Mrs. Harris?'

'Oh I've already had mine, thanks. I'll be needing to get the kitchen cleared to give the caterers free rein for tonight.'

'Ah yes, good thinking Mrs. Harris. I'd go and put your feet up if I were you. Give you a chance to get a bit of a rest before this evening. We'll clear this lot away as soon as we've finished, won't we Harriet?'

'That would be a pleasure. It won't take a minute,' Harriet smiled.

Mrs. Harris beamed as she slipped out of her apron.

'Well thank you both, It will give me plenty of chance to spruce up for Mr. Hansen.'

'So how did you get on back home then Harriet?'

'Yes, fine thank you, I wasn't there long though. There were three messages but I only got to play the first. It was the usual from Mummy until she spotted Daddy through the window soaking Violet Moss with the pressure washer, then she changed tack asking me to go round this morning to re-set her hair. So that's where I've been.' She paused to place a knob of butter on the side of her plate. He laughed.

'Did you have any better luck with hers than your mother's the last time we all landed on her?'

'Oh yes, of course, you all called in. You'd been playing golf with James and Daddy the last time I did Mummy's hair. She took all the rollers out didn't she because they were too tight.' Mr. Sanderson laughed.

'What's the matter Harriet? You look worried, you haven't trussed up Mrs. Moss in the same way have you?'

'Er no, I've managed to spill the beans with regard to Frazer Chambers and his family.'

'Who on earth is Frazer Chambers Harriet?'

'Oh it's Mrs. Moss's daughter's boyfriend, Avril, you know the one who wants our house?'

'Oh I see and how did you manage that?'

'Golly I haven't had chance to tell you yet but before I was kidnapped I was in the chip shop on The Row only to discover the lad serving was Avril's partner.'

'Ah, Chamber's chippy.'

'But surely you don't call it that do you Mr. Sanderson?'

'No, I don't but there's plenty in school who do. So how did you manage to dig yourself into yet another hole Harriet, I'm curious?'

'That vile pawnbroker came in with his wife, started a row and threatened to call in their loans. When they'd gone Frazer Chambers told me the business was almost bankrupt and his dad had pretty much pawned everything then moved on to unsecured loans, the interest rates were creasing him.'

'Oh I expect there would be something in the small print whereby the shop would stand as collateral.'

'Oh gosh I hope they don't lose that. But what happened was Violet Moss thought Frazer had come from a well-heeled business family. She was expecting them to be stumping up half the deposit with them to enable Frazer and Avril to buy a house.'

'Ah I get it now Harriet. So you've enlightened them this morning. Oh crumbs.'

'I didn't mean to, she's a bit like Mummy really, over Mark. She's not fussy on Frazer and had to spill it out. I only told her what happened just like I've told you. I didn't know she was going to go off on one!'

'Crikey Harriet, here let me carve you some more ham.'

'Thank you, that's lovely. Of course it doesn't help Avril's expecting.'

'Quite no, no, it certainly wouldn't. You know Harriet you'll not be needing 4 The Willows much longer. What did Mark say about his share of the house?'

'He's handing it over shortly, he reckons he'll be able to afford to with the salary he'll be getting. He also said it would then be up to me to sort out your legal settlement.'

Suddenly she felt a little uncomfortable. It was still her house, her security and she certainly didn't want to lose it.

'Well Avril won't be able to buy it anyway,' she continued. 'What with no deposit and Frazer Chambers more than likely unemployed.'

'Not buy Harriet, how about renting it? Oh is that a hint of a scowl?'

'But what if I suddenly need to stay on amber Mr. Sanderson? I've got to know it's still mine.'

'Yes, yes of course you have. Look Harriet I suggest we phone the agent tomorrow and take it off the market completely. I'll get this legal option rescinded so once Mark hands it over it will be solely yours to do with as you see fit.'

Harriet took a deep breath, reached for his hand. Oh this gorgeous, gorgeous, understanding man. He stretched forward to kiss her cheek.

'Now stop worrying. You've been through enough. Just one step at a time now, that's the way forward.'

'You are lovely Mr. Sanderson.'

He laughed. 'Now say it again, but this time just try saying Joris.'

She shook her head, looked down to her lap.

'He or she in there can hear you know. I'll never get to be called "Daddy" what's the betting the child's first words will be Mr. Sanderson?' With his hand placed firmly on her tummy he laughed again.

'Joris, Joris, Joris, Joris.'

'Now you're making me sound like a steam engine. Oh forget it Harriet, it will come when you're ready.' He squeezed her hand tightly, kissed her again.

'I love you,' he whispered.

'I love you, too Mr. Sander, er, Joris.'

He laughed, placing one elbow on the table to rest the side of his face in his hand. Serious now.

'Three months Harriet. You know it's high time you registered yourself for a spot of prenatal care.'

She looked down almost refusing to accept the reality of her condition, then decided she was close enough to this doctor if she needed one, so what would be wrong in pretending?

Chapter 13

Harriet slipped into the long white dress, delicately trimmed at the neck and hem with swirls of tiny embroidered pink rosebuds. She loved the way it swirled out at her calves but touched at the white lace edge of her bra showing at the neckline, fearing the cut to be just a little on the low side. She clasped her silver pendant closed to finger the tiny cross, anchor and heart charms at her neck. Molly would be coming. Harriet knew she'd be pleased to see her wearing it. A quick brush to her hair and a spray of Channel No 5. She was ready.

'My word Harriet, you look absolutely stunning.' From the bottom of the right handed staircase Mr. Sanderson beamed up at her.

'All thanks to you,' she smiled, as she tried to lift the rosebud trim to cover the lace edge of her bra.

'No just leave it where it is. It's inviting, beautiful.' He swung her from the bottom stair to twirl her in his arms.

'Come, come, let's have a quiet five minutes together in the drawing room for cocktails before the guests arrive.'

She sank into the armchair by the window. This was their very special room. The field of flowers, the rush of excitement from a glance at the huge picture hanging on the facing wall, flooded her mind, her body. She watched him, his blonde hair resting at his shoulders, looking good in his dark virgin wool dinner suit from the Burberry collection. His pristine white shirt left open at the neck, his white cuffs resting low from the sleeves of his jacket. She turned as he sat down looking splendid in the chair opposite.

'Ah Mr. Reeves. Good to see you again.' Mr. Sanderson stood to shake hands with the barman.

'I presume you are au fait with the latest additions out there?' Mr. Sanderson enquired. The barman smiled across to Harriet then nodded.

'Certainly Sir, now would you like me to take your orders?'

Harriet felt a little flummoxed, she looked across to Mr. Sanderson for help.

'How does a Fraise Sauvage sound Harriet? Plymouth gin mixed with a strawberry puree, a hint of ginger with the zest of lemon.'

'Oh lovely, yes please.'

Mr. Sanderson nodded at the barman.

'Yes, we'll both have the same, thank you, Mr. Reeves.'

She watched him sit down to take his customary position. His right leg angled across to rest his foot against his left knee. He was smiling.

'My beautiful Harriet, my beautiful pregnant Harriet. Have I finally caught my beautiful amber butterfly, would you say?'

She looked down, could feel herself flushing. Scrambled for something to say.

'I think it would take me some time to get used to this lifestyle Mr. Sanderson. What if I couldn't? What if couldn't fit in?'

'What kind of a breed do you think we are Harriet? We're no different from anyone else. You're no different from me. Why indeed, your brother James and his wife mix very comfortably in our circles, I'm wondering if your mother's right about Mark, in that his Bohemian attitude to life has maybe rubbed off a little on you?'

'Oh I don't think so, it's not so much to do with Mark as Mummy. She's always been a snob and I've always railed against it. Look how beside herself she was when she thought we were going to get married. Still is actually. She never lets go of wanting me to sort out the date.'

Mr. Sanderson reached for his glass, serious now, he watched her intently as they sat in silence for a few moments.

'Not that I mean you or your social circle are snobs Mr. Sanderson. It's just Mummy and her social climbing. James, Paul and I all had the same start. We're all her children, we're all basically OK, but in her eyes James is the only one who's really made it.'

'Oh I see and what about Paul, what does he do?'

'Apart from getting Susan pregnant you mean?'

'Yes apart from that Harriet.'

'Paul's an accountant.'

'Ah could that explain it?'

'What do you mean?'

'Not a profession particularly noted for its excitement.'

'Well no. Anyway Mummy certainly can't get her head round them having five children, thinks it's lower-socio but she'd never admit that. She just thinks that's why they still live in "an over-stretched semi", they've never given themselves chance to better themselves.'

'She might be right.'

'No, no Mr. Sanderson she's not right. This is the conversation we had in school, remember? We can't make value judgements regarding anyone. Apart from the fact having children is a very worthy thing to do and to be honest I've often envied Susan. Which of her grandchildren would she do without in order that he and Susan could have had a detached house somewhere posher?'

'None of them Harriet, I'm sure of that.'

'Well then, why did you say she might be right? I've told you before happiness is the only criteria for success.'

'Well I'm certainly up for making you happy Harriet, we can have as many babies as you like.'

She watched his eyes twinkle. The corners of his mouth moving towards a smile. Could feel herself blushing as the door opened.

'Ah Mrs. Harris, how pleasing you look.'

'Oh thank you so much Mr. Sanderson, er which room will we be taking the guests prior to dining? Oh there's the phone, I do hope it's not someone pulling out. Just a minute Mr. Sanderson let me go and answer it.'

'Well you never know Harriet, if both Clive and Belinda lose their guests we might make a match yet.'

'Oh it's for you Harriet. A Barry Giordano. Wasn't that the chap you had to phone in a hurry on that dreadful day you'd been captured?'

'Yes Mrs. Harris, that's him, thank you.' She looked at Mr. Sanderson. 'Shall I take it in your study?'

'If you must Harriet. I think I'd better have a word with the PM, see if I can't get that damned man posted permanently out of our lives.'

Harriet stunned for words, smiled briefly towards Mrs. Harris as she rushed from the room, fuming at Mr. Sanderson's comment, her mind instantly whirling silent spasms of indignation.

"OK so he painted that disgusting picture of me but only to sabotage my relationship with him. OK so I was furious at the time but he's apologised since and he and Andy were lovely the way they looked after us after being kidnapped. No, no, he's no right to say that. There he goes using his influence. Barry's a lovely guy. I'm not being part of getting him posted anywhere. I'm going home tomorrow!' Suddenly she couldn't wait to see Tricia. She looked at her watch. 'Just about five minutes now.'

'Hi Barry, you alright?'

'That's a relief, I wasn't particularly keen on speaking to *him*. I was wondering the same about you Harriet. I left you a message, have you not been home? What are you doing there anyway?'

'It's a long story Barry but I'll be back home tomorrow. I promise to phone you then. Did you want something in particular?'

'Yes Harriet, I want my picture back. No one seems to know anything about it. The shop's all locked up and I can't get any sense out of anyone. Of course it's all in the hands of the lawyers that place. I don't suppose Sanderson's any better informed?'

'Well I really wouldn't know about that Barry. I'll ask him if you like. I'm sure he'd like to see the painting back with you. He certainly won't want that floating around.'

'Yes Harriet, please do. So what's all this about anyway? What are you doing there Harriet?'

'Oh I'll tell you tomorrow, unless of course you're phoning from Somalia?'

'No I'm back in Manchester and I want to see you. You at school tomorrow?'

'Yes but I'll try and leave straight away, though it might be difficult with Mr. Sanderson there and me now being his deputy.'

'His deputy, since when?'

'Well I was acting head if you remember while he was away but he came round and told me Lucinda Lawton had resigned. He left her at that school in the Galapagos Islands, she's hoping for a permanent post there.'

'I can't say as I'm that interested Harriet. Has he given you her job then?'

'That's it. Well I'll have to do the interview but it's in the bag.'

'So what are you doing there? Are you back with him?'

'No, no of course not Barry. Look he's having a small dinner party that's all. It's OK Tricia will be coming. Clive Engells is also up. We'll be taking the opportunity to discuss the new food bank we set up at school. Oh that's the doorbell, it's probably Tricia now. Look I'll have to go. Come round at four-thirty I'll make sure I'm back by then.'

'I'll be there Harriet.'

'Mind how you go Barry.'

Harriet put the phone down desperately hoping Mr. Sanderson wouldn't ask what that was all about, better to mention it later. She pulled back the study door to find him marching impatiently towards her.

'First guests Harriet. What was that all about? What did *he* want?' She hesitated.

'Come, come Harriet I want to know *exactly* what that was all about.'

'Oh it's only the picture Mr. Sanderson. He wants it back. He was wondering if you had any idea where it is?'

'No, not. Absolutely not. His MI6 expertise not serving him too well at present then?'

He strode ahead to open the door. Harriet not insensitive to his distinct change of mood though aware it now better matched hers.

'Ah Molly, Percy. Good evening to you both, do come along in.'

'Let me take their coats Mr. Sanderson.'

Harriet shot upstairs to lay them on the bed in her room, grateful for the few moments on her own. Peered at the cat fast asleep curled in the bag of knitting.

'Oh it's no good asking you Pepper. What am I going to do now?' She lifted her away from the needles to place her ready curled in the cat basket. For a moment she rose to follow her tail then sank back into oblivious slumber.

'We'll leave this open Pepper. Don't want you trapped in this thing.'

Just a fleeting sense of relief at being able to confide in something as she stroked the shiny, flattened fur between her ears, then that old familiar spread of nerves panging across her stomach almost overtaking her annoyance with Mr. Sanderson. She wanted to see Tricia again. She felt a cold shiver down her spine, the evening closing in to unlock the strange fear she'd experienced in the night. She needed to know if Tricia would be sensing it too.

'Harriet!' She jumped at the sound of her name.

'Oh Mr. Sanderson, I'm just coming.'

She rushed down the stairs expecting to find him at the bottom. Just Mrs. Harris crossing the fireplace in the huge square hall.

'Oh that's strange Mrs. Harris, I thought I heard Mr. Sanderson's voice then. He's just called me.'

'I don't think it was him Harriet, he went straight to the wine cellar taking Molly and Percy with him, as soon as you took the coats upstairs.'

'Oh no Mrs. Harris, please don't say that. This place is spooky enough at night.'

'Oh don't set me going on that Harriet, I've had my suspicions but I'm a level headed woman. I've not experienced anything like that in this house after all these years but it's the tunnel I don't like. I steer clear of that passageway if I can. I think that's why I came over all funny and fainted when you and your friend were shouting for help from the other side.'

'Well you wouldn't have needed any more than that Mrs. Harris, it must have been a real fright for you. No, thank goodness you were there at that moment to hear us. But it was last night Mrs. Harris, I was so scared I had to wake up Mr. Sanderson.'

'And he wouldn't hear a word of it?'

'Exactly Mrs. Harris. I'd got over it by the morning and felt very silly about it when I woke up but now it's evening. Oh I don't know, hearing that voice just now, it's brought it all back.'

'Now you listen here Harriet. You know I've referred to the trail of young ladies Mr. Sanderson has brought back over the years and there's only one he's ever opened up to me about.'

'Oh, really?' Harriet wasn't sure what to expect.

'Yes really Harriet and it's you. While you were out this morning he told me he'd never been happier. He asked me did I think he'd finally caught his "beautiful amber butterfly". My eyes filled with tears Harriet, you know I've been here that long he's almost like a son to me. He hugged me Harriet and when I looked up, his eyes had misted over. I shouldn't have been talking like this. We're both being ridiculous Harriet. There's no ghosts, just a long, dark tunnel. That's enough to make anyone feel scared. Don't break his heart over that Harriet, I couldn't bear to see you break his heart again.'

Suddenly Harriet was clasped to her matronly bosom.

'You know Harriet, it's not just him. This place lights up when you are around, I know I'm being selfish but it's just as much for me, too. I want you to stay here. The two of you together, here. It felt so empty this morning once you'd gone.'

'That's lovely Mrs. Harris, really lovely. One day I'd like to explain everything to you. I must seem so callous in the way I've treated Mr. Sanderson but it just been fear, really, and I'm always digging huge holes for myself and dragging everyone else in with me. It's a wonder he's still interested. To be honest I thought he'd gone off to marry Lucinda Lawton, oh I didn't like that one bit, but who could have blamed him?'

'No, no Harriet. If you didn't know it, I certainly did. You've been the only one he's really cared about for some time now.'

Harriet smiled, stepped back to the sound of them laughing, coming back from the cellar.

'Cocktails in the lounge, shall we?'

Mr. Sanderson ushered them all forward, Harriet hanging back as the doorbell rang. She rushed to answer, wanting to be first to say hello to Tricia.

'Oh, er, hello Belinda, it's good to see you, you're not on your own are you?' she enquired.

'Oh *you're* here Harriet Glover. He actually didn't say anything about that. What is it, some kind of school staff meeting?' Belinda Oxfordshire peered down her classically shaped nostrils. Where is he anyway?'

'Oh he's just chatting to guests in the lounge. Would you like me to take your coat?' said Harriet wondering who she'd brought along.

'Indeed not. Let's wait for them shall we. I know Joris's house far better than you Harriet Glover, I didn't need you to be opening the door for me, either,' she announced sneering as Harriet's cheeks flushed bright red.

Harriet could feel herself going bright red. Belinda Oxfordshire had grown up with Mr. Sanderson with both sets of parents being friends. Harriet suddenly felt excluded, like she didn't belong at all. It had been different in the drawing room. Just the two of them and the beautiful reminder of the field of flowers, but this was his world and she'd scarcely entered it. Even with Mrs. Harris's beautiful words still in her mind she suddenly felt her confidence drain away, a deep sense of inferiority running through her. She clung onto the door holding it open whilst Belinda Oxfordshire breezed straight past and into the lounge. She could hear Mr. Sanderson's welcome. Like he'd never ever broken off their engagement. Then all of a sudden Tricia's voice, raised, just closing the door on Clive Engells' beige Bentley. Harriet stepped out. Convinced she was hallucinating.

'No, no it can't be, Belinda Oxfordshire surely hasn't brought Bob along?' Shocked at the thought, she rushed back to the lounge to stand in the doorway.

'Ah Harriet. You haven't still got that front door open have you? My word there's quite a draught coming through here.'

For a moment she froze, hardly hearing Mr. Sanderson's words.

'Harriet what ever is the matter? Belinda's guest is surely here by now?'

Mr. Sanderson turned to Belinda Oxfordshire.

'Lewis, it will be, Belinda. I haven't seen him for some time. So looking forward to meeting up again.'

She spoke briskly as she followed them both through.

'No actually, not him. No, rather more of a surprise than that,' she replied, briefly scratching her head. 'Actually Joris I've brought two guests along and there might be a third. I didn't think you'd mind. It was all a bit last minute actually so difficult to let you know. Still Mrs. Harris is always so accommodating I'm sure she won't mind setting another two or three places at the table.'

'Mrs. Harris isn't on duty this evening Belinda, I've invited her along with Mr. Hansen which, according to my reasoning, makes them both guests.'

'Joris whatever's got into you?' She shot Harriet a sour glance. 'Or have you taken *her* on now instead, as the housekeeper? I can't think why else she'd be here.'

Just at that moment Harriet felt like one. Trust Belinda Oxfordshire to hit exactly the right spot.

'That is quite enough Belinda. I think Harriet deserves a full apology for that remark.'

'No, it's quite alright Mr. Sanderson, that's exactly the way I feel just at this moment, anyway. I think I'd far better fit in as one actually.'

'What rubbish is this you are talking now Harriet? What's that fucking secret agent been saying over that damned phone?' Furious, he turned back to Belinda.

'Just exactly who *have* you brought along this evening, Belinda and what is the reason for doing so?'

Unfazed, she placed her hands on her hips. Actually Ross Farquerhart was my first choice but I couldn't catch him. I left a message and he didn't get back to me until after I'd decided to ask someone else. Oh and I thought I'd better cover just in case, so there's a possibility Caroline might turn up but as yet I haven't heard. Not that it would matter if they all arrived. It is a buffet evening, is it Joris? You didn't think I'd be arriving here on my own did you? I could hardly turn Ross down once he'd been invited.'

'You're not leading that young man astray I hope Belinda? You are aware he's my PhD student and not to be distracted from the task in hand. When did he get back from the Galapagos Islands, anyway?'

'He arrived this morning, didn't you realise he'd missed his flight? He was supposed to be coming back with you?'

Mr. Sanderson looked across to Harriet.

'I'm afraid I had far greater issues on my mind.' In that brief, sharp glance Harriet could feel the intensity of his annoyance. 'Mrs. Harris would you be so kind as to ask the caterers to set another couple of places at the far end of the table, it would seem we could have another two guest to cater for.'

Mrs. Harris stopped in her tracks.

'Oh right Mr. Sanderson. Er is there any sign of Mr. Hansen at all?'

'He could be out there for all the noise that's going on. Anyhow it's early yet Mrs. Harris. Do give the poor man time.'

She looked sideways at Harriet then scuttled off to the kitchen. Mr. Sanderson raised to full height.

'Good heavens, it seems the whole place is to be filled to the gunnels with surprise guests this evening, just make sure it doesn't turn into a complete fiasco will you?' Harriet decided he was definitely looking at her just then. That was meant for her! 'How dare he?' she fumed to herself, 'Oh I'm so on my way home tomorrow!' she watched him stand tall in his Burberry dinner suit whilst slipping his fingers through his hair at the same time as clearing his throat.

'We'll all feel better after a glass of wine or too. Let's retrieve the evening as best we can, shall we? Ah the doorbell, come along Harriet, some fresh air. Let's see who's out there. Let's get them onboard shall we?'

Harriet twisted her lip then bit on her thumb as she turned to follow him through, past the fireplace in the hall, to the open door.

Chapter 14

'Ah Clive, good to see you again. It would seem we're surrounded with surprise guests this evening. Now let me see, might I ask who you've brought along?'

Clive Engells looked behind him.

'Oh do come along in Clive, now where is she?'

'It would seem my dear surprise guest has met up with her ex out there Joris. What a strange coincidence!'

'What are you talking about Clive?'

'Well just listen to them. The pair of them are at it already.'

'The pair of who? Oh dear, I know I've been plying the cocktails but surely I'm not that far gone already?' Mr. Sanderson looked at Harriet.

'Er Harriet, have you any idea what's going on here? Didn't I just hear the doorbell?'

'Oh they're all on their way over now,' Harriet replied, sidelining the question.

'Oh no, stone the crows, that's not Mrs. Harrington I see stomping along with her hands in her pockets? Good heavens, indeed, it is. I'm damned sure Belinda wouldn't have invited her. What the hell's going on Harriet?'

'Clive's just as good as told you Mr. Sanderson. There's only one person Tricia would be fighting with,' Harriet replied, not wishing the involvement flowing from enlightening him.

'My surprise guest Joris!' declared Clive Engells.

For the first time in her life, from under the porch light, Harriet was looking straight into the face of a truly embarrassed Mr. Sanderson.

'Oh I do beg your pardon Clive, there's nothing wrong with the girl, it's just a fucking nightmare when these two get together.' He turned to Harriet as she swiftly landed her gaze to the ground.

'So who's Belinda brought that Mrs. Harrington has so obviously taken a complete dislike to on first meeting?'

'Oh has she now?' Belinda Oxfordshire suddenly piped up, stalking towards them. 'What the hell have you been playing at Joris, surely you've got better sense than to ask me to bring a guest, suggesting *any* guest and then invite *her* along as well.'

'No, no Belinda, what you are unaware of here is the fact that kindly, I was also invited to bring a guest. Joris and Harriet here had no idea who would be arriving,' explained Clive Engells, anxious to calm things down.

Harriet could feel the deep crimson blush to her face spreading like a bush fire through the whole of her body, convinced her hair had turned bright red, too.

'*Harriet!?*' demanded Mr. Sanderson. One word, one tone, one single facial expression reserved especially for her. She looked up, then down again, fuming at his insinuation it was all her fault.

'Oh can I come in then seein` as how the door's already open?'

'Ah Mrs. Harrington, yes indeed, do come through. What's happened to our other guest then? Not dumped him in the nettles I hope? Mr. Swift's growing the damned things for nettle beer. Apparently that fussy little wife of his can't get enough of the bloody stuff. Lives on that and steak and ale pie by all accounts. Er, Mrs. Harrington might you refrain from such familiarity. Do stop poking me like that.'

'Ah Mr. and Mrs. Swift, how very nice to see you again.'

'And you Mr. Sanderson for sure. It's Vivian but do call me Viv, just as Mrs. Harris does. Oh and he's Ken but you already know that Mr. Sanderson. Oh look, there, she's on her way over, now, your Mrs. Harris. Hello Daisy, Reg here yet?'

'I was just on my way to find out. It sounds like everyone's arrived at once.'

'Yes well I would greatly appreciate if you could all call me Joris, if only for this evening. I've never quite understood why people have such difficulty with it.'

'Oh, is that someone driving in Mr. Sanderson?'

'Sounds like it, let's hope it's at least someone we know!'

'Oh yes that'll be Mr. Hansen now. As punctual as the dawn is Reg, always bang on time!' Viv predicted, exuding an air of confident satisfaction.

Mr. Sanderson raised his eyebrows, momentarily wondering which planet she'd just catapulted from.

'Splendid, now Mrs. Harrington, now where has this husband of yours got to? He's a long time coming in,' Mr. Sanderson said briskly, convinced he'd finally got it right.

'Don't ask me, ask her. I didn't ask him to come.'

Belinda Oxfordshire opened her mouth then closed it again as she jumped to one side.

'Oh let me get through, let me go and see to Reg. He's a quiet man, he'll want me by his side until he gets used to the company,' flustered Mrs. Harris.

'Ah Ross, good evening to you. Good flight? I believe you are accompanying Belinda here, this evening.' He shook hands, smiled as Ross Farquerhart pushed his spectacles further up his nose. He caught Harriet's eye. She caught his very wide beam as he stopped in a gaze of admiration.

'Wow!' He pushed his glasses further up his nose, then took them off to wipe them with his handkerchief only to return them to the mist blowing upwards from his disbelieving mouth.

'Wow Harriet, you look gorgeous!'

'No that wasn't Reg at all Mr. Sanderson, that was a car driving out.'

'Where's Mr. Harrington then?'

Belinda Oxfordshire squeezed her way through.

'Well that's our lift home gone! Look what you've done now Patricia Harrington. It took me all that time talking Bob into picking up Ross here and now you've chased him away!'

'You'll just have to make do with one man tonight then won't you Belinda? I told you Bob was no good in bed, he probably didn't fancy freezing up with you tonight. Still I suppose you could have tried the two of them together. It's always quicker defrostin` a freezer with two.'

She glowered at the snigger from behind.

'That's not funny Ross Farquerhart. There's no way either of you would have got your hands on me tonight.'

He tried to lose the smirk rapidly gaining momentum.

'Lighten up Belinda. It was supposed to be a good night out. You didn't want him in the first place, or so you said,' snorted Ross Farquerhart.

'Well you can get home any way you want. I'm staying here. JORIS, will it be alright if I spend the night with you?'

'I'd be just a teeny weeny bit more subtle about it if I were you Belinda. he won't be wantin` you turnin` him into an ice-lolly in the middle of the night. You might find yourself `avin` to walk home.'

'What was that Belinda? Did I miss something here? Sorry I was just showing our guests to the lounge,' Mr. Sanderson enquired.

'It looks like Bob's changed his mind. He's left, in any case. You've already been drinking and I can't bear the thought of taking a taxi. Would it possibly be alright with you if I stayed the night?'

'Oh no problem whatsoever Belinda. Now relax, come along, the barman's taking orders.'

'Oh thank goodness for that Harriet, we've got the hall to ourselves.'

'Come up Tricia. You can leave your coat in my room.'

'Oh I say Harriet, it sounds like you've well and truly settled in.'

'Oh no I am not Tricia. Here, just lay it on the bed. Look, sit down a minute they won't notice, they're too busy chatting down there.'

'Oh it's really good to see you Harriet. I'm so sorry you had all that with Mark. You didn't need that after being kidnapped. You know Harriet we've had a very traumatic time. I can't tell you how helpful Clive has been in helpin` me to get over it. And how about our friend Joris, has he been any help to you?'

'Well he has Tricia. Actually he's been lovely, so kind and generous. Look he bought me this and two others.'

'Oh I was admirin` that Harriet, it's very pretty. Wow, you certainly lit Ross Farquerhart's firework. You should have seen the way he's just been lookin` at you.'

Harriet smiled, she wasn't interested. In fact the less said about him the better, allowing him to kiss her like that on the cliff top during the school camp was something she could not let go of easily. He'd even slipped away the straps from her shoulder. It took that to bring her to her senses, he was a lad young enough to be her son. On the rebound, gazing out to sea, desperate to be back on the beach in Cornwall with *him*. *Him* on the verge of marriage with Lucinda Lawton, or so she'd thought. Mrs. Harris's words suddenly came back.

'Look Tricia, he's gorgeous. He's absolutely gorgeous but Barry phoned here, this evening before you all arrived. He wants that picture back. Mr. Sanderson was so horrible about him. Spoke of getting him posted abroad permanently. Him and his friends in high places!'

'Well he's forgettin` it was only Barry actin` so quickly to get us all out of here that we stayed safe. They might have had a way of openin` that door. No that wasn't very nice of him at all to say that.'

'No it wasn't and you're absolutely right. You should have seen him change. He was furious about the call. I'm not going to be party to that. Barry can be so lovely. He's been good to us Tricia. I'm not having anything to do with that. It's been magical being here until then, oh apart from the ghost last night.'

'Ooh Harriet whatever do you mean by that?'

'I definitely heard something here in bed last night, a scary high pitched yowling sound. It must have unsettled the cat because she disappeared. Oh I was terrified. I had to get Mr. Sanderson out of bed. He ended up coming in here with me.'

'Ooh you wouldn't be feeling very much like havin` the good time I was then Harriet?'

'No, no, I don't know what he thinks of me. I wouldn't even take my pants off.'

'I wouldn't worry Harriet. he knows you're expectin` and bound to be a bit more sensitive in any case. I wouldn't have felt like it either if I'd have been in your shoes.'

'Well that's not all, I know Mrs. Harris is terrified of that tunnel. She won't go down that passageway leading to the wine cellar for fear of going past the door. She said it's always cold as ice there even on a hot day.'

'Oh spooky!'

'And I could have swore I heard Mr. Sanderson call me from the bottom of the stairs when I was in the bedroom earlier but no, he'd taken Molly and Percy down to the wine cellar. Mrs. Harris told me that.'

'It doesn't sound good Harriet. No wonder you're scared. Do you remember when we were runnin` back through the tunnel and we stopped the other side of the door to see that picture of the Madonna and Child gleaming. We only had one torch between us and it was not shining on that. It was still gleaming when we started running again, don't you remember how we looked back?'

'Oh I do. I don't think I could ever live in this house. You know Mrs. Harris wants me to, she said she'd love me to live here.'

'Maybe that's why. She probably spends quite a bit of time on her own here one way or another, the way our friend Joris comes and goes. I don't mean that she doesn't like you as well Harriet. I'm sure she does.'

'Oh I know exactly what you mean Tricia. Do you know I've wanted to see you all day to tell you about this.'

'Well I wouldn't worry about tonight. he's got plenty of bedrooms here. This place is more like a hotel. The way they're drinking down there, I can't see Clive in a fit state to take me `ome, er home. Oh sorry Harriet I'm still tryin` very hard to improve my elocution for `im, er him. That's a bedroom next door, isn't it? I'll insist Clive and I have that one. We'll meet on the landing if we hear anything funny.'

Chapter 15

'Ah there you both are. You two down at last. We've just about ten or so minutes before dinner is served.'

Mr. Sanderson ushered them into the lounge.

'Now are we all here?' He looked around the room. 'Mr. Hansen not yet arrived Mrs. Harris? Ah that sounds like the doorbell now. You might as well get it Mrs. Harris. I'll be with you in a tick. Do sit yourselves down you two, you're blocking the doorway here.'

Tricia followed Harriet to the double sofa just to the right of the door.

'Oh no Harriet, that's not Bob's voice I can hear, is it?'

'No that's got to be Mr. Hansen. Bob drove off remember?'

'No it *is* him, I'd know his voice anywhere. What's he doing back here?'

'Oh oh, we're about to find out.' Her hushed words hardly finished, Harriet looked up to see Mr. Sanderson guiding them all through. Moving across he turned to Belinda Oxfordshire, now fully engaged with Clive Engells, swamping him with her presence.

'Mr. Hansen broke down on the way and Bob Harrington, here, being the kind of person he is, stopped to offer assistance. As you can see I persuaded him to join the party after all as he's insisting on honouring his pledge to take both you and Ross home,' he announced.

Harriet watched Belinda Oxfordshire's face drop whilst Tricia consumed his every word with delight. It was almost worth having Bob around for that, seeing as she was very obviously on track for stealing the father of her unborn child he'd be a useful distraction!

She nudged Harriet's arm, whispered,

'Just look at her all over my Clive. Serves her right! Now she'll be stuck with fat-face-four-cheeks until she gets home.'

'But Joris you've already said I could spend the night here. You're simply not allowed to go uninviting guests. It's not on, going back on your word like that!'

Instantly Bob cut in.

'That's alright Belinda, Tricia and Harriet here will both need a lift back and with young Ross in the front there wouldn't be room anyway.'

Tricia paled, digging her elbow into Harriet's side.

'Oh bloody-hell I don't want to go home with him,' she whispered.

'I do,' replied Harriet to the sound of Mr. Sanderson elevating his voice.

'It's no problem whatsoever Belinda, certainly you may spend the night here.'

She blew him a kiss.

'You're such a sweetie, Joris.'

'When it suits him,' Harriet muttered.

'Look, he's not making any difference, just look at her still all over my Clive. I was hopin` for a night here with you Harriet. Trust big feet Bob to put his size nines in it. I do hope they don't put me next to him at the dinner table.'

'If you'd all like to come through, I believe dinner is about to be served,' Mr. Sanderson suddenly announced, raising his hand to one of the catering staff in the doorway. He weaved his way through the crowd spreading the message like some duty-bound missionary.

Tricia shot up making a rush to the door, beckoning her to follow, Mr. Sanderson just gaining the edge.

'Er you'll find your seat at the table, they're all place-named Mrs. Harrington, I believe you to be seated at the window end next to Clive. Harriet you're next to me at the top.'

'Look Harriet he's parked Bob at the bottom end on the other side of me. Oh I'm not `avin` that, here let's do a quick swap, he can have him up his own end seein` as he insisted on askin` him back.'

'Tricia he'll notice. Who are you going to swap it with?'

'Yours Harriet. he can `ardly move us once we're sat down.'

'MRS. HARRINGTON what on earth are you doing?'

They both jumped as he strode in.

'Look Mr. Sanderson it's bad enough `avin` my ex here without `avin` to sit next to him. How could I ask anyone if they'd be willing to move when there's only Harriet here? She very kindly agreed. Anyway it's too late now I can hear them all coming.'

'Indeed it is not too late Mrs. Harrington, replace those cards immediately. The both of you kindly conform to the original seating plan and take your seats right now.'

'Oh I'm swappin` over with Clive then.'

'You'll do no such thing Mrs. Harrington. It won't hurt you to be civil to your husband for once. With the exception of Belinda he barely knows anyone else here. You've children to consider Mrs. Harrington, it's high time you got this marriage of yours back on track!'

Mrs. Harris wishing she'd hung back caught Harriet's eye, then smiled.

'Oh I'm not intruding am I? It's just that we all got caught up chatting again. We're all on our way through now Joris, if that's still alright?'

'Yes, yes Mrs. Harris, er, Daisy. Hurry them along will you, we can't keep the caterers waiting all night.'

Mr. Sanderson quickly pulled Harriet's chair out to allow her to sit down, immediately marching to the other end of the table to do the same for Tricia.

'Ah yes, do come in all of you. Belinda I think you'll find yourself seated on the other side of Clive here, when he turns up. Bob you're at the end next to your wife on the corner there and Ross you're next to Belinda. Molly and Percy, this end on that side for you, er Mr. Swift, or should I say Ken and Vivian, I believe you're next to them. Mrs. Harris, that is Daisy and Reg, I have got that right, haven't I? Er you're both seated over here on this side, next to Ross.'

The shuffling of chairs fell back to the polite chatter repositioning itself to the formality of the dining room. Harriet glanced across to Tricia, watched her fury blazing crimson as she turned her face as far away from Bob as she could manage. Harriet felt her own anger rising:

'Oh just give over chatting with Clive Engells and the barman in the doorway, will you Mr. Sanderson?' She thought, as far as she was concerned the sooner this dinner party was over, the better.

She watched Mr. Sanderson stretch his arm to take a set of burgundy leather-backed menus from one of the caterers. One between two all the way round the table then he finally sat down to take Harriet's hand under the cloth.

'Now let's see what treats we're about to partake of shall we?'

Grateful for the opportunity she released herself to take hold of the menu, this mood wasn't about to shift lightly. It sat over her mind like a tightly woven hairnet, not allowing any sense of forgiveness to permeate. 'First Barry, now Tricia,' she thought. 'If Belinda Oxfordshire hadn't made a play for Bob in the first place, their marriage would still be intact. Not Tricia's fault.' She looked down the table. Tricia silent. Belinda and Clive chatting away. Ross Farquerhart silent. Decided this mix of guests was never going to work.

'Right for starters, "Salmon and Scallop Aspic Terrine, served on a green leaf salad vinaigrette" or "Pheasant Pate with chilli jelly and side salad", mmm, sounds good Harriet, what will it be for you?'

'Salmon please Mr. Sanderson.'

'Yes, I'll go for that too, I think. Now "Clear Duck or Mushroom Soup"?'

'Oh mushroom please.'

'I'll part company with you on that one Harriet, and go for the Duck. Now "Apple or Lemon sorbet"?'

'Apple please.'

'Yes I'm with you on that. No choice on the next one I'm afraid, we'll all be having "Coq au Vin served with Croutons and buttered Noodles". Now, I wonder if it's up to Mrs. Harris's standard? He smiled. 'Now let's see what's for desert. Ah yes, Mrs Harris asked if they could use up the remainder of the soft fruits. Yes here we are, "Fruits of the Forest Merangue served with Fresh Double Cream or Iced Clotted Cream". Yes, well done them! There were rather a lot left, or "Crème

Caramel with Whipped Cream and Fresh Berries". We've plenty of time to consider these, Harriet.'

He sensed her mood and smiled her that smile, confident of regaining his ground.

'So from what you've said Avril Moss and Frazer Chambers are still interested in your house then Harriet?'

'It would seem so, but they're hardly in a position to proceed. It doesn't look like Avril's working and Frazer Chambers won't be much longer for the takeaway by the sound of it.'

'Mm, maybe it's time for a little sympathetic assistance, do you think Harriet?'

'Sympathetic assistance? I'm not sure I understand what you mean?'

'It needs work Harriet. It needs money spending on it if we're to attract a firm buyer.'

'But it wasn't that long ago Mark and I did it.'

'Quite, quite. Have you worked out exactly when that was?'

Harriet hesitated.

'Well, I suppose it could be getting on for four or five years since we actually started. I've got to admit it did drag on a bit and I suppose some of it didn't actually get finished. Still it's not that bad or Avril and her mother wouldn't be as keen as they are.'

'That's the point, the agent's been bending my ear over this one for some time now. This couple are keen but it's probably more to do with what they can get it for.'

'Oh, so they've been putting pressure on you to try to get us to sell have they? Is that what you're now suggesting Mr. Sanderson because I'm not about to give my home away to anyone?'

'It's unfortunate Harriet but with the economic mess the country's in it's going to be years before property becomes a sound investmest. We've been selling off much of the business portfolio. Renting has become a time consuming non-profitable liability I'm afraid and I'm certainly not looking to add yours to the books.'

'Oh, well you don't have to because even when Mark hands it over to me I'm not selling.'

'In that case you'll be needing to take the mortgage on yourself, I presume?'

'It's not a huge mortgage. Forty-seven thousand isn't a lot these days.'

'It's debt Harriet, unless Mark's agreed to take some of the responsibility for it.'

'No, he didn't say that. If he's planning on buying something in Basingstoke he's not going to be able to support two mortgages. Anyway I'll get a permanent pay rise for this deputy post so I won't have any trouble meeting the payments.'

Overhearing, the waitress bit her lip as Mr. Sanderson paused to pass the menu back. With all orders taken and wine glasses filled he stood to propose a toast.

'To you all for being here and especially to Harriet, my lady in waiting.'

'Oooh well now?' Percy looked up, smiling.

'Lady in waiting, eh?' Ross Farquerhart suddenly grinned.

'Waiting for what, that's the question?' enquired Bob almost innocently from the far end of the table. He turned to Tricia. 'And will you stop kicking my feet.'

'Come on don't leave us in suspense Joris,' declared Belinda. 'Or have you got her lined up for the maid's job here?'

'Ouch! I've just asked you to stop doing that!' Bob winced.

'I haven't a clue what you're talkin` about,' Tricia shouted over the noise.

'Good old Tricia,' Harriet decided to herself, 'she'll fend all this off.' She bent her head, furious with Mr. Sanderson, waiting for the cacophony of curiosity to die down.

'To Harriet,' they chorused as they raised their glasses to her blushes.

'To Mr. Sanderson for appointing me to the post of Deputy. Just waiting for it to be made official,' Harriet gabbled sensing she'd successfully dampened the atmosphere.

He caught her eye, started laughing. Then spoke gently to her as normal chatter resumed.

'First the house, now this. So I'm being stonewalled am I? You'll not slip through my fingers this time Harriet, I promise you.'

'Why did you say that? It was absolutely loaded.' She watched his eyes signalling disapproval at the question.

'They are all going to know sooner or later, I'm being realistic. Just preparing the ground.'

Interrupted by the bustle of starters arriving she knew he'd said just as much as he'd intended, knew she'd have to let it go.

'Look you've embarrassed her Joris. Don't take any notice of him Harriet whatever he's just said,' Mrs. Harris smiled.

'Oh it's herself she embarrasses, it's poor Joris you should be feeling sorry for. Now Clive where were we?'

'Nowhere you should be Belinda Oxfordshire with my partner yet again! I'll have you know it was Clive who invited me here not you. You've hardly looked at poor old Ross sittin` there gazin` at the embroidery on the tablecloth. I bet you wish you hadn't bothered coming Ross don't you? OUCH! he's just kicked me! Oh I'm not stayin` here next to him. Here Ross you come and sit by me, swap places with fat-face-four-cheeks here so he can talk to her. I might stand a chance of gettin` my Clive back then.'

Ross grinned totally bypassing Tricia.

'No I've been thinking actually what the chances are of the Roman ninth lost legion sculling around here. There's plenty of Roman history going on in these parts. That tunnel the kids went down. I don't suppose there's been any ghostly goings on down there while you've lived here, has there?' Mr. Sanderson looked up to take a very deep breath. The whole table hushed, turning to Ross in anticipation of his next words.

'You see I've been researching it and the whole of Britain is littered with anecdotal evidence, heresay, old wives tales passed from generation to generation particularly around the Scottish borders. But it's really got me going this. I've been delving into the archives and this place is as bloody near a match as I can come up with.'

'Language young man!' Mr. Sanderson declared.

Ross Farquerhart pushed his spectacles up his nose frowning at the interruption.

'Now where was I? Are yes! Now I've discovered there was a Celtic monastery built on the island at the start of the fourth century A.D. in line with the introduction of Christianity to Britain just after its inception on Holy Island. But, with regard to this island here, there's some evidence to suggest the monks were driven from it early in the four hundreds which generally marks the end of Roman rule, with the exception of pockets around the country of course. Now given that the Romans were meticulous record keepers, there's actually no record of this very strong 9th legion as to where it ended up. There's all kinds of speculation as to what happened to it but the monastery was definitely taken over and there's archaeological evidence of Roman remains on the island. Apparently one source suggests the monks on re-occupation of the monastery recorded their findings of skeletal remains shrouded in Roman battledress, somewhere on the walls of the tunnel. So it's not difficult to suppose this to be the lost 9th Roman Legion who were overthrown by the marauding locals who got their revenge on those that weren't killed by throwing them in the tunnel to leave them to their fate. Story has it the Romans attacked and pilfered valuable cargo, like spices and gemstones, from passing cargo galleys and on finding the haul, the monks created the image of the Madonna and Child from the gemstones, by way of atonement for the atrocities committed on their land. Apparently the sound of ghostly wailing coming from the tunnel to both the house here, and the old house on the island has been recorded down the centuries in various sources.'

Harriet went white. Tricia instantly forgot Belinda Oxfordshire, shivered her next sentence across the table to Harriet.

'Oooh Harriet and we got put in there. Oh Ross Harquerfart...'

Mr. Sanderson cleared his throat, instantly raising his eyebrows.

'Er sorry Ross, er Farquerhart, are you quite sure you've been readin` about the right house? You do know `arriet and I had a very ghastly experience and you're not really helpin' our post traumatic stress, especially as poor Harriet heard somethin` in the night.'

Harriet turned to Mr. Sanderson.

'Sorry I'm definitely not selling my house now, not ever!'

'What foolishness. Sheer nonsensical rubbish. Deviating a bit from your original idea for this PhD I rather think young man,' he snapped, glaring at Ross.

'No, not really.' With a forceful index finger travelling swiftly up his nose he suddenly twitched, instantly blinking soup away from his eyelashes as his spectacles somersaulted with a splash into Belinda Oxfordshire's delicious consommé.

'Oh Ross now look what you've done you menace,' she spluttered. 'Mushroom soup sloshed all over my best cashmere. Oh no Clive, don't start dabbing with a napkin, you'll rub it in. Here let me get out. Let me take all this to the kitchen.'

Suddenly Ross winced to a sharp slap on his hand.

'Look I've just told Clive, now you just get out of it Ross you're shaking the stuff everywhere. Leave them in for goodness sake. I'll wash them in the kitchen.'

'You see,' Ross continued sucking at the back of his hand, 'once this legion had been annihilated the monks regained the fortress and returned it to its original state.'

Harriet caught Tricia's eye, their shoulders starting to shake.

'Oh well what `appened…?' She enquired of Ross desperately trying to contain herself, she tried again. 'What `appened to all the bodies then Ross?' She exploded.

'Do stop hooting, just calm yourself down Mrs. Harrington, it really isn't amusing,' Mr. Sanderson cut in. With her ribs bursting and cheeks sucked in Harriet decided to excuse herself.

'Oh I'm goin` too,' declared Tricia struggling with the words.

'No, neither of you will leave. It's high time you two learnt to control yourselves.' Mr. Sanderson turned to Ross.

'Do wipe that piece of mushroom from the end of your nose boy, it's beginning to look like something else.'

With her whole body shaking Harriet screeched laughing, trying to catch the tears running down her face as Ross continued regardless.

'It's been postulated most of the bones were gathered up and tipped in the river.'

'Still don't quite follow the connection, I'm afraid,' declared Mr. Sanderson rattled with impatience, barely managing to smile at Belinda as she returned to sit herself down.

'Oh sorry Ross I clean forgot about your spectacles.' Instinctively he touched at his nose moving his fingers swiftly from its high bridge down across his right cheek.

'Oh Ross what's that grey thing there. Just there?' Belinda suddenly demanded as she pointed with her soup spoon, 'It's making me feel quite ill!'

Harriet had watched the small piece of mushroom dislodge from his finger nail to rest like something just slid from his nostril to almost touch his top lip.

'Oh Ross Farquerhart it's a bogey, you revolting boy. Get rid of it this minute before it makes me be sick. Oh I can't look,' continued Belinda, cupping her hand around her left eye.

Impatient to continue a blank briefly crossed his eyes as he swiped his hand across his mouth to land it on his ear.

'Back to your question Joris, there were amber fossils in amongst these gems and apparently they were used in the structure of the mosaic. Now as amber is the earliest of all the fossils ever recorded, therefore I give you the link. There's an amazing wealth of history down there and if we can corroborate the evidence for the lost legion I'm going to be able to take the prize.'

'If I were you I'd take that bogey off your right ear first Ross,' howled Tricia shaking and shrieking from the far end of the table, 'how come it's `angin` off the end of that wire?'

'Oh do be quiet Mrs. Harrington. This really is most tiresome. Mr. Sanderson turned to Ross. 'I think your suppositions are highly unlikely! All a bit far removed. I'd advise you to stick to your original idea young man,' he announced.

'Well I haven't actually submitted the proposal yet but I can see a link in all of it. Don't worry my trip to the Galapagos Islands won't be wasted either.'

'Oh I'm not worrying, not about that, at least. I am concerned that you could be disturbing my guests, rather.'

Ross hastily went to push his spectacles up his nose just as they appeared on a small silver tray.

'Oh thanks,' he mumbled at the waitress, impatient to further explain. 'Of course it's not proven. No one really knows. If you wouldn't mind I'd like to inspect the tunnel walls for those drawings.'

'Oh you won't find anythin` there only sheep, will he Harriet? We saw some drawings of sheep on the wall the other side of the picture when we took the children down. They didn't look like Roman soldiers to me. Ouch!' Instantly she turned to her right. 'And you, Bob just keep them `obnail boots, them size nines to yourself. I'll talk if I want to.'

'Drawings! You say there are drawings down there! For certain there'll be more than those. Am I OK Joris to go down there with my torch and camera?'

'Certainly young man. You may do so right this minute if you feel so inclined. But have you got the equipment?'

'Er yes thanks Joris, especially this. Oh hang on a minute it's fallen off.'

'I told you that `alf an `our ago. What are you doin` with an old grey hearin` aid anyway Ross Farquerhart? Who have you been tryin` to listen in to?'

'Excuse me, if you don't mind it's part of my paranormal seeking equipment,' then he grinned, lifting his plate and serviette. 'They'll keep mine warm won't they?'

'Good gracious boy I was joking. You aren't leaving this very minute, are you?'

'I need to, I've got to do it. Is it locked, the door through?'

'It's the long black key on the end of the row hanging from the board on the wall in the kitchen,' Mr. Swift piped up.

'Oh don't you be lettin` any ghosts in Ross Harquerfart,' Tricia piped up. 'That thing's whistlin` already. You'll be attractin` them with that thing goin` off like that in the tunnel.'

'So I'm hoping. Now let me get to it!'

'What a strange young man,' Mrs. Harris suddenly decided, 'and what was that grey thing hanging from his ear?'

'Highly academic Mrs. Harris. Let's just put it all down to that shall we?'

'Grey thing Mrs. `arris? If it was the ear next to her over there, it was somethin` that wandered off from `is nose. Oh and you can just stop kickin` me under here again with them big feet. Go on Bob the hob you can have `is chair now. Try kickin` er under it, instead.'

All humour had long since drained from Harriet. She shivered, as she touched the faith, hope and charity charms threaded on the silver chain resting at her neck. All she wanted was to go home.

'Er Bob,' Mr. Sanderson declared, 'It might be a better arrangement if you came and sat by Belinda here. My apologies, of course, you having declined the invitation it was rather a case of squeezing you back in once the table had been set.'

'I've already suggested that, could do with Ross's hearin` aid, you. OUCH you bugger, just you stop that. Move him will you Mr. Sanderson before I `it him one with this.'

'Return that pepper mill to the table this minute Mrs. Harrington. Now what do you think Bob?'

'If it's all the same with you Joris, Ken and I are, or were trying to have an interesting conversation. It's her, for some reason she can't keep from driving those bloody high heels into my shins. Sit her up your end or banish her to the tunnel with that funny lad. He might be able to lose her in there for good.'

'Right, quite. Er I do beg your pardon Bob, er Ken. Mrs. Harrington come and sit this end. I told you to put that pepper mill down. You'll be starting on Clive next.'

'Yes I will if he doesn't stop talkin` to her. he was the one who asked me to come in the first place and she's never stopped gabbin` at him. Look neither of them have even heard what I've just said. Oh very well then, I'll come up to that end, at least I'll be nearer Harriet.'

'If you would do so with as little fuss as possible Mrs. Harrington. I see you've finished the starter, you only need to bring your wine glass along. This cutlery hasn't been touched. You know the meal's barely started and I was rather hoping this would turn out to be a pleasant evening for us all.'

'Excuse me Clive I'm `avin` to move my seat.' She scowled back at Bob feeling an intense and overpowering need to inflict massive pain. With glass in hand she shuffled her chair sideways only to get her feet twisted, jabbing her heel straight into the wrong leg. Tumbling to a helpless wedge between the various legs on the floor she grabbed at the swinging chair only to cartwheel it into the table, jolting the guests as she sat stunned clutching her glass to see the wine trickle down Clive Engell's stinging leg.

'OUCH! FUCK ME! WHAT THE HELL'S GOING ON? That'll do my varicose veins a power of good.' He rubbed furiously at the side of his leg whilst trying to pull the chair out from under.

'Bloody hell I was only tryin` to get out from here. Oh so sorry Clive that was meant for him. I got my feet all mixed up.'

Mr. Sanderson jumped to his feet to stride round the table.

'Here Mrs. Harrington, get up this minute. Are you alright Clive?'

Tricia, furiously spurred on by his unsympathetic tone refused to budge, swinging her right leg round to take revenge on Bob's left ankle, digging her heel straight in.

'Bloody hell you evil bitch of a witch, what was that for?'

'Well now you know just how it feels!'

'Up, up, right this minute Mrs. Harrington before you decide to go for anyone else.' Mr. Sanderson glanced up to see Mr. Swift nervously shifting his chair back.

'Oh fuck this for a good night out you can sodding well get yourselves home.'

'Oh but surely you're not leaving us Mr. Harrington? Come, come Mrs. Harrington, given that you've just seen fit to engage in a double attack, with only one apology coming forth, the least you can do is say you're sorry to your husband and try to persuade him to stay.'

'Well you needn't think I'm apologisin` to him and if he's goin` home, I'm certainly not. I'm stayin` here with Clive.'

'With Clive? You have so got to be joking Tricia Harrington. With Clive? He's a barrister for heaven's sake. What on earth would he be wanting from the likes of you?'

'Well maybe you'd better be askin` him that for yourself Belinda Oxfordshire,' Tricia finished looking for support with an appealing glance at Clive Engells.

'Mrs. Harrington will you not embarrass my house guest,' Mr. Sanderson commanded.

All eyes turned to see Clive Engells remove his patterned silk handkerchief from his top pocket to pretend to blow his nose.

'Oh Clive,' Tricia suddenly shrieked, 'that's much too good to do that with, here, have this!' She snatched Bob's bunched-up knapkin just as he made a grab for it.

'There Clive, blow your nose on this.'

Clive, embarrassed and harassed, unthinkingly dropped his silk patterned, ornamental handkerchief, to bury his nose in the knapkin, Mr. Sanderson watching in horror as first one, followed rapidly by three green peas fell from under the white cloth dangling towards his chin.

'Oh Bob, you haven't been pickin` your nose again have you and puttin` it all in Mr. Sanderson's nice white knapkin, I `ope? Oh no you haven't. They're peas. It's alright Clive, carry on, they're only peas. he never eats `is peas. Now that's not a nice place to put them is it Bob? I'm sure you've picked up that very bad `abit from her,' Tricia shouted, pointing an accusing finger at Belinda Oxfordshire.

'If you must know they rolled off the fucking plate and in my experience you don't go passing over knapkins to use as handkerchieves!'

'It was an emergency if you remember. Clive's eyes were still waterin` from my accidental kick.'

'Enough, that's quite enough Mrs. Harrington. Mr. Sanderson turned. 'Er Clive, you've er managed to… '

'Ooh Clive you've just got a bit of green sticking out of the end of your nose, now. It'll be one of `is peas. Oh here, come here. First Ross and now you.'

'For goodness sake Mrs. Harrington leave the poor man alone.'

'No, keep still Clive, I've got it, yes I've got it.' She turned, 'Next time keep your peas to yourself! Oh where's he gone now? Oh no, I don't think this one was a pea after all Clive.'

'Mrs. Harrington, leave this poor man alone WILL YOU! Your husband's just limped out and Clive here does not wish to have his nose excavated in such a manner. Leave it! RIGHT NOW!'

'If you'll excuse me, thanks but no thanks, I'll be on my way now.'

'Oh and what's made you come back?' Tricia declared glowering at Bob, his head popped round the door.

'You coming Belinda? You don't have to put up with the likes of her. I'll give you a lift home.'

'In view of your wife's atrocious behaviour Mr. Harrington, might I suggest you offer her a lift home? I assume that's alright with you Clive?'

Clives Engells threw his hands open then rubbed at the side of his leg.

'On this occasion I feel it's most probably in your best interest Clive. Mrs. Harrington will you kindly depart with your husband now.'

Tricia stood, filling her cheeks with fury. Desperate to leave, Harriet glanced nervously across the table, first to Molly and then Mrs. Harris, wondering if she could get away with walking out, too. She looked up at Tricia, glancing back, then caught the fury in Mr. Sanderson's eyes.

'No, don't even think of it Miss Glover. Just let them be. It will give them the much needed chance to sort themselves out.'

'No, I'm sorry Mr. Sanderson, I need to get back. I need to go home, right now! Excuse me please, I'm really not feeling too well at all but thank you, thank you all for the evening. I'll get a lift while I can.'

Harriet grabbed her bag from the side of the chair and dashed through the hall slamming the front door behind her only to see Bob's car scattering the stone chippings as it screeched to turn left out of the drive and into the road. She froze, wondering what on earth she was going to do now.

Chapter 16

Tricia leapt in surprise. 'Oh Harriet it's you, thank goodness for that.'

'Yes indeed Mrs. Harrington, now might I ask why you are still here?'

They jumped to see Mr. Sanderson appear like the rabbit from the hat, wagging his finger in such a manner normally reserved for deviant pupils.

'He went without me Mr. Sanderson, he told me "to bugger off" then said "That jumped up git needn't think I'm takin` you home. Who the hell does he think he is?" Then he marched off.'

'I'm sure you've put your own construction on that one Mrs. Harrington, I've never taken the impression Mr. Harrington's been lacking in good manners.'

'Well whatever he said he wouldn't let me into `is car, that's why I'm still here. Harriet and I will just have to curl up on your step Mr. Sanderson.' She turned to Harriet, 'Oh unless we get a taxi and stay the night at yours.'

Harriet's hand was already in her bag fishing for her mobile.

'Yes, home to 4 The Willows, Tricia.'

'You'll do no such thing! Come in the pair of you and resume your places at the dinner table. Perhaps with your husband out of the way you'll be better inclined to exercise your best table manners.'

'It was him Mr. Sanderson. Oh he can't see further than the end of `is nose, him. Belinda Oxfordshire chattin` up my Clive and still he was givin` her droolin` looks. She has to have every man in sight that one. It was Clive who asked *me* not her. No, he deserved a damned good kick, him.'

'That's enough Mrs. Harrington. You'll both spend the night here and kindly keep your feet to yourself on your return. I will not have you kicking Belinda or anyone else for that matter. Go through now; er, Miss Glover, a word please.'

Tricia marched off, glancing back to Harriet before disappearing into the dining room. Harriet stopped to the sound of a car, tyres crunching to a halt on the gravel. She followed him back to the front door.

'Oh now who the hell's this? Surely it's not that scatty girl's husband back again? Highly unlikely I would think. Oh wait a minute it's a woman getting out.'

They both looked across to the tall, thin figure, knees buckling as her high heels battled with the chips of golden stone, refusing to carry her forward at her intended pace. Feeling uneasy Harriet wrinkled her nose. There was something familiar about this woman.

'Crikey it's not that one from the department store is it? Good grief it is! Hell's bells what's the matter with her now?'

Mr. Sanderson shot a look of desperation at Harriet.

'Well it's nothing to do with me Mr. Sanderson. I don't know why she's decided to come here.'

'Oh I'm quite sure it's got everything to do with you Miss Glover. I thought we'd got away with all that rather too lightly.'

'Absolutely not my fault,' Harriet insisted as Mr. Sanderson strode forward into the evening air to greet her.

Harriet, unsure of whether or not to follow, clung to the door in a state of utter disbelief. She could see him chatting away, putting his arm round her, ushering her forward as if a long lost lover.

'Er, Caroline Worsnip, Harriet. You do recall?' He took her coat, passing it to Harriet.

'Pop it in the cloakroom will you Miss Glover? As it turns out Caroline here is a good friend of Belinda's. An uncertain invitation but I've persuaded her to stay a little while since I'm sure Belinda will have finished her meal by now.' The atmosphere drenched in charm, he smiled Caroline Worsnip that most gorgeous of smiles, much to Harriet's fury.

'Here, let's go into the drawing room Caroline. I'm so grateful to you for taking up Belinda's invite, calling in after that disaster, you know Miss Glover's feeling so bad about the whole thing. You are indeed welcome, we appear to be losing guests right, left and centre this evening.'

'Oh so you're losing guests are you?' Harriet silently fumed to herself. 'Miss Glover indeed! Fancy reverting to calling me *that* in front of her!'

She hovered in the cloakroom not wanting to come out. Decided she'd wait for Belinda Oxfordshire to cross the hall first when suddenly she heard Tricia's voice. 'I'm in here Tricia,' she whispered.

'It's Rappin` `ammer Harriet. he phoned me in there.' She pointed to the dining room. 'I've just come out here to take it.' She beckoned Harriet over to join her on the stairs.

'I'll have you know you've still got my "save Venice" tin Rappin` `ammer, that's why you've had a threatenin` letter from my barrister friend, Mr. Engells.'

Chapter 17

Rapping Hammer slouched across the makeshift sofa in the back of his pantechnicon, flicking the pungent ash deposit to the floor from the brown thing curling towards his lips. He pushed his shades further up his nose gesturing rudely with his fingers to the rest of the band sat there, smoking and smirking in unison.

'So what? It don't mean a soddin' thing.'

He turned to the lads, grinning. 'Chick Lips is getting all worked up down the wire. Just listen to it!'

He increased the volume, scanning the phone round the van as if he was making a video.

'Alright Chick-Lips, now just shut it and listen will yer? I want this crumb of a legal arse-hole off my back, understand? Me and the band are stuffed to the eyeballs with you and Mummy-Mama. We'll get our fuckin' way with the both of you, you see if we don't, that scramble in the tent was nothin' to what we'll make the pair of you do for us. The old ditchwater won't hear of growin' the mush again thanks to prissy arse, nothin' doin' there thanks to Mummy-Mamma swipin' all the bleedin' plants. The only way he'll do it is if he gets to lay her flat. You get that bastard Engells off our backs or we'll be comin' for yuse sooner than you think.'

He held the phone out again to allow Tricia's voice to hit all sides of the van. From the bottom of the stairs in Mr. Sanderson's house, she babbled incessantly, her voice piercingly high with indignation. Creased with laughter, Rex, Rox, Rux, Rix and Rax thumped the putrid smoke-laden air with their fists.

'Yea, yea, you tell her Rappin'. They aint makin' fools of us. Tell her we all wan' a fuck or she don't get her tin back!'

The phone went round again as Tricia squawked in disgust at the dope-laden Rapping Hammer.

'Oh and tell prissy-arse to make sure lover-boy gets me on the next Fastnet race will yer, seein' as that same legal arse-hole he sticks with all but promised me he'd fix it with him?'

Rapping Hammer threw the phone down.

'She's hung up, the evil cow. We'll teach the pair of them, eh zats. We'll teach them a lesson when they're least expectin' it and it won't be one of those lessons Miss Prissy-Arse teaches the kids in her class, either.'

The van rocked as the scruffy lads raised themselves from the dirty floor to return to their makeshift seats. Rapping Hammer's mood becoming decidedly more ratty as he thumped his heel on the floor demanding their full attention.

'It's no flaming joke this. We've already got half of Interpol after us for defacin' them fuckin' statues in that stinkin' place full of ditch water they call Venice.

Chick-Lips has already done for us. We don't need that gold chain danglin` spore up our backsides, threatenin` legal action over her stupid tin, or puttin` us away on her hearsay.'

'It's not just that or her tin though, is it Rap? She's blasted our campsite threats right into his bleedin` dial. `is alarm will be goin` off if she doesn't get him off our backs. What with him and Sanderson and the connections like, we'll all get fuckin` rumbled. We'll be banged up for years for that lot.'

'We need a plan, man. It's a dead cert she was at Sanderson's place. I could hear him fussin` and fartin` in the background. he's had a quay built down there.'

'So?'

'Don't be so bleedin` thick Rix. We've gorra get down that river now and catch them comin` out. We'll take the rib, let's just check what time the fuckin` tide is. Here, pass me that.'

He pressed a dirty thumb into the centre of the stapled pages to keep the booklet open.

'High tide, nine forty-seven.' He took a quick glance at his watch. 'Let's get this baby back to the shack now. We'll load the rib on the trailer and get down there. There'll be enough piss in the pond for the draft by the time we get launched. We'll frighten the fuckin` life out of them that'll make sure they keep their slats zipped!'

Chapter 18

Tricia switched off the phone to fling it across the highly polished woodblock floor.

'I'm fumin` Harriet. I didn't even know Clive had sent a letter off. Rappin` `ammer wants him off `is back. he's still threatenin` those not very nice things they'll do to us both if I don't warn Clive off. It doesn't look like he's about to give me my tin back anytime soon, either.'

'Look Tricia, the only thing to do is to explain all of this to Clive. He'll know exactly how to deal with it,' Harriet whispered, fearful Tricia, in her rage, would be overheard.

'Well that wouldn't stop them from finding us. I'm startin` to get really frightened now. He sounded to me like he was well away. You just don't know what they'll do, especially when they're high.'

'You two brewing up trouble again? I would have thought you'd have had enough by now.' Belind Oxfordshire diverted her steps to pick up Tricia's phone.

'Oh and how long have you been standing here listenin` in Belinda Oxfordshire?'

'Oh don't flatter yourselves. I'm looking for Caroline. Oh has she got a bone to pick with you Harriet Glover!'

Harriet panicked, wondered just what she meant.

'And there's no need to look so astounded. Caroline phoned to tell me all about the ridiculous woman running round the store in her underwear, embarrassing Joris in the extreme.'

'Oh I do beg your pardon,' Harriet returned, 'I was getting changed and if she hadn't insisted on checking the contents of the basket for a baby, of all the stupid things, the cat wouldn't have escaped. I had no choice but to run after it.'

'You could have thrown your clothes on first, I'm sure. I really don't know why Joris puts up with your childish behaviour,' she retorted.

'She phoned you to tell you all this? Mr. Sanderson didn't seem to know her, and I certainly don't, so what's the connection?'

'Oh so Joris didn't recognise her again? You wouldn't believe how many times he's snubbed her in the street. Of course she always goes along with it, always finds some excuse for him. She's still in love with him you know. She wouldn't want to compromise him, not after the do with that baby. After nearly losing her job she's keeping her head well down. He'd never have gone to that store if he'd realised she was still there. There's been other people in his life before you Harriet Glover.'

Harriet, dazed, resisted the temptation to remind her she'd been one of them. Then it clicked into place, the way he'd greeted her just now as if long lost friends, … or lovers?

'Anyway that's exactly why I extended Joris's invite to her. He could do no other than be polite. He owes her! With all the kafuffle over that baby the papers decided she'd been dismissed, fat lot they knew! She knows all about you though, in fact most people round here do.' She paused to glare at Tricia. 'Both of you in fact. You don't really think the scrapes you two get into go unnoticed do you? We're good friends Caroline and I. Both been dumped.' She flared her nostrils whilst taking a deep breath, staring hard at Harriet. 'Oh, yes indeed, she knows all about my engagement to Joris and just who broke it up.'

Harriet looked down, went very quiet, her curiosity overriding the remark. Harriet needed to know what this was all about, needed to know just why she'd agreed to come.

'Oh so she thought Joris had invited her? She hasn't exactly arrived in time for dinner.'

'After dinner drinks as it happens, I wasn't going to let her miss such an opportunity to square with him at the same time as dealing with you!'

'So what's that all about then?' Harriet asked, her stomach starting to churn at the thought of whatever it was this Caroline woman had in for her.

Belinda Oxfordshire delivered a whimsical little smile.

'That's for you to find out Harriet Glover, once I've seen my way to having our little chat.' She moved to go, then turned as Tricia demanded her phone back.

'Oh it's yours, is it? I can't say Joris will be too pleased to find out you flung it across the parquet floor.'

Tricia snatched it back.

'I can't say Joris will be too pleased you've spent all evenin` flirtin` with `is `ouse guest, either. Especially as I was the one who got invited to the dinner party.'

'Oh rubbish Patricia Harrington. Why do you suppose he sat you by your husband? He feels it's high time you two grew up and started acting like the grown up parents you're supposed to be.'

'Oh Harriet, did you just hear that? It was her who pinched my Bob in the first place. She's had him on and off like a light switch ever since. She only switched him off tonight because she'd found better fish to fry.'

'You and Clive Engells? What a joke! He's a barrister, if you did but know. You expect me to believe that? No, Joris invited me especially to give us the opportunity to get to know each other better. It could just be why he seated us together.' She paused to consider. 'In fact Joris is insisting I stay the night. He can't move it along quickly enough for my liking!'

'Yes, well Clive and I had such a good time last night, all warm and cuddly we were. I can't see him, myself, wantin' to swap me for a fridge-arsed bat like you, tonight! '

'Oh let me get to Caroline. All lies, complete lies. You're obviously unaware Joris has ordered a taxi to take the pair of you home!'

She threw the mobile into Tricia's hands then clicked her way across the hall to the drawing room.

'But he told us we were both going to spend the night here? Surely he hasn't change his mind?' Harriet said, confusion cutting into her nerves.

'In any case I don't know what this woman's decided she's got on me and I don't want to hang around to find out.' She pulled her bag to her midriff, scrambling in the bottom searching for Mr. Sanderson's keys.

'Never mind a taxi, it's quicker if we use the car, come on let's get out of here while the goings good. I did say you can stay at mine if you like.'

'Oh I do like Harriet but he'll go ballistic when he finds out.'

'We'll just tell him we preferred it to taking a taxi as it was far less likely to cause him any further embarrassment.'

'Good one Harriet! Come on let's go!'

Quickly but quietly they closed the door behind them.

Chapter 19

Belinda and Caroline simultaneously placed their coffee cups down as Mr. Sanderson swung the drawing room door open to intrude on their hushed exchange.

'Ah not in here I see. Any sign of the terrible twins at all?'

'How apt Joris. It would seem you've finally got the measure of them,' hummed Belinda Oxfordshire, positively delighted. 'The last time I saw them they were sat on the bottom of the stairs colluding over something or other.'

Mr. Sanderson ran his hand through his hair.

'No, no, the terrible twins? That's Molly's latest name for the cats Belinda. She was hoping to take hers back with them tonight.'

Belinda Oxfordshire fidgeted her legs, looking decidedly uncomfortable.

'No we haven't seen any cats around here have we Caroline?' She bristled.

'No, not that we've noticed,' Caroline smiled, relishing the opportunity to admire Mr. Sanderson all over again.

'If you've got just a couple of minutes Joris, I think Caroline would want to tell you about her predicament, especially as you were there at the time as a witness.'

Mr. Sanderson, still filled with a sense of obligation to Caroline Worsnip, closed the door behind him, lifting the upholstered chair from the corner, to place it between them both. He glanced at his watch, conscious of deserting his guests sat around the dinner table.

'Go on Caroline, tell him. He might be a knight of the realm but he doesn't often take to his sword.' Belinda congratulated herself, amused at her efficient piece of ice breaking.

Mr. Sanderson cleared his throat as he bent forward placing his hands on his open knees.

'I'm afraid Caroline's been given instant dismissal as a result of the incident Harriet Glover started. Go on Caroline, you tell him all about that feeble boss of yours, Roger Boxsocks.'

With a purposeful, simultaneous slap of both hands against his legs, he raised his head towards Caroline, giving her the go-ahead to proceed.

'You recall the incident Mr. Sanderson?'

'I think we have enough behind us to dispense with the formalities, Caroline! Look just call me Joris will you?'

Caroline Worsnip scrunched her face in delight. Instantly relaxed she let forth.

'You do recall Miss Glover causing an absolute riot in the department?'

She strained to search his eyes for the desired response.

86

'I do recall your insistence on opening the basket just to check we weren't about to dump a baby!'

'Regardless of other things that was absolutely necessary Joris, after the one that was left by the fire extinguisher we've been told to be very cautious. A lot of company time was wasted in respect of that incident, customers departed hastily at the sight of the police and the publicity had an adverse effect on sales for a while. Mothers became frightened to bring their babies into the store for fear they'd be suspected of dumping them. Roger Boxsocks insisted it is only through vigilance we can be sure such a thing will never happen again.'

'Perfectly understandable, perfectly understandable Caroline. I can see you were only acting on instructions. However, I do fail to see how Harriet has impacted on all of this as she was perfectly within her rights to rescue her own cat.'

'Not to the point where chasing it caused a rotating display stand of expensive perfume to topple to the floor, I wouldn't have thought,' replied Caroline Worsnip, gaining in confidence. She crossed her legs and smoothed out her skirt, more than satisfied with her case building abilities.

'Actually it could have hurt somebody,' she continued.

'But it didn't, now let's stick with the facts, if we may, Caroline. I don't see a case emerging against Harriet, or your dismissal, for that matter.'

Immediately she uncrossed her legs, bolting her knees together to brush her hair from her face.

'In fact,' Mr. Sanderson continued, 'I seem to recall a woman whose child let loose one of those damned battery driven hamsters; the ensuing chaos could well have been a considerable factor in this stand toppling over. As I recall I compensated this woman fairly generously for any part the cat might have played in causing her to fall. Indeed she was certainly more than happy to accept my offer.'

He rubbed his chin then took a deep breath. 'Let's get to the point here Caroline, why exactly have you been given notice and to what extent do you feel Harriet has been responsible?'

For a few seconds Caroline Worsnip faltered.

'Actually Roger Boxsocks has dismissed me on the grounds of stealing stock.' She pursed her lips then covered them with a tissue pulled from her cuff as she attempted to wipe her nose.

'Stealing stock? And have you?'

'Of course she hasn't Joris. Go on Caroline explain. You were only giving away a couple of bottles, only doing the same compensation thing as him.' She glowered at Mr. Sanderson.

'That's enough Belinda, quite enough. Let Caroline continue.'

'I only gave her a couple of bottles of perfume from those fallen to the ground as compensation. Of course Roger Boxsocks flies to the computer, does a stock check and finds he's four short. He said not only did I not have any right to steal company stock to give away in that manner but there were still two bottles unaccounted for. He accused me of keeping a couple for myself. Anyway it seems he's acted within the law. Instant dismissal I'm afraid. I haven't got a job to go to on Monday.'

Mr. Sanderson leant forward to pat her shoulder.

'Look, as it happens, I have a Mr. Engells staying for a few days. He's a lawyer, a damned good one at that. You were only acting in the best interests of the company, on the spur of the moment, as you saw fit. I'm sure he'd be more than happy to help you out with this one.'

Belinda Oxfordshire narrowed her eyes. This seemed to be taking a turn not quite to her liking. Anxiously she jumped in.

'We need to know where the other two bottles went. Caroline and I wouldn't put it past Harriet Glover to help herself during the chaos! No lawyer can clear Caroline's name unless we find the culprit. At the moment she's the one suspected of theft on two counts.'

Mr. Sanderson took a very deep breath, turning to look at the painting behind him. The painting of the wild flower meadow, their painting. Slowly he turned back, measuring his words before speaking.

'You might just as well accuse me, or anyone else in the place for that matter. Belinda, your notion is ludicrous and I trust you haven't planted that particular seed in Caroline's head.'

Belinda Oxfordshire stiffened and fearful of overstepping the mark pulled the accusation right back.

'Oh no, no, not at all. It's just that Caroline is in very serious trouble here. Her good name and reputation is at stake. Harriet's the only one you saw round the stand at the time, so naturally we were starting to put two and two together.'

Caroline Worsnip nodded in agreement.

'They've gone missing, someone's taken them and it wasn't me!'

'Well I can categorically state that it wasn't Harriet either! Here, let me bring her in. Let's sort this out now, once and for all. Let's deal with this preposterous accusation whilst it's fresh in our minds.'

He strode to the door, marching round the house calling her while they sat waiting, in silence. The door swung open.

'I don't seem to be able to locate either of them, unfortunately.'

'And that could well be the reason Joris,' Belinda Oxfordshire smiled, in triumph.

Chapter 20

'The car Tricia the car, where is it? Oh sod no! Look the garage door's closed. Oh no I bet Mr. Swift's locked it away in there for the night. Clive's Bentley's gone too. They're probably both in there,' Harriet's panic sank to despair, she grimaced at Tricia, unable to believe she'd not even considered the possibility.

'Oh Harriet, we're locked out now. We're going to have to wait here until he opens the door to let everyone go home.'

'We can still call a taxi. Look, let me call a taxi. We can't wait here all night.'

'Mr. Swift won't have locked the gates as well, will he?' Tricia panicked. 'Here I'd better go and see.'

Harriet watched her run back and forth in front of them, leaning on the stone pillar, pressing each button in turn. Still the automatic gates refusing to budge. She put her phone back into her bag wondering what on earth they were going to do now.

'We could always climb over the wall and start walkin`.'

'But it's miles Tricia and it's going foggy. It was bad enough having to walk all the way home from the opening of Starboard Marine North West that time. This is twice as far! Anyway with those huge shrubs and bushes in the border we'd never get to it. Not to mention it's higher than us, we'd never get a foothold. Come on, let's take some thinking time, a walk round the back down to the river. I'll show you his new quay while there's still enough light. We might just come up with something.'

Caught in the autumnal chill carried on the mist rising from the river they hurried past the big greenhouses hugging themselves to keep their bare arms from freezing. Cutting across the helipad, the damp grass beyond tickled at their peeping toes with every step as their stilleto heels sunk into the lawn.

'Ooh Harriet I didn't realise his garden was as big as this. How many steps have we got to go down? I'm wonderin` if this is such a good idea. We won't be able to see much in this mist anyway.'

'It's a better idea than waiting on his doorstep Tricia. If he has to come looking for us at least we can deal with it out of earshot of those two.'

'Oh yes you're right. It's those two that should be out here in the cold. Ooh so this is it. How big's his boat? You could park a Mersey ferry here.'

'He's got two don't forget. One at the sailing club and the really big one's still in Falmouth. He's asked me to bring it back with him.'

'Ooh try and get an invite for me and Clive, I'd love to sail round the coast all the way back to here.'

'Now that's a great idea, would you really be up for it?'

'Of course I would, oh eh, what's that Harriet? I can hear the sound of somethin` comin` up the river. It's gettin` quite a bit foggy up here. Oh I do hope they know what they're doing whoever they are and don't get lost. Listen it's gettin` louder.' Filled with fear she suddenly remembered the call. 'Oh no, suppose it's them. Just suppose it's Rappin` Hammer! No, they wouldn't be coming up the river in this surely? Unless they're high.'

'Yipes Tricia I hope not, we won't stand a chance down here. Quick let's get into the mooring shelter, it's best we're not seen. Come on run, it's just this other side.'

They tottered at speed along the quayside throwing themselves on to the patio swing housed inside the quay house.

'Ooh Harriet, don't breathe, I can hear voices. I'd know `is anywhere. They're here, get your feet up quick and crouch, we might just look like a pair of cushions in this fog.'

'Listen, someone's landed,' Harriet panted. 'Oh no I've just seen a light flicker. It's torchlight!'

'If he comes in here he'll get a shove up `is bum. He'll be back in `is boat before he knows what's hit him.'

'Tricia he might drown you can't do that!'

'Just watch me Harriet!'

All the piercing yelps of a horror movie rose from the foggy sea as the plunging jib tipped to a plummeting body crashing sideways into its foul cargo, emptying them into the water; struggling to right itself amidst the scramble of wet bodies cursing, heaving, hurling themselves over its gunwales, all desperate to get back in. The sound of the outboard motor fading fast for Harriet and Tricia as they fled up the steps and across the lawn, soaked to the skin.

'It was them, wasn't it Tricia? Oh gosh I do hope we don't get done for assault and attempted murder.'

'Course it was them, didn't you hear their language. I couldn't say which one it was I shoved in though, still it sounded as if they all went in. No it's a good night's work Harriet.'

Harriet wasn't so sure, she shivered as they approached the greenhouses, yanking at the door.

'Come on, come on, open!'

'Here let me have a go.'

'No Tricia no, there's no time, they won't give up just like that, we're going to have to get back into the house double quick.'

Harriet caught Tricia's arm hurriedly steering her towards the kitchen garden and the back door.

'With a bit of luck we'll catch Mrs. Harris in the kitchen, she might hide us in a spare room,' she panted, half-turning.

'More like the caterers Harriet, she's a guest tonight, remember. Ouch, that was me foot!'

'Watch these sprouts Tricia...'

Too late, she struggled to her feet, shell shocked, trapped in green netting covered in wet sprout leaves, sticky brown soil completing her military camouflage; her screeches sending a wide beam of light straight at them as the back door rapidly opened.

'What in the name of goodness are you two up to now?'

They watched Mr. Sanderson striding towards them, shaking his head, tossing his blonde hair back in a fury.

'IN,' he boomed, 'IN the two of you, THIS MINUTE!' Little did he realise they'd just fended off that gang of yobs so utterly abhorrent to him.

Chapter 21

Rapping Hammer looked back to the slumped shivering mass, exhausted, demoralised and too wet to curse, as he steered the rib in a laboured return down the river. He hoped they were all there and trusted those who weren't were near enough to the quay to be able to haul themselves out.

Anger raged within at the smart arsed fool who couldn't wait to reap revenge, whose impatience to get ashore had literally sunk their plans. He glanced back at the band again, wondering which one it could be, wondering if he was even in there.

'Damn and blast!' He muttered trying to get more response from the rib.

'You say somethin` Rappin`?' came a shivery chatter from below.

'Which of you fuckers arsed us into the gravy then?'

'What you on about Wayne we're dead `ere.'

'`e will be dead if I ever get to find out!'

'Are we driftin` then? It's bloody freezin` down `ere.'

'Get the water out of them lug `oles Rix, we're not on the back of a bloody broomstick.'

'Can't even hear the frigin` motor goin`, power it you big melon.'

'You fuckin` talk like that to me again and you're out on your ass!'

Rix struggled for comfort, grabbing a bucket rolled into his back.

'You pisser do you want this jammed on your melon head?'

'Just get soddin` bailing snail lugs, then we might have a chance of crawling from this thing alive!'

Chapter 22

'Remain in the kitchen both of you. You Mrs. Harrington look like you're ready for combat. What the hell have the pair of you been up to now? No don't bother, I really don't wish to know. Just remain in here will you whilst I check with Mrs. Harris the ensuite rooms in the South Wing are prepared for guests.'

He strode off leaving Harriet and Tricia trying to avoid the smirking caterers busy loading coffee cups and saucers onto each of their trays.

'You two let the nobs down, have you? Can't think how you got invited here in the first place. Thought 'is friends would have been a bit posher than that.' She turned to Tricia. 'Anyway who was that poor sod you had to move away from at the table? On the way out he told me you'd been stabbing him all night with your bloody 'igh heels.'

The white aproned woman took a very deep breath, turning as she folded her arms.

'That's right isn't it Melanie, you heard him.'

Melanie shook her head. 'He wasn't one of them either, He was more like one of us. He winked at me I know he had his eye on me all evening.' She paused to glower at Tricia. 'I'd have jolly well got a date with him if you hadn't sent him off home early kicking him like that. Can't blame him for throwing you into the sprouts.'

Trays in hand the pair of caterers left the kitchen oblivious to Tricia's instant ranting.

'It's got sod all to do with you, bugger off will you!' Tricia shaking like a wet dog shut the door behind them.

'Come on Harriet, we're not spending the night here. He can keep 'is soddin' ensuite rooms.'

'Too right kicking me out of my room just like that. Let's go home!'

Mrs. Harris's pristine quarry tiles succumbed to the trail of mud and wet sprout leaves, the odd one lifting and scattering to the sharp draught arriving uninvited as the back door slammed shut.

'Golly Tricia, what are we supposed to do now?'

'We're going home Harriet, just like you said. We're climbin' that soddin' wall and we're walkin' home. To yours if that's alright?'

'You know it is Tricia I'm just not sure if we'll make it, it's miles, we're in these and it's freezing cold.' Harriet pointed at their muddy heels barely visible after aerating Mr. Sanderson's lawn all the way down to the steps.

'We haven't really got any choice, have we? Come on take them off and run. I'll stand on your shoulders and then pull you up.'

A doubting Harriet unleashed her aching feet, shivered and flew behind her to the gate post, heaving herself up on the wall.

'Bend over Harriet like you're givin` me a piggy back then stand me up. Hurry up, oh hang on, I can hear a car.'

'It's a lane, doesn't mean anything. Come on let's get out of here.'

Harriet jerked as her bent back winced to Tricia's weight, clinging to the gate edge she tried to straighten up, the load lightening as Tricia swung to her right, finding foot holes in the wrought iron, now already rising on her shoulders, moving sideways, heaving her leg towards the top of the wall.

'Bloody hell what's `appenin` to this thing Harriet, I'm goin` for a ride `ere.'

'It's the gates, they're opening, come back Tricia, quick down let's get out now, quick.'

'Bloody hell Harriet I'm up here now, there's a car turning in. Get to it now, quick Harriet, it might be a taxi.'

Harriet, gratefully mobile, leapt from the wall, shot between the gates waving her arms to stop the car. Already the driver's window sliding open.

'Your lucky Miss I spotted you in this fog, I'm trying to turn in here, what you on, some kind of suicide mission?'

'You a taxi,' Harriet demanded.

'Sure am, two young ladies to be collected just about now!'

'Yes that's us!'

'That a gargoyle or a bag of sprouts swinging off that gate, no wonder the bloody thing won't open properly!'

'No, that's my friend, she's stuck. A hand please, if you don't mind helping me to get her down.'

'Are you two pissed or something?'

Harriet glanced across to the house, panicked, could just see Mr. Sanderson's tall figure hanging around, wavering at the front door, batting the fresh air at the hall like he'd just lost to game, set and match. 'Catch me Harriet, I'm comin`.'

'Not the way it usually `appens when the girls are with me! She alternative or something, you two been `aving kinky sex up there?'

'I beg your pardon... Quick get out help me catch her, NOW!' Harriet demanded, stepping back tripping the rotund driver into a roll to land on him with a thump. 'Your sittin` on him Harriet,' screeched Tricia as she half slid, half fell from the gate, tumbling on top of them both. Harriet winced, feeling the painful thud to his head as he hit the gutter, she watched him depart from consciousness all the time struggling to unearth herself from underneath it all.

'We've knocked him out Tricia, quick support his head and shoulders while I grab his feet. Let's get him moved onto the grass.'

No lightweight, they struggled, relieved to lay him down still breathing.

'Done, get into the cab Harriet whilst it's still tickin` over, we're goin` home!'

'We can't drive that Tricia!'

'Who can't? 'Get in before he comes out, that front door's flappin` like bats' wings'

They slammed the doors closed, grateful for the fog, Harriet praying Tricia would be able to find reverse gear. She crunched and scrunched until they finally went backwards, then a determined shove sent them hopping forwards like an inebriated kangaroo all the way down the lane.

Chapter 23

'Can't see a damned thing out here,' Mr. Sanderson boomed, not in the best of moods. 'Now where's this flaming taxi? Everything's in vanish mode tonight. Heaven only knows where that mindless boy Farquerhart got to. No doubt wandering through the tunnels of Cheshire by now, the lad will probably end up in a salt cellar if he's not careful. At least those two harum-scarums are in their beds, or so I'm told by the caterers. I'm not inclined to investigate just now, that particular roasting can wait until the morning.'

Belinda Oxfordshire glanced at Caroline Worsnip, a knowing smile passing between them.

'Is that a car engine I'm hearing? That damned man phoned at the gates, he's hardly going to lose his way on the drive. Where the bloody hell is the cab?'

Mr. Sanderson marched towards the open gates, scratching his head, unable to see a thing, unable to recall his reason for requesting a cab in the first place.

'It's too bad out here, no-one's going to come out in this, the guy must have panicked and turned round. Come back inside you two, er it was for you, wasn't it? I'm afraid you're both going to have to stay the night, after all, along with the rest of the guests I'm afraid.'

He closed the door behind him, ushering them through to the lounge.

'I'll organise coffee and see if Mrs. Harris can't warm a couple of spare rooms in the south wing. Should be enough accommodation for everyone if we open that side. You girls can use the flat over there if you like, Mrs. Harris has already prepared it for the PM and his family, they're paying a visit shortly. There's a bathroom and one ensuite you can sort it between yourselves, that will leave the other two rooms for Molly and Percy and Mrs. Harris's friend. She does, of course have her own private accommodation here. Anyhow, do take a seat and make yourselves comfortable, coffee will be along any minute.'

They sat together on the end of the sofa nearest the fire, a silent sense of achievement pervading the room as they nudged each other delighting in the secured circumstance, their mutual smile of satisfaction so very apparent as Mr. Sanderson opened the door to let the catering staff through.

'I believe you were the last to see the two tearaways,' declared Belinda Oxfordshire not noticing the blush of pink suddenly colouring Melanie's cheeks.

'Joris says you saw them go off to their rooms, is that right?' She continued, not wishing to miss the spectacle of the morning should these catering people be wrong.

'Couldn't wait to get out of the door quick enough,' Melanie spouted into the coffee cups.

'No no no, white for me if you would be so kind.' Belinda Oxfordshire requested, momentarily lost the plot.

'Creamer's there, take it or leave it, sure you wouldn't bloody well like me to wipe your arse, too?'

'Oh, indeed not! Joris!' She called, turning to see the door swiftly close behind them.

'I'd leave it if I were you Belinda, Joris isn't exactly having the best of evenings, wouldn't you say?'

'No, perhaps you're right, so lower socio, still it goes with the territory these days, Mummy's always saying that. You've still got a soft spot for Joris then, Caroline?'

She allowed the cream to slide into her coffee, deliberating. Took a sip and finally replaced the fine china cup to its saucer.

'Sorry Caroline, do go on.'

'You know Belinda we had a baby? Yes, sorry, of course you do, we've been friends a while now. It's too painful I've tried so hard to block it all out.'

Belinda visibly shocked straightened her back into the sofa, crossing her legs, steeling herself for what was coming.

'I know you went away Caroline and we lost touch, but I'd no idea you were expecting, is that why you went?' She uncrossed her legs, fidgeting, trying to look unphased by this nightmare revelation. All the time she'd been engaged to Joris Sanderson, she knew they'd been an item, but no he'd never told her that. She'd wanted his baby all along, she couldn't bear to know this, instantly she seethed. He'd never wanted one with her, how many loose kids could he handle, anyway? Her thoughts raged, couldn't square their brief engagement in her mind, was it because she'd finally told him she couldn't ever have children?

'You OK Belinda, you've gone a bit white and very quiet, sorry I thought you knew, didn't mean to shock you but yes we had a baby, she was beautiful. Beautiful blue eyes and blonde hair, just like Joris. We called her Amber because we met in the autumn and she was born in the autumn.'

'That's a lovely name Caroline...'

She stopped speaking as the door opened.

'Ah they're in here Molly, we're all having coffee in here.' Percy pushed hard on the door, holding it open as the rest of the party straggled their way in.

'A corker of a meal that, not up to your cooking though Daisy, mind.' Mrs. Harris smiled, catching Reginald Hansen's wink with secret delight.

'And it's a good job you said that Reginald Hansen or that's the last you'd be seeing of me at the bridge club.' Her face wrinkled into that teasing smile he knew of old. They'd been good pals since she'd lost her husband. He never ceased his gratitude to Joris for introducing them. Of course they'd have crossed paths anyway at the bridge club but somehow this was a nicer way to meet, the right way to do things. Marriage had often crossed his mind but he couldn't expect to uproot her from here. Couldn't take her away from housekeeping at this fine old residence.

Belinda Oxfordshire, downed her coffee, irritated they'd lost their privacy to talk. She was impatient to know more, to know what had happened to the baby, the real reason why Caroline had come back. She wondered why she had never chosen to tell her any of this sooner. She looked up as her legs cooled, Mr. Swift momentarily drawing off the heat from the burning fire, rubbing his hands as he turned to her.

'My word it's a sharp night out there, just as well you'll both be staying over. Strange though, this taxi chap making it all this way only to turn back. Still there's nowt so queer as folk, or so they say.'

Chapter 24

'Sorry Harriet that was a bit of a swing coming out of there, it's this gear stick, I feel like I'm stirring the Christmas puddin`. Oh eh I do hope that fella's not dead, I thought I heard a groan as I was climbin` off him, I do hope that wasn't `is last breath.'

'Don't Tricia, please don't. We've stolen this thing you know, not to mention drowning Rapping Hammer. Look Tricia I think we should turn it round and leave it. At least it would look like the driver's abandoned it in the fog. If he's a bit concussed he's bound to be confused when he has to tell the tale.'

'Confused Harriet, he's probably swingin` on heaven's pearly gates himself by now. I `ope he stays on a bit longer than me.'

'Tricia, don't. You're making him sound dead.'

'If he's concussed he wouldn't know the difference, now let's keep goin`.'

'Oh please turn this thing round, we'll just have to try walking it.'

'That's if we're still on the road Harriet, I haven't a clue where I'm going.'

Harriet could feel the flood of nerves spreading from the pit of her stomach, wondered if the baby inside her would survive another adrenaline surge on top of all she'd been through.

'Well let's get further on,' Tricia pleaded, 'Once we get to the traffic lights by Starboard Marine North West we'll dump it, we do know we can walk home from there because we've already done it once.'

A quivering Harriet briefly recalled abandoning the opening of Mr. Sanderson's prized marine business after the Prime Minister striding to the edge of the stage, unaware of her bag perched precariously on the front edge, caught his toe in the strap and almost flew through the air to land with a huge thud at her feet. Yes she could see the sense in it then, it was daylight and the pair of them ran for their lives. Now though, thick fog, but at least they'd have the street lights on the main road for most of the way, far better than this joint guesswork while driving. Taking a deep breath Harriet agreed, hoping she knew these country lanes to Mr. Sanderson's house well enough by now to have kept them on the right route.

Tricia, trembling, crawled the taxi along hoping she was still in the lane that would take them to the crossroads on the corner of Starboard Marine North West.

'Tricia, when we get there I think it's probably better if we take it into the car park then turn it round to leave it just at the start of the lanes. We'll have to walk back I know but he's more likely to have abandoned his taxi in the lanes, don't you think?'

'You're joking me Harriet, the fog might have lifted up there, I'm not riskin` being flagged down by any townies lookin` for a good night out; and if it hasn't lifted I'll never find the back entrance anyway.'

Harriet bit nervously at her lip, 'No, no, sorry, it's just that this is so thick how will we know where the end of this scary lane is?'

'I don't know, we'll just have to keep goin` until we find it.'

Harriet felt sick, felt a griping pain across her stomach, wondered if it was the first signs of a miscarriage. She'd been there before, she marvelled her baby had survived so much… 'Only to lose it now,' the words were so loud in her head, she needed to swallow hard on her fear and just focus on getting herself and Tricia through this. Instantly the negativity returned, she was now over three months pregnant, had never seen the doctor, never been for a scan, what kind of a start was she giving this baby? The only thing she was sure of her breasts were constantly feeling tender and full.

'They wouldn't still feel like this if the baby wasn't still alive,' she thought, trying to convince herself as the taxi started to shudder.

'You `aven't gone to sleep have you Harriet? I do hope we're not on the road to Vesuvius, or is it Rome all roads lead to? How much longer do you reckon we've got to go? Oh bloody hell what was that we've just rumbled over? It sounds like we've got four flat tyres.'

'No, no that's got to be the cattle grid, that's it, oh thank goodness.'

'What's one of those then?'

'Oh you know, it keeps them in the lane and off the main road if they get loose.'

'And there's me been puzzlin` over them for years.`

'Oh thank goodness, at least it means we're here, I'd forgotten all about those in the road. We'll need to turn it round here if you can manage it.'

Tricia changed from second to first gear desperating hoping she'd get it round in one.

'I think you'll need to do a three point turn, if you can. There's ditches either side of this lane.'

Tricia promptly stopped, couldn't for the life of her remember how she'd backed it away from Mr. Sanderson's gates. They leapt forward only to halt with a jerk.

'Oh bloody hell it's stalled, hang on a minute.'

The engine sparked then died, sparked and died, then fired. 'Hang on Harriet I think I tried pullin` this gear stick up after pressin` it down when it wouldn't work. There got it, we're goin` backwards.'

'Well done you, gosh, stop Tricia or we'll hit the ditch, forward, NOW, go forward!'

Harriet glanced back to see the rear seats tilting, the whole rear end slanting precariously over the edge. She had visions of 'The Italian Job' climaxing on the cliff face during the excruciating wait prior to Tricia losing then finding first gear. They jerked forward in three leaps on the diagonal to end up facing the way they'd come, the rear wheels stalling just a straw's width from the edge.

'This is goin` to have to do Harriet, let's get out of here.'

Simultaneously they grabbed the door handles, Tricia jumping out to instant yowls and screams from the other side.

'Bloody `ell I thought there was enough room your side, you haven't gone and landed in the ditch have you?'

Harriet struggled to right herself.

'Come this way, `ere let me give you a hand.'

It was her good fortune she'd landed upright, feet first into the mud; shaking, she scrambled out, glad of Tricia's help.

'You alright Harriet? Bloody hell I wondered what had `appened then! Hang on just let me get back in and close your door, we don't want that swingin` in the wind when they find it. Oh and I'd better be leavin` the keys in here as well, make it look like he panicked, left it in a hurry to start walkin`.'

Harriet could barely concentrate, couldn't believe they'd got themselves into another load of bother. What was it about that man? That house? His friends? What was it that always got them into so much trouble? The thoughts swirled inside her head as she hobbled along the lane, keeping close to Tricia, hoping not to meet with any oncoming cars. Then a yelp.

'Watch the pavement `arriet, I nearly went flyin` then. Hang on while I take these things off.'

'Are you OK Tricia? I lost you for a moment then, just had to get out of these things,' Harriet panted, swinging her pair of muddy heels in the air along with her evening bag.

'I do hope you've got your keys in there and not just your hanky.'

'Too right I have, I always keep a spare key in this, but that's about it.'

'Oh thank goodness for that, I had visions of spending the night in your shed again!'

'Keep walking Tricia I think we should be hitting the traffic lights any minute now. YESSS! We're here!'

'Now how do you know that? I can't see a thing further than the end of my nose in this.'

'It's those lads Tricia, just listen, they're swinging on the lights again. Yes I can just make them out, shouting and whooping for Britain as usual.'

Tricia stopped, cupped her hand round her ear.

'Oh yes that's them alright, I can hear them now. Silly sods, they could end up gettin' run over in this. One of them only has to fall off.'

'Oh no, please no, was that the sound of police sirens?' Harriet trembled.

'Oh don't say I spoke too soon, we don't want to get caught up in that lot.'

They smartened their pace, the traffic lights in sight as the fog lifted towards the top of the incline.

'That is a police car there, you were right, looks like they've caught the silly sods, we'd better take a left here and hide in the back doorway of his place.'

They took a swift left round the corner, then, without looking, hurriedly crossed the road bringing the police car to a screeching halt.

'What are you trying to do, get yourselves killed?' The officer demanded, getting out of the car. 'What are you both doing anyway, carrying your shoes, no coats on in this?'

'Oh, we've been waiting for a taxi over there. We just left a party we weren't enjoying didn't we Harriet? Just started walking home seein' as he didn't turn up.'

Harriet sank into the depths of disbelief. Why oh why was Tricia mentioning taxies to the police. Even in Venice, even being kidnapped, at this moment she'd never felt fear like it.

'Get in the back, both of you.'

'But we haven't done anything you're not arresting us are you?' Tricia panicked. The plain clothed gentleman sat in the front passenger seat, turned, face as straight as a ruler. 'Detective Chief Inspector Jones, pleased to make your acquaintances.'

Harriet wasn't so sure, wished Tricia would have the wit to realise it was time to move on.

Chapter 25

Caroline had barely replaced cup to saucer before Belinda Oxfordshire decided it was time to move on.

'Ah, Mr. Swift, er Ken, why don't you and Vivian sit here, by the fire, Caroline and I are needing to cool off.'

Caroline Worsnip, now extremely comfortable, stood somewhat reluctantly to follow Belinda out of the room into the large square hall.

'Come on Caroline, let me show you the rest of the house and then the south wing where we'll be tonight.'

Caroline brightened, in all the time she'd known Joris she'd never seen upstairs, only the grand staircases each one set either side of the huge chimney breast running up to and meeting on the galleried landing.

'Oh wow this is grand!' Caroline declared, 'No wonder he needs a housekeeper!'

'And the rest,' retorted Belinda Oxfordshire, savouring every word. 'This place is more like "Upstairs, downstairs" when he's fully staffed.' She knew that was a gross exaggeration but wasn't going to leave an opportunity begging to air her insider knowledge, put herself ahead of the game as far as Caroline Worsnip was concerned. 'That's why I just don't get his obsession with Harriet Glover. She's nothing, just one of his ordinary teachers. No class, no style, no money worth speaking of, always making a show of herself, it still won't come to anything, you'll see.'

'Well he was busy buying her dresses, fussing over her and that stupid cat. It looks like he's totally obsessed with her, to me. What's wrong with her, doesn't she want him or something?'

'She doesn't know what she does want, except causing trouble with that stupid girl I have to work with every day. I don't know why her husband doesn't let go either. You know Caroline, Bob and I have been a bit of an item for a while now, I don't feel bad about it either. She's asked for it the way she treats him, especially as he took her and her baby on. It wasn't his you know but he's that kind of guy. He took them both on when he married her. Didn't deserve to have a baby, her, never mind have another one by him, I mean, to complete their marriage. It's so unfair, I can't have any myself, just born like that and there's nothing they can do about it.'

'Then we're both in the same boat now Belinda, I was told not to try for any more after I had Amber. It was a complicated caesarean birth, it went badly wrong. It broke my heart, I love babies, I'm desperate for another one. You'll never know how tempted I was to keep that baby left in the basket. I had to sit on an impulse to run out of the store with it. I'd adopt one but I couldn't afford the childcare. I've always got to work to keep myself. Unless I can get back with Joris of course, it's hopeless.'

Belinda Oxfordshire quickened her pace, now busting with curiosity missed the look of jealous determination hardening Caroline's features as she bypassed his room to cross the landing, pushing open the door where Harriet had slept.

'Come in Caroline, oh of course her things are still in here, she'll be needing to collect those. Take a seat here in the window, too foggy to see anything, not even the lights twinkling in Wales, still, we'll come back in the morning and I'll show you the views. They are fantastic over the river from here.'

They seated themselves, Caroline feeling uncomfortable at being where she was. Harriet's room, she looked at the bed, wondered if he'd made love to her right there.

'Are they getting married or what?' She needed to know.

'Oh don't ask me,' replied Belinda Oxfordshire. I just don't know how long that man is prepared to wait around. Don't get it!'

She rose to her feet, started inspecting the bits and pieces Harriet had laid out. Picking them up, putting them down. Finally she sat on the bed.

'Do you know Caroline I just can't stand the thought of him sleeping with her.'

'Me neither.' Caroline snapped.

Belinda Oxfordshire, curiosity spilling, seized the opportunity to find out more.

'Now Caroline, if it's not too painful for you, do please tell me all about Amber.'

Caroline breathed in hard, she'd suppressed her sense of guilt for so long but the turmoil from being in such close proximity to Harriet released the need to let it all go. She felt she had first right to Mr. Sanderson, not Harriet Glover, not Belinda Oxfordshire either, though it helped to hear of her inability to have children. She tried to hide the sudden rush of guilt from her face. She'd only managed to restore their friendship properly once she was certain Joris had broken off his engagement to her. Belinda had walked from one fiancée only to find another, her man! All she knew was neither Belinda or Harriet Glover had had his child, in her own mind, on the face of it, that put her first in line. She'd refused his massive settlement out of sheer pride. That's when he'd told her to get on with it. Oh no she wasn't going to let him near Amber after that. That was her last weapon, though mistaken in her belief he'd come back on her terms for the sake of his daughter. Furious she'd moved away deliberately leaving no forwarding address. Unrelenting she spilled her version out.

'Oh I see,' faltered Belinda Oxfordshire, not seeing very clearly at all.

'But if you'd have allowed him to help you out, you wouldn't have had to continue working. You could have stayed home to look after her right up until the time she went to school.'

'He wouldn't marry me Belinda. Money would have been the easy way out for him. He didn't want to be the father of my child, in the end, did he?'

'Well obviously not on your terms Caroline or he would have married you.'

'That's exactly right, oh I expect eventually he'd have popped by every now and then to get the nice bits while I was left with all the responsibility. No, it was all or nothing as far as I was concerned. Amber and I did alright especially as Aunty Sharon shared the load. Single, living on her own, she fixed me up with a flat down there. I couldn't have done it without her.'

Belinda needed to know more, couldn't keep from asking.

'Is she still down there then, your Aunty Sharon?'

'Oh yes, I go down there most weekends, she's never given up. She's pursued every possible avenue. Of course we're both financially limited, it's really out of our hands now, it was never in our hands really, all we could do was our best.'

Now Caroline was talking in riddles to Belinda's increasing frustration. She left her seat suddenly curious about Harriet's belongings; walked around the bedroom, started opening drawers, then tried the wardrobe door.

'Wow, what's this? I wonder how this got in here? She's absolutely beautiful. What on earth is going on? Why would Joris have this stashed away, do you think?'

She took the framed portrait standing upright at the back of the top shelf turning it round for Caroline to see.

'That's her, that's Amber, that was the very last portrait I had done of her before she was taken.' For a brief second she held herself together then started sobbing violently, shaking so much with grief and anger Belinda was forced to hug her in an attempt to calm her down.

'I'm so dreadfully sorry for you Caroline, I really am but wow all this has come as a huge shock to me. I've known him all this time, was even engaged to him, he knew we were friends but he never mentioned you or having a child.'

'Had Belinda, had,' Caroline managed as she attempted to take control. 'We've never had anything to go on. I was sat on a park bench watching her on the small slide, a mother came and sat beside me, just for a couple of seconds I was distracted and when I looked up she was gone. I heard no crying or anything. I was distraut, frantic, phoned the police, drove round and round trying to spot her. One minute she was there, the next she was gone.'

'Oh no, what an absolute nightmare! I'm just so sorry to hear it. When did it happen?'

'Twelve months ago, she was just three at the time. It was autumn half-term, her nursery was closed and the park was very busy. I sat only a couple of yards from where she was, literally three or four strides away. It was the tots end of the park, the equipment was small and mums always sat around the edge, you could honestly see everything from those seats. I used to go over and over it in my mind and then I just had to block it all out because it's just too painful. Very few people know, only those that had to know, we were instructed that way so as not to push the position further underground.'

'Does Joris know?'

'Yes, he had to know being her father. That's how he got this.' She lay the portrait down on the duvet, turning it face down, as if it was more than she could bear to see it again.

'Oh this is so painful Caroline, it must be for you both. Don't give up, you never know, please don't give up on her.' Belinda quickly blinked the tears away.

'He didn't blame me entirely and I'm thankful for that. He said we both carried the responsibility, though had I accepted his financial support and not lied to try to prevent access before disappearing things might have worked out differently.'

'What did you say to that?'

'Had he married me things would have worked out a lot differently, we might both have had our little girl now.'

'And what did he say?'

'He just said I knew marriage was never on the cards and it was my fault I got pregnant.'

'And did you know that Caroline?'

Caroline flushed, looked down, clasping her hands together.

'Promise, please promise you'll never tell anyone this?'

'No, I wouldn't dream of it, I honestly wouldn't do that.'

'I was desperate to marry him, who wouldn't be? It's the same old story I thought if I got pregnant he couldn't refuse. What man isn't going to believe a girl when she tells him she's protected herself?' Joris isn't the belt and braces type, he likes his sex to be good and that's exactly what he got.'

'Oh!' Belinda declared, not sure if this wasn't just a bit too much information. 'I see that, he does rather see the good side of people, I mean he tends to trust people but I'm not saying anything about you here. He's a doctor and he knows the score. If he wanted to be that certain he should have perhaps gone with the braces?'

Caroline forced a smile.

'So you see this is why I came back. I couldn't bear to stay down there after that. It's cold comfort, I know, but it is a comfort to just be living back here and being that much nearer to him.'

'Do you ever see him at all?'

'Only a couple of times he came in when I was working on the ground floor. I could see from the china and ornaments everyone coming through that revolving door. I hated being moved upstairs to fashion and perfume. I just hate it. Do you know you wouldn't believe it, there wasn't a flicker of recognition in his face when he walked in with Harriet Glover yesterday. I can hardly believe I'm here, in his house now. I actually told them my weekend was booked, I didn't dream you would ask me to come here, tonight, it was almost prophetic. I wouldn't have come but I've got to get my job back. I'm not having that woman getting away with having me fired.' She paused, then continued. 'Still in a way I'm not sorry, he's been quite civil with me so far, this could just be the chance I've been looking for, a way back to him. I'd almost forgotten where he lived.'

Chapter 26

The police officer closed the door on each of them then marched round the front to assume his driving position.

'Where is it you each live?'

'Where are you takin' us we haven't done anythin' wrong have we Harriet?'

Rigid with fear, Harriet couldn't find it in her to respond.

'Home, that's where you were going wasn't it? Unless of course you'd both rather walk in this?'

'Oh no we wouldn't would we Harriet? Thank you Officer that's very kind. It is isn't it Harriet? We've 'ad enough of taxis for one night.'

Harriet rolled her eyes, knew if Tricia didn't shut up she'd drop them both in it there and then.

'How many didn't turn up then?' The officer enquired, half turning as he raised the question.

'Oh just the one Officer, this is so kind of you to take us home. I know Harriet thinks so too but she's too frozen stiff to answer, aren't you Harriet?'

Her thoughts had never been louder: 'Oh bloody hell Tricia do shut up, I mightn't be the only stiff around here.'

'You alright? Is there something you two are not telling me?'

Harriet had never found her voice quicker.

'Oh no, I'm absolutely fine thank you, it's just that we got cold hanging around, waiting.'

'Why did you leave your coats at the party, then?'

'We didn't take them, they're always a nuisance trying to find them and as we were getting a taxi down we decided not to bother.'

Harriet could feel herself blushing to the core, she wasn't very good at this, she was just grateful to be sat behind him in the police car's dimly lit rear. She saw him look at his watch after he'd turned around. 'I presume it's a right turn here?'

'That's correct Officer, we stay on the main road after that,' declared Harriet.

'That would be forward, right or left at Joris's place then?' The officer seemed to lighten a little.

'Oh so you know Joris then do you? He's my boss that's just where I work, there.' Tricia pointed to Starboard Marine North West on the corner. Harriet wanted to get out. She dug her elbow into Tricia's side hoping she wouldn't say any more.

'Yea old Joris, decent chap is Joris Sanderson, great pals with our colleague here, Detective Chief Inspector Jones. Does a hell of a lot for the local community.'

108

'Oh really,' Tricia continued, 'that's good to hear, I really wouldn't know as he's only my boss.'

'No one knows the way that guy helps people. One of the country's great philanthropists if you ask me.'

Harriet hoped against hope Tricia would keep him on this tack until they got home.

'Now which way, quick girls, which way?'

'Left at the lights, then follow the road down to Stetmead Village, then left into The Willows, er, number 4.'

'Yes, I'm staying at Harriet's tonight so you can drop me off there too, if you would be so kind.'

'Ah yes, I know it, not all that far, then?'

'No, well it is when you come to walk. We've walked it once, haven't we Harriet?'

Harriet felt her stomach churn again, dug Tricia in the ribs, this was somewhere she just shouldn't be going.

'Yes and it would have been for a second time had this very kind police officer here not taken pity on us. Thank you so much we really do appreciate it.'

'No problem Harriet, my pleasure, and what line of work are you in?'

'Oh I teach in a primary school, just been promoted to deputy head actually.'

'You're not the young lady who was honoured for her outstanding performance are you? It was someone from this area as I remember. In fact I'm not sure if old Joris didn't get his knighthood at the same time?'

'Oh we're here now Officer, that was quick, not that I think you've been speedin` or anythin`, well you couldn't in this fog, not that you would if it wasn't foggy. Oh eh you'll need to take a left just here.'

He swung a left turn, coincidentally parking right outside no. 4.

'Well how did you know this is Harriet's house?'

'Now that would be telling.' The officer said, touching the side of his nose, smiling briefly. 'I'll hang on until you're both inside. Oh and keep this lift to yourselves will you otherwise we'll have every Tom, Dick and Harry flagging us down.'

Relieved to get out they thanked him, waved the car away, then opened the front door to the rush of the cat meowing and brushing against their legs.

'Oh Tricia, what on earth did he mean by that and why did Detective Jones never say a word?'

Chapter 27

'Ah Mrs Harris, do forgive me, just a word if I may. I'm aware this was supposed to be an evening off but Mrs. Chesterfield says she can spare her live-in, so I've organised for Bethany Evans to pop along to set up the guest rooms. She's just two houses down from here, you know the one up for sale anyhow I've asked Mr. Swift to escort her. Nasty out there, still if he keeps to the walls he'll be alright. Now if you wouldn't mind giving her a hand, I'd prefer she works under your direction.'

'Oh no, not at all Mr. Sanderson, that'll be no bother to me.'

'Make up Harriet's room, too, will you, I've just taken a call we'll need that for tomorrow. Sod's law, why on earth do people think it's fine to land without notice? Anyhow, you've no need to disturb the South wing apartment, she's safely tucked up as with Mrs. Harrington. There's no way I was allowing the pair of them through the house in the state they were in - nothing more than a pair of hyper muddy scarecrows, there's enough mayhem in the place already. In any case there won't be any time for a spring clean tomorrow, I'll detail you later. Now that boy! Heaven only knows where he's got to. We don't need an emergency on our hands right now. Been pacing that damned tunnel all evening, if he hasn't added to his PhD by now, he's never going to.'

'Oh Mr. Sanderson what on earth's going on all of a sudden? I'm not liking the sound of that. I've gone all shivery at the thought of him still being down there. How do we know he's alright? He might have tripped and broken his ankle, or something.'

Mr. Sanderson took a very deep breath, cupped his hand to his chin, thought for a moment pointing his finger firmly at the door.

'Yes, yes, of course, you're absolutely right, I'll send Mr. Swift down the tunnel to look for him and I'll walk down to escort Bethany Evans back myself. Swift's used to that damned tunnel, he'll soon see what's what.' Sentence barely finished, he turned as Belinda and Caroline entered the room.

'Keep the guests happy will you girls, I'm just off to find Mr. Swift and then I'll be popping out for ten minutes, or so.'

'Out Joris, in this? Are you mad? Don't tell me the prisoners from South Wing have escaped again? You'll never find them in this. Good riddance, I say.' Belinda looked at Caroline.

'Do you really have to go out in this?' Caroline questioned, not wishing to lose one precious minute of his company.

From behind he gathered them in his arms. 'Your concern is touching Caroline but yes, I do, I really do, I can't let this young lady arrive unescorted and we desperately need the help just now. You two keep an eye on the guests, I won't be long.'

They watched him stride out, each looking like they'd just won the lottery and lost the ticket.

'So he's finally got someone else in tow,' Belinda suddenly declared. 'Another young lady, or should I say fool offering to help him? Must be the people down the way, he's got everyone at his fingertips. Still it's only fair we let Harriet Glover down gently. Come on Caroline, let's tell her the news.'

Caroline's face assumed an expression of almost sinister determination. This was an opportunity too good to miss.

'Where are they Belinda, which part of the house did you say?' She rubbed her hands at the prospect, oh this was so much better than Harriet Glover getting him.

'Oh Mrs. Harris, just a moment...' Belinda cut in.

'What is it dear? I'm just off to check the linen cupboard.'

'Where exactly did Mr. Sanderson say Harriet and that friend of hers are sleeping tonight?'

'Oh that'll be the South Wing, in the apartment, I think. Yes that's what he said because he told me to check if the bedrooms were made up. We've got to make up the other rooms on that side, I expect that's where you two will be staying.'

'He promised us the apartment didn't he Caroline?' Belinda returned instantly feeling aggrieved.

'Oh I don't know, it sounds like they're all tucked away for the night. I can't understand why he wouldn't let Harriet go to her own room, the poor girl won't know whether she's coming or going. He's acting like the head of a boarding school if you ask me, bossing people about and who on earth's coming tomorrow, I don't know? This was supposed to be my evening off.'

'Well if they will behave like naughty school girls.... Just a minute did you say someone's coming tomorrow, and just who would that be?' Belinda Oxfordshire, now thoroughly irritated, could barely contain herself.

'Well I don't know, do I? I just told you that. It must be royalty the fuss he's making about it all.' Mrs. Harris stomped her way out of the room. Belinda Oxfordshire raised her eyebrows, this was indeed something of a first for Mrs. Harris, loyalty had always been her mantra.

'No, we're not losing out on the apartment Caroline, he promised us that. They won't be asleep yet, they'll be slugging the drinks cabinet dry. Come on let's kick them out!'

Chapter 28

'Oh it's a relief to be here Harriet, at least no one can kick us out.'

Harriet agreed, shaking with relief at being out of that police car. 'Yes thank goodness it's still my house. She stumbled her way round the cat in a panic to close the front door behind them.

'How did you get back here again? Mummy been looking after you properly, Pepper? Hope you haven't been hiding from her again. Why she phoned the police last time, I'll never know.'

'That could be it, that's why he knew your house. Well that's a relief for a start.'

'Let's think that for now Tricia, I'm trembling all over.'

'Same here. You haven't got something very strong to ease our nerves have you?'

'Yes, let's go for it, there's half a bottle of gin here, shall we start with this?'

They sat, exhausted...

Chapter 29

...whilst the taxi driver having recovered consciousness limped his way back down the lane wondering where the hell his taxi had got to. He rooted in his pocket for the keys then it dawned on him that pair of lesbians, having stolen the family jewels, had seen fit to knock him out to make their getaway in his cab.

'Bloody cheek, the little bastards, I'll have them for this.'

There was never a man in the whole world spurred so rapidly into a fast march along a foggy lane nor with such a steely determination to reach the police. He knew this route like the lines on his face. This route always meant money, you almost had to pay them to get a smile out of them. 'Serves them right, hope they stole the lot them two, aye and did a few others while they were at it. Filthy rich snobs, all they are round here.'

Then a better idea, he decided to leave the police out of it. Thought he'd come off better for a share of the booty. He'd get them. His mates in the business knew everyone round there. Always got to know when a house had been done, usually because it was one of their own who'd done it. All it took was a quick slide in for a glass of water while the nobs flapped around outside.

"Oh fine yes, just pop in will you, you'll see the house-keeper she's around somewhere."

They always said that, 'The last person we want to see is the bloody housekeeper.' With thoughts whirling he turned right at the end of the lane, slowed his pace, his head now refusing to cooperate with his feet. 'Oh fuck this!' he muttered, wandering over the road, every step born of sheer determination. With one hand pressed to the side of his face he pushed forward then wham, his knees buckled against a steel grill and for the second time that night he slid sideways, but this time he rolled straight into the ditch.

* * * * *

'This your cab Gov?' He awoke the next morning to a couple of police officers lifting him out.

'That's it, yeah that's it alright.' He pulled himself together recalling this was a story he wasn't going to tell. 'Pea-souper last night, I remember getting out to walk but don't know how I ended up in that.' He pointed an accusing finger at the ditch.

'Easily done mate, you must have passed out for some reason. You OK?'

'Fine Gov, nothing wrong with me, thanks.'

'Let's just check, have you got the keys?'

He pushed his hands into his pockets hoping against hope he'd left them in the cab.

'It's OK they're here, must have left them behind in your rush to get on your way.'

'That's it Gov, just on my way home I was.'

'You live on this side of the river, then?' He enquired somewhat sceptically.

'Oh not in one of those big houses I don't, this is the way I always go home, takes me away from the traffic, it's further but I get there quicker. Didn't realise it was going to turn as thick as it did.'

The officer seemed satisfied, tossed him the keys then walked with Detective Chief Inspector Jones to their parked police car on the far side of the road.

Chapter 30

…'Ooh Harriet we've finished that bottle between ush. Do you reckon we've immortalised that cabbie?'

'Letsh dishcush it over a sherry, shall we?'

'We'll get life if we finished him off, you do realishe this, don't you?'

'There Trishia, thatsh yoursh, take it shlowly.'

'Thanksh, Harriettia, Jorish'll get us out, yesh?

'Yesh, yesh and Clive, too, he ish a sholicitor, don't forget.'

'Not mush of one I say, he ashn't got my Venish tin back yet.'

'Really, then we mush take shsteps to chivvy him up. Wobble him like a jelly until he doesh.'

'He doesh wobble very well Harriet, he short of wobblesh when he'sh, well you know?'

'No I don't know Trishia, sorry Tricia I mean what do you mean?'

'When he'sh puttin` on his protection of courshe.'

'What protection are you talking about Tricia?'

'You know Harriet to shstop you `aving babies.'

'Oh sho you won't be pregnant then Tricia. How long did it take for him to shstop wobbling?'

'He never did shstop wobbling, especially when he knew it had come off.' That'sh when I shstarted wobbling. We were wobbling together then.

'Oh sho you might just be pregnant like me?'

'I might just be Harriet, do they let you have babies in prishon?

'More sherry Tricia?'

* * * * *

And there the conversation ended as they took a sofa each to lie prostrate until the rattle of keys in the front door jolted them to consciousness at approximately 10.33 the next morning.

'Stay still Harriet we're being burgled.'

They heard footsteps going upstairs.

'Quick Tricia the shed!'

They were out like dynamite with the inside bolt firmly locked on the shed door.

'Oh no, who do think it was?' Harriet said, trembling.

'Oh I do hope it wasn't the police, my head can't deal with it this morning.'

'Well who else could get in, unless of course it's Mr. Sanderson, he's the only one with a spare key, apart from Mummy but she knows I'm away. Maybe Mr. Sanderson's come looking for us.'

'Let's hope that's all it is Harriet. Oh bloody hell how do we keep getting ourselves into all this mess? If it is the police, they're bound to look in here.'

'Get behind these sun-loungers and pull this canvas over ourselves. They won't see us, hopefully!'

'Oh Harriet how many times have we had to hide in here? I think it would be safer to stay here, don't you? At least until lunch time, they'll have all given up by then.'

The tarpaulin moved backwards and forwards as they debated the best way to prolong the inevitability of their fate.

'I do hope it's not my Clive in there, I wouldn't want him thinking I was trying to hide from him,' Tricia whispered, pulling her feet in, hardly daring to breathe.

Chapter 31

'Yes, yes, had a quick look around, that'll do me fine for the time being. I've been online, there's a couple of promising properties, need to look at them, set the ball rolling on something.' Clive Engells looked at his watch. 'What time are you expecting the PM?'

'Not until two, or thereabouts. Need to get the last of the house guests cleared. I'm hoping that disconnected student of ours doesn't land in the middle of it all. I can't think where he's got to, I rue the day I took him on.'

'Is he at school?'

'That's it, goodness knows what his PhD's all about, I'd have thought the field trip to the Galapagos Islands would have done the trick, but no, the boy's deviating like the devil. He'll get nowhere with it if he keeps changing tack. Anyhow it's about time those two were on their way, or at least one of them. Forgive the bluntness of the question Clive but are you and Patricia Harrington an item or was she just a one nighter?'

'Oh no, no, no Joris, I'm extremely attracted to the girl. She's such a change from the type of women I've ever been involved with. Totally scatty, so sweet, and naïve in a way. I don't think that husband of hers has got much about him.'

'Enough to suit Belinda, or so it would seem.'

'You know I'm not sure about her. I think she's so gone on you she'll use any strategy she can to get her way with you. I'm sure this guy's just a stop-gap, someone to keep in the frame until she gets what she really wants.'

'Really you surprise me Clive, though I shouldn't be, you are a lawyer, must know a fair bit about relationships or at least the breaking of them.'

'Yes Joris, I've seen plenty in my time, of course. Now what about this other young lady that's appeared on the scene, you obviously know each other?'

Joris Sanderson shifted his stance, he wasn't too keen to enter into this discussion. 'Oh yes, yes, she was a former friend of mine, left the area and returned. A good friend of Belinda, that's how she came to be here.'

'Ah I see, and what about you and Harriet, now where's that going?'

'Right to the altar Clive, right to the altar, I'll catch that amber butterfly if it's the last thing I do.'

'Good luck Joris, I think if we can distance the pair of them you might stand half a chance.'

'Yes Clive, indeed, do me a favour will you and just marry that damned girl.'

'Steady on Joris, she's still got a husband remember?'

'Another good reason, that poor guy needs a break!'

'You mean a permanent arrangement with Belinda?'

'He could do worse.'

'She'll never settle for him and well you know it Joris.'

'Well I want her and Caroline Worsnip off my back, any ideas Clive?'

'Be straight Joris, you're not obliged to relate to anyone you don't wish to. Besides she'll be focussing on this unfair dismissal case for a while and no doubt Belinda will be supporting her. Let them both get engrossed in that, you worry too much. Concentrate on Harriet, get this business over with the PM whatever it is and round that girl up.'

* * * * *

'Ah Belinda, Caroline, slept well? On your way, I see.'

Clive departed as Mr. Sanderson turned to the sound of high heels reverberating off the parquet floor.

'Yes, thank you for a great evening. We couldn't wake that childish pair you placed in the South Wing apartment last night, hope you have better luck this morning.'

'Yes I'll see to it now, we need the house cleared as soon as possible. Belinda, now have you got your taxi organised?'

'I phoned Patrick, should be here any minute. Yes, ah that sounds like him now, he seems to love speeding in, crunching his tyres through that gravel of yours.'

'They all do, unfortunately,' replied Mr. Sanderson, narrowing his eyes. 'Right off you two go then, Clive says he'll be in touch regarding this employment issue but I've asked him to let me have a word with them first,' he said, turning. 'Oh there you are again Clive.'

'Yes that's how we'll work it Caroline, I've taken your number, just give me chance to get some context around it all, I'm sure there's no need to worry, there's no case whatsoever as far as I can make out,' Clive reassured.

Caroline smiled, nodding her head at them both in appreciation as they left to get in the waiting cab.

'I'll get my things packed then,' Clive said. 'Are you sure this is going to be alright with Harriet?'

'Oh absolutely Clive, I want her here, under my nose where I can keep an eye on her. This is the best place for her, she'd be moving in anyhow once we get married.'

'Ah yes, I see, didn't quite realise the relationship had progressed that far.'

Mr. Sanderson placed a hand on his shoulder. 'There's much we need to catch up on Clive, there'll be far more opportunity now. Now I'll just pop along to the far side, see if I can wake the pair of them.'

'Ah Mrs. Harris, how's it all going, I did tell you it's the PM arriving, did I not?'

'Well no actually but I thought it would be someone like that. Anyway we're pretty much there, Bethany and I got through most of it last night, it's surprising the difference an extra pair of hands makes. Do you know she's actually a trained nanny? She's looking to get back to that, I think the job with the Chesterfields is just a stop-gap, she's not staying with them when they go.'

She noted Mr. Sanderson's instant focus on her words, thought it best to keep quiet as she went on down the stairs.

'Any sign of Harriet and Mrs. Harrington along there?' he called back.

'The beds haven't even been slept in Mr. Sanderson.'

He leant over, his face reddened, his blonde hair falling forward as he banged the banister hard.

'Now where the hell are they? I can do without another crisis right now!'

Chapter 32

'Oh it's awful under this thing, I swear I'll never get hung-over again. Gosh my head's going. Oh let's get out from under it, it's sliding all over the place. Oh flip that's the bike gone over now. You alright Tricia?'

'No I'm not, I think I'm goin` to be sick, I'll have to get out of here and outside quick Harriet.'

She pulled the bolt across and dashed to the Rhododendron bush in the corner, just managing to squeeze between that and the fence. Harriet, having deja vu crouched down crawling to the back door, peering through the cat-flap before cautiously reaching for the handle.

'OK Pepper let's get you fed. I just need to see the coast's clear. It wasn't Mummy then?'

Pleasingly, the brush of black soft fur caught her legs.

'Right Pepper, *food*, I'm coming, just let me put the front door latch on so no one can get in.'

Head thumping Harriet forced herself to hurry then froze on the bottom stair as she heard movement on the landing.

'Mummy!'

'Harriet! Oh you made me jump then! I thought you were supposed to be staying with Joris, over the weekend at least. Oh no don't tell me you've reneged on that poor man again. You know Harriet he's going to lose his patience good and proper one of these days.'

'Yes Mummy, it's just that I needed to come back for some things.'

'Well, thank goodness for that Harriet but where's your car? Oh I see he's dropped you off, he's so kind no wonder he got a knighthood, just get him down that aisle before you miss the boat completely. I suppose Mark still hasn't signed the house over to you yet. Just what's going on with that useless ex of yours?'

'Do come into the kitchen Mummy, we can talk while I'm feeding the cat.'

'I'd be surprised if he had anything to say on the subject Harriet.'

'Give him chance, he's not long gone down there, he's got to get his head round that new job. He'll do it when he's ready.'

'Getting his head round that new girlfriend more like. Do you know there's talk of marriage?'

'Who have you been talking to Mummy? How can you be saying all this?'

'I phoned his mother to see if I could get a bit more sense out of her with regard to this house. You never tell me anything these days Harriet. In any case it looks like Mark's got other things on his mind to be bothered keeping in touch with you. It looks like it's his mother will be getting all the news now. Full of his new girlfriend after him letting you down at the church like that, I'll never forgive him. Well we'll see if he does any better with this one, won't we?'

'Oh,' that's all Harriet could bring herself to say.

'He'll not be wanting to hang on to this house Harriet. You need to be pushing for a legal conclusion. In the meantime tell me, just what is the point of this place lying empty when poor Avril could be renting it, at least. They've got to find somewhere before the baby's due, poor Violet can't be putting them up in that little bungalow, you know it's no bigger than ours. Anyway I've already told her you'll be more than happy to let her have it, you're not going to be wanting to live here as well as in Lower Tideside.'

'No Mummy you should not have done that, you're just going to have to go back and tell her she's not on. You can't just turn into a landlord overnight you know. There's all kinds of legal issues to be addressed before you can rent to people.'

'Well that's even better, she won't need to be paying any rent, you can just let them borrow the house until the whole thing's sorted out. You know she's set her heart on this place Harriet.'

Harriet's head throbbed, she looked out of the kitchen window hoping her mother would go before Tricia materialised from behind the Hydrangea.

'Please just leave it Mummy, I'm always going to be needing to come back here, I can't just move everything into Mr. Sanderson's house, just like that. Just tell Violet to lay off.'

Mrs. Glover bristled into despair.

'I'm off now Harriet, Daddy's in the car, we're late, supposed to be meeting Ivy and Arnold for lunch, they'll be there by now, I'll be getting told off for keeping them waiting.'

Harriet about to breath a sigh of relief paused as her mother swung round to have a quick look out of the kitchen window.

'You'll be wanting to get that shed down before Avril moves in as well, Violet says she can't stand them cluttering up the garden. And what's that resting on the side fence at the back Harriet, it's not another shed is it? Really it was most unfair of Mark....Oh no, I'm off, it's that awful girl what's she doing struggling out from the back of that Hydrangea bush? Let me get out Harriet I haven't got time to be dealing with that one. Do you know I'm on the verge of giving up. Please don't let Sir Joris slip through your fingers again Harriet, it's high time you broke that association, she's a bad influence. You'll never grow up while you've got her in tow. She's got a husband, you haven't and your not likely to the way you're going on.'

Mrs Glover bounced down the hall, slamming the front door closed behind her. Harriet waited then hurriedly put the latch on, for a moment sitting at the kitchen table with head in hands, stunned, hurt and angry.

'Is it alright to come in Harriet? Only I think I saw an apparition in your kitchen window, but my head's so far gone, it might have just been me.' Tricia peered round wondering whether it was safe to enter.

'No Tricia, you did. It was Mummy, she gave me the fright of my life when I heard her on the landing, I thought we were both gonners you and me.'

'Oow but they wouldn't have found me behind the Hydrangea, you'd have been off on your own with who ever it was Harriet.'

'Oh please don't say that, it could have been the police back. I wish I knew that taxi driver was going to be alright. Why, oh why, do we do these stupid things Tricia?'

'It's because of the way we get treated, we get bossed about, picked up and put down, it was never like that before Joris Sanderson came into our lives. Him and his upper class friends. If we hadn't fallen for him our lives wouldn't have taken this horrible direction.'

'No you're right. He's from the land of high places where there's far more influence, selfish vested interest, corruption, competition, money, media spotlight then we have ever been used to. We keep getting caught up in all of that so we're out of our depths really. That's why we're always running away, hiding, frightened. The only trouble is Tricia, we can't turn the clock back now.'

Chapter 33

Joris Sanderson looked at the clock, he couldn't decide whether to phone the police or not. He'd been for it, then against, swinging back and forth ever since Clive Engells had left the house. The fog of yesterday evening concerned him but having heard the taxi last night, he felt the most likely scenario to be they were both in it and away. Of course he'd closed the front door not hearing all the kafuffle and having left the house to escort Bethany Evans both ways and no sign of anything untoward going on out there, that was sufficient to take the edge off his concern. He knew he'd reacted badly to Barry Giordano's phone call, Harriet was bound to rail against that. He didn't like the man. Couldn't stand the man. Couldn't fathom why Harriet insisted on defending him, wanted to have anything to do with him after that disgusting work of art he'd presented them both with as a wedding present. He'd known for long enough this undercover guy would fight him to the death if necessary to get his hands on Harriet. This was one streak of anger, disgust and jealousy Mr. Sanderson was unable to control. Of course he'd been obliged to be civil to him, he was part of a very efficient, highly organised team working for the government and with the Prime Minister holding him in the highest regard it was difficult for Joris Sanderson to exert his will. Not to be defeated, however, he stood tall, decided there was no time to waste as he squashed all negativity knowing this thing must be done with haste. He looked at his watch, finally decided against reporting them missing, what with them and Ross Farquerhart he could at best be accused of carelessly losing house guests. Besides the P.M was due to arrive in forty minutes, this wasn't the time to stir things. It could be the time to have a quiet word in his ear though. Joris Sanderson brushed his fingers through his hair, then hoisted his trousers. 'Yes, it's time to use my connections to advantage,' he thought then sat down in the drawing room to think it through.

Joris Sanderson looked through the French doors at the helipad, tapping his watch, his attention suddenly caught by the low drone of chopper blades crossing the river.

'He'll be landing any minute now Mrs. Harris. We'll enjoy a light lunch in here if you would be so kind.' He looked at his watch again. 'Say about one-ish.'

'That'll be fine Mr. Sanderson, I'll make sure neither of you are disturbed.'

He delivered her the most charming of smiles which always made Mrs. Harris run her hands swiftly down the sides of her white apron to steady her legs before hurrying away.

'Good to see you again Mac, flight comfortable?'

'Best part of the job,' Mackenzie Lyons grinned. 'Great view, she's berthed nearer the sea than I imagined. Fine looking ship, I'm all in favour of keeping them out of the scrap-yard. Private enough, too. Just thinking aloud here, could we hire a motor launch say to carry forty or so? I'm thinking a trip along the coastline, around Anglesey and back, something different for the guests to enjoy and plenty of privacy.'

'Sound great Mac, we can arrange that for you no bother! Now how's Rosemary and the girls, I wasn't sure, but it looks like you're on your own Mac?'

'Yes, sorry old boy just a flyer this one Joris, no point in bringing the family. I thought I could at least overnight but something urgent's cropped up. If we could just run through these wedding plans then leave it all in your capable hands, I know both myself and Rosemary will be eternally grateful. Anyway how are things with you? Fine residence this, you know Lower Tideside must have some of the best properties in the country. Rosemary loves it here, don't be surprised if we end up as neighbours one day.'

For a fleeting moment Joris Sanderson thought of Harriet and Tricia. If it was ever going to work he either needed to educate or get that girl Tricia Harrington out of their lives. Maybe Clive could exert some influence. He had noticed Tricia's inconsistent attempt to improve her accent of late but it wasn't even that, it was all the scrapes they'd managed to get themselves into, he was convinced she was the driver. 'Of course,' he reminded himself, 'she's even less used to mixing in these circles than Harriet, not used to fending off all the less obvious paraphernalia that goes with it.'

They each sat either side of the French doors, looking across the garden towards the sea.

'Yes Joris, I wouldn't mind retiring here at all. Fabulous views, equitable climate I understand and so well placed for the rest of the country, the rest of the world even with Manchester Airport virtually on the doorstep. Plenty of privacy, too, just what Ida needs for this wedding of hers. No press, can you assure me of that Joris?'

'No press Mac, I guarantee it. Ida's had a hard time at the hands of the press, let's hope this one works out for her.'

Ida Lyons had spent some years modelling, strutting the Italian catwalks. She'd met Savriato Cello during that time. Fallen deeply in love with him, managed to persuade her father to use his influence to get him lined up for a constituency seat "anywhere in Italy would do for Savriato", he'd told the Italian PM, Bruno Bello. He'd never known his daughter so happy, the least he could do would be to give him a leg up in the political stakes. Well settled in Italy and more than ready for the role of PM's wife Ida Lyons hadn't a clue his ambitions were set on the UK. A second generation immigrant, his Italian father had married a Scottish girl and between them had run a successful restaurant business. Much to their disappointment Savriato had shown little interest in it and on graduating he'd entered the world of finance, eventually becoming a stockbroker. His strong political leanings soon had him elected to the European parliament where he'd first met Mac Lyons. They parted, he'd been returned for a second term while Savriato Cello had lost his seat. Disillusioned he changed tack, and having been successful in his application for dual nationality, went back to full-time finance settling in Milan. Every inch the playboy though always on the lookout for an opening that would get him back into the world of politics. Meeting Ida Lyons had been heaven sent, it presented an opportunity too good to miss. Her father, in the know, would prepare the ground for his candidacy, he would ensure his selection to a safe seat in order to fight the next general election. It was only when Mackenzie Lyons inadvertently heard of his ambitions to return to British politics in support of the extreme right he cried a halt. Mac Lyons, furious Savriato Cello had fudged his intentions with Ida completely missing the signals and now embarrassingly messed up with Bruno Bello, he insisted Ida put Savriato Cello straight. In a shot he terminated their relationship, furious with them both, decided to go for it himself. Oh yes, he'd make damned sure he was elected a Tory MP, make damned sure he'd take Mac Lyons' place by swinging his party to the right. One day he would be PM, it was his burning ambition, he'd settle for nothing less. He started there and then giving serious consideration as to how best to smear their names.

When Ida came home she became anorexic, it took a long time to sort her out. Not surprising it's her therapist she's about to marry. Not surprising neither of them want publicity. Once Mac Lyons was set for a second term in office Savriato Cello hatched a better plan, switching political allegiance to the opposition. He soon scaled the party ranks to become leader. Now rising fast in the opinion polls, just waiting his chance to win the next general election. At all costs Ida Lyons must keep her marriage to Patrick White secret. At all costs the relationship between Savriato Cello and Ida Lyons must not come to light during the forthcoming campaign. How would it look, the electoral battleground speared with lies and innuendo? This guy was dangerous, he could bounce Mackenzie Lyons straight out of a job, no it was better for all concerned this wedding be kept well under wraps.

They ate and chatted for a couple of hours whilst Mrs. Harris busied herself serving lunch then coffee. Logistics of the forthcoming marriage agreed, Joris Sanderson saw fit to mention his concerns over Barry Giordano.

'Ah I see,' Mackenzie Lyons tapped the side of his nose. 'That shouldn't be too difficult. I'll put a word in, Get Charles Bird to revise his contract make sure this chap gets posted somewhere well away, maybe something more permanent, desk bound even. There's always that kind of work going at the far flung corners of the globe. Don't worry Joris, I'm delighted to have this opportunity to reciprocate your kindness. Now Harriet Glover, yes very pretty girl as I recall, rather accident prone though. Not too sure I get on with her handbag. Get her another, something smaller, will you old boy. I want to stay in one piece in order to be able to attend your wedding!'

'I'm rather hoping she'll be carrying a bouquet, Mac.'

Chapter 34

Harriet still stinging from her mother's revelation decided to keep the latest news on Mark to herself. Just now she couldn't deal with any more anxiety.

'Well what are we going to do now Harriet?'

'Look Tricia we're quite entitled to be here. I just wish I knew what had happened to that taxi driver.'

'Oh so do I, put the radio on and let's see if anyone's died in last night's fog.'

They sat and listened to the local station, relieved there was no such incident reported.

'It would be on there if someone had died, no reports of a taxi going missing either! Keep your fingers crossed he might just have recovered and walked back to find it.'

'That's some hope Harriet, but they love talkin' about deaths on there. They wouldn't have left that one out. Anyway he would have died outside Joris's house. Him and the police would have been round here as fast as they could but they haven't.'

Suddenly they jumped up. The sound of the key in the door.

'They can't get in,' Harriet whispered, 'I locked it, let's crawl to the lounge and see who it is.'

They could hear the key wrenching back and forth as they crawled along the hall pushing the lounge door open walking in a sideways stoop to the front window.

'Oh look, it's Clive with his cases Tricia. Mr. Sanderson must have sent him round here to stay. He wouldn't be carrying his cases otherwise, what a cheek, he's as bad as Mummy!'

'Harriet, I feel really sorry for him, can we call him back?'

'Oh OK go on then, we've got to come clean sometime,' Harriet decided.

She stood in the window watching Tricia running alongside the car as he geared up to move away. He stopped, got out, hugged her. Lifted the boot lid and with a suitcase in each hand he walked up the path, Tricia almost skipping alongside him.

'Well I'm not playing gooseberry to you two lovebirds,' Harriet declared. I'll get a taxi back to Lower Tideside right now, my things are there anyway, but mark my words I'll be back tomorrow, Barry Giordano's meeting me here at four-thirty prompt.'

'You'll see nothing of us Harriet,' Clive Engells declared. 'This is really very kind you know, Patricia and I have a great deal to discuss, not an easy one in Joris's place, always difficult in someone else's house, especially when they've guests.'

Harriet made a quick call, grabbed her bag and coat, knowing full well the taxi would be there almost before she'd had chance to open the door.

'Lower Tideside, you say Miss? Oh I'm always going there, that's where the posh people live. They're always getting done them houses. Done a few round there myself, just waiting for the proceeds of another one. Er keep that under your hat.'

Harriet trembled, kept her head down whilst the rotund driver heaved himself into the front seat. At least she knew he was alive!

Chapter 35

'Well life is full of surprises Clive, who would have ever thought you and me would be here today, all on our own?'

'Well, I have to agree and isn't it such a nice thought petal. You know our night together has never left my mind.'

'Oh no, me neither Clive, it was very special indeed. Did you enjoy the dinner party last night?'

'Yes, I certainly did, not a little hung-over this morning, I have to admit.'

'Me too Clive, I can't really remember how Harriet and I ended up back here. Still glad we did, otherwise we wouldn't be having this chance to be alone together, again.'

'Well certainly I don't think old Joris would be expecting this outcome. He was most concerned at yours and Harriet's disappearance.'

'Oh good that will be nice for `arriet, er Harriet then. Hopefully he'll be in a good mood when she gets back. The least he can do is let her go back to her own bedroom.'

Clive Engells smiled, 'So you were intending to stay here again for the night I presume. Let's dine out shall we, and then see where the evening takes us?'

'Oh Clive that would be wonderful. I see you've got your suitcases, I'm afraid I haven't got anything to get changed into with me. I only packed for the evening. Is my case still in your car Clive? At least I'll have a clean pair of knickers and my make-up.'

'Yes but in any case I'll nip you home dear, it's not too far from here, as I recall you saying?'

'Well no it's not but I wouldn't want us to be bumping into Bob right now would I? He wasn't in a good mood when he left the party last night.'

'Well maybe not petal. Let's order in, there's bound to be a restaurant will do that for us. We'll enjoy it better here and who knows what the night will bring?'

Chapter 36

'You wouldn't believe the change in the weather from last night,' the cab driver half-turned to Harriet. 'What a night that was. Oddly enough I was at that very house you're going to last night collecting a couple of girls.' He half-turned again. 'You write stories, at all?'

'Er no, not at all, that's not me,' Harriet declared still keeping her head down.

'Well that's a pity because what happened to me last night would make one hell of a story!'

Harriet went cold, didn't answer.

'Not that I remember much, got there to a couple of girls swinging on the gates, last thing I remember they all fell on top of me, knocked me out good and proper they did. Probably gate-crashed the party, knocked off a few gems. The cheeky buggers escaped in my taxi. Well it had to be them didn't it. No other bugger would be wandering along there intent on stealing it. I was going to report it, you know to the police...'

Oh yes, Harriet knew alright, she began shivering with fear.

'... But then I thought better of it, decided to hunt the pair of them down, I'd know them, I'd only ever see them together. Lesbians them, not that that's got anything to do with it, we've got some great girls working the taxis, just the same, but boy there's a pair there you can't get them apart. Carl only employs one of them, the other's always there for the ride. He's a soft bugger him, he should be charging them the fare.'

Now approaching Starboard Marine North West, Harriet was grateful for the green lights, the sooner she was out of this taxi the better. He took a right turn driving towards the lane.

'Anyway where was I?' Suddenly he pointed to his left. 'Look, see there, that's where they left this sodding thing. I shuffled miles in the fog from that house, couldn't see a damned thing, to walk straight into this bloody thing, then slid off the bonnet and ended up comatose wedged in the ditch.'

'Oh I'm so sorry to hear that,' Harriet said, trying to smarten her accent for fear of recognition.

He retracted into a considered silence which ate the last few remaining miles of this nightmare journey, then he went off again.

'Yes you would be, anyone would be, no-one would have wanted to go through what I did last night. Anyway I had my reasons for not telling the police. Oh it would have been easy, they were the ones that pulled me out but I decided I'd find them and demand a share of the booty.'

Harriet remained silent, glanced over to Molly's house on the corner as they turned down the narrow lane leading to Mr. Sanderson's place.

'Does he know you're coming? It's just those bloody gates, I've never liked them, especially with a pair of gargoyles hanging off them.'

Harriet took a deep breath, panicked she'd not got her handbag with her. Remembered it was still in the house, desperately didn't want him to know that.

'You'll need to beep actually, oh no it's OK looks like the gates are open. There's Mr. Swift, he must be up the ladder, you can just drive straight in. Er Mr. Sanderson will pay you, does he have an account with the company?'

'Him and the rest of them round here, they don't know what cash is, never get a tip, that's why they're always getting robbed. I hate coming here, you go and find him, I'll need his signature.'

Harriet stepped out of the taxi to see Mr. Sanderson storming through the gravel. She waited.

'Were you done here last night Gov? `Ad anything swiped? A couple of lesbians they were, swinging off them gates. Knocked me for six, flat out then nicked me taxi to escape with your valuables!'

'Oh good heavens no, certainly not here. You must have the wrong house, the fog was dreadful down here last evening, it would be easy to get confused.' He glanced sideways at Harriet waiting for him to mention the call out.

'What's he doing up that gate then if he's not fixing it?'

'Merely rubbing it down for repainting, anyhow I see it has little to do with you. My guests are all of impeccable morals, not a thief amongst them and certainly the house was not broken into, I can vouch for that. Here let me sign for this trip and I would advise you to be extremely careful what you say unless you want to be prosecuted for slander.'

'Alright, alright, don't get all heavy Gov. I could swear I got a call out to this one.' He scratched his head, 'I can't be certain I'm remembering right if that's what you're saying Gov.'

'Sir, if you don't mind, you are talking to a knight of the realm here.'

Harriet looked down at her feet, whilst Mr. Sanderson returned his pure gold Shaeffer pen to the inside pocket of his jacket. She couldn't believe she was hearing him speaking like this. They both leapt out of the way whilst the cabbie did a quick swerve in the gravel to turn his taxi round.

'Oh go fuck yourself you stuck up arse-hole,' he bellowed, trailing two fingers from the open window, raging, vowing never to return to this dreaded place again.

'Harriet, what the hell do you think you've been playing at? Inside! We'll discuss this in the study, *right now!*'

She sat in the upholstered chair by the window. Normally she would love to be in this room with its white walls and furnishings, the jade rug at her feet, each picture, each piece of glass, reflecting every shade of the sea. Normally it would be restful, peaceful, but not just now, Harriet was in utter turmoil yet again. She placed her hand across her stomach wondering how this tiny baby could ever survive, wondering if it would turn out to be an adrenaline junkie. She knew she needed to calm down, get some kind of stability back into her life. She thought about Mark, about Barry, about Mr. Sanderson. She thought about her mother's words, Tricia could well be on the way to acquiring a second husband, never mind the one she's already got. Harriet could feel herself beginning to get left behind. It wasn't as if she hadn't fallen deeply for Mr. Sanderson, maybe it was the menopause like Mummy said, maybe all these competing pregnancy hormones were responsible, maybe she just hadn't recovered from being dumped at the church by Mark, maybe she only wanted what she thought she couldn't have. She slumped into the chair, through the small Georgian panes could see Mr. Sanderson striding back. Tears spilled, filling her eyes until they could be contained no longer, rolling down her cheeks, falling to her clasped hands like first drops of rain. Quickly she dabbed them away as she heard the door opening.

'Now Harriet, what's this all about?' He drew the opposite chair closer, sat facing her, placing his hands firmly on his knees.

Harriet, aware his voice had softened, kept her head down, her firmly knit hands tightening resting on her baby. She felt him lifting her chin, closed her eyes for fear of him seeing the tears, felt him gather her up in his arms, breathed deeply into his neck as he carried her slowly up each stair to his bedroom.

He sat her upright on the bed, sat beside her, drew her once again into his arms.

'Harriet surely you can understand my anger? Why oh why do you keep running away from me?'

She looked into his eyes, took a very deep breath, turned, sinking into his chest, sobbing, just like she did when Mark had let her down at the church.

'Harriet, listen, now listen to me. Think about this very carefully before you answer me. Since Clive left for your house, I've been thinking, very deeply. I think you know as well as I do 4 The Willows isn't the best place for you to be right now. You've the memories of Mark and all that's gone wrong for you over the last couple of years. Now I don't want you to do anything against your instincts, your finer feelings if you like. Yes I want to marry you, I want you to be my wife, and this is nothing to do with the fact you're carrying my baby. It's simply this, it's because I love you deeply and therefore your happiness is my priority. I know this is not the right time for you to settle here, but I am thinking and I do know Molly and Percy are with me on this, at least until you've had your baby, why not stay with them? Molly has such a strong instinct to care for you, if you should need it. You know it's not going to get any easier as this pregnancy progresses. You've just another three months in school if you can make it that far, but it certainly won't matter if you don't feel able to, or don't want to remain there. Molly has an independent suite attached to that house. I've offered to fund its refurbishment. You can design it to your liking, have complete freedom to do exactly as you wish. Have the comfort and security of good friends and of course I am just down the road from you should you want me. You've now got the Mercedes, that's yours whatever you decide to do. Think about it Harriet, your happiness is all I want, you've given me more than you will ever know. Please think about it. Give yourself a chance. Get off this merry-go-round, that's really not so merry at all. I know you place a premium on this friendship with Tricia, well that's fine, but Clive's serious about her. Things are not going to remain as they are now once they get married. He's a fine lawyer Harriet, he'll have her whipped out of that marriage before she knows it. And Mark, the chances are he's going to meet someone else you know, things move on. Please think very seriously about all this Harriet. I want you to have space to make the right decision, to be where you want to be, who you want to be with. I have to be honest now, I've dropped the word to Mac to get Barry Giordano out of your hair for a while. You need space to decide what it is you really want Harriet. Do you think you can go along with this?'

Harriet blew her nose, released herself from his arms. 'I love Molly, and yes, I don't even need to think about it, I want to be with her and Percy but you can't do that to Barry, it's so unfair, you can't interfere with his work, his life.'

'Isn't that exactly what he's trying to do to me Harriet? That guy's insidious. He's trying to destroy by degrees all we have together. That painting was hideous. He tricked you and well you know it. I don't know how you could wish to have been associated with him after that.'

'I know it was very wrong of him to do that but he proposed to me, he said he just fell head-over-heels in love with me. That wasn't my fault. He's not the bad guy you're making him out to be. If it wasn't for him getting us away and out of here after Tricia and I had been kidnapped who knows what would have happened to us all.'

'Quite Harriet, I do indeed take your point. It was of course, partly his job, you'd inadvertently become embroiled in his work, though I know this last episode was to do with the aftermath. Look, as I said, you need to have space in which to decide exactly what you want to do with your life. Obviously Molly is very concerned about you, she didn't hesitate at the suggestion, but would, of course understand if you don't want to take up her offer. Nothing's been arranged, Clive won't have difficulty finding a rental if he can't use your house, 4 The Willows is still yours, it's your choice. You know you've got me up and down like a yo-yo Harriet. You're carrying my baby for goodness sake, I make decisions based on the assumption you want to marry me, but even now I don't know where I stand.'

He walked to the window and back again sitting down beside her.

She reached for his hand, recognised the truth in all he was saying. Could feel the tears welling again, tried to sniff them away before speaking.

'I don't know what's the matter with me.'

'It's probably got a lot to do with being pregnant, I'm convinced things will settle down once you enter the second trimester.'

She tied to smile.

'Mark's met someone, according to Mummy it's serious, they're going to get married.'

'It was always a possibility, I recall only just saying exactly that to you. I knew from the conversation we had in the Galapagos Islands he seriously intended to move his life along. Promotion, relocating to Basingstoke was a God-given opportunity. Your first break from home, university and getting pregnant. Neither of you had chance to live, find your feet. At least you had your maternal instincts to hold your lifestyle together. As soon as your children flew the nest you wanted more even though you couldn't let go of the need to marry him. It was exactly the same for him. It's hard Harriet I know, but you really do need to face facts. You can't continue behaving like a deviant school girl. You've considerable, acknowledged talent. You've two wonderful daughters both happily married, could well be returning to the area. You've so much to be grateful for, certainly this isn't the time to be feeling sorry for yourself.'

'No, I know that Mr. Sanderson. Mummy spoke to Mark's mother and she's come away with the impression Mark's about to renege on giving me his half of the house, after promising.'

'Well I never expected that to materialise. It'll be going back on the open market then? It looks like your time in there will inevitably be limited, anyhow.'

'I know I need to sort myself out,' said Harriet, reaching for a tissue from her sleeve. Just now anyway I think, if it's not putting Molly and Percy out, it would be better if I do go there. I didn't realise there was an apartment attached to their house.'

'Probably nearer the mark to call it a house, anyhow it's self-contained and accessed from the lane side, there's a drive so you wouldn't even need to worry about parking your car. It's not used, I understand they naturally use the main entrance off the top road.'

'Thank you Mr. Sanderson, thank you so very much. I never expected things would turn out this way, today. Will you sort it out with Molly, please? I don't mind what state it's all in, I just want to be in there. I don't want to see Mark arriving home with his new partner, I just couldn't stand that. I just want to be away from that house now and the garden shed with all its memories. Is this place furnished, do you know?'

'Yes indeed it is, Molly said it's all modern beech furniture, but the kitchen's white flat-pack stuff, anyway it will tide you over Harriet.'

She caught the word "tide", thoughts of the sea immediately flooding her mind, remembered that dream she'd had.

'Tide, Mr. Sanderson, that's what I really wanted to say, I'm drowning in the tide, I've tried but I'm so very out of my depths here, with you, this house, your friends....' Her voice trailed off, exhausted she rolled away from him, stretching out on the bed, then with her head on his pillow curled into immediate, gentle sleep.

He walked round to her, brushing the corner of his eye, the side of his face damp from his fingers.

'No, no, no, you've got it so wrong. This is where you truly belong, in this bed my sweet amber butterfly. Harriet I know you'll be mine the day you can comfortably call me by my name.'

His gentle whispers fell to a kiss on her hair, he walked away, swallowing the lump in his throat, quietly closing the door behind him.

Chapter 37

Molly and Percy closed the door on the annexe then followed the garden path to the back door of their house. It was late September, with sweeps of fallen leaves painted every shade of autumn blowing at their feet.

'Do you know Percy I so very much want Harriet to come and live here, even for a little while. That poor girl's gone through so much. It was a terrible do you know when Mark let her down at the church. No wonder she's in such a state, not to mention the run of nightmares she and her friend have been through. I don't know how they've survived it all. She really doesn't need to be on her own, oh I do so hope Joris will phone with some good news.

'He's going to have to find her first, I can't make out why she causes him so much worry. I hope you're doing the right thing Molly, volunteering us, we haven't been here a year yet and we've already had the police knocking on the door suspecting us of growing cannabis. I hate to say it but Harriet played no small part in that.'

'Oh let's get inside Percy, you get some more logs on the fire while I put the kettle on. You know she's a very responsible young woman, they don't give out damehoods for nothing, she's done wonders for that school, far more than any of us are likely to hear about. You know I've helped out from time to time at the coffee club Joris holds at Starboard Marine North West. I've spoken to some of those parents, they absolutely think the world of her. She's been known to open her purse rather than see some of them go hungry. And look now, she's got this food pantry going in school. It was her idea and I do know it's making a big difference to those children and no doubt their parents.'

She stirred the tea and sat each mug on the small tables either side of the fireplace by the armchairs.

'There Percy, that's yours, I really don't think we have any need to worry about Harriet. Do you remember how we all met on that cruise ship? My what a girl, I swear if it hadn't been for Harriet we wouldn't have got married. You were at such a low ebb after losing your dear wife and I was still feeling just as low as you. Time didn't heal for me, it's only since I met you I've really found life to be worth living again.'

'Come here Molly, put that cup down, give us a kiss. Of course it'll be alright. We'll do all we can to help her settle in, that's if she wants to stay here, of course.'

'Oh there's the phone Percy, it might be Joris, quick let me get to it.'

Chapter 38

Mr. Sanderson replaced the receiver, pleased at Molly's reaction to his message. Pleased Harriet would at least be within reach. He was increasingly concerned about her, convinced she'd not yet seen Dr. Holden, not had any pre-natal care. As doctors they did of course know each other and as much as Joris Sanderson was driven to enquire, he always withdrew, knowing full well it would be unethical to expect Dr. Holden to betray a patient's privacy or for him to go behind Harriet's back in this way.

'Ah Mrs. Harris, there you are. Would you be so kind as to return Harriet's belongings to her original room. She'll be with us at least for tonight, I'm not too sure for how long after that.'

Mrs. Harris nodded, wanting to find out what was going on with them, as far as she was concerned Harriet was moving in. She held her counsel, vowed to keep her ears pinned. The house came to life with Harriet around, she couldn't understand what the matter was with that girl, she'd met so many that would have snapped Joris up, given the chance. Stifled she gave in, felt the need to ask something of last night.

'What about that nice young man, what was his name again? What about him? Will I be needing to make a room up for him, too?'

'Oh Ross Farquerhart you mean. Mr. Swift scoured that tunnel last might looking for that boy, he was that long gone for a moment or two I was beginning to think he'd gone the same way as him, then he appeared. "No luck, not a trace, it seems the lad's disappeared into thin air", he said. I can't tell you how my heart sank.'

'My goodness me Joris, I'm not surprised. What will you do about it?'

'I contacted the police, they just told me to get back if there was no sign of him in forty-eight hours. The lad's probably discovered a hidden exit, I've no doubt he's found his way home. He's probably at his computer right now pumping all sorts into his thesis, forging scurrilous links to the Roman ninth lost legion. That lad's too clever for his own good.'

'Oh I see,' Mrs. Harris declared, suddenly taking liberties, frustrated, desperately needing to know what was going on with Harriet. 'Well then, we'll let his mother make up his bed shall we?'

'As you like Mrs. Harris, just as you like. I don't wish to alarm his mother by enquiring. He's well old enough to look after himself.'

Then instantly feeling guilty should the boy appear she had a better idea.

'The PM's room's untouched, that would do, if need be?'

Mr. Sanderson turned to go,

'No, on second thoughts I'm not having this place turned into a hotel for every Tom, Dick and Harry. Let his mother look after him.'

Sensing his impatience she scuttled off, none the wiser, brooding on the downside of the job. For the staff there was always a limit to the dissemination of information.

Chapter 39

A soaking wet Ross Farquerhart wanted his mum. It had been almost eighteen hours since he'd been pulled out of the icy waters of the River Dee. Dragged over the plump gunwale of the rib to land hard on groaning bodies veiled by heavy fog. Grateful to be alive he'd thought it best to keep quiet, besides he wasn't sure if it hadn't been one of them pushed him in though he couldn't for the life of him think why.

He looked around the van, longing to be in his mum's clean house, longing to be sitting at their kitchen table tucking into the Sunday roast. He was hungry, he'd left most of his evening meal in his rush to get down the tunnel and since then had only had a piece of bread thrown at him and a swig of water from an old plastic bottle, looked like it had been kicking around for ages. Then they'd all disappeared locking the door behind them. He knew they were on the run, druggies the lot of them but it wasn't for that, they were after them for defacing those Venetian statues, he wasn't exactly sure what they'd done, just that Rapping Hammer was now feeling a whole lot better about his manhood, oh he wasn't going to part with the banana he squeezed into his leathers to get the girls going at the gigs, but nevertheless he was now a whole lot bigger than those ancient buggers standing around the canals.

Wondering what they were going to do with him he tried the door again, gave it a good rattle, nothing doing. He couldn't even wave his hand or call for help from a window, all locked of course. He sat down again, at least grateful to be out of that tunnel, it was sheer accident he'd stumbled on a way out, he was beginning to feel a bit like he'd suddenly acquired a leading role in 'Alice in Wonderland'. It was all a bit too surreal, he needed to go back for fear of getting completely lost. He was now on the wrong side of that heavy, old door. He'd viewed the jewelled mosaic image of the Madonna and Child, marvelling at it, wanting to know more. If only he could get back to that he knew he'd be safe. Inching his way suddenly the side of the tunnel fell away from his hand. He'd knelt flashing his torch into the gap. It was barely more than a burrow, he ran the beam over the ground dropping the torch, his heart leaping at the muted light just visible from the far end. He'd weighed it up, decided even if he had to scrape the earth away with his hands he'd reach the daylight at the end. He'd wriggled along, hitting places so close to his head he feared he would be buried alive. He prayed to the image of the Madonna, crossing himself; did this totally alien thing as if he were destined for the priesthood. Panting, covered in soil, cobwebs and much else he heaved and elbowed himself out against an ancient wooden cover partially sunk into mud and a thicket of wild brambles growing all the way down to the river bank. Stunned to see the holy bejewelled image clearly standing before him, he once again made the sign of the cross against his shirt between the open lapels of his jacket, he moved to thank her, saw her gently smile, reached as if to take his hand. She faded leaving the cross he'd just signed glowing a magnificent warmth into his chest. Whatever else happened to him he knew this would be the most significant moment of his life. Something made him run the beam of his torch across the old wooden cover he'd just been struggling across. His body had lifted the covering of earth to partially reveal a Latin text carved into the wood. His excitement mounted, had the Romans left a clue as to the demise of the Ninth Lost Legion? He'd fought his way through the brambles, excitement numbing the pain until he'd been shoved into the drink. The icy waters of the Dee, swamping, dragging him down; the image of the Madonna coming and going. Then he understood why. He understood this was his end until the second miracle of the day. Rabble as they were he owed them, they'd saved his life. He'd do whatever to repay them, it never crossing his mind who might have landed him there.

He sat puzzling, familiar with the saying 'God works in mysterious ways' but couldn't get his head round the bunch of scallies been chosen to save him; couldn't quite comprehend the bizarre series of events that had overtaken him. His mind now fluctuating, on the horizon a move to the priesthood or would he opt for fame and fortune. The latter seemed to be winning out. He could so easily visualise the accolades, in his mind he was already world famous, the media couldn't get enough of him, his PhD paled into insignificance as he saw himself being presented with the Nobel Prize for the most significant historic find of all time. He was confident they'd recognise this, it might be a first for a historian, of course, but why not? Especially if he had solved the enduring mystery of the Ninth Roman Lost Legion single handed. No, he'd shifted again, his conscience couldn't agree to that. He'd have to declare the role the Madonna had played in all of this. Ross Farquerhart drummed his fingers on the small melamine table top where the plastic bottle stood. He had plenty to mull over whilst waiting for their return. He jumped up as Rapping Hammer leapt in, leaving the door swinging on its rusty hinges.

'You can go if you like!'

Ross Farquerhart nearly fell over.

'What just like that?' he said, mouth falling open in disbelief.'

'Yeah we don't want you gettin` in the way, we're on a mission. Just a mo haven't I seen you somewhere before?'

'Er I don't think so,' he racked his brains to try to generate a little co-operation. After all they were letting him go, there must be something he could say. Then Rapping Hammer lit with recognition.

'Yeah that's it. You're the tall scrawny lad went camping with that arsehole's school. Yeah I thought you looked familiar.'

Ross Farquerhart beamed, didn't recall him or any of them really, too busy collecting fossils for the kids from Chesil Beach but certainly he'd been there.

'What were you doing there then?' grated Rapping Hammer, as the very thought of Joris Sanderson tightened his vocal chords to rope. He stepped back to swing the door closed. Ross Farquerhart's sense of imminent freedom rapidly evaporated.

'You'll know Chick Lips and that tight arsed Mama then?'

Ross Farquerhart scratched his head.

'They call one of them Tricia, the other's her mate.'

'Yea mate, yea, yea I'm with you now.'

'She wants her "save Venice" tin back, I'll be arsed.'

'Well I could deliver it to her for you, save you the bother.' He raised a weak smile, grateful for this opportunity to be able to show his appreciation.

'Fuckin` not.'

Ross Farquerhart stepped back. 'Well anything at all just let me know. Look I'll give you my number, here.' He struggled to pull his phone from his soggy pocket.'

'Well fuck me, that things not still working, is it?' Rapping Hammer rasped.

Ross Farquerhart grimaced, he'd rather not, wondered what was coming next, decided to move it all along.

'It's a camera, too. Got this one for the Galapagos Islands, got some great underwater shots with this little thing.'

'You been on that bastard's yacht or something? He's promised to take me on the next Fastnet Race, never heard a piss from him.'

'Your joking me, I don't know one end of a boat from another, me.'

'That guy's got friends in very high places, useful you're still hangin` out with this fucker.'

'Yea, work experience in his school,' replied Ross trying to make it sound cool, desperately wanting to get out of the door. 'Want to pump this into yours?'

'Yeah OK splash them digits out.'

He turned it on, read out his number, relief rushing through him as it caught a signal, he'd be needing this to get himself home.

'Zat's the zits man I'll tell you what I'm thinkin`. We're on the run. The cops are after us for crackin` them fuckin` statues. Finished them off, defaced the buggers, got pissed after the last gig already flying on weed if you get me drift, took a hammer to the lot of them!'

'Oh I see,' returned Ross Farquerhart wondering what on earth he had against the amazing productivity resulting from the Renaissance.

'You gonna tell that Sanderson gov to get them to hell off our backs. He's in with the PM, they're always doin` it for the boys and all the other old farts holding the establishment together for their own ends. Freedom man, let's make this the start of the revolution. Fix it man! Here give us that.' In a tick he'd added his contact number to the end of Ross's not inconsiderable list.

'Well I'll try, er do my best but I'm not sure he'll listen to me.'

'He'd better bucket-head, if he doesn't want Chick-Lips and her prissy-arsed mate kidnapped. We're just waitin` to get our way with those two alley cats. We'll get them fagged alright.'

'Oh right, yes, I'll get on to it right away, wouldn't want any harm to come to them. Would you like me to tell Joris Sanderson this, or not?' 'Tell him what you soddin` like, just get us off the hook will ya? This is worse than the jail, no gigs, no money, we can't spend the rest of our bleedin` lives hiding!'

'Right, no. I'm off then. I don't suppose you've any idea where we are?'

'We're parked in them fields the other side of Fuck-head's school. There's a hole in the fence man, the school's just behind those trees, keep stalking that fence, it gets ya to the main road.' Don't end up in that fuckin` school, we don't want our arses whacked by him, as soon as the bards land we're away. Dunno where they've soddin` got to.'

He stood in the doorway, smirking, watching him squelching his way across the field.

Trembling and trudging some distance, finally Ross Farquerhart dared to look back, relieved to see the trees now obscuring the view of the van. He continued until he could hear the traffic then hit the key on his moby that would hopefully bring the taxi. He hurried forward, this last bit was longer than he'd expected. As he reached the main road he could see its bulky black form in the distance. It was to his great relief they'd arrived in sync.

'Bramley Court, Chester, please,' Ross Farquerhart almost begged.

'Card or cash?' The rotund cabbie replied.

Ross fished once again down to the far reaches of his trouser pocket, heaving a sigh of relief to find his cards still there.

'Card, if that's OK, otherwise my mum will have to pay you.'

'No that's OK, jump in the back. You're covered in mud lad, you haven't spent the night in a ditch have you like me? Got done by a pair of lesbians would you believe it - ahh I'm not going through all that again. That big `ouse facing the river, that posh fella with the blonde hair, loaded the bloody lot of them down there. Supposed to be collecting a couple of guests to find these two swinging on the bloody gates like a pair of gargoyles. Landed on me like big bats, knocked me out.

I had to walk miles down them lanes, a bloody pea-souper of a fog too, walked straight into this bloody thing, they'd parked it alongside the ditch, rolled off me own bloody bonnet. The pair of them hanging on to them gates like that, I could see the squawking skinny girl about to drop - ahh I'm not going through all that again.'

Chapter 40

'Ooh Clive, you are a naughty boy. Bob never thought of exciting me like this in bed. It was so boring being with him.'

'Let's put him out of your mind shall we petal. Now if this were a four-poster bed, I'd teach you a thing or two.'

'Oh Clive, what exactly would you have me doing?'

'I'd have you swinging my little nymph, completely naked all the way along the rails.'

'But how would I get round the posts Clive?'

'Ooh now let me see, most probably on my shoulders, you'd catch the corners whilst I lift your beautiful legs from my neck. I'd be looking up of course!'

'Ooh Clive you've got me melting here, when are you going to let me take all these off?'

'In my own good time petal. We need to savour each delightful moment.'

'I'm quite good at swinging Clive, I had a practice for all this on Mr. Sanderson's gates.'

'Oh my dear, you weren't naked I hope?'

'Well no, I wouldn't be would I Clive, I'd only do it naked for you.'

'Oh come here you little tease, let's start with these shall we? On second thoughts, I'd first like to learn a little more of your domestic situation, your marriage, your children. You know I don't want to be tossed away like an empty crisp packet my petal. Are you serious about divorcing him? You have two children I understand?'

Tricia snuggled into his chest, playing with the button closing off his open-necked shirt.

'Yes, our Adam and Michelle. Well I say *our* but Adam isn't Bob's. I do have to say though he was very good taking him on. I was pregnant when we got married, it didn't matter to him, though.'

'Then you must have been very special to him indeed.'

'Yes I was, it tailed off once the novelty wore off but we were alright together until that Belinda Oxfordshire came on the scene. He didn't think twice about jumping into bed with her, the little tart. She was only making use of him to get back at Joris for breaking off their engagement. She still fancies him you know. Of course Bob won't have any of it, daft bugger. They're poles apart him and her yet he's forever coming and going, grabbing at any little crumbs she feels like doling out. No, I've had enough of him, I'm not putting up with that any more, never knowing where he is, when he's coming back. It's not fair on the children either. It's a good job they've got my mum.'

Clive Engells instantly experienced an intense sense of relief.

'Your mother, petal, does she look after them a lot?'

'Yes quite a bit, they're older now, they never want to be at home much anyway, they're always going to friends' houses.'

'And how would you like to see all this working once you were divorced?'

'Oh I don't really know, never really thought about it seriously, we've been living our lives separately under the same roof for a while now.'

'Well I suggest you give it all some very serious thought petal, I'd like us to be able to plan for the future.'

Instantly swamped by a huge surge of excitement she rolled on top of him.

'Ooh I think better with my clothes off Clive, when are you going to undress me?'

Chapter 41

Joris Sanderson crept into his bedroom just as Harriet began to stir. She turned over, barely opening her eyes.

'Would you not be better getting undressed Harriet, you'd be far more comfortable you know?'

'Oh no, what time is it? I've got to get to school.'

'No you're alright, it's still Sunday, you can stay here, there's no rush for anything.'

Gently he stroked her hair away from her face. In her barely conscious state she liked that. She liked the elongated dimples either side of his smile. The smell of sea-salt on his arms. That look of his, those clear blue eyes narrowing slightly, concerned, serious, questioning, betraying the joviality of his smile. He had much on his mind, her pregnancy, her propensity for disappearing, her deputy headship and how that would work out. Still she'd be leaving work at Christmas, he was sure they'd make it working together until then. Then the question of marriage, he couldn't force her down the aisle, he just hoped her hormones would settle down and it was nothing more than that. He could have married anyone of the girls he'd dated. It wasn't arrogance that led him to such a conclusion, no, he'd been asked as many times as the girls he'd taken out, not one of them hadn't tried. He wasn't vain either, all his own insecurities flooded in when it came to Harriet. She was different, cautious, always on amber, she was the biggest challenge of his life. His thoughts moved to Caroline Worsnip, the last thing he needed right now was her complicating his life. He cursed himself for allowing her to get pregnant. He'd trusted her implicitly. She'd never so much spoke of wanting children, she never struck him as the maternal type. He'd never be rid of the searing guilt until their child was found. They'd both agreed to keep it out of the public eye, already he'd laid out thousands of pounds engaging private investigators offering promising leads only to come to nothing. He'd often thought of confiding in Mac, getting MI6 on the case but held back. This was private business and with a world full of missing children his conscience wouldn't allow him to go that far. Caroline Worsnip had seen fit to leave the area, seen fit to refuse all financial support, seen fit to make it virtually impossible for him to see his own child; then the portrait sent because she'd gone missing. She'd grown from a toddler to a little girl all behind his back. He swallowed hard as he continued to smooth Harriet's hair away from her face. No he wanted Caroline Worsnip and Belinda Oxfordshire for that matter out of his life. She was instrumental in him having to come face to face with Caroline Worsnip last night. He didn't want the pair of them tripping round whenever it took their fancy. Unsettled, he'd hoped Clive would have taken a fancy to Belinda Oxfordshire, he'd certainly informed them her parents were both of the same profession as him. 'Bad timing, oh such bad timing,' he told himself. He was aware of Clive's sexual proclivities, he liked to man-chat over a glass or two. Just a brief mention, always eyeing up the talent. Until today Joris wasn't sure whether or not it was merely prowess, bravado, and it may well have been until he'd got the chance to bed Tricia Harrington. The man was positively glowing, brimming with innuendo, oh yes it would seem Mrs. Harrington was capable of feats Belinda Oxfordshire would have slapped him for.

'And now that damned boy, no word whatsoever, all this and overseeing Ida Lyons wedding,' he thought. He knew it was increasing the pressure having to bring the main boat back from Falmouth in a hurry. They'd be needing to use it, Mac Lyons had specifically requested it. The PM would owe him one, or two, very rarely he called in favours but this one was going to be a quid pro quo that would not fall to the ground. He decided he would not let go until he got Barry Giordano out of his hair for good!

He looked down to Harriet lying on his bed, wanting her, every force in his body needing her, aching for her, crying out for her. She looked into his eyes, recalled them lying in the grass surrounded by wild flowers. Remembered the buttercups he'd picked for her. Could feel how he'd unbuttoned her blouse, taken the fullness of her breast into his hand, kissing her, her writhing body aching for him; recalled how he wouldn't make love to her for fear of making her pregnant. Her thoughts moved to The Bangles in Cornwall, how they'd left his yacht to lie on the sand in that magical bay; just from the corner of her eye a tiny pile of blue lace tossed away, the full force of his body deep inside her, the tide lapping gently, both at one with each other, both at one with the sea.

Sensing her desire he took her into his arms knowing exactly where she was and without a hint of resistance she felt him unfasten her bra, feeling it fall away to the gentle touch of his hand on her breasts.

'Well swollen now Harriet, with all the magnificence of full-blown roses.' He spoke gently, all the time aching to take the taut, deepening pink buds between his finger tips. He moved gently, wave after wave of desire running her whole body she felt his hand move down to her jeans, across their baby. He slipped the button away, then slid the zip down, she arched her back a little, as he moved to leave a line of kisses stopping just short of her lace panties.

'Now this is an improvement Harriet, I know these very well.' He slid his hand across and down as far as would have to go to satisfy his desire for intimacy, glancing back, a semi-serious smile.

'I have against my hand something more beautiful than any rose bud ripe for opening. As much as we ache to finish this, you are still unsure of me and that's not the way I want it, we'll save that for our honeymoon Harriet when we won't be fettered by anxieties or clothes, we'll be as the flower to the bee and our nectar will run to the sweetness of honey, amber honey, and there will be no other connotation to the word "amber" other than joy and fulfilment.'

He lifted his hand away, closed the zip on her jeans, fastened the button at her waist. She lay back, her body throbbing for him, knowing full well he was right, she also knew however slight the risk he would never take it to lose their baby by making love to her right now.

'As you are surely aware not least of my concerns relate to you and the baby. You understand Harriet, we're still not sure whether you were undergoing a miscarriage last time you thought yourself to be pregnant. We can't risk it, it's not just the baby, important as it is, it's you Harriet, I would never put you in that position ever, miscarriages are not without risk.'

She lay snuggled to his chest, liked him for what he was saying, just wished he hadn't been like that towards Barry.

'That's why I'm thinking of bringing the boat back from Falmouth myself. I need to be getting her back now before the weather breaks. The long term forecast doesn't look good, there's a series of deepening lows crossing the Atlantic and coupled with the spring tide it could be pretty wild out there.'

'But if we go this weekend it would be safe enough, surely?' Harriet pleaded. She'd been looking forward to this. She loved 'Mare Libertas', loved the name, loved the meaning, "From the sea freedom". 'In fact Tricia was wondering if we could all go, you and me, her and Clive. Clive does have sailing experience, doesn't he?'

'Certainly, in spades, he and his brother are both noted yachtsmen.'

'Oh please Mr. Sanderson. We'll be alright the four of us. Three out of four sailors isn't bad.'

'Oh it's the fourth that worries me, that girl could sink us all single handed.'

'She's not going to be wanting to do that now, is she? She's dotty on Clive, couldn't wait to get me out of the house fast enough.'

'Really? Indeed! Oh I see!' Mr. Sanderson rolled off the bed, walked over to the window, stood for a while thinking. He'd secure Harriet whatever it took. Those two were inseperable, he knew he'd stand a far better chance with Tricia Harrington on board than without. 'Done!'

He turned as Harriet slipped into her shoes.

'I'll have a word with Clive, if he's up for it then we'll do it. Did I mention the PM is planning on having his daughter's wedding from here? We'll need "Libby" back before that.'

'Here?' questioned Harriet. 'Why here? Wouldn't something like Westminster Abbey be more appropriate?'

'Not in these circumstances I'm afraid. It needs to be as low key as possible for security reasons. The wedding ship over the water, he wants that booking. We'll be working from here but he's planning on some kind of cruise out and about in the afternoon for the guests. Not on mine, of course, we'll be sailing them all out from here. Fortuitous I went ahead with the new quay otherwise it would have been impossible.'

'Oh golly, when will it be then?'

'They're hoping for mid to late October, it depends on availability of course. Mac wouldn't dream of having the hosting company cancel anyone's wedding to accommodate them. He's just not that kind of guy.'

Harriet panicked. She and her handbag didn't wish to meet this man just yet. Still she'd be at Molly's, out of the way, he hadn't mentioned anything about her being invited.

'Naturally we're both invited Harriet, Clive too and no doubt Mrs. Harrington will be on his arm. In fact I was rather wondering if you might oversee the arrangements from our end of it. Booking the venue, transport, flowers, additional catering, things like that.'

She gulped, felt she could hardly refuse. Wondered what Barry would think of her getting embroiled like this. This was going to be so difficult now. She began agonising over whether or not to say anything to him about his job, wasn't sure if it was her place. She knew one thing, she wasn't looking forward to seeing him after school tomorrow, hoped it would be all about trying to find where that horrible painting had vanished to. She wanted it found and out of the way just as much as he did.

'Ah Belinda's just driving in. I wonder what that's all about now? You get yourself sorted out Harriet whilst I see to her. I'm hoping this won't take long.'

She crossed the landing to her bedroom. Dressing table cleared, her case and bags closed, half-expected as she'd been the one to leave the house yesterday evening.

'Er I take it you'll be staying here for a few days whilst we get this annexe of Molly's sorted?'

Harriet jumped, her hand springing to her chest.

'Oh I thought you'd gone to see to Belinda?'

'She's just been commandeered by Mrs. Harris. No I've just popped back to ask the question, Mrs. Harris is beside herself with joy at the prospect, you're not about to let her down are you?'

Harriet smiled, 'No, no, thank you that's very kind. I'm alright for school tomorrow I loaded the boot, but I'll need to pop back home for a couple of hours after.'

Mr. Sanderson beamed. 'Great stuff. Oh apparently Mrs. Harris is making a pot of tea for Belinda. Out of my hands again! You wouldn't care to join us in the drawing room would you?'

'No,' thought Harriet as she nodded her head in agreement.

Chapter 42

Caroline Worsnip closed the door on her ground floor apartment after waving Belinda Oxforshire off. They'd met for lunch and then back to hers for coffee. She was pleased their friendship had been resumed on a more secure basis, after all they both had one negative in common, Joris Sanderson. Even now, either would do the other down to get him back, but with no prospect the horizon looked bleak and their renewed association truly cemented in their dislike of Harriet Glover, she felt was one that would last a lifetime. After all just by sticking with her she had far more chance of keeping in touch with Joris Sanderson. Over lunch they'd hatched a determination to find Amber. Belinda would pull all the strings available for the chance to be this child's surrogate Aunt, to be closer to her than Joris Sanderson ever could be. They'd both sell their apartments and try for adjacent town houses on the new development in Westhall Lane. For Belinda not too far from Starboard Marine North West, either. A small development down the lane more or less opposite where Tricia and Harriet had ditched the cab.

Yes, Belinda had promised to get Daddy on the case. As a lawyer he'd had experience of divorce, missing children, all that kind of thing. She'd said he'd know the best way to tackle this. Caroline had felt the need to slow her down, didn't want anyone to know of their plans just yet. Besides she wasn't in any kind of financial position to be employing lawyers and private detectives. She told Belinda she had a hunch about the whole thing and wanted to explore this privately before pursuing new avenues. Belinda, feeling a bit deflated had shrugged her shoulders but very quickly decided it was still OK, she was not to miss this opportunity to get one over on Joris Sanderson.

Caroline Worsnip hunched her shoulders embracing herself to the buzz of excitement running through her. This was beyond her wildest dreams. If she couldn't have Joris Sanderson she'd make damned sure this way he'd be a substantial part of their lives. She'd have Belinda Oxfordshire fighting her corner now, all she needed was to nail Harriet Glover and this would be nothing short of game, set and match. She went to touch the silver dice pendant resting at her neck, momentarily panicked at its absence, couldn't stand the thought of losing it, she hoped she'd left it at Joris Sanderson's house.

An evil smile crossed her face, she must phone Belinda immediately, oh this was now working so well for her.

'Sorry Belinda, hope this isn't too inconvenient for you, just leaving a message to see if you've come across my silver dice pendant at all? I think it must be at Joris' house.' She replaced the receiver hoping she hadn't lost it, Sav Knight had given her that before he left the company to work abroad. She missed their regular tennis matches and much else. It wasn't everyone that got to play tennis with the SEO, it was, however, nearly everyone that got to sleep with him. She knew that well enough, found it irksome but if that was the way it had to be, so be it. In any case he'd introduced her to Joris Sanderson at the tennis club, she was so grateful to him for that. Her infatuation for Sav Knight instantly melted like candyfloss under boiling water. Joris Sanderson had oh so much more going for him, this guy was all she'd ever dreamt of and more. How oh how could she get Harriet Glover out of the way? She collected the coffee cups, thinking hard, it was after all Harriet Glover caused all the rumpus she'd been sacked for. She needed a lawyer and fast. Then it dawned on her, glory oh glory she'd just been offered one. She'd phone Belinda again once she'd reached home. In the meantime she needed to call Aunty Sharon immediately.

Chapter 43

Harriet showered, dressed, quickly ran the brush through her hair thinking how very much she didn't want to meet with Belinda Oxfordshire just now. She hung back on the landing, could hear her cultured, though strident voice, something about Daddy not minding at all, then "Oh no you needn't worry about that, Daddy wouldn't dream of charging."

Harriet waited before reluctantly descending the stairs to see her hurriedly terminate the call, dropping the phone back into the burgundy kid leather bag swinging from her shoulder.

'Now Belinda, Mrs. Harris says you'll stop for a spot of afternoon tea. Er is there anything in particular I can help you with?' Joris enquired.

'Caroline phoned, she's missing her silver pendant. It's very special to her, has great sentimental value. '

'Good gracious me was that cabbie prophetic or something? We haven't had a burglar in the place have we? Must get searching, come along let's get this cup of tea first. Harriet, tea's ready,' he called.

Harriet heard it all. 'Just on my way Mr. Sanderson.'

Taking her time she descended, catching her hand on the oiled teak bannister wondering just what was going on with Belinda Oxfordshire. She knew she was in the clear as far as Caroline Worsnip was concerned, certainly Mr. Sanderson would defend her position but she sensed something afoot. Felt there was more to Belinda Oxfordshire's visit than mere pendant hunting. Knew her parents to be lawyers and it could only be a friend she would offer her father's service to for free. Her stomach sank, she knew she'd worked it out correctly. Charles Oxfordshire would be defending Caroline Worsnip in court against her. Her stomach churned again, nerve ends panging, she was just grateful to have Mr. Sanderson by her side.

'Ah there you are Harriet, come in, do sit down. Look I'll leave you two girls to chat whilst I have a word with Mrs. Harris about this. You never know she might just have found it lying around.' He took his tea with him leaving Harriet face to face with Belinda Oxfordshire.

'Actually I was hoping to see you here,' Belinda declared, reaching for a shortbread finger as she lifted her cup.

'Why's that Belinda?' Harriet politely enquired, bracing herself.

'It's just something that might be of interest, though it doesn't really concern you.'

'Well that's OK Belinda I don't need to know then,' said Harriet raising her cup. 'Look let's see if we can't find this pendant shall we? I know how easy it is to lose things and if they're of great sentimental value it can be so upsetting.'

'Oh I think what I'm about to tell you is far more than being of sentimental value Harriet Glover and you'd never be able to appreciate the sense of loss for those concerned.'

'Maybe but I'm not too sure why you're wanting to tell me this right now.'

'I think it might be as well for you to know you're not the only one in Joris's life, you know.' She placed her cup carefully back to the saucer waiting for the response.

'There's all sorts of people in Joris's life Belinda, this isn't making much sense at all.'

'Oh but it will. Actually I don't have to tell you. I'm doing you a favour, something you might want to factor into the equation should you be thinking of marrying Joris, yet again.'

Harriet began to bristle, curiosity well aroused now, she needed to listen.

'Well if it's that important, I'm sure Joris will tell me, in the event.'

'As he hasn't told you himself yet, it's most unlikely. Probably keeping his fingers crossed you won't find out.'

'So what makes it your place to tell me Belinda, this isn't being very fair to Joris?'

'Oh we're being very fair to Joris, Caroline and I are making one huge drive to find his daughter for him.'

'Find his daughter!' Harriet could feel herself paling, the shock seemed to drain her blood away.

'Yes that's what I said. Did you not know he and Caroline were an item?'

Harriet breathed hard. He'd not said anything.

'Golly Belinda he's allowed to have had girlfriends, surely?'

'Is he allowed to get them pregnant, though?' Experiencing the ultimate satisfaction, she lifted her cup again, the calories blown to wind as she reached for another shortbread biscuit.

'You see Harriet Glover, he and Caroline are the parents of a little girl called Amber. There's a portrait of her in the wardrobe. You may have noticed it whilst you've been staying in that room.'

Harriet felt like she'd just been slapped in the face. It hurt to breathe. Felt like she'd been physically sawn in half. She tried to steady herself.

'Of course he wouldn't marry Caroline, accused her of deliberately deceiving him to get pregnant, which she hadn't. He tried to buy her off but she wasn't having any of it. She moved away to have the baby, didn't want him around at all.

He hardly ever saw their child, Caroline thought he didn't deserve to.' She paused waiting for a reaction.

'So she's moved back, he'll be able to see her more now. Caroline doesn't appear to be holding any grudges.'

'Well that's not for you to decide. You have no idea what he's put her through.'

'So why has she come back if she was happier away from here? She must have had a change of heart, decided it's better for them all to try to be a family again.'

'I know you're not thinking the way you're talking Harriet Glover. You're ice cold, you'd never let your true feelings show.'

'Look Belinda if you're telling me all this for your own satisfaction, stop right now. I'd far better hear the whole story, the whole truth from Joris. Yes I've seen the portrait, Joris actually showed me, told me when he was ready he'd explain. I doubt if he'd be too pleased you got in first.'

Belinda Oxfordshire's demeanor instantly changed, suddenly needing to babble the last of it out for fear she'd miss the punch line.

'Amber's missing, she was taken a while ago, it's an open case. Fortunately Caroline got her old job back, until you got her dismissed, that is. She came back here to try and persuade Joris to get onto it. She wants her daughter back, and even if he's not interested, the least he can do is help her. She's every intention of driving him hard, she's not letting him get away with it this time.'

Harriet's throat tightened as she tried to swallow, she would never let Belinda Oxfordshire see her cry. She stood, walked away, she'd find Joris Sanderson and tell him she needed to go home after all, she really needed the time at home to get ready for school tomorrow, then she panicked remembering Tricia and Clive were there, but still she had to go.

Chapter 44

Clive Engells strode down the path, pressing the remote to instantly unlock the car. He glanced across to see Joris's Mercedes coming down the road. For a second he wondered what he wanted, then realised it was Harriet behind the wheel.

'You OK Harriet? I'm afraid my things are still in there. Patricia needed to get back to see to the children. Look, in view of her need to be at home I've arranged to go back to Joris's for a couple of nights but if you'd rather I found rented it's really no problem. It's just that he was most insistent there was no point in yours remaining empty, he was rather under the impression you'd be staying with him from now on.'

She smiled with relief, 'No, no, that's not a problem Clive, you're more than welcome to this. It's far better being lived in, I certainly don't wish to be here any more, it holds no sentiment whatsoever.'

'Thank you Harriet, that's fine then, no doubt I'll be seeing you again shortly.' He turned to open his door. 'Looks like you've got another visitor Harriet. I'll be off then, away in the nick of time.'

She looked up, her sense of relief short-lived as her stomach churned yet again. 'Oh no it's Mark, the last thing I need right now!'

She waited as he marched up the path.

'See you've got the Mercedes then. Great stuff, I told you, you were in with the right guy. How's he doing, anyway? Does he know you've got yourself a sugar-daddy on the side?'

Harriet chose to ignore that one, she simply didn't have the energy.

'Yes, he's fine, got a lot on his plate just now. Anyway what are you doing here? You might have rung to let me know.'

'Oh I did Harriet, you've not bothered with the messages then?'

'No Mark, I haven't had chance. In any case Mummy's updated me with all your news. That didn't take long, did it? Was it love at first sight or something?'

'Come on Harriet, let's get in, we don't want to be airing our dirty washing in public.'

'Too late for that Mark. What's happening anyway? Hang on just let me put the kettle on, I presume you want a cup of tea?'

'What's up Hat? I thought we parted on good terms. You haven't called it off with him already, have you? That geezer just left isn't the latest is he?'

'No he is not. He's a friend of Mr. Sanderson's if you must know. He's staying with him just now until he can find a house to buy.'

'Oh I see, you've been showing him round. Great stuff! You reckon we've got a buyer then?'

He pulled out the chair, sat himself at the kitchen table.

'Gosh this place seems strange, it feels like ages since I was last here.'

'Out of site, out of mind. You've obviously had other things to think about like going back on your decision to give me your share of the house.'

'Who told you that?'

'Oh your mother's passed all the information along. She phoned Mummy, couldn't wait to spread the news. Terrified I'd sell the place or something before you had chance to get here.'

She plonked the mugs down, sitting to face him.

'Anyway what's her name? Have you told her yet about your marriage phobia or are you planning to dump her at the church like you did me?'

Mark wrapped his hands around the mug, his elbows firmly planted on the table.

'Look Harriet that's all in the past, I refuse to go over old ground again. You made your choices, not me, and no I'm planning on living with Sasha but we want to get a decent property between us.'

'So I suppose that's where you're coming from. I thought your salary was so good you had no need of the collateral in this? Not that I ever really wanted you to do that. This is her, isn't it? This is her.'

'Look, property's more expensive down there. I thought you knew that?'

'No! It's not as if you're buying in London. It must be some house.'

'We've seen the perfect house for us and that's the measure of it, we now need to get this place sold as soon as possible.'

'It's her, isn't it Mark? She's pushing you on this. And where am I supposed to live in the meantime?'

'So you have split with him then?'

'No!'

'So what's the problem, he's loaded, you could easily afford to give your half to me for that matter.'

'It's in both our names, let's just leave it like that shall we?'

'OK, OK let's just get it sold.'

'I'm not ready to sell yet Mark, I'm afraid you and Sushi are just going to have to wait.'

'It's Sasha Harriet, Sasha.'

'Sorry getting confused with a fast takeaway.'

'Very funny Harriet and believe you me we certainly won't be waiting. This thing's still under the agent's counter, it's never been taken off the market, you've already consented to selling it. In fact that agreement with Joris Sanderson still stands, he only gave a verbal release, he could insist on the sale by now, it was a condition of compensation. I'm sure I only need to have a word with him.'

Harriet knew she was beaten.

'Oh don't bother Mark, I've had enough of the place anyway. Why would I want to hang on to this when my enduring memory is one of years of excuses for you not wanting to marry me. Too many bad memories here, you just get on with it, you deal with the whole thing, I've got enough to cope with right now. Anyway where are you staying, at your mother's?'

'Yes I'm on my way there right now. Just need to collect one or two things from the bedroom and I'll be out of your hair.'

The cat flap opened as Harriet sat the mugs in the sink, she felt the brush of fur against her legs, heard Mark thumping down the stairs.

'It's OK Harriet, your secret's safe with me - be in touch.'

He was gone leaving Harriet wondering what on earth he was talking about. She went upstairs to see metres of pink ribbon woven through the spindles below the right-angled turn of the banister and the cheval mirror tilted now standing opposite in the doorway of the smallest bedroom.

'Oh no,' she said out loud, 'what on earth have those two been up to?'

Chapter 45

'You're the last person I expected to see here. What brought you back then?' Tricia said, glaring at Bob.

'What's it to you? You're never here yourself. Black and blue I am after you kicking me like that under the dinner table. It's finished you and me, it's divorce time. I've never been so humiliated in all my life. You can stick your posh friends, they only laugh at you anyway, your way out of depth with that lot. Go and pick some one up who goes for cheap common little tarts.'

'Oh my you should talk. Aren't you just a teeny weeny little bit out of your depths with Belinda Oxfordshire? She `ardly looked at you all night. Had her eye on my Clive she did.'

'Your bloody Clive, are you in fantasy land or something?'

'No, not really, he's just asked me to marry him so a divorce is fine with me.'

'He's bloody what? There's no way I'm making it that easy for you, the guy must be off his head. A lawyer wanting to marry you, you've got to be joking.'

'Oh no I'm not Bob Harrington, you're the one that went wanderin` off with fridge bum, it wasn't me that broke this marriage.'

'Oh come off it Tricia, the way you've been flirting with Joris Sanderson, you've tried every trick in the book to get him and you know it. It was Mark Glover before that, goodness knows how Harriet felt watching you falling all over him.'

'Harriet knew I was only joking, anyway I wasn't leaping into bed with any of them like you, me never knowing when you'd be comin` home.'

'You've been no better, those poor kids, what kind of a mother are you to them, they spend most of the time with your mother.'

'Oh no they don't, anway she likes having them around during the school holidays, most of their friends live near there. They're not exactly babies any more, it's good for them to find their independence.'

'Good for you, you mean. No I'm not making it that easy for you Tricia, I think these kids have enough to deal with as it is, divorce would send the pair of them off the rails completely.'

'Oh you didn't think of that when you went off with Belinda Oxfordshire in the first place, you haven't given a toss for me or the kids for long enough. Don't start gettin` all sanctimonious with me fat-face-four-cheeks. Don't you worry about the kids, Clive's already said there would be a home for us all. I'll be takin` them, they'll have a far better life with him than you.'

'That's rich, what kind of a life would Adam have had without me? You've got a very short memory Tricia Harrington.'

She took her coat off, a sense of guilt dampening her fury. She knew he'd never hesitated to marry her, take her unborn child on.

'That's why it hurt me so much, you did all that for me yet never thought that much of me to stop you sleeping with her. Oh just go and marry her, get her off all our backs will you. Don't worry she's right up your street, she won't refuse you the cheap little tart.'

She turned to hang her coat up, found she could hardly move.

'What the bloody hell's happening here. What you doin` now?

'It takes one to know one,' retorted Bob, letting go of the tail of pink ribbon hanging down the back of her jeans.

Chapter 46

Monday morning, Harriet drove in, noticed Clive's Bentley parked in Mr. Sanderson's spot by the front door. She looked for a space to park the Mercedes as far from him as possible. School was the last place she wanted to be right now. She could still feel the stinging hurt of Belinda Oxfordshire's revelation regarding Amber. Why hadn't he told her? Why would he be wanting them to use that name should their baby be a girl? Why would he be wanting to have two daughters by the same name? None of it made any sense to Harriet whatsoever. They'd been in the department store and he'd acted as if he'd never met Caroline Worsnip before let alone fathered her child. She was oh so glad to be moving in with Molly for a while. Her whole life was falling apart and she wasn't sure just how much more she could take. She'd do her best to avoid him, then the rapid realisation she was now officially his deputy, this wasn't going to be so easy.

She unloaded the boot hoping Mr. Brown the caretaker wasn't around. She didn't want anyone to see she'd arrived in Mr. Sanderson's car. She sensed a shuffling behind her.

'Oh I see, I was wonderin` why the boss had turned up in a Bentley...'

Harriet jumped, he was forever appearing like the genie out of nowhere.

'Good morning Mr. Brown and how are you?'

'We still haven't found an answer to those wagons delivering all this food stuff, it's getting to be just too much is this.'

'Mr. Brown I do believe the school governors discussed this and our new Chair, Mr. Engells, our distinguished lawyer, established as long as the deliveries take place during school lessons there isn't a problem. All supermarkets have agreed to this, so there really isn't a problem at all.'

'Ugh and what does he know about schools?'

'Must get along Mr. Brown, if you'll excuse me,' said Harriet dancing around him anxious to be gone.

Relieved to arrive in her classroom without further interruption, she closed the door standing behind it for a few seconds to catch her breath before sorting through her briefcase and bags. At least she wasn't taking a new class. Mr. Sanderson wanting to minimise the change the children would be exposed to had seen fit to keep them together since she would be taking maternity leave at some point.

She sat down feeling just as she did the day she started. Nervously wondering how she was ever going to get through the day, hoping against hope Mr. Sanderson wouldn't have need of her.

'Miss, Miss, I'm glad to see ya, you're not goin` again are you Miss? I didn't like the other Miss Curtains.'

'Oh hello Danny you gave me a fright then. Everything alright? Did your Mum and Dad get to take you to Butlins?'

'Yes Miss I mean no. I told Miss Curtains we couldn't go because that horrible man had stolen me mum's money and she just told me to be quiet and go back out.'

'Oh I'm sure Miss Curtiss didn't mean to upset you Danny, she was probably very busy, teachers are just like the children you know, they have lots of things to do.'

'No she wasn't doin` noffink, like you now. I came in like this and she was horrible to me. I told me Mum of her but she was `orrible too giving that man my new silver trophy to get some money.'

'Look Danny your Mum and Dad like many of the parents here just haven't got enough money to live on. That's why we've set up the food shop.'

'Ooh me Mum loves it, she's always saying how good you and Mr. Angels are for gettin` such a brill idea. Me Mum's hot rod for Mr. Angels, she told me not to tell me Dad.'

'Ah Mr. Engells, Danny, yes he's working very hard making sure we can keep the food bank operating. Have you had anything nice from it yet?'

'Yes Miss I can have my banana again, me Mum gets seven every Friday. It is seven isn't it?' He did a quick count of the days of the week on his fingers then smiled in triumph at his mathematical skills.

'I'm gonna gerr it, and me trophy Mr. Farmercart gave me for winning the best fossil prize. Look here he is Miss!'

Mr. Farmercart, better known to Harriet as Ross Farquerhart just missed skidding into the lunch trolley as Danny swung the door open with force enough to break the sound barrier. 'It's him Miss, he's here.'

Landing in a skid at her desk he pushed his rimless specs up his nose a protrusion looking essentially larger set in his very pale face.

'Steady on Ross, you OK? Glad to see you alive at least. Whatever happened, where did you get to?'

'Fucking nightmare Harriet, I can't tell you now, where's the boss?'

'He should be there, his car was there when I drove in.'

Agitated he galloped to the window.

'Oh yes, his car's there alright, so where the devil is he?'

'The bell's about to go Ross, you'll just have to catch up with him at break.'

'I need to see him, I've been all over the school. No, no I don't want to see him at all. No, I can't tell him. Oh sod Harriet I'm in one hell of a fix.'

'What on earth's happened to you Ross?'

'You wouldn't believe I've been to heaven and hell and back. Literally!'

'What happened Ross, what do you mean?'

'That tunnel I had an amazing experience, found a way out, it was then. I'm on the river bank, on my way back to the house when I'm pushed into the water by someone, fell into that fucking rock group's rubber dinghy and bounced out.' Harriet instantly covered her blushing cheeks with her hands, said nothing. He continued, 'Well to be honest I don't know what really happened I just know they pulled me out. Ended up in that stinking van of theirs. Fucking nightmare. There's more but I've got to go. Tell the boss I'm in if you get to see him first, will you Harriet?' Flustered, Harriet now on a guilt trip, watched as he held the door open to allow Enid Frost in.

'Worse than a main line station in here this morning,' Harriet tried smiling at the school secretary. 'What can I do for you Enid?'

'Assembly Harriet, the boss told me he's had to go out, wants you to take charge of the school today.'

'Right you are Enid, is he getting a supply in?'

'Susan Curtiss is on her way right now.'

'Great, I'll work in his office then.'

Harriet couldn't have been more pleased, a quick decision to make the food bank the subject of assembly this morning, emphasising the need for helping one another. Oh yes she knew she could rattle that one off the top of her head, Danny had given her a wonderful introduction talking about the bananas. She'd bring Danny up to do the counting on his fingers, they'd talk about the need for food and drink seven days a week, then of how we all need love seven days a week, yes she'd focus on kindness and caring.

To the hush of the assembly hall Harriet delivered.

'Now Danny would you like to come up and tell the children what you told me, this morning?'

All heads turned.

'No Miss you can tell them what you told me this morning. I'm not going up there for you. You said you were stayin` here and we've got Miss Curtains back and you know I don't like her!'

All heads turned to see Susan Curtiss going scarlet, glowering at Harriet.

Suddenly she upped and went.

'I'm comin' up now Miss, she's gone.'

Danny proudly mounted the platform, a double triumph, he'd make the most of it and announce he'd got his silver trophy back Mr. Farmercart had given him for the best fossil.

Ross Farquerhart fidgeted on his chair at the side of the hall glancing out at the silver Mercedes wondering if Mr. Sanderson had been abducted by that weird Hammer lad and his gang. His sense of reality began to come and go. He pushed his spectacles further up his nose, everywhere went hazy as he tumbled from his chair his world transformed to a huge veil of white. Immediately the staff surrounded him, brought him to his feet, had him sat with his head between his knees.

Harriet called for order, curtailing assembly, instructing the teachers to take their children back class by class in the usual manner.

'It's her, she's back again, it's horrible Miss Curtains, I'm not goin' back to her.' Before Harriet could hold him back, Danny Bustard had fled aiming for one of the darkest reaches of the school. At least she knew he'd be in the building since security had been stepped up.

'You OK Ross? You'd better come back to the boss's office with me, he's out today, all day. Come on I'll make you a cup of tea.'

She sat him in Mr. Sanderson's chair for comfort, leaving him quiet for a few minutes with his cup of sweet tea whilst she had a word with Enid Frost.

'We've lost Danny, he's got to be somewhere around, would you mind asking Mr. Brown to find him please Enid.'

'What happened Harriet? Susan Curtiss has just been down, filing a complaint against you. Said you'd been reinforcing Danny's dislike of her.'

'Look Enid, once you've seen Mr. Brown would you mind keeping an eye on the class for me please and send Susan up to me. I'll be in the boss's office.'

Enid nodded whilst Harriet returned to see the colour returning to Ross Farquerhart's cheeks.

'Everywhere went white,' he said, 'how long was I out?'

'Not even a minute Ross. Thirty seconds at most. Now don't worry Ross I've had that happen to me a few times. Mine was stress and it's more than likely the same with you.'

'I want to talk about it but I've been warned not to. No I can't say anything more than I've told you.'

'They're a bunch of scallies Ross, don't for goodness sake let them intimidate you like this.'

'Ah do come along in Mr. Brown,' Harriet rushed. It sounded like he was dragging Danny along by the ear.

'Thank you Mr. Brown, where was he?'

'Hiding between the coats outside your classroom.'

'OK, thanks a lot, I'll deal with this now.'

Mr Brown grunted his way out of the room. Harriet put her arm around Danny.

'Look Danny poor old Mr. Farmercart's not having a good day either, why don't you both go to the hobbies room and check out all the fossils in the cupboard. Let's display them in the glass cabinet in the entrance hall with your silver cup in the middle. Ross can you take a photo of Danny to stand by it and make a plaque saying Danny Bustard won this for finding the best fossil.'

Ross Farquerhart grinned. This was more like it. He'd been itching to go through all of those again. He'd take a few notes in school time, rework his PhD thesis somehow to incorporate his amazing experience, linking it to the lost legion, the tunnels, the gems and the amazing wooden board covered in Latin.

Danny Bustard grinned, Miss Glover was the bestest teacher in the whole wide world!

'OK Susan you can come in now,' said Harriet, closing the door behind her.

'It's just one of those I'm afraid. You've done amazingly well with my class, Mr. Sanderson wouldn't have asked you back if it hadn't been the case. Everything was in top order for me when I came back. As you know Danny's sometimes a difficult child to deal with and I've certainly had my share. I'll let you read the whole file on him, it's easier to understand where he's coming from if you know the background. It might be as well to prove you can turn this thing round with Danny, there's always going to be at least one in any class you teach, especially in this school. The trick is to get him on your side. He loves fossils and he's so proud of this trophy. Work on a bit of interest and praise this afternoon. He'll soon respond.'

Sat facing in Mr. Sanderson's chair, Harriet could see Susan Curtiss relaxing a little as she spoke.

'Are you looking for permanent work eventually Susan?' Harriet enquired.

'Yes, I'd love a permanent post, it's so difficult though, usually they're already spoken for.'

'The way in is to get yourself covering for longer periods, like covering for maternity leave or sabbaticals or for teachers out on training courses. Look there could well be something coming up here, if you can sort Danny out I could put in a word for you.'

Susan Curtis assumed a look of intensity, suddenly hanging on every word.

'Would you, please? Look I'm sorry I'll withdraw that complaint, it was done in the heat of the moment. Sorry Harriet, I'll make sure you see a difference in Danny by the end of the day. I'd love to come back here to do a really good stint.'

'Right Susan, in that case I'll leave it with you.'

Harriet sank in the chair to stay there most of the day, checking files, updating lists, browsing reports, minutes and all else that would have been in Mr. Sanderson's domain this day. Almost home time, she looked at her watch, she needed to be away sharp, Barry was calling at four-thirty.

A knock on the door, Ross Farquerhart on the other side wanting to thank her.

'No, no Ross, not at all. You did me a big favour with Danny. How did it go?'

'Fine, Susan, that her name?'

Harriet nodded.

'Yes well that stand in teacher Susan spent the whole of her break time with him and they're both filling the glass cabinet in the doorway, right now. Getting on like a house on fire, the two of them.'

Harriet smiled, breathed a sigh of relief as she picked up the ringing phone. She stiffened. Made a concerted effort to be civil.

'Oh yes Mr. Sanderson I'll write that down, now. Half term you say, that would be October the 24th so we're looking at Saturday the 25th for the wedding. The PM and his wife will be up on the Friday to stay with you, oh yes and his daughter, of course. Right, yes I'll see if we can't get a late morning booking for the wedding on the ship, I'll give them a call when I get home. Yes, OK, that's OK the weekend after this to Falmouth to bring the boat back. Does Clive know? Great and Tricia too. Looking forward to it.'

Harriet replaced the receiver not noticing Ross Farquerhart's relieved expression. He'd duck out of passing Rapping Hammer's message across to Mr. Sanderson, they could do their own dirty work. After all he'd just been party to all the information they needed and what's more this cool phone in his pocket had recorded every word.

Chapter 47

Harriet slowed down as she approached the traffic lights outside Starboard Marine North West. The amber lights changed to red which was exactly where she felt her life to be right now. She looked across to see Tricia's car parked alongside Belinda Oxfordshire's, driving away wondering what kind of a day the two of them had had together. She hadn't had chance to phone Tricia with the depressing news, in any case she was reluctant to cast blight on her ecstatic state, it could wait, just now it was more important to see Barry, she desperately needed to talk with him. The traffic was heavy, she'd be lucky to get there before him. No sign, she turned into The Willows parking the Mercedes on the drive of No.4.

She opened the door nearly falling over the cat to reach the ringing phone.

'Barry, are you OK? Where are you? You've not hit problems I hope.'

'I'm parked at the top of the road Harriet, I've no desire to get caught up with Sanderson right now. What the hell's going on? I thought we were supposed to be meeting up at yours right now.'

'Oh Barry we are, come on down, he's not here I just borrowed his car that's all.'

'Right with you Harriet.'

Quickly she peeled back the lid on the tub of meat chunks in jelly shoving it under the cat's nose with just time to wash her hands before the door bell rang.

'Sorry Barry, come in, just been feeding the cat. I know you haven't much time so what would you like to drink?'

'Just a weak coffee will do, thank you,' he said briefly kissing her cheek.

'How are you doing, anyway?'

'Come in Barry, let's get the drinks sorted and we'll go in the lounge. I had Mark sat at the kitchen table yesterday, I'm trying to forget.'

'As bad as that is it?'

'Oh that's not the half of it, I hope you're ready for all this.'

'Broad shoulders Harriet, don't worry about me. Anyway how's it going, how's that baby in there doing? Is he practicing for Everton yet?'

He smiled, tossing his long black hair away from his shoulders. She liked him, he'd always been a reliable friend from the day they met in Venice. Barry was undercover, working for MI6. He and his mate Andy were tracking the mafia, or so she and Tricia thought. Certainly they got themselves well and truly embroiled, the repercussions still very fresh in all their minds. Divorced, he'd fallen for Harriet big time making enemies with Joris Sanderson as he'd tried to win her over. Every single detail came flooding back as she followed him through to the lounge.

'Anyway Barry, how's life treating you?'

'Bad news Harriet, they've posted me to planet Jupiter, or feels like it. I've got a choice of course, I can take it or leave it. They're telling me they can't afford to carry contractors any more. Most of them including Andy have been given the chop. It would appear in recognition for the work done bailing out the PM and all else besides, I'm one of the very few contracted been offered a permanent position abroad. I've got something like three or four days to get back to them. It looks like a certain Joris Sanderson has been exerting his influence - old-boy network and all that. Fuck Harriet I don't want any favours from that load of crap.'

Harriet could feel herself blushing, wasn't sure how to deal with this now. This is what she was supposed to be telling him, she had no idea Mr. Sanderson had moved so quickly on this.

'Golly Barry, where to?'

'Bloody Alaska of all places, some military base or other, as obscure as it gets!'

As Andy and most of the others had been made redundant she decided it best not to pile it on. Decided Mr. Sanderson must have been thwarted and when briefed he'd pulled all the strings to make sure Barry kept his job to get him right out of the way.

'I'm so very sorry to hear of all this, what are you going to do?' Harriet asked, biting her lip.

'They'll be back Harriet. Andy and I are no fools, we've kept plenty of stuff back, we've always had an inkling this would happen.'

'Wow Barry that's fantastic. You mean you've got the key pieces of a few jigsaws and they're going to have to come back or they're stymied.'

'Exactly Harriet, they'll crash like a bloody ice comet's hit them in a few months time. Andy and I are setting up in business, we're broadening out the field, we'll take work from where ever it comes, we're setting ourselves a base in Manchester right in the centre of the shopping mall. We're calling it "ab extra", it's Latin for "from outside".'

'That's spot on, Andy Barry Extra, love it!'

'Yea, thought you'd appreciate that one. He's not the only one can throw the old Latin around.'

'I'm just so pleased for you both, I'm really glad you're not going to Alaska, that would be so isolating, what a nightmare thought.'

He smiled, looked at his watch, I'm afraid I've got to move this along Harriet. I wanted to know if you've picked up anything at all about the whereabouts of this damned painting? You know I just wish I'd never done it. Didn't get me anywhere and you driving his car now, he's well and truly got you caught.'

'It may have been that way just a couple of days ago but now I'm not so sure. You know he's still stinging like hell over that painting. He wants it found as much as you and I do. I haven't got a clue, I'm sorry Barry. What have you managed to do about it, if anything?'

'I contacted the local police who said they'd send someone out to the pawnbroker's to search the place but nothing came back, it's weird.'

'You're good at this Barry, I bet you'll get it back, wherever it is it doesn't seem to be doing any harm, you've got enough to think about right now.'

'No it's got to be found for all our sakes, one of these days it'll pop up to bite us all.'

'Oh please don't say that Barry, I don't think I can deal with any more.'

'Come on Harriet, spill the beans, tell me all about it.'

He put his cup down to sit alongside her on the sofa facing the window.

'Completely out of the blue, yesterday, Mark arrives, wants the house sold as soon as possible, can't wait to shack up with his new partner, they've seen the house they want to buy.'

'Let go Harriet, that was finished with long since.' She felt his arm around her, it was good. There could never be a straighter guy than Barry. If only she'd met him years ago. Those Latin good looks, his sensitive artistic nature, his lack of worldliness, complete disinterest in social self advancement. He'd proposed, more than once, just now she was thankful he'd felt that way and though she'd turned him down she knew he would always be in touch, always in the background ready to pick her up from her latest fall. He'd told her that, he'd said he would wait for as long as it took. Not confined in any shape or form by convention this caring guy would still welcome Harriet and her baby into his life, for the rest of his life. He was about to tell her again, then decided she was struggling as it was.

'So Harriet, what is it that's really bothering you?'

'Mr. Sanderson has a daughter, a little girl called Amber by a woman I only met on Friday. The department store in town, he insisted on buying me some dresses for this dinner party he'd organised. The woman behind the till, you wouldn't have ever guessed they'd been an item, no recognition whatsoever. Anyway to cut a long story short she left the area because he wouldn't marry her. She's only back because the poor little girl's gone missing. She wants to get him involved in getting her found.'

Barry took his arm away, stretched his long legs full length, briefly covered his chin with his hand stretching his back hard into the sofa. He then gathered her against his chest.

'This is probably something in his past he felt you probably didn't need to know about right now. He must have got a hell of a shock seeing that woman there.'

169

'Yes I suppose he did, managed not to show it though. Not that long ago when I was there he showed me a picture of Amber and to be fair he did say one day he'd explain. He went as far as to say if this baby's a girl we'll call her Amber. I agreed, thought it was a lovely idea. I didn't have the faintest idea what the story would be though. How could he say that, how could he want to have two daughters by different women and call them the same name? Oh Barry, I just can't deal with this.'

'How did you find all this out Harriet?'

'Belinda Oxfordshire, you know the snooty one Tricia and I can't stand, did she enjoy rubbing that one in.'

'So how did she know all about this?'

'This woman, Caroline Worsnip happens to be her friend.'

'Ah, I see.'

'There was a bit of a disaster in the store, I won't go into all that now but the upshot was she ended up at Mr. Sanderson's on Saturday night, missed the meal, but obviously not the after dinner chat with Belinda Oxfordshire.'

'Right Harriet, the first thing we need to do is get this little girl found. Yes it's the first case-load for "ab extra", I'll be back in touch just as soon as I've sorted out with the spooks at MI6. Will you still be here Harriet, you're not likely to get it sold any time soon are you?'

'Oh as far as I know there's still a young couple in the wings, though I'd need to check that out. On no, just a minute, no, Clive Engells, he's Mr. Sanderson's lawyer friend will be staying for a while, he's moving up here and looking for a house.'

'Might be helpful to have him on side Harriet. So you'll be back with golden boy will you?'

'No, I'm staying with friends Molly and Percy, they're just up the narrow lane from Mr. Sanderson, the house on the corner facing the road.'

'Great, what have they got, an annexe or something?'

'That's it, self contained.'

'When are you moving?'

'Tomorrow, I'm back at his tonight. Separate bedrooms of course.'

'Bit late for that Harriet,' he laughed.

'But finding Amber, Barry, that would be absolutely wonderful. You'll need to be paid, I'll pay you Barry even if it's only for trying.'

'It will be more than that Harriet, I assure you. I'll find her, and there's no way you'll be footing the bill. He's loaded, it's not going to be any kind of problem for him, you'll see.'

Chapter 48

Just one more night at Lower Tideside and then tomorrow with Molly. Harriet couldn't wait, she'd phoned her saying it didn't matter what state the place was in as long as she could just be with them and away from the chaos pursuing her. Of course Molly had been delighted to hear this from Harriet, Joris had suggested as much, told her Harriet needed immediate peace and quiet with as much rest as possible. Molly had already spent the day making the bed, sprucing the place up and tomorrow she would pick more apples from the tree to make a pie. She'd invite Joris for dinner, a good opportunity to return his kindness. They'd really enjoyed the dinner party, never had so much fun since they'd been on that cruise with Harriet. My oh my, she'd never be done thanking Harriet for one of the best times of her life. The laughs, looking for the cat. It was nothing short of a miracle Harriet's cat found its way home.

Harriet, pleased to have seen Barry, turned to make sure the cat was still firmly in its basket on the back seat.

'And don't you be wandering off back here from Molly's. I won't be coming back and I've got to tell Mummy where I am, you were just lucky she called in to find you. You've got Timmy to play with at Molly's, a lovely big garden and lots of fields, you'll have a whale of a time Pepper, believe you me.'

Silence as expected, Harriet drove along checking she'd got all she needed for school at the same time wondering what was afoot, that he should desert the place first day of term. She'd be needing to tell him she now knew about the picture, about Amber. In his rush to get away, she hadn't had chance to ask Barry if he'd be informing Mr. Sanderson of his intention to find her. She decided to keep quiet on it all, keeping her fingers crossed it would all work out for the best.

'Stay green, stay green, please!' She pulled up sharply as the lights at the crossroads outside Starboard Marine Northwest changed to amber then red. Looked at her watch, it was 5.30 pm, she was surprised to see the Bentley parked alongside Belinda Oxfordshire's car. No sign of Tricia's. 'Ah there she is Pepper she's just turning out now, she'll catch the green if she's lucky.'

Tricia wasn't, Harriet watched her jump the lights, was all set to wave when a blast of horns suddenly had her fumbling for the gear lever the pair of them stalling centre road. With traffic circling they wound their windows down.

'Ooh 'arriet, he isn't half 'avin' a go at her in there!'

Chapter 49

'It was bad enough being called away from school, first day back, start of a new term without having Caroline Worsnip on my back. What the hell's going on with you two and what damned business is it of yours if her child's gone missing?'

'*Her* child Joris? *Her child,* that's a bit rich coming from you!'

'I beg your pardon Miss Oxfordshire and kindly address me in a like manner at least whilst in the work place. Regardless of misjudged past association, you are still my employee, for the moment that is.'

She uncrossed her legs to sit to attention, fuming at his treatment of her. Decided she would continue to hold her ground.

'Caroline only has me to lean on. You've no idea how this is affecting her. That's why she's up here for heaven's sake. Can't you see that? And now she's lost her job all because of you and Harriet Glover. Just how can she support Amber, I mean the search for Amber on unemployment benefit, I ask you?'

He stopped dead, stared hard at her, wondering if this was some kind of Freudian slip. There was much that didn't make sense over Amber's disappearance. For a start when he'd first enquired of the police he was told there was no one missing by that name. Then he got a call back from someone else whose particularly northern accent was very difficult to understand to say two children from that area had disappeared from the nursery by the park, one by the name of Dawn Knight who apparently was found pretty quickly and the other Ember Anderson unfortunately was still an open case. When asked what his interest had been in this Mr. Sanderson had told them the sorry tale. They'd come across this lack of co-operation before between estranged parents and perfectly satisfied the officer had promised to keep him posted on any new developments. He hadn't heard anything positive and felt his constant enquiries were becoming a nuisance so he let them go. 'Ember Anderson', he'd often mull over this piece of confusion. It had to be her, the officer had got himself tongue-tied surely? He'd hoped he hadn't frightened the poor man knowing on occasions he could sometimes sound a little officious, deciding it was the scourge of most head teachers and probably doctors for that matter. No, Amber Sanderson is surely what he meant to say. Then after convincing himself he'd toss it around, he'd never heard of such a name as Ember but Amber Enderson, sounded more like it could be Amber Henderson which would mean, as devastating as the terrible event was, it would not have anything to do with him or Caroline Worsnip. And so it had proved difficult on the occasions he'd try to employ private investigators as he was unable to give them much to go on and for some reason known only to Caroline Worsnip she simply refused to co-operate with them, saying she didn't

172

want it taken out of the police's hands in case it would cause them to lose interest in the case. Mr. Sanderson knew there was more to it than that but couldn't get to the bottom of her game. The woman infuriated him as with the one sitting opposite, right now.

'What exactly has Caroline told you about this case? A damned sight more than she's ever told me, I'm sure.' He stood up, pacing the floor, then returned to her grand swivel chair, looking out of the window as he spoke, decided she wasn't worth the courtesy of eye contact.

Belinda Oxfordshire fumed, this was her office, her desk, well his but most of the time he wasn't here anyway. She ran the place for him, it would never have been profitable if he'd had to rely on that airhead Patricia Harrington who was barely competent at opening the till never mind anything else, oh apart from her mouth, of course.

'I'm waiting Miss Oxfordshire. I demand to know everything Caroline Worsnip has confided in you. If I find you've left just one single thing out, your job's on the line. I need to be able to rely on someone trustworthy running this place and at the moment you aren't shaping up too well at all.'

Chapter 50

Harriet crunched the car through the golden gravel screeching the tyres to a halt sooner than intended, distracted by the sudden. demanding ring of her phone. She was relieved to see Mr. Sanderson not yet back though it did little to quell her churning stomach. With indecision creasing her, she couldn't decide whether or not to tell him about Belinda Oxfordshire's revelation or to try and quietly keep it to herself. After all it was not her affair, oh yes she was hurt, very hurt but essentially she appreciated it had nothing to do with her, or Belinda Oxfordshire for that matter. She didn't want him to think they'd been tittle-tattling behind his back. Yes she was furious with him, but now wasn't the time, she was too stressed to take on any more. She'd leave the whole thing with Barry now and focus on more immediate things like getting the house sold, organising this wedding for the PM, settling into Molly's place, yes she'd have almost two weeks there before they'd all be off to Falmouth to sail the boat back.

She reached for her bag, jumping as the cat yowled, scratching at the lid on her basket. 'Hang on Pepper, just let me answer this. Hi Barry, you back home already? I've just got here this minute.'

'My Lamborghini knows the way Harriet. Look, this portrait you were talking about. Could you possibly get it to me?'

'Yes I think so Barry, it's in the bottom of the wardrobe, I think it's just too painful for him to see.'

'That's helpful, he'd miss it if it was displayed anywhere.'

'Are you not telling him about any of this, then?'

'No Harriet, I think it's best for us to do our own investigations first. I need the addresses of this Caroline woman, present and former. Do you think you could manage that?'

'Oh golly, I'm not sure, I'd have to go back to Belinda Oxfordshire.'

'Do what it takes Harriet, I need the portrait though.'

'What now? Where are you?'

'I'm parked in the narrow lane just past the place where you're going to be staying. Get it now, I'll start walking we should just about meet half-way.'

He finished the call. Harriet in a fluster rushed round the side of the house and in through the back door. Grateful there was no one around, she hurried upstairs, found the department store carrier bag, popped the portrait in then dashed across the landing and down the stairs, cursing at the sound of the gravel as she crunched her way through and out of the gates, running up the narrow lane towards Barry strolling down.

'Well done Harriet. I'm sure we could find you a job in "ab extra" a superb response!'

'Go Barry quickly, now. I don't know when Mr. Sanderson's going to be back. He's probably on his way now.'

'OK, OK you're not coming back with me are you? Shouldn't you be going that way?'

'Look just run, I'm going to pop in to say hello to Molly, I want to see her anyway. You just mind how you go'

He slowed down, quickly kissed the side of her face to sprint away, Harriet marching forward, relieved to see no sign of Mr. Sanderson as she clicked open Molly's gate.

'Harriet what a lovely surprise.' Molly flung her arms round her as if she were her long lost daughter.

'I've really only just got back to Mr. Sanderson's. I had to pop out again so thought I'd make a quick call. How are you both doing, anyway?'

Molly beamed, 'Yes thank you, we're fine Percy and I. We're so looking forward to you moving in tomorrow. Do you want to take quick look at it now?'

'Oh yes please, but I don't want to hold you up or anything.'

'Not at all Harriet, come on, I'm sure you'll like it.'

Harriet followed her along the path to the back door entrance. She liked it being attached to their house, a bit like a small end semi to the main building.

'This is just perfect Molly, I love this kitchen overlooking the garden and wow, yes, I can see the sea and the mountains.' She flung her arms round Molly in an attempt to express her gratitude then followed her through to the sizeable hall leading to the front entrance. Moving along to the lounge, she gasped, this was so much bigger than hers at home, then on into the small dining room.

'Oh Molly, I've never really noticed there was all this to your house. It's fantastic.'

'Looking at the deeds this side was split from the main house and refurbished about ten years ago. To me it looks like it's never hardly been lived in. The kitchen's your standard flat-pack stuff but they may have had it done for a relative or someone who didn't want to invest too much money in it. It might even have been a holiday let, I just don't know.'

'Oh I love it Molly, it's a lot better than the kitchen back home. This is so light and airy. The sink looks brand new, it all does. I got the impression from Mr. Sanderson it needed a lot doing to it.'

'Well he's a keen eye Harriet and he spent some time in here, but there's no damp or anything nasty, he was probably talking about it needing redecorating.'

'It's absolutely fine for me Molly, I honestly couldn't ask for more.'

Molly smiled, shrugging her shoulders in delight. 'Come on then, let's go upstairs, there's an ensuite bedroom and then a slightly smaller guest room, that has its own ensuite, too.'

They wandered through the three bedrooms, Harriet gasping at the views as the river widened into the sea, she knew if she'd been searching herself she could never have found anything more perfect.

'This is the bathroom, then Harriet, oh and I forgot to show you the cloakroom downstairs. Same white fittings and ivory wall and floor tiles as this.'

Harriet was lost for words. It put her in mind of Mr. Sanderson's house. Maybe they'd had the same interior designers in. The woodblock floor to the hall, the same colour carpets in the lounge and dining room, the little touches here and there, paintings, ornaments, minimal but giving the whole place the stamp of the sea. Yes she was sure his interiors would have been in their client portfolio.

'There you go Harriet, I'm sure you'll be wanting to be adding your own bits and pieces but it's fully equipped, Mr. Sanderson organised one of those cleaning companies to go through the lot, down to the last teaspoon.' She started laughing, 'I've been over it again mind, there's nothing like the feeling of having done it yourself. Cut corners some of these people.'

Harriet smiled, put her arm around her. 'Thank you so much Molly this is unbelievable. I can't wait to move in. Look I must get the rent sorted out with you.'

'No need at all, Joris tried that one but Percy and I just want you to be here, give yourself chance to recover from all the terrible times, one on top of the other, you've been going through. We're not interested in the money, we're comfortable, very comfortable. I had to say the same to Joris, out came his cheque book but I chased him away. He'll be in trouble if he finds a way round, like he said. No Harriet we want you to have this chance for a bit of peace. We're here if you need us for anything whatsoever, but we won't come pestering. You're more than welcome to join us for meals, or just a bit of company. Anything we can do for you, we will, but we agree with Joris, what you need most just now is a bit of peace and quiet, time to relax and recover.'

Harriet could feel the tears welling, for a second blurring her vision. She knew Molly was right.

'Oh and as you'll be busy tomorrow getting moved in we wondered if you'd like to join us for dinner? I have asked Joris, I wanted it to be a thank you for the dinner party and all he's done here, of course. See how you feel tomorrow evening Harriet. There'll be plenty for all so no need to let me know until the last minute.'

'That's lovely Molly. What's there to do here? I'd love to come, thank you.'

Molly beamed, 'There Harriet let me take you out this way, this side garden is all yours and you've plenty of driveway for the car.'

They walked to the gate on the narrow lane, Harriet could scarcely believe so much had just fallen into her lap.

'Oh and the cat Harriet, she's already got a friend here, I expect they'll sometimes be dining together.' Harriet laughed, hugged her.

'Gosh Molly, that's if she's not passed out, she's still in the basket on the back seat of the car. I forgot all about her.'

Chapter 51

'Hello Harriet, that's a fine place to leave the car almost blocking the gates, where have you been?'

'Oh couldn't wait to see the house. I thought I'd just run back to Molly's to let her know I'll be moving in tomorrow. It's gorgeous Mr. Sanderson, I had absolutely no idea, it's perfect and I can't thank you or Molly and Percy enough.'

Mr. Sanderson smiled, his eyes betraying a hint of suspicion. 'Do you know Harriet I'm almost sure I saw a black Lamborghini launch itself from the traffic lights on my way out of Starboard Marine North West.'

Feeling engulfed in deceit she opened the rear door of the Mercedes making a grab for the cat basket.

'I must get her in Mr. Sanderson, I thought she was sleeping, she hates it in here.'

'She seems to hate it in there, too,' Mr. Sanderson declared, nodding towards the house. 'Where did you find her?'

'She'd got herself back home.'

He laughed, 'Talk about nine lives, surely she's used them all by now? Let's hope she settles in at Molly's.'

'She'd better because I know I will, I can't wait to move in.'

'Good stuff Harriet. I've arranged for Susan Curtiss to cover your class for the rest of the week, it'll give you chance to get yourself sorted.'

She smiled suddenly feeling sorry for him. She never liked to admit how dreadful it must be for him, always running away, never wanting to face up to anything. She had to admit to this guy having the patience of a saint.

'That's brilliant, I wasn't expecting that at all, thank you Mr. Sanderson.'

'No problem, I'm sure there's provision for moving house somewhere in the rules and regs, anyhow, did you have a good day? I'm sorry I had to disappear like that, urgent business, one way or another it's always popping up.'

'On the whole it was OK, bit of a tantrum during assembly from Danny Bustard but it was sorted in the end, everything fell back to routine.'

'It always does with you Harriet, I have to say. You're an absolute whiz down there, I just wish you could get your private life organised as efficiently. You've channelled too much emotional energy for too long into wanting to marry Mark. You've rebounded off this going in various directions totally to your detriment. I am really hoping this quiet period staying up the lane will give you a sense of perspective, enable you to find yourself, find what you really want out of life.'

She took a deep breath, couldn't understand what was the matter with her. This amazing guy, all six foot and more of him, his blonde hair cut, now curling at his collar, his pure blue eyes forcing her attention. This man, all she ever wanted and yet she was so caught up in this plethora of emotional baggage she felt she couldn't connect any more with her true feelings for him.

'Come on in Harriet, make youself at home. Ah Mrs. Harris if you would be so kind some food for the cat if you wouldn't mind. I'll put the kettle on, or would you prefer a drink Harriet? Yes, we'll relax a little by the fire before dinner, what would you be having?'

Harriet warmed her hands, her delight at the prospect of moving into her new place eased the fury of Belinda Oxfordshire's revelation. She smiled as he pushed the door open from behind, holding two glasses filled to the brim with sherry, the bottle slid precariously under his arm. She jumped up to slide it away.

'Yes, that's the one.' He placed them down on the woven drink mats sat on the small table, Harriet had moved along.

'Right, there we go Harriet, any more school news?'

'Oh yes, Ross Farquerhart was in looking for you.'

'Well that's a huge relief I must say. Did the boy stick it out or bunk off to this damned tunnel again? Where on earth did he get to? Did he say?'

'Well no, not really Mr. Sanderson, it was you he wanted to talk to as I said. Actually he wasn't feeling too good at all. He passed out in assembly.'

'Oh dear me, was he alright?'

'Yes he soon recovered, I sent him off to the library with Danny to go through all the fossils.'

'Excellent Harriet, excellent move. I'm sorry you appear to have had a day of it.'

'Super end though, I'm so excited about moving into Molly's house, I can't wait.'

'Well I am hoping you won't be making it a permanent arrangement Harriet. I'd rather like to think of it as an interim, we have got the baby to consider after all.'

Harriet had to sit on an instant impulse to tell him Belinda Oxfordshire had filled her in, had put rather a different perspective on things now.

'You know Harriet I've had a bit of a tussle with Belinda Oxfordshire just now. She's thick in with that damned woman Caroline Worsnip, apparently it's our fault the woman's lost her job. I don't see it that way, do you?'

'No, no not at all. In fact she was the one who insisted on seeing into the basket. Is she a bit loopy or something? Who'd bring a baby into a shop inside a closed basket?'

He breathed an enormous sigh stretching his legs full length then suddenly downed the rest of his sherry in one. He reached for the bottle. She reached for her glass.

'You know Harriet, you know the portrait of the little girl I keep in the wardrobe?'

She coughed uncontrollably, the sherry hitting the back of her throat burning the wrong way down.

'You alright Harriet? Oh goodness me, it wasn't something I said was it?'

'No, no, I'll be alright, thank you,' she managed to say, eyes watering, patting her chest as she spluttered.

'Harriet, it's something of a mystery to me. There's something about its history I'm uncomfortable with, always have been. It is indeed a portrait of a beautiful little girl but I was given it in circumstances I won't go into right now.'

He topped up her glass, then his own again, standing as he placed the bottle back on the table.

'Let me just get it, let me explain what I mean.'

He disappeared leaving Harriet on the verge of death, unable to think fast enough to enable a suitable response on his return.

'It's that damned woman, the pair of them, seen fit to take it. I'll bide my time on that one, see what comes out of it. My word Harriet, you're as bad as me, got through that one already? Here let me fill you up again.'

Harriet didn't refuse, needed to get on fast with changing the subject.

'I've booked the venue and that's been confirmed to the PM's office, not as a wedding ceremony of course. What are the plans following the wedding breakfast Mr. Sanderson, do you know? Do they have any preferences at all?'

'Only as much as I've mentioned to you already. I'll have a word with Andrew Norton and get this afternoon cruise under way. We'll be hosting dinner in the evening for say twenty to thirty guests. I must get the numbers cleared with Mac. Naturally they'll be organising the invitations etc. but they have allowed some leeway to invite a few of our friends. Clive and no doubt Mrs. Harrington will be coming. Oh yes Geraldine and James, I think it would be rather nice for you to have your brother along and possibly Molly and Percy, what do you think? Anyhow those have all gone through.'

Harriet perked up. 'Yes, oh yes that would be lovely.'

'Pop them on our list then Harriet and if there are any more I'll let you know.'

'Wow Geraldine will be beside herself. Who's arranging the seating?'

'They are.'

'Oh, oh I hope we don't get put next to her.'

Chapter 52

'Just wait until I tell Violet Geraldine and James are invited to the Prime Minister's daughter's wedding. She will tell everyone at the WI and I'll become quite a celebrity there. Talking of celebrities we've got Gregory Goldman, the gardening man off the television coming to speak at our meeting today, now there's a thought. Are you listening George? I need this little boost It's not been the same since I got voted off the committee. That Mrs. Harding, "Time for a change, time for a change", she chortled in that squeaky voice of hers. I'll never forgive her!'

'What are you going on about Frances?'

'Oh George you weren't listening. The PM's daughter's getting married. James and Geraldine have been invited to the wedding.'

George pushed his plate to one side to make better room for the morning paper.

'What's that all about they haven't been knighted as well have they?'

'I hope you're not casting aspersions on Harriet, George, saying that. You know as well as I do they haven't. No it's all about dear Joris, they've been invited as close friends of Sir Joris Sanderson.'

'Oh I see,' he said smiling at his wife's enthusiasm. 'When's Harriet going to marry him? It's about time she got herself sorted out. I don't think that girl she goes round with is a very good influence you know.'

'Exactly George, exactly. Harriet's got a good head on her shoulders but these last couple of years she seems to have gone right off the rails. Oh it's not just Patricia Harrington, I blame Mark. For years he's led her a right dance over getting married and then what does he do, I ask? Leaves her stranded at the church. What that poor girl felt like I can't imagine. I'll be forever grateful to Joris for stepping in. She'll be starting the menopause, too. It's a very difficult time all those hormones fluctuating, oh I do think nature has been very unkind to us women.'

George laughed, 'And what about us having to put up with you all? No you've got it wrong Frances, she's not menopausal, to me she's got all the bloom of youth.'

Frances started clearing the table, just for the briefest of moments it crossed her mind Harriet might be pregnant, then she couldn't let go of the thought. 'Don't tell me Mark's left her holding another baby.'

She finished the washing up just as George folded the paper closed. 'Not much in that today,' he declared looking out of the window. 'A good day to be getting on with tidying the garden.'

'Would you mind driving me to Harriet's, first, George. If we go now we'll just catch her before she goes to school.'

'If I must.'

Unable to sit on the compulsion to find something out, she jumped from the car, leaving George behind the wheel with the engine running. He looked across to see her rushing back, shocked.

'George, no sign of Harriet but there's a strange man in there, says he's moved in temporarily until the place gets sold. I told you Mark's mother had said that, she must have been right.'

'Where's Harriet then? She might have let us know what's going on.'

'According to him she's with Joris. What were we just saying over breakfast? Let's hope she's seen sense at last. She's taken the cat again. It won't stop there you know, it'll be back, you mark my words. I'll be on the go feeding it again. He doesn't look like the sort who'd know how.'

She cleared her throat, fastened the seatbelt taking a very deep breath. 'You know George I insisted on going up stairs to look for it. He's a very funny man that, already he's tied yards of pink ribbon to the corner of the banister rails at the top of the stairs. You know where I mean, and he's moved Harriet's cheval mirror into the doorway of the small bedroom opposite. He's turning that house into a brothel!'

George tried to resist from smiling.

'Take me to Joris this minute George, they need to know what's going on. I'll find out if the cat's still there, too. You know he asked me for the key and I refused to give it to him. I told him it belonged to Harriet not me and it was in my safe keeping. Hurry up George we might just catch them before they go to school.'

'Oh no Frances, we're not doing that. It's not up to you to start interfering in other people's lives, just let it be will you. We're going home.'

She remained silent, refusing to look at him, sat staring out of her side window all the way back. Irritated at seeing Violet Moss busy in her front garden, she wasn't in the mood for talking and there was no way she could keep her head down this time.

'Have you heard any more about Harriet's house,' Violet launched, 'Avril's desperate to know. You know with the takeaway business going under, they're not going to be able to afford to buy it but Avril was wondering if they'd be willing to let it to them until they get back on their feet and are able to get a mortgage.'

'It looks like it's already being let Violet, Harriet tells me nothing. It might be better if Avril and her boyfriend give the estate agent a call.'

Violet Moss sensed this wasn't the best of times for this, thought it better to change the subject.

'The WI should be good this afternoon, Frances. Have you got your questions lined up for Gregory Goldman? He's such a handsome man, can't wait to see him in the flesh.'

'Steady on Violet,' George winked across as he went ahead, hadn't quite lost the image of trailing yards of pink ribbon. Frances glared at him then turned to smile at her.

'Oh yes Violet, I've already thought of my very special question. What about you?'

'Yes, well I want to know exactly what the law is on growing conifers, big ugly things blocking out the light.'

'You mean those at the back of you?'

'Yes Frances, he's bound to know. Bethany managed to get hold of Simon Barnes so I've every intention of grabbing him and getting him to raise the issue in the press. There should be a law against planting trees right on top of people's fences. I'm up for getting a protest going, let's see if we can't get enough of a protest going to lobby parliament. Oh it's all starting for me this afternoon.'

Frances nodded a smile in tacit agreement, hers was a different agenda for now and there was no way she was going to miss this opportunity.

Chapter 53

Rapping Hammer asked for a couple of packets of cigarettes from the corrugated steel blind behind the counter, at the same time glancing across to the newspaper stand, unable to believe his eyes. He grabbed the top one, although any one of them would have done, they were all sporting the same headline:

" 'CELEBRATION CRUISE STOP' TO BE LOVE BOAT WEDDING VENUE FOR PM's DAUGHTER, IDA LYONS ON SATURDAY 25th OCTOBER 2014"

He stood blocking the doorway as he read on. "The party will sail from Sir Joris Sanderson's quay adjoining his mansion on the Lower Tideside banks of the River Dee to take the bride, her family and select guests to this once great liner now permanently moored on the opposite coast of beautiful north Wales."

Forced to the door and out the other side by a series of impatient customers he folded the paper under his arm walking quickly towards the van determined to ignore the moby ringing until he'd sat down.

'Oh yeah so you've got some news for me. Go on then…'

Ross Farquerhart needed to get it over and done with. This wasn't his forte at all, he'd never quite envisaged spying as a career, not least because he was doubled-up with nerves at the very thought of engaging with the undesirables of this world and just now was no exception. He began only to be cut stone dead as Rapping Hammer continued reading it word for word down the phone.

'It's all in here fuck head. Go back to playing with your toys and keep out of our way in future. Next time you drop-arse into our rib, we won't be fucking pulling you out! Got it!'

A strange fury instantly gripped him, unable to leave well enough alone he could barely contain himself. 'Well there's something I know that's not in there you git.'

'That sounds more the hot stuff. Spill it now or you're done in sock face.'

'They're picking the boss's boat up from Falmouth the Friday after this.'

'What the hell has that got to do with anythin`?' Demanded a furious Rapping Hammer, visions of freedom disappearing like the puff of smoke shot from between his teeth.

Ross Farquerhart stepped back, stunned, thought he'd dropped a prize, then quickly realised his error. Thoroughly confused he just couldn't make out where Rapping Hammer had got the information from. He straightened his back, puffed up his chest and sneered into his cool moby: 'All in where? What do you mean? How can you possibly know what's going on?' Then he panicked. Wasn't he supposed to be getting the boss to have a word in the PM's ear to get him off this

Venice hook? He was all set to approach Joris Sanderson this morning but for sure he wasn't going to bring this up. He terminated the call almost choking on a double surfeit of fear and nervous energy. He sat down to breakfast trying to look normal.

'Oh look Ross, the PM's daughter's getting married next month on that ship down the River Dee. Oh your dad and I will have to go and have a nose around on that day. I bet the river will be full of yachts and dinghies and motor boats waving the flag. I remember reading she's had a bit of a rough time that girl. Let's hope she's found the right one this time.'

She held the paper up to show him, he buttered his toast in relief. Rapping Hammer, for certain, now had enough information to do his own dirty work, now he could really concentrate on piecing together all he'd discovered in the tunnel. Could it have been his paranormal equipment brought the Madonna to light? He made a decision. He'd complete his PhD and turn it into a book 'What Really Happened to the 9th Lost Legion' and he would be the most revered historian in the land.

Chapter 54

George Glover picked up the morning paper landed nose first between the plant and the side of the door, tucking it under his arm as was customary before wandering to the window to admire the fruits of yesterday's labour.

'George, it's ready,' Frances called, seating herself down at the kitchen table, sporting two softly boiled eggs.

'Oh I see it all here about the PM's daughter getting married. It doesn't take long for news to leak out. After all the press coverage she's had I'd have thought they might have wanted to keep this one quiet.'

Frances stared at the yolk yielding to the buttered finger of toast she'd half-dipped into her egg. That hadn't even occurred to her. She went very quiet.

'Any mention of an anti-conifer campaign?' She piped up, trying to change the subject.

'Unless of course they've been phone-hacking again,' George declared, not hearing. 'No, surely not?' he continued, 'it's already touch and go as to whether or not some of them will get the jail. What did James say about it when he told you?'

'It wasn't James it was Geraldine, at least I think it was her. I spoke to them both you know but I don't remember either of them saying it was confidential.'

'Why you haven't been spilling the beans have you Frances?'

'Hardly George, don't you think I've got enough on my mind to be doing that? What with Harriet and the cat, Violet after me for Avril to get the house and that strange man, don't you think that's enough to be going on with? Do you know, on the way home I was sat on the bus next to Violet, and it stopped at the bus stop outside that adult shop. It's immoral putting a bus stop there. Well if it wasn't Harriet's car parked outside, I got such a shock and then he got out of it and went inside that disgusting place. I don't know how the council ever gave them planning consent. That man, George, I'm telling you that man renting Harriet's house, using her car and going into that sex shop. He's a pervert, a total pervert. He may be a lawyer but I can't understand Sir Joris having anything to do with him.'

She sank the remainder of the buttered toast fingers into the egg-yolk suddenly aware of her need for a lawyer. Rapidly decided she'd speak nothing of this sighting if he and Sir Joris could keep her out of jail. Yes, she decided she'd pop back to Harriet's and be nice to him.

Chapter 55

Harriet sat down to a plate of scrambled eggs peppered with smoked salmon, a tinge of excitement gleaming in her eyes. Today she would be moving in to her very own place. She'd be close to Molly and Percy, and Pepper, she felt sure, would be happy enough with Timmy to play with. Well yes, sometimes they scrapped, cats aren't supposed to be same species sociable but these two had been seen on occasions washing each other, falling asleep nose to tail in the sunshine streaming through the window on the top of Mrs. Harris's laundry basket under the window in the utility room.

'Ah good morning Harriet, sleep well?'

'Yes thank you, Mr. Sanderson and you?'

'Yes, very well indeed, thanks. Up early actually, working, the sooner I get to school the better. A couple of hours down there should finish it off, I'd like to be around just in case you might need me for anything.'

He loved the special glow the morning gave her beautiful face. Catching that sparkle of joy in her eyes, he smiled, pleased with his decision, hoping this move would settle her into eventual marriage.

'Also I'm having the new car delivered today Harriet, so poor old Clive will at least get his wheels back. He'd be a bit marooned at your place yesterday, though I suppose he could always have used your car, pity I didn't think of asking you.'

'The spare key's in the basket on the window sill, he may well have put two and two together.'

'Quite, Harriet, quite. Ah Mrs. Harris, do I see the morning paper tucked under your arm?'

'You do indeed Mr. Sanderson, now don't you be letting that go cold.'

'Just the headlines, that's all. Ah, thank you.'

He seated himself musing over the global warming debate.

'Well we've always been subject to diverse weather patterns of varying levels of intensity from time immemorial. Let's hope it holds off, we're needing to be getting the boat back in time for this wedding.'

'It's going cold Joris, now put that down and get on with it.' Mrs. Harris winked at Harriet.

'Right now!' He smiled only for it to fade rapidly. 'My goodness me what's this all about?' He'd caught a column inch against the margin, began reading out loud ' "**PM's Daughter to wed on Wirral**". Hells bells how on earth did they get hold of this? Mac insisted on complete confidentiality as far as was absolutely possible.'

He turned to the pile of post sat on the sideboard behind him. 'Ah yes this will be ours Harriet. "*Confidential*' It couldn't be plainer, oh and there's an explanatory note here in the folder. How on earth did they get hold of this? It could only have been through phone hacking, my word those journalists will never learn. He'll have the lot of them and make damned sure the bill gets speeded up through the Lords to get the curbs on the statute book. It'll be a circus you mark my words, that's if they don't cancel.'

Immediately Harriet felt guilty, racked her brains to see how it could have been her but nothing would come to mind.

'Are they likely to do that?'

'They all want it out of the way before the election. It'll be too late now, Savriato Cello will already know about it, the guns already loaded for firing the dirt. Anyhow I'll give Mac a call, find out what's going on. Don't you worry Harriet, there's no reason to let this spoil your day.'

She smiled and then realised, there was every reason to let it spoil her day. Ross Farquerhart had been in the office when she'd taken the call, she remembered repeating every last detail to get it right as she wrote it all down. He couldn't help but hear. Instantly she dismissed the thought, going to the press wasn't him at all, that's the last thing Ross Farquerhart would do. Then she had another thought, wondered if Belinda Oxfordshire had been invited, wondered if it was her couldn't keep her mouth shut.

Chapter 56

'Hi Caroline, I'm at work, though he's lucky I'm in today. I got a right pasting last night, and it looks like the portrait of Amber's gone missing. Good as accused us of taking it. Damned cheek! How did he react when you spoke to him?'

'Not best pleased at all, he didn't mention that though. He had the cheek to say there was a lot that didn't make sense over her disappearance, so I told him it wouldn't seeing as he couldn't be arsed to get involved.'

'Good one Caroline, good for you. What's he going to do about it?'

'Not a lot Belinda, you wouldn't think it was his daughter missing. He said he'd already had private agencies looking into it and they'd all drawn a blank, he didn't think there was much more he could do. He said he was getting a bit of a reputation always phoning for news, and decided it was probably hindering the case, he said these people are professionals, they know their job and he didn't want to get their backs up.'

'Oh so that's it then. It looks like we're going to have to see what we can do for ourselves. We need to go back and see those show houses again. It's no good the way it is. Amber will need to be somewhere settled, she'll be pretty traumatised if and when we do find her. I don't think we stand much of a chance ourselves though Caroline, I think you're going to have to let me ask Daddy.'

Caroline stalled, she'd save him for sinking Harriet Glover. 'Well maybe Belinda but I've got to focus on trying to get my job back, I can't think of buying anything until I'm back in employment.'

'Well maybe Daddy could help with that?'

'Actually Joris touched on it, for his own ends and Harriet Glover's of course. He's going to make an appointment to see Roger Boxsocks and he's taking that lawyer guy with him, to clear their position; he said it was up to the company to decide whether or not to rescind the dismissal.'

'Very big of him, I'm sure, especially when he's got all the strings to pull. Anyway stay in touch, I must go I can hear bird brain just in chatting to someone. It sounds a bit like Tarquin Bridgewater to me. Bye.'

'Oh hello Mr. Bridgewater, you're an early customer, what can I do for you? Just a moment while I take my jacket off.'

Tricia slung it over the back of the chair.

'Just popped by to see if old Joris was about. We're looking to bring the big boats in a bit earlier this winter, he was talking about a more sheltered spot this time and I've got the very place. Just wanted his OK before we get shifting.'

'Oh I see,' said Tricia as Belinda came stomping out of the office.

'He was here last night wasn't he Belinda, did he say he'd be in this morning?'

'I presume you're talking about Joris and no he didn't.'

'Ah Belinda, my dear, and how are you doing? Still keeping up the good works? You never know that OBE might turn itself into a damehood one of these days, just like Harriet's got.'

She froze to the spot. Tarquin Bridgewater touched his hat, made his excuses and scurried away.

'I wouldn't worry about him Belinda, he most probably hasn't had an invite to the wedding probably feeling a bit miffed.'

'Oh so Harriet Glover's finally made up her mind has she?' Belinda Oxfordshire sniffed. 'I think Joris has lost his marbles hanging on to her by his finger-tips. She's the one that's got Caroline fired, oh it's alright for her, not everyone's quite so well in with the boss.'

Tricia shook her head, fished in her handbag for her lipstick peering into the mirror.

'I don't know what you're talkin` about Belinda, I'm talkin` about the invitation Clive and I have had to the PM's daughter's wedding by courtesy of our close association with Sir Joris.'

Belinda Oxfordshire fumed and bubbled like a boiling kettle, over-filled with hot steam rattling its lid.

'When did you get that?' She snapped.

'Oh I can't remember now, haven't you had yours yet?'

'NO!'

She retreated to the office slamming the door closed behind her. Opened it again. 'Oh and I suppose Harriet Glover's had hers, too?'

'Oh yes and James and Geraldine. Not her mother though, I don't think she'll be getting one, so you're not alone Belinda. You couldn't really expect them to invite everyone, now could you?'

Chapter 57

'I won't be a minute George, I'll just make sure the cat's not there again. He won't know how to take care of it. I'll need to show him where everything is.'

Frances Glover waddled up Harriet's path taking care to ring the doorbell this time. Clive had already seen her getting out of the car, his face turning red from acute embarrassment. This awful woman wouldn't have understood for one minute what she had seen on the landing. He pulled the door back.

'Oh I'm not here to take up your valuable time Mr. er?'

'Engells, Clive Engells. I'm afraid Harriet's not here.'

She thrust her hand at him leaving him no option but to shake it.

'May I call you Clive? You know Harriet has mentioned Joris's very nice handsome friend, a lawyer I believe. You know when I got home it struck me it could have been you staying in Harriet's house, all along. It's just that you look so young, like a ripe tomato. So sorry I meant ripe matador, er almost mature if you like. Those same swarthy good looks and of course those with the darkest hair always seem to go prematurely grey. "Far too young to be him," I thought, you'll understand just why I didn't form an association. Yes I'm sure she said his name was Clive. Met you when they were down camping with the school in Falmouth. Is that right?'

No it wasn't! She'd messed the whole thing up after having written it out so many times and then practiced it to perfection. She just wished she hadn't done it in the greenhouse, didn't expect to be met with such a red face. She knew those tomatoes should have been picked long since, George never listens, it could well have helped if he'd picked them.

'Look could I come in for just a minute? You won't want me bothering you if the cat comes back. She does that you know, found her way all the way home from Belgium, goodness knows how. Stowed away in Harriet's bag when she went on that mini-cruise. Was back here just the other day when Harriet had taken her to Sir Joris's, good job I keep popping in when Harriet's away, just to make sure.'

She bustled forward, steering Clive into the kitchen.

'Let me just show you where Harriet keeps the cat food, there, and these are the bowls. Oh and I'll give you my number just in case you have any problems.'

'Thank you Mrs Glover, most kind.'

'Oh you may call me Frances, please do. So you're the legal brain behind Harriet's food bank at her school. Do you know Clive, she's never done singing your praises. I'm so pleased she's got such a good friend in you. She's had a bad time you know, what with that hippy boyfriend letting her down at the church. There we all were, and he's coming up the path full of excuses telling her he can't go through with it. I don't think her daddy and I will ever recover. No we're very thankful she has such good friends in you and Joris. She doesn't seem too keen on Belinda, is it? Yes Belinda that's the one. Used to be engaged to Joris, I suppose that's not the best of starts but all that was nothing to do with Harriet, I've told her that. Do you know Belinda at all?'

Clive nodded his head.

'Well yes, I'm sure you do. I think Harriet would have been far better making a friend of her than that silly, common girl she insists on going round with. I'm sure she's a bad influence on Harriet, she wouldn't have been in half the trouble she has of late, if it hadn't been for her. I don't know how Belinda tolerates her, they work together at Joris's place, you know, what's it called now?'

'I believe it's Starboard Marine North West, Mrs. Glover.'

'Now do call me Frances, Harriet would like that, and take a tip from me, Belinda has a lot going for her, she'd be far better off with the likes of you than that scatty girl's husband. I'd steer well clear of her Clive, just not yours or Joris's class at all. Oh she'll be wanting an invite to the PM's daughter's wedding alright, she'll be lucky, that's one occasion she won't be able to mess up. If you get an invite, just you bear Belinda in mind.'

'Thank you Mrs. Glover and good-day to you.'

She bustled down the path and into the car convinced she'd done him a favour. Oh there'd be no problem at all now, should she be needing a lawyer.

Chapter 58

'The sooner we get this bill through parliament the better. Get this phone hacking stamped out once and for all. I'm outraged this should have been leaked. We're completely stymied now. I'm in two minds whether or not to go ahead with the wedding plans. It might be better to wait until the election's over. It'll put them on a false trail. It'll completely wrong foot them if there's no wedding. Leave it with me Joris, I'll have a word with Ida, see what she thinks.'

Joris Sanderson replaced the receiver, deeply saddened the wedding plans appeared to be rapidly disintegrating. He looked at his watch, popped his head into Enid's office to tell her he'd be going at break time.

'I've had a word with Miss Frost, she'll keep an eye on the place and I am, of course only a phone call away.' Mr Brown grunted to himself as he wandered off to find Miss Frost, 'He thinks it's him that runs this sodding place, he'd be nowhere without his caretaker.'

Mr. Sanderson piled into the Bentley, not his style at all, he was looking forward to his new car. Well reviewed, he'd decided his new Mercedes-Benz SLS AMG was just the ticket. Silver Metallic, "voluptuous sports car", so aptly described; the time to move on was indeed now. He could picture himself next to Harriet with the top down, the wind blowing through her hair. There were so many places he wanted to take her, so much they could do together, why oh why was she so reticent, so unable to grasp the opportunity to live life to the full with him? This was a question he just couldn't answer. All understanding failed him.

His mind wandered to the wedding, he wondered what Ida's response would be. It could indeed be that the girl has no intention of cancelling and with the damage already done she could feel there'd be too much to lose. Now approaching the traffic lights at Starboard Marine North West on impulse he decided to pop in. He was unsettled about Amber, decided he'd get Belinda Oxfordshire to run it all past him again.

'Oh good morning Mr. Sanderson.' Tricia jumped back from the mirror promptly popping her lipstick back into her handbag. 'Mr. Bridgewater's been in here looking for you. He said something about moving your boat to a more sheltered spot. Wanted you to OK it, or something like that.'

'Oh right, thank you Mrs. Harrington.' He nodded towards the office, 'Miss Oxfordshire in, is she?'

'Oh she is Mr. Sanderson but I don't think she's in a very good mood. I think she's a bit miffed she hasn't had her wedding invitation yet.'

'Really? On second thoughts Mrs. Harrington I'll be on my way.' He marched towards the door, then turned. Tricia straightened, instantly pulling back from her handbag. She wished he wouldn't do that, always finding an excuse to turn on his heel. 'Did Clive mention we're looking to bring the boat back the weekend after this?'

'Oh yes he did Mr. Sanderson, I'm really looking forward to it. Are you thinking of going down on the Friday or Saturday?'

'Subject to weather conditions and the forecast's indicating a bit of a calm before the storm, it had better be the Friday. We can overnight on the boat and set sail on Saturday, home on Sunday. Oh, on second thoughts I'd better have a quick word with Belinda, put her in the picture. See if she can't organise Tarquin Bridgewater to cover for you.'

He stepped back to let an enthusiastic looking young couple through.

'Are you Sir Joris Sanderson? We want to buy a dinghy and have sailing lessons, have we come to the right place?'

Mr. Sanderson beamed. You have indeed, come through.'

He closed the office door behind them to send a furious Belinda Oxfordshire scurrying out.

'What's going on in there now? Bloody cheek kicking me out like that. He's always up to something. It's about time he got Caroline Worsnip her job back. He doesn't give a damn about her or their child.' She shut up as the office door opened. Tricia aghast at what she'd just heard ,refrained from enquiring further as they both stood to attention, Mr. Sanderson's voice loud and commanding now, as the door wavered back and forth.

Chapter 59

Roger Boxsocks stood to his office door opening. He'd been expecting Saville Knight to call in but not quite as soon as this.

'Do take a seat, Mr. Knight. Familiar surroundings for you these.'

'Yes indeed, it's not somewhere I'm particularly pleased to be but I was extremely disturbed by Caroline Worsnip's call. I understand she's been dismissed without a full enquiry, that's wrong for a start. She should have been suspended on full pay if you were intent on that kind of thing.'

Roger Boxsocks was somewhat taken unawares by the speed with which this former CEO was homing in. 'What's she supposed to have done, anyway?'

Roger Boxsocks, playing for time, reached for his handkerchief.

'Miss Worsnip had this department in complete chaos, insisting a couple of customers carrying a cat in a basket, open it. She was off her head believing there to be a baby inside. Of course we had that incident a while back where someone did leave a baby in a closed basket and she doesn't appear to have recovered from that. Shortly after she left and was indeed very fortunate to get her job back.'

'Fortunate I was still around to re-employ her Mr. Boxsocks. Now whilst it may appear somewhat irrational, given her sense of unease at the incident you've just cited, it wasn't that unreasonable and certainly not a sacking offence.'

'The cat ran the place ragged, the woman with the tall blonde guy shot out of the changing room, running round half-naked trying to catch the bloody thing. There was a collision not too far from the perfume stand which crashed by the way, involving one of our regular customers who insisted on immediate compensation. The blonde guy handed her goodness knows how much and Miss Worsnip saw fit to hand her a couple of bottles of Channel perfume which had fallen to the floor. A stock check revealed far more than that missing and I'm afraid Miss Worsnip was the only one in the vicinity.'

'So you accused her and sacked her.'

Roger Boxsocks remained silent.

'How do you know a certain Harriet Glover didn't help herself? According to Miss Worsnip you were in here, didn't see anything of it. Are you sure you've not been piling all this on simply to save your own skin? By all accounts this department's revenue has well fallen since you took over. Apparently you've been consistently anti with regard to Miss Worsnip's career path in this company, consistently marking her down, when in actual fact she's as capable of you of running this floor, if not more so. It has occurred to her you might just want her out for fear of her taking over your job. Believe you me she's hell bent on taking this to court and if you don't want it to get very messy I suggest you reinstate her immediately along with an apology and an explanation if you can devise one fit enough to placate the CEO.'

'Well I certainly don't see that any of this is your concern Mr. Knight, as I recall you left the company some time ago.'

'I'm still on the Board of Directors, Mr. Boxsocks, see to it now or your fired!' His angular face reddened under his tight blonde frizz and his blue eyes darted vehemently towards the phone. 'You get it sorted this minute whilst you've still got chance. I want to see her back in here tomorrow!' He stood, tall and fit, Roger Boxsocks went to shake his hand. 'Point taken Mr. Knight, consider it done!'

Handkerchief in hand he blew his nose once Saville Knight had closed the door behind him. Then the phone rang. 'Mr Boxsocks there's a certain Sir Joris Sanderson wishes to speak with you, shall I send him up?'

Chapter 60

Joris Sanderson looked at his watch deciding he'd take the short cut back from town, he didn't like the single track lanes but he was needing to get back to see how Harriet was getting on. It hadn't been his intention to get involved with Roger Boxsocks just then, but he was furious at overhearing Belinda Oxfordshire's remark to Tricia regarding what he wasn't doing for Caroline Worsnip, after promising. Amazed at how effortless the quest had been, barely with the man five minutes and he'd committed to reinstating the woman just as soon as he could. He'd assured him it would be today and by tomorrow Miss Worsnip would be back in store. At least that was one problem solved but the finding of Amber was a different matter. Frustrated with his inability to make sense of it all, for the moment he decided to put it to one side. Hard as it was for him, just now he had to press on with things he could press on with. In his heart he knew Amber's disappearance may for ever remain one of those unsolved mysteries. He hoped the portrait wouldn't become one either.

Grateful for no oncoming traffic he was back at Lower Tideside in less than fifteen minutes. He turned left off the top road past Molly's place and with no sign of the Mercedes on Harriet's drive he decided to go straight home.

'Good timing indeed,' he said, stopping to beam at the driver offloading the new Mercedes from the back of the truck onto the gravel drive. Harriet, Mrs. Harris and Mr. Swift were all there, gasping at this prize of an acquisition. He veered left, then right, bringing the Bentley to a halt in front of the greenhouses. Harriet watched him striding over, looking like a kid with a much wanted new toy. 'If only, if only he'd told me first about Amber.' This was something she couldn't easily erase from her mind. 'If only he hadn't wanted to use the very same name for our child should it be a girl.' It stung, the thought pierced her very soul. 'How could he already have a child and have not told me.' She could see the swelling across her stomach now, her breasts full, she'd so much wanted to be the first to carry his baby. At times she'd tried to be more rational about it, after all she knew this guy had hardly been living in a monastery. He hadn't wanted her to get pregnant and maybe that was why but then he'd always said "Save that for me". That was in the early days, of course when she'd admitted to taking chances with Mark, always longing for just one more child. In the brief time it took for Mr. Sanderson to crunch his way towards her she'd had the full realisation of the complete mess she'd made of all their lives since turning forty.

'Like it Harriet?' Mr. Sanderson ran his fingers through his hair as the spanking new car finally rolled gently off the truck.

'It's quite amazing, absolutely gorgeous, golly you'll turn a few heads in that.'

He hadn't heard, he was busy taking all the documentation from the driver before waving him off. He walked back tossing the keys between his fingers.

'Not bad eh. Every guy should have the chance of one of these before they reach fifty. I guess I'm very privileged.'

He scooped Harriet into his arms, 'But there's only one of you Harriet and I'm the luckiest guy on earth.'

Taken by surprise, she knew she'd gone bright pink.

'There you go Harriet, what have I been telling you all along? This man's potty about you and I want to see that thing trailing ribbons and tin cans.' She turned to Mr. Swift. 'We'll make the "Just Married" plaque for the back, won't we Ken and no one will see the pair of you for all the confetti we're going to be throwing.'

Mr. Sanderson laughed, he liked the sound of that. Harriet smiled, she'd just seen Barry, right now she wasn't so sure.

Chapter 61

Harriet woke to her first morning in the new house. She gasped at the view. Looking up the river, the sunrise flicking all the pinks and lilacs across a pale blue sky promising a beautiful day and on the sea reflections so deceptive as to confuse a stranger as to east and west. The cat, soft and warm curled at her side, a special first night concession. She looked around, enjoying her new surroundings. She'd enjoyed last night's dinner at Molly's, too. It was a wonderful evening. She'd not known this kind of contentment, ever. Today she would sort the bits and pieces Mr. Sanderson had arranged the collection of from 4 The Willows, then she'd get on with writing the change of address cards. She lay between clean sheets just thinking of where she was at, marvelling at still carrying her baby, their baby. Her mind moved to Barry Giordano and the painting, wondered if he'd ever find it, then she began wondering if he would ever find Amber. Thought Mr. Sanderson might feel differently towards Caroline Worsnip in the event. Decided how difficult it would be for him having two children by different mothers. Barry had always wanted children but his wife didn't which was the prime reason for their marriage breakup. All along he'd made it clear he would welcome Harriet and the baby into his life with open arms and she knew his feelings hadn't changed. Harriet was very fond of him but she'd met him on top of falling in love with Joris Sanderson so he never really stood a chance. She wondered how she would have felt towards him had she not been so in love with her boss. She hated what he did to her, painting that picture of her lying pregnant, naked on the sofa. He did it to break them up and Mr. Sanderson whilst furious, at least he said he believed Harriet would never have posed like that but sometimes she had her doubts. As much as she wished Barry had never gone there she could understand his motive which of course was very flattering but the whole affair still rankled with her, as kind as he'd been, just as Belinda Oxfordshire's revelation about Joris Sanderson did. She'd woken happy, wanted to stay that way. Brushing negativity aside as best she could she swung herself out of bed, stroked the cat and went down to make a cup of tea. A tap on the hall window made her jump then she realised it was Mr. Sanderson moving across to ring the bell.

'Sorry, just down the stairs hope you haven't been here long?'

'No, no Harriet, don't worry. Just thought I'd pop in on my way to school to see how your first night went.'

He smiled that gorgeous smile and for a fleeting second she felt she could forgive him anything.

'Have you time for a cup of tea, I've just come down to make one?'

'Oh I'll make time Harriet as long as you stay just as you are while I drink it.'

Her silk slip barely covering her breasts and where it did her nipples taut beneath it. Her blonde hair, natural, falling like silk just over her shoulders. Her arms, bare, beautiful, lifting her hands to her head, the rising slip wrapping her legs in one clean run. He drew her close, running his hand down her side knowing this was all she was wearing.

She had the same sudden realisation. 'Just a tick I need to..'

'No Harriet you don't need to go anywhere. I haven't got the time. Just a quick cup of tea with you.'

He sat on the tall stool at the breakfast bar just looking at her. The flush to her cheeks, the shyness governing her smile, watching her sorting the cat out. He decided there and then he would let absolutely nothing stand in his way of marrying her.

'How does the new car feel? Pleased?' Harriet asked sitting alongside him.

'It's ace, can't wait to take you for a spin. How about I collect you at lunch time, we'll eat out?'

'Fantastic, thank you.' She smiled, the corners of her mouth lifting, widening to a beam, her blue eyes sparkling. He swore he could see Amber in her.

'Then how would you like me to pop round this evening and I'll cook dinner? It'll give us chance to run through things. Apparently Ida Lyons is not up for cancelling the wedding so we can talk through our side of that and I do, of course want to get the boat back before the weather breaks. We can run through this as well.'

'No, let me cook dinner for you. You'll have been at work all day. I'm dying to try my new kitchen out. I'll drive along to the village butcher, in fact I can get all I need from the shops there. I really would love to do that tonight.'

He swallowed the last of his tea, swivelled round to slap his hands on his legs then stood.

'Right Harriet, you're on. But don't enhance the rice with drawing pins will you?'

'Wow you've got a good memory. That was ages ago I did that to Mark. I didn't know the drawing pin had landed in the rice when I pulled the calendar off the wall. Anyway you're not having rice.'

She jumped off the stool to land in his arms.

'You're beautiful Harriet, It's strange how I can see so much of the portrait in you. "Tu pulcherrima muliere ego numquam accelerant", here let me write it down so you can look it up.'

He passed her the slip of paper. 'I want the translation at lunchtime, you can use your laptop. Oh and find out what the maritime weather forecast is for a week on Friday whilst you're there.'

She followed him through the hall, briefly stepping out to see him slide into his prized car, not closing the door until he was out of sight. Smiling, in her hand the line of Latin, ripe for translation. In her mind the thought of Amber, wondering how he could pinpoint a resemblance, thought about the photograph her mother had given her of when she was a little girl, thought about the striking resemblance between the two. Yes, she needed to phone Barry, she wanted the portrait back. He'd have to photograph it or something, but she needed it back. Goodness knows how she'd smuggle it back into the house but decided she'd worry about that later. For now she must phone Barry Giordano.

Chapter 62

La Belle Cafetiere graced the entrance to Manchester's busy Arndale Centre and was a convenient enough meeting place for Barry and Andy sat in the window chatting intently about their new business plans. Both were glad to be free of MI6. They'd been contracted for some time and had travelled the world as undercover agents, cracking espionage, gang thieves, the mafia. But the issue today was two-fold. How to find Amber with only a portrait to go on and during the course of this, Barry was hoping at least to throw some light on his own missing painting. It was a huge call. He moved the conversation along.

'We've done all the Wirral art shops, galleries, charity shops and no joy. It's time to widen the search Andy. If we could find who painted this portrait it might give us a clue. It's a bit of a long shot but it's just possible the artist could help kick-start the investigation.'

'If she's Sanderson's child shouldn't that be the starting point?' Andy sounded confused.

'Therein lies the problem. According to Harriet, according to this Belinda woman who sounds a bit of a busy B, the mother has had very little to do with him. Apparently she moved away taking the baby when he refused to marry her. He's had minimal or little contact since. It's only when the child went missing the mother established contact, giving him the portrait. Not long after that she moved back to the area, got her old job back so she could be around to chivvy him into finding her.'

'Hoping for a "happy ever after scenario"?'

'Exactly and that's what I'm hoping for Andy on all counts, it's in my interests to get this child found. Harriet's already hacked off, the fact he's got a child he's not yet mentioned to her. She's pregnant by him, she must be feeling pretty cut-up about it all right now,' Barry explained.

'Any chance we could get Harriet to raise this again with B?'

'It's worth a try. It might work better with Tricia though, remember her, the scatty one in Venice?'

'Not likely to foget that one Barry! Yeah didn't you say they work together?'

'That's it, Sanderson's marine place. Ideal, we'll need to get Harriet to persuade her to put the screws on this B woman. We need all the information we can get.'

'Ahh whose that now?' Barry reached to his inside pocket, held the phone to his ear. 'Oh it's you Harriet, speak of the devil, how's the new pad going?'

'Love it Barry, thanks. You and Andy OK?'

'Buzzing! We're trying to get a grip on this missing child. Look Harriet any chance you could persuade Tricia to grill this Belinda woman. We need as much detail about the circumstances of the mother as possible. At the moment we've only got this portrait to go on.'

'Oh I need it back please Barry, he knows it's gone missing.'

'So it's missing? What can he do about it? Just keep shtum! We've no chance without it. Sorry no *buts* Harriet'

'OK, I'll try.'

'Now how soon can you get hold of Tricia?'

'Immediately Barry, I can phone her at work, now.'

'Has she got a direct line?'

'Yes at the counter, she takes calls there.'

'Great! Her number Harriet, on second thoughts it would be better if I speak to her myself.'

He put his cup down, reached for his pen, swallowing quickly as Harriet returned.

'Right Harriet, that's great. Stay in touch, we can start moving this forward now. See you.'

'Good morning, Starboard Marine North West, how may I help you?'

'What do you know about this missing child of Sanderson's Tricia? Has Belinda mentioned it to you at all?'

'Oh hi Barry, this is a nice surprise. If you've got Andy there, tell him he's missed his chance, I'm already spoken for now.'

'Come on Tricia stop messing about, you can tell him yourself. I need the lowdown on this kid and her mother, as much info as you can manage. Every small detail. Can you extract it from this Belinda woman you work with?'

'Oh I already know it Barry. She was so fuming with him after he'd wiped the floor with her she spilled it all out. She's not here at the moment so I can tell you now.'

He pressed the record button on his phone. 'Fire away Tricia, fire away.'

Barry was fortunate, in her rage, Belinda Oxfordshire had spewed out to Tricia everything Caroline Worsnip had told her. He listened intently as Tricia passed it all along thinking faster than she could speak.

'Great stuff, thanks Tricia, we're on to it now. Look if there's anything specific would you mind giving it a try for us?'

'Oh no, not at all, her and Caroline are so narked off with him, I could get to know anything, especially if I pretend to be on their side.'

'Great stuff, thanks Trica, see you.'

He returned the phone to his inside pocket giving Andy the thumbs-up.

'Plymouth, that's where we need to be Andy. We need to locate Caroline Worsnip's former address. It shouldn't be too difficult. In the meantime we need to get back to Wirral, I've just had a hunch about my painting. I want to get down to the police station there, chat to a few of them, find out exactly who went to the pawnbroker's to check it out. See if they can't let us in to have a look round. You up for it Andy?'

They downed their coffee, almost cold by now and headed for the Lamborghini fast running out of parking ticket. The portrait of Amber in the carrier bag on the bag seat, Barry never parted from it, there was always a chance, someone, somewhere could give him a lead. He'd certainly wave it in front of the police officer at the desk, see if they could run a quick check for him on missing children in the area. He was puzzled, very puzzled there appeared to be so little to go on. A quick call down south to the Soot Street Station proved vague, all Barry had managed to generate was a sense of confusion as the officer checked records both manually and online, coming up with nothing. They arrived geared up for nothing less than success, their determination springing a pleasantly cooperative response from the officer on the front desk. He called to the rear, 'Hey Brian, come and take a look at this, have you seen this little girl at all, can you work a match with anything we've got on file for missing children?'

The officer left his seat to come to the counter. 'Seen that one before I'm sure of it. Yes I remember it now, that guy does all the community work, funny name, er, yes, Joris Sanderson, runs the school by the old pawnbroker's shop, he brought it to us. What do you want to know for?' Barry decided it was a good time to show their ID's, 'Just a bit of confidential private work.'

'Yes that was it, she's gone missing. We've had every force in the land and beyond quietly on this one. Just not enough evidence to go public, bizarre as it sounds, it looks like the case was never actually reported.'

He stopped to study the painting again, scratched his head. 'Yes, it's a mystery to us, good luck with it, if you can get to the bottom of who painted it you might get a lead. Oh I'll tell you one thing though, no point bothering with the pawnbroker's by the school, rum lot they were, we did them alright, we closed them. I had to go in and do the stock inventory for the insurers. There was so much stolen stuff in there, you'd never believe!'

Barry took a deep breath, silently condemning the inefficiency. Managed to refrain from comment, he wanted to hear exactly what this guy was about to say.

'Funny thing, the resemblance to this face and the one on that painting I found down there is quite remarkable. It could have been one and the same person. A grown woman now but same blonde hair, blue eyes and mouth. A beautiful woman, the artist is quite amazing. Oddly enough I dropped a pair of featherheads off the other night, you know the night we had that very bad fog. One of them was a dead ringer for this woman. Teaches at the school I just mentioned.'

Barry now knew, just knew it was his painting he was talking about. Was the man never going to say she was naked, pregnant, draped on the steps of St. Mark's Square with her legs to one side, slightly apart. He took another deep breath and waited but nothing. He desperately needed confirmation but managed to hold his cool.

'Ah that's very interesting, what exactly happened to this painting you are talking about?' Barry asked.

'There was no record of identity, previous ownership, not even the artist's name. We assumed it was nicked, not the sort of work you'd hang up in your lounge. No that one went to auction.'

'Do you have a record of the purchaser?'

'Not here we don't, that kind of stuff doesn't move very well round here. We didn't put it into any of our own auctions, it went to one of the big art auction houses in London. I believe it made around a million. Not bad for an unknown artist, eh? Mind you I'm not surprised I'd have paid as much to have that painting of such a blue eyed beauty naked, hanging on the wall.'

Barry could feel every drop of blood drain from his face.

'You must know the auction house it went to. If there's such a resemblance between the two I might surely get a lead. It's interesting both works are unsigned.'

'You're right there, just give me a few minutes, we should have it on record somewhere.'

Barry looked at Andy in utter disbelief, they stood silent for what felt like hours waiting for Police Officer Brian to return.

'Yes, got it. Here, let me just write it down for you, "Rossenthorn's Art House Auctioneers, London" Let me just add the phone number for you, there.'

'Well thank you, you've been extremely helpful.' Barry shook his hand, Andy following suit.

'No probs, we like to help our own,' he said as Barry pulled open the door.

Dazed, they sat in the car for a while, unable to come to terms with their findings.

'I've got to get it back Andy. I'll never stand a chance with Harriet unless I get it back. Here, let me get hold of this auction house right now, find out where it went to.'

'You'll never get that back, Barry, where are you going to get that kind of money from?'

'Just a minute Andy, the proceeds must have gone to the Treasury. I should have a claim on them. In effect the picture was stolen, it was mine, Sanderson must have given it back to Harriet, neither of them wanted it so it should have been returned to the rightful owner, surely?'

'No I'm not sure of the legal position on that one, but you could end up getting Harriet sucked in trying to make a case. I'd forget it if I were you Barry.'

'You may be right but don't forget the police listed it as stolen property, I can prove ownership with all the sketches, it's worth a go. Think what that money would do, or even a tenth of it, for the business. We could set ourselves up for life!'

Andy wasn't into fantasy, he looked sceptically across at Barry. 'I suppose it's worth a try you may as well phone this auction house, it might be interesting to find out who bought it and where he lives, if they'll part with such details, which I doubt.'

'We'll see,' said Barry punching the number in, getting impatient with the all calls are recorded dictum. He took a deep breath, pressed the record button, then finally a reply.

'Ah yes, I do recall the purchase of that one, a most unusual composition set in Venice, St. Mark's Square if I'm not mistaken. It went through the roof. Just hold the line please whilst I check. You do understand I'm not at liberty to disclose the owner's name but certainly I can give you the location.'

Barry glanced at Andy giving him the nod.

'Sold to a gentleman residing in Cornwall.'

'Ah whereabouts in Cornwall?' Barry asked.

'Is there any particular reason you would wish to know this Sir?'

'Look I'm working undercover, we have good reason to suspect this work was stolen and we've located the artist.'

'And what might your name be Sir?'

'Barry Giordano seconded to MI6. You may check me out if you wish. I'll give you the number of the Stetmead Police Station who have seen our credentials, this is the place from where the painting was sent. We're parked outside now.'

'Er yes, I'll take the number if you would be so kind Sir.'

They waited and waited, Barry drumming his fingers on the dashboard, impatient to get on with it.

'My apologies for keeping you waiting. Ah yes, let me see, we're looking at a gentleman by the name of Arend Achterbeg residing at 15 Breakloch Apartments, The South Quay, Falmouth. Oh yes and this is his telephone number…'

Barry basked in the moment of triumph, he had a good feeling about this.

'Your co-operation is much appreciated Sir and you can be assured your confidentiality is protected.' He finished, grinning at Andy.

'So the guy's Dutch and he's currently living in Falmouth. It might at least get me a new Lamborghini Aventado, that would knock the socks off Harriet alright, he laughed, the phone suddenly ringing in his hand. 'Oh hang on, who's this now?'

'Yes, Giordano speaking. Ah Tricia, more information so soon?'

'Well yes, in a way, I haven't got Caroline's old address in Plymouth yet but Belinda did mention she's got an Aunty Sharon who lives in a flat near to where she used to be in Brambles Court. Apparently this Aunty Sharon of hers helped her out with looking after the child.'

'That's great Tricia, thanks a lot. We've got something to go on now. Keep us posted.'

'A very interesting day so far,' Barry rubbed his hands together. We'll be needing a trip down to the South West shortly.'

Chapter 63

'Pleased with the new car Joris?' With a long drive to Falmouth ahead, Clive steered towards the gates crunching the Bentley through the golden gravel for the last time.

'Indeed, it's superb, goes like a rocket! That right Harriet?' He turned catching Harriet's smile.

'You girls comfortable in the back there?' Clive asked.

'Oh yes thank you Clive.' Harriet felt the nudge from Tricia's elbow. 'We are aren't we Harriet? We're so looking forward to spending the night on your boat Mr. Sanderson and then sailing it all the way back to here. It's very exciting.' She nudged Harriet a bit harder, scrunching her shoulders in sheer delight, never thinking she'd see a time such as this.

'So the Aston Martin's being delivered here tomorrow Clive. It's the Vanquish you've gone for, then?'

'It is Joris, all change for me and Patricia here.' He half-turned. 'You helped me choose it didn't you petal?'

'Well sort of, you made me say which car I like the best out of a whole pile of brochures and I just happened to like the one you'd already chosen.'

'Well that was just a confirmation of how well we're matched my dear. I'm certain it will be exactly the same with the house, we've a few lined up to view when we get back.'

'Oh yes we have Clive, they're all like palaces, just like yours Mr. Sanderson. Well they're all like that round here. We do want to live round here, don't we Clive?'

He turned to smile at her, 'We certainly do petal, as I say there's a few to look at facing the river.'

'How are you getting on in Harriet's house Clive?' Mr. Sanderson asked.

'Very well, aren't we petal?'

'Oh so you've moved in too?' Mr. Sanderson said, turning to Tricia.

'Well I do a bit of both really, I'm there when my mum's got the kids. Me and Bob try not to see one another.'

'Yes I can appreciate that. It would appear your marriage is over, now.'

'Definitely, it was him that started it all going off with that Belinda Oxfordshire woman. I don't know whether or not she'll have him back either now.'

'Oh and what makes you suppose that?'

'Well from what I can gather she's really chummed up with Caroline Worsnip. They're talking about buying a house each on that new development at the end of the lane, just a bit down on the right from Starboard Marine North West.'

'Yes, yes, I do know where you mean. Good gracious me what would she want to do that for?'

'She never told me but I would think she's trying to shake Bob off. He's enough to get on anyone's nerves after a while, even hers.'

Mr. Sanderson looked unconvinced.

'Your mother's called in a couple of times Harriet,' Clive suddenly popped up.

'Mummy? What did she want?'

'Oh just wanted to show me where to find the cat food should it decide to wander back.'

'Oh right, I'm sorry about that Clive, she can be a bit over fussy at times.'

'Oh no, not at all. I think she's happy enough your house is occupied by someone of suitable professional status. Anyway how are you settling in to your new place?'

'Adore it thank you Clive, it's perfect, just right in every way.'

'Don't get too comfortable Harriet!' Mr. Sanderson said, smiling. She didn't answer, for the moment she knew she was more comfortable there than she'd been anywhere, in years.

They sat in amicable silence as Clive took the short cut down the single lanes to the town bypass and then onto the motorway.

The car hummed into the outside lane, Clive overtaking everything in sight, each with their thoughts were rudely interrupted by what sounded like a rock band tucked away in the shoulder bag at Tricia's feet. 'Oh there's my moby, excuse me everyone while I answer it,' she said struggling to retrieve it.

'Oh hello, it's a bit difficult to talk right now.'

'Yea OK it sounds like you're on the road, where are you off to?' Barry asked.

'Oh we're all on our way to Falmouth, we're bringing Mr. Sanderson's boat back tomorrow.'

'Well that's certainly a turn up for the books, Andy and I are just about to set off.' She strained her ears.

'Set off where?'

'Falmouth, we've got business to do. We're hoping to kill two birds with one stone, could even be three. Any chance of meeting up?'

Tricia, more than a little flustered looked across to Harriet, trying to mouth who it was.

'You two been given a lift by the fuzz recently?' Barry interjected, the memory instantly setting Tricia wobbling.

'It's vital Tricia, we can't not utilise this fortuitous opportunity. I'll phone you when we get there later. We'll pick you up.'

'But...'

'No *buts* just think of something, make an excuse, this won't take more than a few minutes. You'll be back before you know it. See you Tricia.'

He terminated the call, Tricia left floundering, Harriet left wondering what on earth was going on.

Chapter 64

'But we're not in Falmouth, Barry, we're here in Churndale Village, I'm standing outside "The Lantern Box Hotel" with Harriet. She's not too pleased about all this you know. We were supposed to be sleepin' on the boat tonight but they decided they're going to stay here.'

'Where the hell is it?'

'Oh `ang on a minute Barry. I know it's in Dorset. What's the name of this place again Harriet?'

Barry tapped the side of his phone rapidly losing patience.

'It's called Churndale Village. We're in Dorset, not far from where we went campin' with the school. It's just that Clive has to leave his car here. His brother's giving us all a lift down to the boat tomorrow.'

'A lift down Tricia, it'll take you the morning at least to get there.'

'Oh no Barry we're getting off to a very early start.'

'Right, we'll switch it, we'll do Plymouth first, phone me the minute you get there.'

'But he'll be wanting to get away, Barry, I don't see that we're going to have time.'

'Make your excuses, he's going to have to get the thing rigged and all the rest of it. I promise this won't take more than half an hour. Just find out the berthing quay, we'll only be parked round the corner up one of the side roads.'

'OK Barry we'll do our best.'

'Don't you two let me down. We're onto something big here, very big.'

'What's going on Tricia?'

Harriet wasn't liking the sound of the snippets she'd heard. Wasn't up for having her tranquillity disturbed right now.

'Barry says it'll only take a few minutes, they're onto something big. We can't let them down, we'll just have to go and hope he's as good as his word.'

'I don't see it, Mr. Sanderson won't want us going missing, he'll want an early start and even then he'll have to stagger the journey, as much as he thinks he can, I don't think he'll be able to do it in a day.'

'Well we're supposed to be helping Barry. You do want him to get to the bottom of all this, don't you? You don't really know what he'll turn up that might make you feel better. In any case you want that painting back, it might be something to do with that. They're not going to leave us high and dry, now are they? Clive wouldn't let him do that to us.'

'I hope you're right Tricia, I just hope you're right on all counts. So where did you say they're going?'

'They're on their way to Plymouth now to track down Caroline Worsnip's Aunty Sharon. I don't suppose she'll be able to tell them much, though.'

Chapter 65

Sharon Black tidied up, part closed the bedroom door, gently descending the stairs to get on with quickly clearing the lounge. She looked at her watch, turning the oven heat down on the lasagne. All set now she laid the dinner table for two as was customary for her to do almost every weekend since her niece Caroline Worsnip moved back to Wirral. She popped a small posy of flowers into a tiny glass vase, placing it on the table along with her best cotton napkins This evening, however, she was making a special effort knowing Caroline to be pretty distraught over losing her job. Things never seemed to go well for her niece and confident Caroline would stand a far better chance of finding work there, this weekend she decided to make a concerted effort to try to persuade her to come back. She stood back to admire the table then jumped at the doorbell chiming. Caroline always caught the same train, arrived in the same taxi, it was unusual for her to be ten minutes early. It was four minutes past seven, not a quarter past. The rain splattered against the side windows as she secured the door chain. She needed to be careful, there'd been a couple of incidents of late in Brambles Close, she had no intention of being taken for a ride like her next door neighbour. A couple of guys in the dark, it was, in the rain, one leaning on the windowsill tipping a tube like bottle hidden up his sleeve creating a flow of water enough to convince her the torrent was gathering from the far side of the gutter. The poor woman ended up committed to buying not only new fascias and gutters but a house full of new windows, too. She only became suspicious when she spotted the narrow bottle lying on the grass.

Gingerly Sharon Hawker pulled the door back the twenty centimetres or so the chain would allow. Two guys! She was ready for them!

'No thank you, I'm not interested in double glazing, these windows were only done last year. Oh yes and it's raining. I know what tricks you've got up your sleeve now bugger off and get your bloody foot out of the door or I'll phone the police.'

'We are the police madam, may we come in?'

'Oh no your fucking not. Ah their's my niece.'

'CAROLINE CALL THE POLICE NOW.'

Caroline rushed up the drive, swinging them one with her heavy shopping bag then delivered a hearty whack with her case catching Barry's backside hard enough to have him unwittingly dislodge his foot.

Sharon whammed the door closed to quickly open it again piling Caroline and her luggage inside, snatching at the newspaper clearing the letterbox so she could poke her two fingers through just to make sure they'd got the message.

'Bloody hell Barry, she's an Amazon that one. Let's get going! What you doing down there, what's that bloody thing you're picking up now?'

'Let's get the fucking hell out of here Andy. We've got all we need. Let's hope we're as successful in the morning.'

Chapter 66

'Are you comfortable in the back there, Terry? A rose between two thorns eh?'

Terry laughed, he was used to his brother's wise-cracking. 'We're OK aren't we girls? Enjoy the meal last night?'

'Oh yes thank you, we did didn't we Harriet? We have dined in your restaurant before. It was when Harriet and I escaped from that prison camp down your road. Of course we did have Rapping Hammer after us. Do you know Clive, I still haven't got my "save Venice" tin back from that yob.'

'Ah is that the rock star, weren't we supposed to be taking him on the next Fastnet race Joris? I'm sure one of us promised him.'

Mr. Sanderson turned, frowning. 'Never in a thousand years Terry. The boy's complete rabble, I'd rather join the first mission to Mars than do that.'

Terry laughed, 'So you weren't thinking of asking him to crew for you today then Joris, not for a bit of practice? It might have been enough to get us off the hook, I don't think that lad's going to let go of it you know.'

'We'll see about that, I'll have him behind bars first.'

'Oh yes you do that Mr. Sanderson, he's horrible. he calls me "Chick Lips" and poor Harriet gets "Mummy Mama". He's wanted in Italy for defacing all those statues, they're on the run, with my tin, too. I think they've gone into hiding and I hope they stay there until they get the jail.'

Harriet was finding it difficult to engage with Tricia's humour, she was most concerned at leaving the party. She'd made such a play for going on the trip, Mr. Sanderson wasn't going to be understanding any of it. She racked her brains trying to think of an excuse to get away then the obvious occurred to her, they would just need to pop to the high street for something which was in essence what they were about to do. She looked out of the window, recalling the first time she'd gone down to Falmouth with Mr. Sanderson, they'd been to the Palace for the Investiture, dazed she'd expected to be driven home by Tarquin Bridgewater, but Mr. Sanderson had sprung the most wonderful surprise wanting her to join him on his fabulous yacht "Mare Libertas". It proved to be the most exquisite time of her life, a couple of heavenly days. He'd made love to her on the sand, the water lapping, she'd never forget the passionate intensity, the need for him, the deep, deep release, their whole beings reborn into one powerfully beautiful consummation, orchestrated in the splendour of the sunset pouring its whole spectrum of colour to the turquoise sea. His strong profile in her view, drawn to it now, his blonde hair curling at the crewe neck of his navy sweater, his hand lifting, his Rolex maritime watch perfectly reflecting all he was, all he is. This gorgeous,

gorgeous man, Harriet could feel herself going, suddenly her world made complete sense. Carrying his baby, marriage, she was convinced he'd live in her new place. His voice, chatting intermittently to Clive, beautifully spoken she was loving listening to him. His past, well it was nothing to do with her, after all she'd pretty much done the same self thing to him as Caroline, how could she stand in judgement? All Caroline wanted was to marry him, she could well understand that. He'd been having to deal with massive aggravation, excluded from seeing his own daughter. No wonder it wasn't something he'd wanted to tell her about. But why, oh why did he want to use the same name Amber? She knew that was always the place she'd wanted to be but it suddenly occurred to her there maybe another reason, though completely coincidental, even she could see the strong likeness to herself in the portrait . His daughter had not in any way taken after Caroline, only after him. If they had a girl there was a strong possibility of her resembling Amber. For all he knew his little girl may never be found, was it so wrong, was it not too much to ask of her given the significance of the 'amber' concept for them, he should want that name for his next child, be it a girl. No she understood now, completely understood, wanted to marry him before the baby started to show to the rest of the world. She closed her eyes, her mind drifting to their wedding day.

Chapter 67

'Oh Clive would you mind letting Harriet and I out very near to the town? It's just that I need to go to the chemist for something, we can walk back, Harriet knows the way, don't you Harriet?'

Clive glanced across, looking for the OK from Mr. Sanderson.

'Well I suppose if you must, you must but do be quick,' he warned. 'There's three of us to get her rigged and all the rest of it so it's not going to be taking very long.'

'Oh no Mr. Sanderson, we won't be very long will we Harriet?'

'Shouldn't think so,' Harriet agreed, surprised at how well ahead of the game Tricia was. 'Is there anything we can get for the trip while we're there?'

'Oh pick up a couple of bottles of wine Harriet, and some bread and milk. That should do it, I've seen to the rest,' Terry finished.

'Yes indeed Terry, that was most kind of you to organise supplies, save us a great deal of time, thank you.' Mr. Sanderson turned to smile just as Clive swerved left into the park and ride.

'Oh we didn't want to go here did we Harriet?'

'Just get on that bus parked over there and it will drop you off in the high street.' Clive directed.

'And don't get back on it the pair of you,' Mr. Sanderson added, 'you walk towards the end of the high street and any left turn will get you to the harbour. You do remember where the berth is don't you Harriet?'

They scrambled out either side of Terry, waving the car off as if to speed its departure.

'Come on Tricia, he's started the engine, I haven't got a clue the way to town from here.'

Panting they jumped aboard, Harriet scrambling for her purse. Looked down the aisle, standing room only.

'Let's hope Barry won't be keeping us too long, now we've got shopping to do, wish I hadn't mentioned it now. Have you really got to go to the chemist Tricia, you made it sound so authentic?'

'Well I am a couple of days overdue, I wouldn't mind knowing Harriet. Gosh this thing's bumpy, I'm glad we haven't got to climb back up this hill.'

Harriet barely heard, she gasped, wasn't sure if she'd been hallucinating, convinced she just seen the tail end of Rapping Hammer disappear round the corner. She pushed it from her mind, refusing to allow her imagination to get the better of her.

The single decker wound down narrow roads, to halt with a disgruntled snort at a crowd of people anxious to board.

'Well I didn't see them parked at the bottom of that road we'd better try the next one,' Harriet said, feeling uneasy.

'This way girls!' Harriet felt a hand on her shoulder, turned to see Barry looking anxious.

'How did you know we'd be here?'

'Spotted you both standing on that thing.' He pointed to the bus, engine still cranking away.

'We'd better crack on. Breaklock Apartments are on the other side of the headland, that way. He pointed in a north-westerly direction before steering them across the road towards the car.

'You said you didn't see it Harriet.'

'I still can't, how long have you been here Barry?'

'Just! We slid in alongside the bus. We're on yellow lines too. No Tricia not that. We're in Andy's car, here, this blue one.'

'Well you might have warned me Barry, Harriet and I could have been wandering round here for ever. We're in a hurry you know, we've got to get back. We only said we needed to go to the chemist.'

In and away, Andy impatient, jamming the accelerator to the floor to get the car up the hill as fast as oncoming traffic would allow.

'Have you made any progress towards finding Amber, Barry? Is this what this is all about?'

He turned to Harriet. 'Good steady progress, we're on a two-pronged trail at the moment. This one's more about locating that painting. I need to see it. I need to know it's definitely mine before I can take this any further. I'm hoping the guy's in. I want you two to distract him, get him out of the flat while I nip in. I'll go ahead of you, take the lift up, then wander down the stairs. We'll park a bit away from the place.'

'Golly Barry, he's bound to close the door behind him even if he does come out.'

'Not a problem, you should know that by now.'

'But he might have a dog.'

'If he's got a dog it will follow him out.'

'But anyone could be in that place, you'll get caught.'

'Lives alone Harriet.'

'He might have visitors or a woman in bed.'

'I'll take that chance. I'm hoping not to have to touch bedrooms. In any case the painting was stolen. For all intents and purposes I can forge a legitimate case for being there if I have to, I've still got my ID card.'

'Why don't you just use it then?'

'I said "forge" Harriet, we are still on notice but strictly speaking we're only allowed to use them during the course of the department's work.'

'Why don't you just ask him about it?'

'Because in truth a confidentiality was broken when I obtained his address. The guy's not going to take it lightly given the subject of the painting. This is the only way to approach it.'

'So what are we going to say Barry, I hope you've thought of something?'

'He's on the ground floor right on the front, first left off the main entrance hall. You're both going to ring the doorbell and ask for directions. It always works, people can't resist walking out to show the way, especially when it's for two pretty girls. Just ask him to do that if he's not shaping up. Andy will start walking towards you to stop and chat, while I'm wandering out of the apartment block as people do. I'll just carry on walking back to the car.'

'Oh thank you Barry you've never actually said that before. We'll do our best won't we Harriet?' Harriet couldn't bring herself to answer, wasn't feeling best pleased with Barry at all.

'Well I hope it goes to plan and it doesn't all turn nasty,' she said.

'Trust me Harriet, I'll have you back in town in ten minutes flat.'

Chapter 68

'Where the hell have those two got to? We were ready to sail half an hour ago. We need to be away if we're not going to catch that deepening low chasing our tail.' Joris Sanderson looked at his watch. 'We'll give them five more minutes. Would you mind hanging back for them Terry? Get them to the station, they can get the train back. They know exactly what we're up against.'

Clive went down below, made a final check, anxious, he wasn't happy about leaving them, thought Joris was being a bit hard.

'Look Joris we don't know what's happened to them, I'm not so sure about ditching them just like this. If you must leave without them then you and Terry sail the boat back. That's probably the best option anyway given the weather forecast. I'll wait here and drive them back. Would you be up for that Terry? It would of course mean driving all the way back to Dorset but you'd certainly be putting my mind at rest.'

'No, no, not at all, it makes good sense. Not exactly as onerous as bringing her back from the Med what with the Straits of Gibraltar and the Bay of Biscay, this is a cinch. We won't even need to safe harbour for the night Joris, we'll just take her straight through.'

Joris Sanderson twisted his mouth in indecision, cognisant his fury was in danger of leading him to the irrational. He pulled himself up, sharp. 'Right we'll do that, thanks Terry.'

'I'll get back to the car then Joris,' Clive said, 'Safe sailing, keep in touch, get off while the weather's still half-decent.'

He marched away glancing back to see Terry at the slip lines then turned, in his face a gang of yobs shouting, screaming hurtling towards the jetty. 'That's them, there's the fuck heads we're after. He'll get us out of this mess once we've finished with him.'

Clive, horrified, made a snap decision to get back to the car as fast as possible.

Mr. Sanderson looked up, glad Clive had got past them, quickly he moved to the other slip line as he rapidly recognised the fast approaching rabble.

'Speed it up Terry, we're about to be visited.'

'Done, here pass it over Joris, you take the wheel.'

Terry tugged to release the last of the sliplines just as Rapping Hammer joined the jetty, steaming towards them yelling 'Jump bards, fucking jump.' Joris with heart in mouth and engine running, looked back to see the three of them leap from the pontoon, missing the deck by a fraction, as he moved away with the three of them sliding from the gunwales down the side of the boat plunging to the ice-cold water. Under sail they watched them, soaked, scrambling up the legs of the jetty being hauled to safety by the rest of the gang.

'Close shave Terry,' Joris declared. 'How the hell did they know we were sailing today?'

'So you know them do you Joris?' Then it dawned on him. 'Wasn't that the Fastnet guy?'

'Too right it was!'

Chapter 69

They stopped something short of the apartment, the girls hanging back a little to give Barry chance to get ahead.

'Shall we go now Harriet?' Tricia whispered, nervously.

'Just give him a bit longer,' Andy advised.

They sat, the adrenaline curdling their nerves, urging them to flight.

'Take it slowly, the apartments are a new build right on the quay, you can't miss them.'

'Right Andy,' said Harriet, panicking, failing to comprehend how they'd got themselves caught up yet again.

Andy watched as they dawdled along the quay until they disappeared round the bend. He looked at his watch trying to judge how long each stage of the exercise would take.

'I wish we weren't doing this Tricia,' Harriet said. 'I just don't think Mr. Sanderson will wait.'

'Oh don't be worryin` about that Harriet, let's get this bit over and done with first. Look there it is, we're here and no sign of Barry, he must be in there now. Let's stand outside on the cobbles and look as if we're lost, you never know the guy might already be lookin` out of the window.'

Standing on the cobbled path edging the forecourt Tricia first scratched her head, pointed up the way, then across, turning on her heels demanding Harriet do the same.

'Best not overdo it Tricia, we don't want to get the attention of any pedestrians.'

Distracted she immediately looked towards the apartments, saw a short rotund gentleman coming towards them, balding, sporting a thistle of black hair above each ear.

'It's him Harriet, it's him he's coming out to help us.'

'No Tricia, no, don't say anything he's just taken a short cut, he hasn't come out of there.'

'That's the way to catch flies my dear,' he joked as he walked past.

'Oh come on Tricia let's get this doorbell rung, I just can't be doing with any of this.'

Pushing the doors open they looked anxiously around the large square entrance hall before pressing the bell to apartment No.1, both jumping as a tall silver-haired angular looking gentleman instantly materialised.

'Oh we're lost, we're so sorry to bother you but we're looking for the park and ride, and we can't find it at all, can we Harriet?'

'Now let's see, you're a long way out of town, oh dear let me think.'

He stepped out, feeling for the key in his pocket before closing the door behind him.

'Well we thought we would like to see the harbour and then decided we would try walking back instead of catching that rattly little bus, it was packed full, we had to stand all the way didn't we Harriet, and now we're lost. We're awfully sorry we thought we'd better not go any further and there was nobody in the road to ask.'

'No problem at all young ladies, here, it's better if I come right down there's a bend in the road which makes it impossible to show you from here.'

From the last of the second flight of stairs Barry looked over the banister to the large square hall and shot down as soon as the three were clear of the entrance. In a flash he'd manipulated the lock with something the size of his thumb nail. In he went from room to room, glancing the walls, gingerly opening the doors to the two bedrooms. Nothing, absolutely nothing. Defeated, he made to go, irritated at wasting time with no sign of the painting anywhere. Grateful at least for the absence of a dog, he suddenly remembered the kitchen and pushed the door open, cursing as all hell let loose from a snappy little white terrier leaping five inches high from its basket, yapping enough to alert the whole of Cornwall. Instantly he closed the door on it, scooting out of the place, gently closing the door behind him, before trying to look casual as he proceeded down the hall to the entrance doors.

'So we go that way do we?' Tricia queried, pointing in an exaggerated fashion back the way they'd come, holding back a wave to Andy purposefully striding towards them.

'Look let me just nip in and get the car keys. I'll run you back to the park and ride no trouble.'

Airing a sense of satisfaction he marched away, totally oblivious to the guy with the dark shoulder length hair sauntering out. Barry sensed it was him, quickened his pace. With just a brief stop on the cobbles he took a quick look right to see Andy sprinting after the girls making for the car.

'Well done Barry,' Harriet trembled, as he finally jumped in. 'I'm so relieved the whole thing's over.'

'I wouldn't exactly say that, I got nowhere, no sign of it, the whole exercise has been a waste of time.'

'It may not be Barry,' Harriet reassured, still panting. 'He said something about me looking identical to the girl in the painting he'd recently bought. He said it was incredible the likeness. Said he'd show us the painting but it was now hanging in a gallery in Holland. He said they appreciated liberal art over there. He said he was getting a fabulous sum for leasing it to the gallery and rightly so given the amount he'd paid for it at auction.'

Barry immediately recovered, 'Right Harriet, think very carefully and run all that past me again if you wouldn't mind.' Exhilarated, he could hardly believe his luck.

'Tricia you tell him exactly what happened, you're far better at detail than me.'

Their voices receded as she thought of Rapping Hammer, convincing herself it was him. She wondered what on earth they were doing in Falmouth. Wondered what her and Tricia could do if they'd hi-jacked the boat. If Mr. Sanderson and Clive were now hostages? Unable to deal with the terror of it all she back-tracked, deciding she'd imagined it all.

Chapter 70

'It was a crazy idea you lump-head, we were lucky to find the flamin` boat never mind jump aboard.' Rox held his dripping arms out like a scarecrow just been for a dip. 'We could have expired in that lot and I didn't want your hand up my bleedin` arse either pushing me up that jetty leg.'

Rapping Hammer quickened his pace.

'Get movin` you prick, we were all hangin` off the end of it while that bleeding boat of his pummelled us with a bloody tsunami. Pair of toffee-nosed fuck-arsed gits.'

'You've just said that fuck-head, it's the bleedin` dope it's coming out of those purple lookin beets sprouting either side of your `ead, I'm not goin` with any more of your arse hole schemes.'

'So what else do you suggest Rox? You haven't come up with a better idea. We're losing gigs hiding, we need to be exonerated like happens to them in high office so we can get fuckin` rockin` again. We've got to think of something better than this.'

Rex shivered, 'I know,' he shouted trying to catch them up. 'We've got to think of something threatening, we need a bit of leverage, power, man.'

'Are you struggling to catch up wearing them squelchy pixie boots Rex? Just move your arse, Rax, Rix and Roxy are flashing along.'

'They're fucking dry, aren't they? The sly buggers held back, just us sponge heads go falling in.'

'When's that arse-hole's daughter's wedding, did you say Rappin`? 'Dunno, I kept the paper though, why?'

'Just a thought, just a thought, you can pay me for my thinks when I'm good and ready.'

'Splash the mash Rexy, wasn't it you had the good idea we'd fill our poly money bags with flour fleecing the street druggies zero? And what happened? They all came tearing after us with white noses, riding their fury like stallions on hot coals, that's the only high you gave them. I don't think we're in the market for emptying your brain cells again right now, Rex.'

From his rear mirror Clive could see them approaching decided to move along. He turned the key, shifted through the gears slowly driving forward hoping for another parking slot. No luck, he was forced to move, got shunted up a one way street then a right turn through the town then into the system of no return.

'Oh bugger, where's this leading now?' He cursed as he stop-started his way through the traffic wondering just where the hell the girls had got to.

Then he remembered the 'Park & Ride', followed a couple of signs thinking at least he could bus back into town to try to find them.

'Thanks for the help girls,' Barry announced, drawing into the kerb to halt on yellow lines outside the chemist.

'You're not leaving us here are you Barry? What if they've gone without us? We've still got shopping to do yet.' Harriet panicked.

'We've got work to do haven't we Andy? Time's money for us right now. They're never going to go without you anyway, You'd never forgive him and lover boy wouldn't want that.' Barry retorted.

'I'm on yellow lines here, good-bye girls, see you!' Andy revved the engine hard, both laughing as they shot off.

'Bloody `ell Harriet what's their game? Not very gentlemanly I'd say. Just wait until I tell my Clive. Handy though we're right outside the chemist.'

'Do you have to Tricia? I'd rather we go straight to the boat, that's if it's still there. I'm furious with Barry just dropping us off like this, I don't know what we'll do if they've already sailed.'

'Oh it won't take a tick Harriet, just in and out for one of those blue test thingies. I'm so excited I can `ardly wait. Wouldn't it be good if we're both pregnant together? You'll have to stop keeping Joris danglin` though Harriet, he's not going to be waitin` for ever.'

'Let's just get it then Tricia but I'm not going to do any shopping.'

'Oh but we'll have to otherwise what excuse are we goin` to make?'

Full carrier bags in hand they crossed the road, Harriet nervously looking at her watch.

'We can take a short cut through here, I think, round the back of this café and straight onto the harbour. They turned into the narrowest of streets, pretty houses huddled in terraces, hanging baskets still colourful, trailing their flowers into the strengthening breeze.

'The wind's getting up Tricia, I bet you any money they won't be hanging round waiting for us, not with the forecast the way it is.'

'My Clive would never go without me, don't worry, they'll be there. I thought you said this was a short-cut Harriet?'

'Yes, I remember, it bends at the bottom there to the harbour. Come on Tricia let's get a move on.' They paused for a second, heads down, both swapping hands on their heavy carrier bags.

'Bloody hell Harriet look at that lot comin` round the corner. It's Rappin` Hammer and the whole gang of them. Looks like they're soaking wet to me.'

'Run, Tricia run, quick we'll just have to go back to town we don't want to be got by them,' Harriet panicked.

They turned, heads down, hoping they wouldn't be spotted; bags in hand, struggling towards the town, running, rushing, panting, puffing, all the time hearing their loud mouthed insulting bellows through the crowds.

'I can hear them they're catchin` us up.'

'Look there's a bus in Tricia, quick cross over, we're just going to have to catch it. Quickly before it goes.'

They flew, knew the yowling gang were less than ten yards away and fast catching up. Almost on top of them they just managed to jump aboard to see the driver close the doors on them all.

Harriet reached for some change.

'Did you see that gang of louts? Needn't think they're getting on here, messing my bus up. They looked like drowned rats the lot of them.'

Harriet nodded, panting her way to a seat.

'Look there's the next one coming down now,' Harriet could scarcely get the words out. 'They're bound to catch that one, what will we do then?'

'Get a taxi Harriet, here just let me write that number down quick. It's on the side of that bus, there.'

The two vehicles almost collided to a halt. Harriet glanced sideways, through splattered windows she could see incoming passengers beginning to stand in order to get off. She didn't notice the gentleman still seated on the bus, staring at her through two sets of windows, more interested in her bus than his own.

'Damn, that's them!' Clive almost said out loud as the two buses hauled away, scraping each other in the process.

Moving towards the terminus he sat in uncomfortable resignation unaware of the familiar gang on the corner, dripping wet, waiting impatiently for his bus to turn around.

Chapter 71

Tricia fumbled with her bag unearthing her phone in a flurry of white tissues.

'Let's hope they've got a spare cab. We need it to be there just as soon as we get off this. We're not up for being dragged off to their horrible van. Here, read it out Harriet.'

She watched Tricia pump in each vital number, hardly daring to breathe, fingers crossed they'd send someone straight away.

'Yes it's the park and ride in Falmouth,' urged Tricia waving her phone up and down at Harriet, 'Quick he's saying there's more than one, which one was it?'

Harriet blanked, thought to tap the suited gentleman sat in front for the answer, the poor man instantly turning to catch a clout on the side of his nose. Tricia hurriedly apologised, realigned the talking weapon, throwing into it all the urgency she could muster. 'We're going up the hill now, we're on the route that starts just behind the chemist's on the high street in the town.'

'With you, give us ten.'

'Ten what Harriet?' She turned it off, resumed apologising to the empty seat in front.

'Where is he?' She whispered to Harriet.

'Up at the front talking to the driver.'

'Oh eh, we don't want any inquisitions we've got to be off this and into that cab. Oh we're nearly there. I remember that B&B on the corner, how come we didn't notice that taxi place next to it? I hope it's the one I've just called.'

'Probably because we didn't need one then,' replied Harriet grasping at the bulging carrier bag.

'It's just down here, we turn left and it's on the right. Get your stuff Harriet and keep your head down.'

They struggled off the bus trying to decide on the best place to be, where out of site would still allow them to see the taxi. Wedged between the boundary wall and the sub-station, they bent as low as they could, given the space.

'I do 'ope it hurries up Harriet, I'll be stuck like this soon. Oh no that bus is back, I can hear it, Rappin' Hammer and that lot are bound to be on it. Quick pass that bag, let's pile them up to make them look like rubbish. Get down as far as you can.'

'It's driven in, but where on earth's the taxi?' Harriet froze in fear. 'Let's get out of here before they all get off, sit the other side of the wall, we can catch it before it drives in.'

Clive Engells, successfully held his own as the driver tried to chase him off the bus at the terminus. He'd had to keep his head down though, in the face of the rabble sat at the back. With his handkerchief over his nose he stepped gingerly from the bus striding away, stretching his neck in the hope of spotting Tricia and Harriet standing by his car. No such luck! He quickly jumped in engaging the central locking system, resigned to driving around the car park in the hope of finding them. 'After all where else could they be?' 'Oh bugger!' He muttered out loud.

'Oh bugger,' I'm supposed to be collecting someone else from here, straight off that bus.' The cabbie growled, pointing back to the park and ride. In unison Harriet and Tricia looked then sank themselves a low as they could into the back seat until the springs almost hit the floor.

'Oh this might be him now, walking over. Stick with it girls I won't be a tick.'

The engine ticked loud in their ears as they ducked their heads between their knees, Clive Engells now heading for out, oblivious, he looked across, spotted their taxi idling in the entrance, beeped the cabbie marching a suited gentleman towards it. On its way, Clive following right behind, yet again peering through two sets of windows, only this time the girls were nowhere in sight.

'Blimey what a corker,' the cabbie said to the guy seated alongside. 'Do you know, that happened to me once. This blumming woman swings me one with her bag as she's fishing for the fare. It went up like a prize strawberry my conk. It's sensitive there, had a real shiner for three weeks. St Ives, did you say?'

The suited gentleman nodded his head. Harriet and Tricia decided to stay just where they were, all the way to St.Ives.

Chapter 72

Joris Sanderson went down below. Motoring they were making good time, past The Lizard now, skirting the north coast of Cornwall before heading NNW and into the Irish Sea.

'No word from Clive as yet.' He called to Terry from the galley, stroking his chin, his blue eyes registering a furious concern. He'd listened into the local news time after time, relieved to hear nothing, yet this stoked his frustration knowing for sure their absence would be entirely due to trivia. He filled the kettle, called up, 'Sorry Terry, just this powdered stuff, enough for now, we'll have to be without after this.'

'Not to worry Joris, we should get her back tonight. Just checked the shipping forecast, the low's fast approaching, in another hour or so we'll be reaching force 6, it might be worth rigging her to get up speed. We'll get more out of her that way.

'Fine Terry, we're going to be needing as much help as we can get. At least the girls won't be having to face it. I'm hoping they haven't met with those vulgar louts, that's the only thing. Still Clive was waiting, they'd have to have walked past him to get to the pontoon.'

'Looks like our Clive's sold on the scatty one. He's talking about marrying her. Apparently she's wanting a divorce, he's certainly the guy to sort that one out. I've never seen him so obsessed.'

'I must admit not a match I'd anticipated but she has her moments does Tricia. Takes all the ribbing but she's certainly made a go of that place.' Joris handed Terry his tea.

'That Starboard Marine North West, Joris? Pleased it's going well. Not much is these days.'

'We've got "The Bean-s-Talk" corner. I put the coffee franchise in and we link it to the parents so it's pretty much a social club. Again we work with the sailing club, you'd be surprised how those kids have taken to sailing, they learn just like that.' He snapped his thumb across the inside of his fingers, tossing his thick blonde hair to one side.

'Oh damn, I forgot to ask Belinda to ask Tarquin Bridgewater if he'd keep an eye on the place, give her a hand whilst we're away. I'd best call him, I'm not too sure I can rely on Belinda right now. She's not exactly in my good books.'

'This the one you were engaged to Joris? What's she doing with herself these days?'

'Other than making herself a right pain in the arse, I wouldn't know but she seems happy enough doing that.' He stood, put his hands in his pockets, flaring his nostrils taking a very deep breath.

'And what about Harriet, Joris, I thought you'd proposed to her, any sign of the wedding?'

'She's another pain in the arse right now, too. Got this Barry Giordano sniffing around her and she won't let go. Had a word with Mac Lyons, the guy went to no end of trouble to get this arsehole relocated, managed it, and he's damned well walked away from the job.'

'Not great Joris, not great. Friends in high places only works by co-operation or coercion. This guy doesn't sound like he's into either, not the sort to be manipulated.'

'No, the swine painted, or should I say contrived a picture to paint of Harriet, stark naked, gave it us as a wedding present. No one knows where the damned thing is. Harriet wants it back as much as I do, to burn it to cinders. According to Harriet, Giordano hasn't a clue either, though I suspect he's on the hunt. This is why I don't understand Harriet. I don't believe she ever posed like that, I just don't get why she lets him get away with it.'

'She may have more chance of getting it back if she stays in touch Joris, you don't really know what her thinking is right now.'

'Well I know what mine is now she couldn't even be arsed to get back to us, here on the boat. It would seem she's got all she wants where she is now and it doesn't include me.' He took another deep breath, narrowed his eyes, 'At least that's one less wedding to worry about.'

Chapter 73

It was ten excruciating minutes before Harriet and Tricia could find the courage to slowly elevate themselves back to their seat, each sliding sideways, remaining low, each with their head resting against the side window, eyes closed as if asleep. Thankfully the cabbie never looked back, drained by the suited gentleman, in the event a verbose character, stalling only to renew his breath. Forty-five minutes later they watched him march his briefcase up the central steps of "Valender Branton Maynard" Solicitor and Commissioner for Oaths.

'You two have been very quiet in the back,' he announced, sliding the glass partition away. 'Of course I wouldn't be hearing you anyway with this closed. Great when I'm wanting a bit of peace. That's the thing about old Bessie, they don't make them like this any more. Now where was it you were wanting to go? A right gabber he was, nose bulging like a big strawberry, didn't stop him gassing though, no wonder I never got chance to find out properly. Was it the harbour down there?' He said, pointing left. 'Always thronging this place.'

'Oh no, we haven't been concentrating, it's Falmouth harbour we wanted, as near to the pontoons as you can get, please. We're sailing back all the way to Wirral aren't we Harriet?'

'They won't still be there,' Harriet despaired.

'In that case I can take you on to Newquay airport, you'll get there well before them if there's availability on the late morning flight.'

'Yes, yes, do that will you, please,' Harriet blurted having no difficulty making the decision.

'Fifteen, twenty minutes'll do it, forty squids between you, how about that? I charged old strawberry conk your fare to here, it was his fault I got diverted. Loaded the likes of them. He didn't exactly miss the boat! Here, I've got the number somewhere. You should be able to book your flights by phone. No, tell you what let me do it for you. Next flight out you want?'

They both nodded, Harriet swiftly locating her credit card while listening to his gabble. 'Flight out 11.30, arrive Liverpool 12.25.' He passed his phone over, it's OK it's got the app, yep you can use your card.'

The last time they did this they were on their way to Venice. Today she was so thankful to be going home. Couldn't wait to get back to her new house. Couldn't wait to start planning her wedding day.

Chapter 74

Clive, distraught at managing to lose both his bride-to-be and Harriet departed from the taxi in front to turn right. Time was getting on and he needed to be getting back. He dithered whether to try the town again, whether or not to go back to the quay, after all that's where he was supposed to be meeting them. He'd never rest if they were down there waiting. He followed the bus down the hill and then the one-way system round the town and out into the harbour driving down as far as he could. Hurriedly he walked along, checking each pontoon between the boats, just in case. Nothing, he rushed back to his car, decided to try Joris, finger on the keys it rang in his hand.

'Ah Joris, I was about to try phoning you, how's it going?'

'Making good progress on the south-westerlies, getting a bit more bounce now but we're winning. What about you? Any sign of the girls?'

'I saw them on the bus back to the park and ride.'

'What the hell were they going back there for?'

'Wouldn't know Joris, though it might have had something to do with the bunch of rats that tried to board your boat. My best bet is they saw them in town so jumped the bus to get away from them. Look there's no point to this, they're not in the harbour anywhere near your berth. That lot were on their way, sat at the back of my bus, they're probably half way home by now, well away from the girls. They might have opted to get the train home. Don't worry Joris, they're big girls now and there's been no bad news.'

'There will be when I get hold of them. They've both got phones, they could at least have tried. Don't you be so soft on them.'

'You're starting to break up Joris. Look I'm going back now. I'll try Patricia's phone and see if I can get some sense. I'll get back if any news. Safe sailing Joris, just get yourselves back in one piece. I'll take care of the landlubbers.'

That was it, without further ado he drove away, wanting to get the journey behind him before ruffling Joris's feathers any further.

Chapter 75

'Not even a smile for Tarquin, who's been ruffling your feathers my dear?' He smiled, pushing hard to open the heavy glass door.

Belinda Oxfordshire reached for her coat, on the verge of closing the place down for the weekend. 'Bloody cheek expecting me to keep this place running single handed while they all swan off to bring his boat back!'

'Pardon my dear, you appear to be talking to yourself. Spill out the problem Belinda.'

'Just closing shop, no staff, he can stick his customers for all I care.'

'Oh I see, it's Joris you're cross with. He phoned a couple of hours ago, it slipped his mind to ask me, though he did tell me he was going to mention it to you a couple of days ago.'

'Oh what good is that now? For goodness sake Tarquin, I can't be doing with it. Look I'm going, I'm not in the mood for chatting right now.'

'But I'm here to give you a hand, that's why I've come my dear. Apparently there's a young couple coming back to view the video, they want to decide which dinghy's right for them. I can hardly serve and be in there at the same time now, can I? I don't think Joris will be wanting to be losing the commission from this sale. There's sailing lessons, too. A tidy package I might say. Come on now you get behind the till my dear and let me see what's what before they arrive.'

She returned her coat to the stand, livid. Sat herself down to immediately dial Caroline. She was away too, everyone was except her and Tarquin Bridgewater. She grunted, replaced the receiver to the chime of the doorbell.'

'Eh our Danny don't you be touchin` those flamin` gloves.'

'Look Mum they've got holes in the fingers like mine.'

'Give them here, now just leave them alone.'

'Can I be of assistance Madam,' said Belinda Oxfordshire looking straight down her nose. 'I think we do actually have those for children.'

'I want some, I want some, ah ay I want some.'

'Stop jumpin` up and down you little bugger, just put those back.'

'Are you here for anything in particular?' said Belinda trying a different tack.

'Oh haven't you heard, our Danny won the silver cup for the best fossil award when they all went camping to what's a place in Dorset.'

'Yea I did and Boss Farmercart's comin` here now, he is `onest. he's bringing all the fossils here, right here now. We're all goin` in there, he's bringin` cakes and Miss you're doin` all the drinks and we're goin` to have a big fossil party. Aren't we Mum?'

Belinda felt quite ill, watched the woman clinging to the handle of the half-open door desperately hoping for their departure. Hadn't a clue what on earth this hyped-up child was going on about. Joris had mentioned nothing!

'Oh look there's Boss Famercart now, look he's getting out of his car. Eh look Mum he's carrying a big box, that's got all them fossils in. It has got all them fossils in, they were in that one at school. I'm going to meet him.'

'You just come back in here our Danny.'

Too late, she fumbled the wrong way, pulling the heavy glass door open Danny escaping into a stream of chattering kids; parents and barking dogs, suddenly appearing from nowhere.

'Tarquin,' Belinda panicked, '*Tarquin*!'

'Coming my dear.'

'No dogs in here, absolutely no dogs!' She flew to the door, whammed it firmly shut against Mrs. Bustard's backside, locking her out with great satisfaction as she watched her fall to a roll off the step.

'You're not locking out the customers are you dear?' Tarquin Bridgewater enquired. 'That's not going to be pleasing old Joris, now is it?'

'Old Joris can just bargger off! I've had it with him and this whole farcking place.'

Tarquin stifled a grin, he'd never heard anyone quite so posh say it quite like that before.

'Yes you're right Mr. Bridgewater, they are customers and I suggest you serve them,' she said hissing into her jacket. 'You let them in just as soon as I'm out of that back door. Just give me chance to start the farcking engine will you!'

Chapter 76

'What's wrong with this bleedin` engine now?' A soaking wet Rapping Hammer, patience non-existent, ground the engine to a complete halt.

'We can't be `anging around here and we don't want this fuckin' thing stuck here.'

'Call the breakdown skids, let's get the hell out of here even if we have to go back stuck on the back of a wagon,' Rex balled.

'Good thinking Bard brain, where do we get a soddin` number from?'

'Isn't there something in the back, hang on let's see.' He grabbed an old newspaper, it didn't take long to spot a national breakdown service.

'Give it here,' demanded Rapping Hammer snatching it. Done!

His moby back in his jacket before he'd hardly taken it out.

'They'll be here in ten. Get the van cleared Bards, we don't want any anti-druggies snoopin` around.'

There in ten it was. Loaded onto the back of the pick-up truck they opted to stay inside.

'We're not allowed gov,' declared the driver, scratching his head.

'Well the hell you won't get us lot in that cab of yours. Look I'm Guy Hammer, the famous rapper, you won't lose out by us.'

'What you saying?'

'How about we put your sticker on the side of our van?'

'I'd be arsed!'

'Alright then free tickets to the next gig?'

'Look mate we're talking spends here. One hundred smackers and no liability mind!'

'You fuckin` shark, you'd better get us all back in one piece. We've got bigger fish to fry than you.'

Chapter 77

The weekend flew by as was usual for Caroline Worsnip. She packed her case, came quietly down stairs, said her goodbyes to Sharon while the taxi parked outside clocked up the minutes. She reached for her mobile, remembering she'd promised to give Belinda a buzz. Put it back changing her mind. She'd wait until she was on the train, she'd been unsettled during her stay with Aunty Sharon, there was something very disturbing about the two guys trying to flog her more windows. No, maybe it would be better not to mention it after all. For the moment her plans were going well, too well to spoil. She didn't want to panic Belinda out of moving to that new development, she was the best route she had as far as Joris was concerned. Her father could come in handy, too, very handy, should things go wrong, though she considered him to be a last resort. By fair means or foul she wanted to solve her problems once and for all and in the doing of this she was determined to override both Belinda and Harriet Glover to win back the affections of Sir Joris Sanderson. She considered him to be rightfully hers, it would take skill and manipulation until he came to the full realisation of that, but she'd pull no punches to get him just where she wanted him to be.

The train whistled away from the station as she made herself comfortable with virtually the top end of the carriage all to herself.

'You mean he actually wiped the floor with you, then went off this weekend leaving you to cope with a whole squad of parents and kids without saying anything?' She gasped at Belinda.

'That's right Caroline, he did just that. Oh he did make a last minute call to Tarquin Bridgewater. The man infuriates me, parked himself in my office under the pretext of achieving it big with some couple wanting a sailing package. He was in there setting up the promo video when this awful woman came in. Her ghastly lad kept trying on the sailing gloves, oh it was such a complete nightmare you wouldn't believe! The woman tripped over me, rolled off the step so I slammed the door on the lot of them and locked it. Came out the back way and left Bridgewater to it. Anyway enough of that, I went to see the show houses again Caroline.'

Caroline Worsnip perked up, this conversation was going exactly the way she wanted.

Chapter 78

'Has Avril not seen the new development going up just down the road from Sir Joris's sailing boutique? You can see it from the bus Violet. You know the road that quickly runs into the country lanes, it's just on the right at the start of the fields.'

'I'm afraid it's Harriet's house she's set her heart on, Frances. The agent says it's being rented right now but they expect an instruction shortly to resume marketing it.'

Harriet's mum pulled the two edges of her lilac cardigan together, the wind whistling down the side paths between the two bungalows, a place often frequented when the desire for gossip or one-upmanship could no longer be contained. Many a time had Violet Moss politely shot her down in flames.

'Well they look like starter homes to me, you know Harriet's house needs a lot of work doing on it. That partner of hers was a good-for-nothing if ever I came across one.'

'As I understand it, he's the one that's finally made the decision to sell, isn't he?' Violet brushed at a few hairs of moss dared to migrate to her elbow as she removed it from the cap on the fence post. The irony wasn't lost on Frances Glover. Moss by name, moss by nature, she couldn't stand the stuff, invasive, slippery, cheeky. Absorbent though, oh yes in spite of all that Frances Glover would be lost without Violet Moss to offload to.

'Oh yes he was supposed to be handing the whole house over to Harriet, his salary was supposed to be that good he just wanted to wash his hands of the whole thing. Oh he's good at doing that Violet, washing his hands of responsibility. He never did right by Harriet anyway let's hope she'll get this wedding done and dusted that's if Sir Joris hasn't changed his mind. She's not in the prime of youth now you know Violet, Joris could have anyone he wanted. James can't understand his sister at all. He plays golf with Joris you know.'

'Yes I think you have mentioned it once or twice before Frances. Now this person renting the house, have you any idea what his situation is? How long he's likely to be there?'

'Oh don't mention that man! He's turned the place into a complete den of iniquity. You've no idea what Harriet's landing looks like now.'

Violet immediately repositioned pressing herself against the fence slightly turning her head to maximise the most efficient delivery of scandal straight to her ear drum.

'Yards of pink ribbon tied round the banister Violet, trailing ends longer than your clothes line, all facing Harriet's cheval mirror he's plonked in the doorway of the little bedroom at the front. Goodness only knows who he's had tied up there and what they've been getting up to. The place is tainted now, completely tainted. Avril and what's his name would be much better off in a nice new build, no sordid history with those.'

'Oh my goodness me but you might be jumping to the wrong conclusion Frances.'

Frances Glover frowned mercilessly.

'Oh no, I popped in there only this morning just to make sure the cat hadn't returned, empty the place was empty, he's obviously gone away for the weekend. Nearly broke my neck up there. I slid on something long and rubbery, saw myself go flying in that damned mirror, landed in a whole box of the things.'

'Well what sort of things were they Frances?'

'You know that place where the bus stops right outside.'

'You mean that place Frances, the one we don't look in?'

'Yes, exactly Violet. Well I sat on the bus the other day, remember on the way back from the WI and watched him go in.'

'You didn't say anything Frances.'

'Just flabbergasted Couldn't believe my eyes when he got out of Harriet's car. He's tainted that, too. Oh I don't know what's going on at all, I'm very shocked Joris should have a friend like that and I can't understand Harriet letting such a pervert over the threshold. Where he picked the girl up, I wouldn't know! What kind of girl do you suppose would indulge in all that filth?'

Chapter 79

The plane had bumped its way from Newquay to Manchester and Harriet never felt quite so relieved to be off and into the taxi, though it felt strange to see Tricia jump out at 4 The Willows. She waved glancing back as she continued to Lower Tideside. She couldn't wait to return to her own place, wanted to do things, make it a cosy love nest for her and Mr. Sanderson. She felt no pangs for 4 The Willows, especially now the girls had fled the nest and married. Rachael and Clare were very happy, they'd had a double wedding in the Seychelles, there was a strong possibility of them all moving up, too. That would be the perfect scenario. She thought about Mark, of how the girls didn't want things to change when they'd announced their double engagement at the Lower Tideside hotel last Christmas. It must have seemed her and Mark were getting in on the act, the last thing they wanted was for their cool unmarried parents to spoil their fun. Harriet sensed they were relieved when Mark changed his mind at the church expecting normality to resume but when it didn't they sidelined the reality giving her no opportunity to tell her side. They were always saying whenever they'd heard from Dad he was having a great time. It hurt, she wondered what they'd think of his new partner, Sasha. She wondered what they'd think of having a new half-brother or sister, too. She hoped they'd be pleased.

Her thoughts moved on, the lights at Starboard Marine North West already? She could hardly believe it, they turned right, she looked across to the new development across the way. With Mark anxious to sell, one of those would have been the best she could have afforded. Oh she was so grateful to Mr. Sanderson for setting her up with Molly and Percy's annexe. She wondered how far he and Clive had got, felt anxious about the impending low pressure, knew for sure they wouldn't have still been hanging round the quayside in Falmouth waiting for them to appear. Decided to give him a call when she got back.

'Where the hell did you two get to? We're moving into a force 6 now we could have been well on our way if we'd got away as planned. Yes Terry, looks like we're going to have to reef the sails…' The line crackled into a series of break-ups before finally expiring. Taken completely aback Harriet decided to let him make the next call. She paced the hall for a while, this was unusual for him but then so were the conditions he was now met with. He'd mentioned Terry, she decided he must have volunteered to stand in for her, 'Probably better to have the three men sailing her in those kind of conditions,' she tried to reassure herself.

The wind was well up now, blowing off the sea, funnelling up the river. She looked for the cat, it was always helpful to feel her soft black fur under her chin in times of anxiety.

'Pepper,' she called. 'Pepper where are you? Ah the doorbell.'

'I saw the taxi Harriet, here you take her. I don't like the idea of them wandering out in this, it's certainly going some now.'

'Oh thanks Molly, come on in. How's it going? Thanks for looking after her,' she said, lifting the cat to her chest.

'Oh yes I will Harriet, I've got some very exciting news for you.'

'Go on Molly, here, sit down. Spill it all out while I put the kettle on.'

'Well…, but I thought you were all coming back tomorrow. Has Joris berthed the boat then?'

'Oh no Molly, they're out in this.'

'Oh good heavens Harriet, I hope they'll be alright. What happened?'

'Tricia and I got caught up in Falmouth, they had to go ahead and it's just as well they did. We flew back from Newquay, I've just spoken to Mr. Sanderson now, they're having a pretty rough passage.'

'Where are they then?'

'The line broke Molly but I imagine they'll be somewhere due north-west of Pembroke.'

'Oh I'll get Percy to keep an eye on the shipping forecast Harriet. It's just as well you and Tricia did miss the boat.'

Harriet smiled, 'As long as he sees it that way.'

'Yes, of course he will. He thinks the world of you Harriet. There's only one thing he wants in life and that's to marry you.'

Harriet smiled, 'Well I'm hoping it's not going to be too long Molly, of course we've got the PM's daughter's wedding to get out of the way but once that's over I'm going to start making plans.' Her words caught up in Molly's cardigan, squashed against her ample chest in one huge hug.

'Oh Harriet, Percy will be so thrilled and as for Daisy Harris she can't wait to see the pair of you married off.'

'Well thanks Molly, you can rest assured I won't be letting any of you down. Mummy will be in her seventh heaven, too, so it looks like the sooner the better.'

'I would say so,' Molly sat herself down, her face catching the steam from the hot cup of tea. 'Now let me tell you my news Harriet, Percy and I have been invited to the PM's daughter's wedding, such a lovely surprise. Would you believe we are special guests courtesy of Sir Joris Sanderson.'

Harriet delighted in Molly's joy, touched her hand. 'I know he would never have left you and Percy out.'

She beamed, 'It was in the paper you know, we read all about it, never dreaming we'd be invited. It'll be very exciting to be aboard the ship. Just fancy Harriet, it's only the rich and famous can afford that. Do you know how the day will be planned?'

'Mac Lyons and family will be staying with Mr. Sanderson, we'll all be leaving from there, sailing across on his yacht, then we join the ship where the wedding ceremony will take place followed by the wedding breakfast. After that we'll all cruise to Anglesey for an afternoon treat high tea served on board. On return close guests will then board the yacht to return for evening dinner at Mr. Sanderson's house.'

'That does sound very nice indeed Harriet.'

'Yes, we've got to get it all fine detailed fairly quickly now, it's only about four weeks away.'

'And then yours Harriet, oh I can't wait for that one.'

Harriet smiled, let go of a very deep breath. 'Neither can I Molly, neither can I.'

Chapter 80

'Bad judgement this Terry,' Joris Sanderson declared as they each fastened their safety harness. 'The wind's funnelling the sea starboard, it's a struggle keeping her away from the coastal shallows. We don't want to get too far port side either, away from shelter. We're losing speed, the trysail's not helping either, best drop the lot, we'll motor her at least until we get the other side of this cove.'

Terry agreed, was very relieved the girls weren't aboard, told Joris as much.

'Quite, quite, though we'd have been an hour ahead had they got back in time. We'd have maximised speed and been half-way up Cardigan Bay by now. Crikey what a day, I suppose we should thank our lucky stars that gang of layabouts landed in the water. What the hell do you suppose they were playing at Terry?'

'Don't ask me, what do you know about them anyway?'

'They're a vile bunch of rappers Harriet and Tricia saw fit to book into Starboard Marine North West, last Christmas. Caused havoc the lot of them and I can't say I've ever really had them out of my hair since.'

'How come Joris?'

'It's those two, just can't keep away from trouble the pair of them. Of course they've still got Mrs. Harrington's "save Venice" tin which she's never done making a song and dance about and apparently the gang are on the run for defacing statues in Venice. They're off their heads most of the time, druggies the lot of them. Totally irrational they could turn up just about anywhere and probably will.' He reached for his ringing mobile.

'Ah let me just get this, I'll go below to take it, you alright at the wheel for a minute, Terry?'

He nodded, pleased with the trajectory he'd managed to achieve.

'Oh right Clive, you're back, had a call from Harriet earlier. I presume you caught up with them, then?'

'No, no, don't know what the hell they were playing at. I came on back, Patricia said they flew back from Newquay.'

'They did what? This is turning out to be one of those 'Top Gear' farces. I'm wondering who the hell else joined the competition. Looks like there's been a mass migration to Falmouth.'

Joris Sanderson had yet to realise he wasn't that far from the truth.

'Right you are,' he continued to a very concerned Clive. 'We're riding the big ones, nothing for it but to just keep going. We're hoping to make land in the early hours.'

The line broke, he was glad to be able to convey at least that much, relieved the girls were safely back knowing full well neither of them would have been capable of handling the intensity of the storm, especially Harriet in her condition. He flared his nostrils, ran his hand through his thick blonde hair, then caught the rail to go back up, cursing, his mind always reverting to that damned painting. He knew as long as Barry Giordano was a part of Harriet's life, it would never be any different. He braced himself to the boat keeling hard over, wind whistling through the rigging, swirling round the mast, howling down the staircase. Each step climbed taking him back to the freezing spray now hitting his face hard. Legs astride he secured the clasp on his safety harness.

'Damn that man,' he cursed, 'bloody fucking artist. This is where the hell he should be!' Words spat to the wind, swept away to the ferocity of the sea.

Chapter 81

Leaving customs behind at Schipol Airport Barry and Andy pushed their way down to the station directly below, running through their plans as the short train journey allowed. It was unlikely they'd locate his painting in the Rijks Museum or any other such like places, but there were many galleries of contemporary ilk in and around Museum Square where they'd decided to try first.

'So it's de pedals, den?' Andy laughed.

'Only way, we're bound to find them, if not outside the station somewhere along the Damrak.'

Barry took a deep breath, he knew it was a long shot but one way or another he was determined to get his painting back. Oh he knew it wouldn't happen right now, no he needed to first locate it then take up the legalities of being the rightful owner. It was up to those who'd auctioned it to sort it. He felt there was a strong case to be made for copyrighted works of art, and he'd raise hell until he got it back.

'Ah, there we go Andy,' Barry declared as they left Amsterdam Central Station. 'Wheels! Look next to that art shop, "Fiet" on that sign and a load of other stuff I don't get.'

'Great, there's another place over there,' Andy said, pointing the other way.

'Which way, any way,' Barry laughed, 'Look there's another in that flat-roofed place just behind there. Come on Andy it's on the way, let's saddle them ponies.'

Amazed at the intricacies of the paperwork but grateful for the guy's linguistic skills, at least sufficient to give them an understanding of the logistics, they set off, pedalling along the "Fietspad" up the main drag. The place was busy, very busy, buzzing with bicyles, people, traffic, trams and on the canals all manner of small craft, barges, river boats, winding their way through the water like spiders in webs, reflecting the layout of the city.

For them a long straight ride then veering left over bridges to take them into Museum Square.

'You know Andy, I've combed these places on line and I've a hunch about that one over there.' Barry lead the way, making a sudden spurt towards the Nieman Galerie, sat at the end of the terrace, a smart three storied building, double sided running to an angle cornering some way into the narrow side street.

He patted his jacket across the inside top pocket. He'd prepared well, all the documentation to prove ownership was in there. They parked, locked their bikes, brushing themselves down in an attempt to enhance their appearance. Through the grand entrance then an indecisive hover on the marble floor. Barry reached to his inside pocket, waving his documentation at a short, somewhat rotund gentleman with a jolly, ruddy face who promptly steered them away from the entrance doors towards the glass topped counter. He laid down the photographed image of his painting, then the shot capturing his signature. The guy whose badge sported the name Henk Van Leyden, in impeccable English asked the questions. Barry fired back the answers as if gunning to save his life.

'You say it was stolen, but we have heard nothing of this?'

'Check for yourself, it was auctioned at Rossenthorn's London, and submitted by the Home Office. The local force send such stuff to auction assuming it's lost property, but in this instance they made no attempt to locate the artist, me.' Barry reached into his inside pocket, producing an array of identity verification.

'Ah yes, we are a branch of Rossenthorn's, that is most fortunate I can check this out. So you are part of the British establishment and you have the authority to claim this painting? We must wait for advice from Head Office before I can contact the owner. How did the auction house acquire this work? A prestigious auction house such as ours would not deal in stolen property.'

It was obvious to Barry this guy hadn't absorbed a thing. Patiently he began the routine again and again until he was sure the message had been understood.

'Right, yes, let me contact Head Office now. I am not able to hand it over to you so easy, you understand? I suggest you browse our gallery for a short time while I make the enquiries.'

Barry gathered his documentation from the counter top, pushing it back into his pocket. He gave Andy the nod as they headed for the central staircase.

'Er, if you please.' Barry turned back to Henk Van Leyden's outstretched hand to which he returned his documentation.

'At least you hit the right place Barry,' Andy enthused, scanning the huge ceiling, vaulted in parts. 'Now where do you suppose it's hanging? This place is awesome.'

'Oh we'll find it alright. I want it back and I want it now Andy. I'm not leaving this place without it,' insisted Barry brushing previous judgement aside.

'Get real, that guy paid a fortune for it, he's not going to part with it just like that.'

'He might when he finds out he's been bidding for stolen property. The Auction houses live in fear and dread of this happening. It's a stroke of good fortune this place is branch of Rossenthorn's. The onus is on them to ensure everything that passes through their hands is bona fide, they're not going to like this at all.'

'Um, I take your point. Did you see that one? Contemporary's hardly a word I'd use to describe this collection. Makes yours look like it's been nicked from a convent.'

'Wish Harriet could see it that way. No sign here, quick let's do the top floor, I don't want to be hanging round any longer than we have to.'

Andy sensed the tension in Barry's voice, the look on his face always the same just before going for the kill.

'Forget it Barry, sink the pistol. The only way you're going to get the thing back is by diplomatic means.'

'Oh I've every intention of being diplomatic Andy, you just watch me. I've just said I'm not leaving here without it. They can sort the ins and outs of it for themselves.'

'You can't exactly take it from the wall Barry. Calm it, we're on those bloody bikes, don't forget.'

'Come on it's not up here, either, let's get down, it's got to be on the ground floor.'

They leapt down both flights of stairs, Barry's long black hair bouncing off the shoulders of his black leather jacket. He knew all he would need in his defence was Sanderson's and Harriet's confirmation it was a gift returned, in Harriet's safe keeping, stolen from her house, the circumstances of which need never be revealed. The onus had been on her to report the theft to the police but in her defence she may not have even realised it was missing at the time. They leapt from the last stair, doubling back to the walls behind, housing the space under the stairs. They met with a well lit bay and facing them, Barry's picture.

They stalled, gasped, gazing in disbelief at the grandeur of the work. How well it sat with its prestigious neighbours.

'Worth every penny Barry,' Andy declared. 'They'll be tagged, so don't even go there.'

'I'm not that stupid Andy. Come on let's find Henk Van Leyden.'

They circled away from the stairs, casually pausing every now and then to take a closer look at a couple of paintings lining the route to the glass-topped counter just a couple of metres away.

'Ah gentlemen, Mr. Giordano, I've made several calls. Head Office fear there may be money laundering implications with this since payment was made directly from Zurich, a private bank, Swiss Capita. Given your connection with the British Crown they have no reason to suspect your motive. I also tell you, the owner, or supposed owner of your work, was unaware of the source from which it came. On hearing of the strong possibility he'd purchased stolen property, he requested it be returned to the rightful owner without question. I did say we would be carrying out further checks on your authenticity and claim but he requested the painting be quietly returned to you. He does not have the desire to involve the police or any of your colleagues Mr. Giordano in verifying your position.'

'Hells bells!' Barry declared, 'I understood it went for around one million British pounds. Why is he prepared to lose that kind of money if the guy's straight?'

Henk Van Leyden smiled, 'You know the business Mr. Giordano, hanging it here gives the acquisition of it a certain credibility, increases its value. This happens more frequently than you might imagine, ill-gotten gains often end up in the purchase of art works, places like ours are a safe haven for them until the owner is confident his money has been well laundered.'

'Yes it crossed my mind Mr. Van Leyden. I thank you and would appreciate you allowing me to sign my work out.'

Barry scrawled his signature along the bottom of a green form, leaving behind the bare essential documentary evidence, then a quick shot of them both from Mr. Van Leyden's smart phone camera.

'Just to protect myself, you understand. You have your painting back, we here were not involved in the sale, Head Office and our client have agreed to return it to you, therefore I see no reason for the transaction to become any more complicated. Now I will get it for you and Jozephine will wrap it in order for you to take it away safely.'

Andy turned to the thump on his back grinning at the delight in Barry's face. 'We've done it, we've done it Andy, we've fricking done it!'

'Great Stuff Barry but I'm not quite getting this. Wouldn't this guy be wanting his lettuce back?'

'Yeah we've deprived him from selling it on if that was his plan and he wouldn't be short of buyers either, there'd be plenty of them in the black book but I don't think that was his game. It's as the guy said, these dodgers invest heavily in art, it tends to appreciate, it may take years but there's always a black market especially for famous artists. No I think he wants this one for himself but he's not willing to get banged up for it. Theoretically this lettuce was never his to lose.'

'Great with you now, Baz. Great stuff - what a stroke of luck eh!'

'Ah, that's them back again, damn it's bigger than I thought, should have known from the measurements, never dreamed I'd be bringing it home.'

Safely through the doors, Barry weighing the bikes up carefully as Andy unlocked them, decided the only way would be to loosely tie the two together leaving sufficient room between them to rest the painting across the handlebars letting the two seats take the weight.

'Go beg a ball of string off Jozephine, Andy, she won't mind, we should be able to tie it on,' Barry grinned holding them together, as if protecting them, like a mother just given birth to twins. He waited and waited, still the glow of his achievement tempering his impatience but not his desire to keep the bell sat at his fingertips on the right handlebar ringing for Britain.

'You could hear that thing dinging away in there, like Noddy's hat, you know!' Andy declared, a length of wound rope swinging from his elbow.

'Bloody hell, you been harvesting the hemp with Jozephine, you've had time enough to make that lot?' Barry laughed.

'Only wish I had Baz, wow she's a goer that one!'

'Get tying Andy, rope the frames first then the picture and hurry up my arms are dropping off.'

Half pulling, half pushing their improvised trolley, pedals frequently entangled, pedestrians dodging, irritated, in native tongue gabbling thunderous curses at them, still they preferred to push on rather than stopping to rework the rope. Eventually they came to a halt at the end of the main drag, then two sets of crossroads before their final destination; the hire shop that had obliged them.

'Come on Andy, now, quick and watch out for these tram lines.' Reluctant to relinquish all thoughts of Jozeline, Andy barely heard, anxious to cross he veered the unwieldy improvisation straight into the tracks. Had it been by intention, they could not have gauged the width better.

'Oh sod what the hell's up now, this bloody thing won't budge!'

'There's a fucking tram coming straight at us lift the bloody thing Andy. Pull now as hard as you can. Five seconds, one nearly derailed tram and three tyres later, dodging every form of transport imaginable they made it to the other side of the road, gasping outside the cycle-hire shop. They watched the red tram go by, balancing the flipped tyre precariously half over the edge of the moving roof.

Barry tried the door, no one at home. Painting quickly released, bikes shoved into slots between others on the stand, they pooled their spare cash into the envelope made spare by relinquished documentation, hoping their hurried compensation would suffice. They rushed on towards the station, Andy curling the rope round his arm as they went. Traffic dodging led them a diagonal course to the small art shop just to the left of the station.

'Just a quick look in the window Andy, we've seen nothing of the place yet.'

'It wasn't supposed to be a jolly Baz, but it's just turned out to be a sodding nightmare! One quick look and let's get that train and this bloody picture back to the airport.'

Barry barely heard, nose against glass he was absolutely astounded. A shiver caught his spine.

'Hey Andy, look at this! Just look at this! Would you ever have believed it?'

Andy paled, he had no choice but to follow him into the shop.

Chapter 82

Harriet enjoyed her morning walk to the village shop just five minutes down the lane. It had been simply a bungalow for many years until Bill and Sue Cartwright arrived, spotting the potential, surprised that none before had acted on the lack of a store convenient for local residents. Besides, along a short track facing the river, it took her to where she loved to be, just standing watching the river flow to the open sea. The island still, waiting for the incoming tide, proud of its twice daily independent stance.

It was a gentle, autumn day, the sun warm for late September, she'd walked back; in her mind every inch of the way pushing the pram she'd be needing, thinking about Mr. Sanderson, their wedding day. How happy they'd be in her new place. Ready to settle down, ready to put the turmoil and trauma of the last couple of years behind her.

It had been a few weeks now since they'd all got back from Falmouth. Mr. Sanderson and Terry had arrived late Sunday morning, forced to take overnight shelter. Dawn and a fair wind had seen them making good headway home. Terry had been pleased enough to drive back to The Lantern Box Hotel in his own car, just as Clive Engells had been pleased to receive his new one. Joris Sanderson was, of course, delighted with his Mercedes-Benz SLS AMG, though Harriet, conscious of seeing less of him was beginning to feel he was perhaps just a little too delighted, as her occasional weekend visits usually resulted in a cup of tea with Daisy Harris and neither sight nor sound of Mr. Sanderson and his metallic silver voluptuous sports car. Still Mrs. Harris would constantly reassure her of Joris's deep, unfailing love for her. It had been the same at school, too. Hardly there, she'd pretty much taken over the running, much to Danny Bustard's displeasure, though fair to say according to Susan Curtiss they were getting along just fine now. Harriet decided he'd just fallen into the habit of pulling his bottom lip whenever he saw her. A bit like Ross Farquerhart, he didn't sit comfortably with Harriet running the school, either. How many times did she wish she'd never had that two second fling with him on the cliff top, during the school camp in Dorset, never realising that had nothing at all to do with it. No Ross Farquerhart simply dreaded being kidnapped by Rapping Hammer again, dreaded the PM's daughter's wedding, just wanted the whole thing over and done with. He felt so much safer with Joris Sanderson at the helm.

Rapping Hammer was of course plotting his next move, that prick, Ross Farquerhart would have no place in it, he needn't have worried. Ross had already decided, logically they couldn't need him for anything, but still that niggle, hindering the pulling together of his magnificent Phd thesis.

The wedding plans were now well in place. Mac and Ida Lyons desperately hoping the media would fall for the double bluff and they'd all get away with minimal publicity. Harriet was pleased the plans had gone so well. Just one dissenting voice at the lack of an invite, Belinda Oxfordshire never ceased offloading her disgust to Caroline Worsnip over it. She was so obsessed the hunt for Caroline's daughter fell from the front of her mind. She'd also lost interest in the new development, Caroline was needing to be patient assuming Belinda's enthusiasm would return once this wedding was all over and done with. Tricia had had enough of listening to it all. Every day at work Belinda Oxfordshire levelling fury at her, for being invited, for her not being invited. Tricia already had enough to deal with. She wasn't too sure if it was something to do with Clive Engells' new car, or the fact her stay at 4 The Willows had been somewhat short-lived since her mother let it be known she'd had just about enough of caring for the children, whatever it was her Clive had barely been in touch. Harriet hadn't been able to help either, she'd seen nothing of him apart from the school governor's meeting where he'd reported on how well the food bank was going. He'd laughed just a bit too loudly for her liking at Mr. Whittle, the schools inspector's comment 'Now what about this dumpster diver's place, dispensing the largesse...' Harriet recalled his words, didn't like the man, never had, nor his tone: patronising, she'd been inclined to avoid him after that. Felt as Chair, Clive Engells shouldn't have reinforced such a bad attitude. As a consequence she'd felt both pleased and sad for Tricia when she'd imparted the negative coming from the pregnancy test. She sensed Tricia must have spotted a look of relief on Clive's face as she was now convinced he was cooling off. Harriet was beginning to wonder if this love match was to be, after all. Especially as her mother had phoned checking on the whereabouts of the cat, quietly dropping she'd just popped in to 4 The Willows to see that nice young lady friend of Sir Joris, "You know, the one he was engaged to" leave the house. Harriet hadn't told Tricia that, she wasn't about to make matters worse for her. One thing for sure Tricia had already had her invite, they couldn't change that. She just hoped that Tricia would still want to go.

Chapter 83

Friday 24th October, Harriet looked at the calendar, today the VIP's would be arriving at Lower Tideside one day before Joris's special guests. She was grateful Mr. Sanderson had given her the day off ahead of half-term. This morning she needed to check the plans and go down to advise the florist and the caterers of the timings and exact requirements. She was pleased Tricia would be staying with her this evening, coming straight from work leaving Belinda Oxfordshire to manage the counter. She picked up the phone, stopped it ringing into her thoughts.

'Oh Tricia, I'm glad it's you. Are you still OK for tonight?'

'Yes, I've had a good think about it Harriet and it might give me the chance to see just where I am with Clive. It will be very interesting to see if I get to share a bedroom with him, or you and me we might both get put in the South Wing bedrooms, like he was tryin` to do before.'

'Yes, an interesting one that, you know Tricia I've hardly seen anything of Mr. Sanderson since we got back from Falmouth, it's never really struck me until now.'

'Well that's interesting, why would they both decide to do the disappearing act on us. Do you think we've both been dumped?'

Harriet felt the pit of her stomach hit the floor. The thought had just never occurred to her.

'Well they wouldn't dump us for missing the boat, surely? It was them made the decision to go without us, it should be us dumping them.'

Tricia laughed. 'Let's play it cool tomorrow and all over the weekend if that's the way they're going to be. If we're given the west wing they're going to know we're not in the least bit bothered.'

'Hang on a minute Tricia, there's something come through the door.'

She picked it up, to see Mr. Sanderson striding down the drive, closing the gate behind him.

'Tricia it was him, never bothered to ring the bell, he's just pushed this note through the door. "One extra guest, phone the place will you, they'll need to know it's Miss Belinda Oxfordshire OBE."'

'Oh bloody `ell,' Tricia fumed. 'She's got her own way at last! I wonder what changed his mind?'

Harriet dithered, unsure whether or not to come clean about Belinda Oxfordshire calling on Clive, decided against it. If her mother hadn't been busying herself looking for the cat, she would never have known. No this was something better kept to herself.

'She won't be managing the counter then?' It was the only thing Harriet could think of to say.

'Oh I don't know what's going on here. Must go Harriet, she's walking across, grinning like the Cheshire Cat! See you later about 5.30, I'll bring some wine.'

'No, Tricia, no I've stocked up, just get round here as soon as you can.'

Harriet replaced the receiver, her stomach churning, wondering what on earth was going on. That was the first time ever he'd never bothered to ring the doorbell. This gorgeous, gorgeous man, was he seeing someone else, or had he just had enough of her? She couldn't work it out. 'But why had Mrs. Harris been so reassuring?' Words going over and over in her mind until she finally decided they didn't mean a thing.

Chapter 84

'It was such a good idea to leave our overnight cases with Joris yesterday, Harriet. Oh my, don't both of you look beautiful! Don't you think so Percy?'

'Oh I do indeed. What a pair of show-stoppers,' Percy beamed, he'd never cease being partial to the younger ladies.

'Well you both are a picture of sartorial elegance, aren't they Tricia?' Harriet beamed.

'Ooh yes, I would definitely say so, myself,' Tricia agreed 'We'll all outshine the PM and his family. I do hope the PM's not in that shiny suit he always wears on the telly. Always looks like he's been trying to iron it to me.'

They laughed, Harriet always grateful for Tricia's ability to put everyone at ease. She hoped she'd manage it with Clive and Mr. Sanderson, though Harriet felt Tricia's wits were too well sharpened in the face of Belinda Oxfordshire's unprecedented nerve!

'What's the plan then Harriet? I'm afraid you'll need to remind me,' Molly said, apologetically. 'I must say I've got butterflies about it all this morning. I'm banking on saying nothing and just smiling when needed.'

'We're all feeling the same Molly, don't you worry. There'll be enough guests for us not to be noticed, I'm sure. Anyway we'll all be leaving the quay at 11 o'clock sharp. There's a berth booked on the other side close to the ship. We'll all board the ship and wait in the banqueting room where the wedding will take place. Mr. Sanderson, the PM and his daughter will remain on the yacht until then.'

'Oh, I see.' Molly looked at her watch. 'So, it's ten now, we've just got an hour at Joris's before we go.'

'Yes, they'll be serving coffee by now, it's really a chance for introductions.'

'So what happens after the ceremony Harriet?' Molly said, brushing her hand across the shoulders of Percy's tail coat.

We board the cruiser where we'll have lunch, followed by afternoon tea as we cruise round Anglesey. That's where the bride and groom will make their escape, they'll be picked up then whisked off by helicopter from the island. We'll all return to the port, the guests of Rosemary and Patrick will be flown back by private jet to London and the rest of us will relax on the yacht waiting for the tide. We should all get back to his place around 9 o'clock when dinner will be served.'

'Thanks Harriet, I think once you know exactly what's happening, you feel better, don't you dear? So how many of us will be going back?'

'Twenty, er twenty-one now, I think, that includes everyone.'

'Did you phone the company Harriet about them catering for the extra guest?' Tricia asked, hoping she'd forgotten.

'Oh no, golly Tricia, it went straight out of my head. Look I'm going to have to do it now. You go on, I'll follow. Oh no what's this coming now? It looks like it's a wedding car, for us! He didn't say.'

'Oh very nice, we'd better get in then,' Molly said using up her first smile of the day as she nudged Percy to hand the uniformed chauffeur their holdall.

Harriet panicked, felt compelled to get into the car she couldn't recall booking, desperately trying to remember if she had the ship's phone number in her bag.

'All in then,' said the chauffeur stating the obvious with a wry smile. 'I've been told to take you the pretty way.'

'I thought we were supposed to be 'aving coffee with the PM, what happened to that then?' Tricia complained as they scrambled into the back.

'Not the best of ideas for me,' uttered Percy turning, intensely relieved.

Harriet rifled through her bag, at least it would give her time to make the call. She knew she'd written it on the top of the day's plan but did she bring it with her? She tugged at her address book, bits of paper exploding everywhere along with the two pressed buttercups fallen from their special place between the cover and the front page. She swallowed hard, tried to put Mr. Sanderson to the back of her mind as her hat slipped to the floor. Clutching to the phone number she tried it, no answer, turned to Tricia in dismay, her bag rolling from her lap with a thud squashing her hat. She scrambled to retrieve its contents, her twisted foot catching Tricia's left ankle with her heel. 'Ouch Harriet, try keeping them flipping heels to yourself.' She swung her leg up just as Percy turned, lowering his head to catch a jab up his nostrils.

'Oh Percy,' Molly stretched forward, her hat unleashed by a sharp nudge from Tricia's elbow landing to the floor in a tangle with Harriet's foot.

The bearded chauffeur, part turned lifting his shades.

'Yes, that's where we're going, the pretty way unfortunately. I hope you're not doing any damage to my car in the back there. I don't like coming down here, had me cab pinched from this neck of the woods, not that long ago either.'

Harriet and Tricia went cold, kept quiet, heads down trying to ascertain and sort the damage.

'Them big pearly gates I've just pointed at, a couple of lesbians 'avin' it off swinging from them. One of them jumped off, knocked me out, bloody well frightened the life out of me she did. Oh no I don't like going near that house. Swore blind I'd never go there again after that. It's foggy, you know the bad one we had, I come to and me bloody cab's gone, swear it was those two lesbians or the place is bloody haunted, it's got a spooky tunnel you know, I have it on good authority people have vanished in there.'

Percy, with the end of his nose begging for mercy tried to look interested through the pain while heads down, Molly and Harriet tried desperately to punch some kind of shape back into their hats. Bent double, Tricia pulled at the hole in her tights trying to make it sit out of sight, Percy getting on her nerves, suddenly finding his handkerchief, started blowing hard as if trying to break a tune from his nose.

'Stop it Percy you'll make it bleed. It's not bleeding is it?' Molly snapped, cross at the distortion in her hat.

'That's it! I hate this place. I'm not having blood all over this one. I've only just got into wedding and funerals, at least the dead stay fucking still. Bugger off, all of you, we've only just gone past the place. Bloody pretty way, what's with that prick arsed git? Tell him I had a puncture.'

Grateful to be kicked out they watched him drive off then turned to walk back up the lane to the house.

'Who do you reckon booked that one?' muttered Percy from under the huge white handkerchief clutched to his nose.

'It wasn't you was it Harriet?' Tricia asked, 'You did all the arrangements, you never told us we'd be sent a car.'

Harriet put her hand to her mouth. 'Do you know it must have been me, I'd completely forgotten. I'd no idea he'd arrive, I remember now making sure not to ring that place. I just don't know how that one got past me.'

'Oh don't you worry about it Harriet, I know your head's full of Joris and your own wedding,' said Molly, kindly. 'No harm done Percy.'

'Only I'll be blowing my nose all day, you know how easy it is to set my sinuses off, Molly, not to mention my nose bleeds.'

Molly walking between Harriet and Tricia nudged them with her elbows, trying to stifle a giggle, all three dragging behind Percy, their shoulders shaking in short silent explosions of mirth, an uncontrollable outlet as each allowed the humour to release the tensions of the morning.

'Gosh I still can't get through to that flipping place,' Harriet declared, running to catch them up, having tried on and off ever since they left the taxi.

'Well we're here now Harriet, you're just goin` to have to tell him you've been tryin` for days. It was him messed the arrangements up, not you.'

Harriet agreed but the last thing she wanted was to get the wrong side of him now. She struggled with the instant surge of regret. She'd had every chance to marry him but somehow managed to throw it all away. She felt nervous, today was her opportunity to reassure herself the next wedding would be theirs.

'Good heavens you ladies look the worse for wear,' Joris Sanderson declared as he opened the door to the four of them. Where's the car? I thought you'd arranged to be chauffeur driven Harriet?'

Harriet watched him take a very deep breath, rise to his full height, caught the narrowing of those gorgeous blue eyes, then the touch of his hand to the side of his face. Standing tall, handsome, immaculate in his morning suit, the sound of chatter pervading the large square hall.

'Pop along to the west wing,' he said, turning to the sound of Mrs. Harris's voice; he called her across. 'Take them to their rooms Mrs. Harris if you would be so kind, they need to freshen up.' Then a quick glance at Percy, eyes streaming into the white handkerchief now permanently wrapped to his nose. 'You go too Percy, are you alright? I do hope you're feeling fit enough for the occasion.'

'Just a sneezing fit Joris, I'll be alright,' Percy volunteered, recognising the need for diplomacy.

'Right off you go then, er Harriet did you manage to contact this place regarding Belinda?'

Harriet froze, stood with her mouth open going as red as a letter-box.

'Ah I see Harriet, you didn't.'

'I've tried and tried Mr. Sanderson but just haven't been able to get through.'

'Then you should have informed me Harriet, this is going to be very embarrassing.'

'No I'll try again now.'

'A bit late in the day. I take it you'll be the one minus the wedding breakfast in that case?'

Harriet, dumbstruck, rushed away choking on the lump in her throat, felt the rush of tears to her eyes. Could hear Belinda Oxfordshire holding forth, decided she didn't want to meet with any of them.

Head down she flew past Mrs. Harris on the stairs.

'Yes, you'll need to be hurrying Harriet,' she called back. 'Your room's the first on the left and Patricia's right opposite you.'

'Harriet,' Tricia called, her head poking out from behind the door. 'Come in here, oh what's he been saying? Here come and sit down.'

Harriet sniffed out his very words fishing in her bag for a tissue. 'I'm going to try again, I'm not letting him get away with that one.'

She dialled and waited then spoke.

'Oh good morning, this is Harriet Glover speaking, I made the arrangement for today's wedding. Er yes, that's correct. Actually I've been trying to contact you all morning and appreciate this is a rather late request but if you could remove my name card from the table and replace it with one made out to Belinda Oxfordshire, we would much appreciate it.'

'Right, that's no problem,' came the response.

Suddenly Tricia grabbed the phone as Molly knocked on the door bustling in.

'I'm afraid we can't go Harriet, Percy's having a nose bleed.'

'Oh hello, this is Tricia Harrington speaking, please remove my place card and also Percy and Molly's don't know their surnames but they can't go either. So that's three less to cater for and BO is going in Harriet's place. Here Harriet she wants to speak to you again.'

They jumped to a sharp knocking on the door.

'Oh do come in Percy, whatever's the matter now?' Molly queried. Percy stood in the doorway muttering.

'No hang on Harriet, Percy says it's stopped bleeding we can go after all.'

'What's this? What's all this about? What in the name of goodness is going on now?' Joris Sanderson strode in.

'Here Harriet pass that thing over. No wonder I couldn't get hold of them. It's the wedding company, isn't it? Damned place been engaged ever since you rushed upstairs.'

Harriet instantly passed her mobile over, 'Just trying to sort it out Mr. Sanderson.'

'No, no, all we are looking for is one additional cover for a Miss Belinda Oxfordshire. Right, you'll sort it will you? Very good. No really, Harriet Glover and Patricia Harrington will be attending, as will Mr. & Mrs. Pecker, er Molly and Percy Pecker.'

He terminated the call, flinging the thing back to Harriet as if it were a hot coal. He hurriedly lifted his arm, reminding them of the 20 minutes remaining. She watched his immaculate wide white cuff fall back to cover his Rolex maritime watch as he double smacked his hands attempting to speed them up.

The bedroom vacated of males, they silenced, focussing on tidying themselves, none of them in the mood for what lay ahead.

'This is all going to be a bit too posh for me Harriet,' Molly confessed, nervously.

'They're only people Molly,' Tricia piped. 'People just like you and me. Old Mr. Lyons down there wouldn't have been PM if it wasn't for people like us voting for him.'

'Speak for yourself Tricia, I didn't vote Tory, I'm surprised at you Tricia,' Harriet declared, suddenly feigning shock.

'Oh no, nor did I,' agreed Molly.

'Nor did I,' grinned Tricia, 'but that's what I told my Clive, so just make sure neither of you two let the cat out of the bag. I don't want anything ruining my wedding day. Clive says I can have my dress made anyway I like, so I'm having it all white and floating with yards and yards of pink ribbon. I bought some and trailed it round a sheet from your airing cupboard Harriet and it looked lovely. I left the ribbon all tied to the banister to remind me of our beautiful day to come. That's if he's still up for marrying me that is.'

Harriet swallowed hard, she knew exactly how Tricia felt.

Chapter 85

With precious little time for introductions they made their way down to the quay, Mr. Sanderson's yacht looking resplendent on the rising tide, bobbing, impatient to show her prowess to all. Saturday 25th October, he very much doubted the press would fall for the change of dates. He took a very deep breath so very aware of the responsibility he had laid at his own feet. He looked to the sky, grateful for the fine day and a gentle breeze for his crew sailing her across the Dee. He wanted this to be the very special occasion Mac Lyons had long anticipated for the marriage of his eldest daughter. Joris Sanderson would ensure he was not disappointed. Ida Lyons and Patrick White would have that special, intimate wedding they'd always dreamt of.

Extravagance was the order of the day, with some of the most revered fashion houses sporting their identity in the subtleties of designer adornments. Those in the know would know, whilst those less au fait would wait for the odd jacket or scarf tossed over a chair back to reveal their most prized and expensive source. Molly couldn't be doing with labels, she pulled the sides of her jacket together as she stepped on to the deck wishing Percy would put that damned handkerchief away. She knew if he didn't stop flapping it round his face like an exhausted seagull for sure he'd have his nose bleeding again. Harriet stood next to her, wondering if she wasn't in danger of over-doing the pale blue. Maybe that's why Mr. Sanderson hadn't so much as glanced across yet. She'd worn that colour for her own wedding, well truth be known she'd worn the bridesmaid's dress she'd had for Molly and Percy's wedding. She quickly skipped the thought, the worst and the best day of her life, then the wobbles, this ridiculous need to stay on amber. How many chances had he given her? How many chances had she tossed away? How she wished she was in Ida Lyons' shoes. She felt a flutter in her stomach, her baby, his baby, growing fast. A full four months pregnant now and expanding. She'd just managed to find a dress roomy enough across the waist before falling into godets from the lower hips. The matching jacket finally ensuring her privacy.

'I do hope my Clive will come over Harriet. I know Belinda Oxfordshire's on her own but he's making a meal of trying to make her feel at ease. I've got something I want to tell him.'

'Oh you're not are you Tricia? Did you use that testing kit you bought in Falmouth?'

'Of course I did and you'd be the first I'd tell if I was, apart from Clive, of course; but no, I'm not, I'm almost sure I'm not. I'm not telling him that though,

I just want to drop him a few hints to make him think I am, just enough to get him away from Belinda Oxfordshire and keep him away.'

'Oh sorry, I shouldn't have asked, you were so sure I was convinced you'd ended up just like me.'

'I only wish I had. Still there'll be plenty more chances once I get him away from her.'

Harriet nodded, watched her fidget before bouncing away towards them both standing towards the bow. She puzzled at Clive's apparent change of heart, they were looking at houses together, planning for their future. Harriet hoped it wasn't taking on the children he was having second thoughts about. It seemed odd to her they should both be feeling this sense of insecurity. She felt her stomach flutter again, swallowing hard on the moisture blurring her vision, bent on gathering to tears. 'Our baby, our baby needs us both, needs all the love of a happy, secure family life. It was a moment of profound truth. This final, deep realisation, the need for their baby to have the best possible start, brought Harriet crashing out of her amber mind set for good. She watched him, tall, blonde, looking absolutely fantastic as he moved between the guests, then a word in the PM's ear, then a brief instruction to the guy on the winch. She watched the mainsail unfurl proudly fluttering its way to the masthead, knowing full well why the lump in her throat just wouldn't go away. She thought of Mark, their house and his need to get it sold. She couldn't quite believe he was all stitched up with someone else whilst her life appeared, yet again, to be falling apart. She left thoughts of Mark behind, watched Mr. Sanderson smooth his blonde hair down as it caught the breeze, all the while chatting, laughing, then finally giving the all clear to sail. She tried to sit on the temptation to open her heart to him right there and then but each time she crossed the deck he'd moved away almost as if avoiding her.

'Oh there you are Harriet, I'm afraid I had no luck with my Clive, all I'm hopin` is we'll be sittin` together and Belinda Oxfordshire will be well out of the way seein` as she was an afterthought.'

'Me too, I've been trying to get a quick word with him but he's all over the place.'

'That's what happens when the Prime Minister's around with all his posh friends. They could do with a dose of Rapping Hammer, like we've had. That would bring them all down to earth.'

'Oh don't say that Tricia, please don't even go there.'

'Ooh look Harriet, see there, see that little dinghy speedin` up the river, they might just be in that.'

'No Tricia, look it's turning round, probably just someone on the razz.'

"Mare Libertas" rode the gentle ripple of the incoming tide with panache and dignity. This expensive, sleek yacht left nothing to be desired when it needed to rise to an occasion such as this. Tacking across the river with ease, soon they would be moored alongside the ship now draped in all the splendour befitting the wedding of the PM's daughter.

Mac Lyons raised the binoculars, he liked what he saw. From bow to stern the Union Jack bunting fluttering at the sky, the morning sun finally burning off the autumnal mist rising to the green hills beyond, the far mountains anticipating their visibility, standing proud, impatient to give the morning its final magnificence.

He turned to Joris, 'It looks like we've managed to steer the press away. I must admit I half-expected a flotilla behind us. Even that speed boat turned round. All jolly good eh Joris! Great stuff! I can't thank you enough old boy! Now when's your big day to be?'

Mr. Sanderson made his excuses, Harriet watched him stride away though she had no idea of the conversation. She recalled sailing to The Bangles, watching the sun high in the sky shimmering golden light across the turquoise water. Cornwall, beautiful Cornwall, their baby conceived on the sand, this boat moored to reach one small, beautiful cove. 'Do not forget,' he'd written in the sand. She could never forget. She felt that flutter aross her stomach again, with the back of her hand she wiped a tear spilling down the side of her face. She thought about Barry and that painting, why oh why did he do that to them both? Why couldn't Mr. Sanderson understand? She wondered if Barry could find his little girl, if Barry could make it right for them both in the end. She stood quietly by only half-hearing Molly and Tricia chatting, distant, like they were miles away, her every nerve, tussling with every instinct driving her to talk to the man she loved, knowing she desperately needed to be seated alongside him.

'What's up sis, deep in thought?'

'Oh James, you gave me a fright then. Golly you do look smart. Where's Geraldine, I haven't seen her yet?'

'She's off clinging by her fingertips to the top rung of the social ladder. I just hope she doesn't blab about mother's indescretions.'

'What's that James? What do you mean?'

'Didn't you know Harriet? She's the one who gave the game away about all this at her WI meeting. She's so like Geraldine it's unbelievable. Couldn't resist showing off about her family connections to Joris and of course by virtue of that, the PM as well. Apparently they had some garden celebrity there along with the press and bingo, the cat was out the bag!'

'Oh no, poor Mummy, I don't expect she realised for one moment,' said Harriet.

'Well no but she's got herself into a hell of a state, terrified the PM will find out and she'll end up getting the jail!' James laughed.

'Oh I hope you did your best to reassure her James?'

'No way, it'll teach her a lesson. Anyway if she gets banged up it will give Dad a break!'

'That's so mean, I can't believe I'm hearing this.'

'Well how do I know what the consequences would be? She's damned lucky there's no activity here. It looks like the double bluff worked.' James turned, raised his hand to Geraldine, Harriet caught a half-wave as he strolled back to join her. She watched them go down below, obviously Geraldine had managed a private audience with the PM himself, much to Harriet's short lived amusement. She felt a hand on her back then turned to see Clive Engells intent on whispering something at her which needed to be said in a hurry.

'Just a touch of reassurance needed Harriet, if you would be so kind. I say this is such a grand occasion, not too long now before we berth, these tidal rivers are the devil's own to predict, I must say. You know Harriet, Joris and I have been very busy of late, hardly a moment to spare - you may well have noticed. What with getting our new cars and fine-tuning the arrangements for today, and various business issues arising we've not had much time at all. No, what it is, I spoke with your mother a few days ago and I'm sorry to say she doesn't seem to hold a very high opinion of Patricia, not that I'd let that influence me, of course. Your mother seemed most intent I should associate myself with Belinda when I do strongly feel it really isn't any of her business. Now would you be so kind as to make her aware of this and I'd also appreciate greatly if she refrains from calling round to 4 The Willows whilst I'm in occupancy there. I'm afraid Joris isn't appreciating her reference to Belinda and his broken engagement, either, but don't get me wrong here, I haven't discussed this with him, apparently it's got back to him through a friend of a friend of the Chair of the WI. It would be as well Harriet if you could gently persuade her to think before she speaks. If you could do that for me dear, I would be eternally grateful.'

Harriet nodded, walking to the stern of the yacht, choking on the tears finally getting their way. 'So that's it, it all makes sense now,' she told herself, 'It's Mummy, he probably knows she's the one who blabbed to the press, too. No wonder he's been cool with me, no wonder he doesn't want to marry me any more.' She fished in her small pale blue bag for her white lace handkerchief, trying desperately hard to control herself hardly aware they'd dropped the mainsail and the jib was bringing them rapidly in to berth.

'Oh Harriet this is where you are, I saw you talking to my Clive what was he saying Harriet? Oh no, what's the matter? He hasn't upset you has he? Look if he's told you he's finished with me don't worry I can take it, he hasn't gone cool like that for nothing Harriet.'

'No Tricia, it's not that, it's Mummy she's been blabbing, calling at the house, he doesn't want that any more. But what's worse from what he said I'm sure Joris knows it's her who went to the press with this wedding.'

'How do you know that?' replied Tricia, aghast.

'She confessed to James, he's furious with her, says she deserves all she gets.'

'Look Harriet, try not to worry, you aren't sure of that, are you? The last thing the PM's going to do is make a fuss about it even if she did. There's a general election coming up, don't forget. Anyway it won't matter after today.' Harriet felt Tricia's arm around her. She took a deep breath, 'They've been busy Tricia, he said that almost apologetically. I don't think you've any need to worry about your Clive.' She watched Tricia's face now almost engulfed in her smile, thought just how wrong her mother was.

'Tricia, I'm not getting off this, I don't want to be in there, I just can't deal with it.'

'Well I'm not goin' in there without you Harriet, I can tell you. They're all getting off now. Look, there's Joris, oh and there's the bride and the PM, duck down Harriet, we can stop here for five minutes until they're all in.' They crouched to the sound of fading chatter.

'Oh Harriet, it looks like the guests are off, the crew are just at the end of the line now.'

Harriet popped up to see them leaving the grand gangway duly installed for the occasion, relieved they'd soon be down it and away themselves. She would only need to explain to one of the staff she wasn't feeling well. She looked up, her thoughts interrupted by the familiar chopping sound of helicopters rapidly approaching.

'Four of them! That'll be the security set I should think,' she said turning to Tricia hoping she was right.

'Come on Harriet let's get down below before they get any closer, we don't want them seeing us.'

They stooped to crawl their way round the cabin port side, descending the steps without looking back.

'Oh that's alright they've gone now,' said a relieved Harriet, 'They'll probably circle around for the rest of the day, at least until Ida and Patrick leave Anglesey.' She fished in her bag yet again, but this time for her phone. 'I'm going to phone them Tricia, get them to tell Mr. Sanderson I'm not well before they all sit down to the wedding breakfast and we're missed.'

'That's a good idea, oh there's one of those helicopters back again. Oh eh Harriet it sounds pretty close, sounds like it's landing to me.'

'Well they will do I expect, put some ground forces in. That's OK, let me just get this call out of the way. Here Tricia can you read out the number please? The sooner we're away from here the better.'

Tricia swamped by the luxury sat on the urge to investigate the series of doors surrounding them. 'Right, I'm with you now, read it out.'

Frozen by the sound of voices. Instantaneously they both felt the blood drain from their faces as the cursing got louder and louder. Harriet thought of the gangway, heard the first thud. 'Tricia, quick, into this one.'

They shot into the bedroom Harriet knew. She grabbed the covers from the bed, pushed Tricia into the ensuite, quickly closed the door, crouching with her under the lot, hoping against hope they would look like a pile of dirty bedlinen. Their hearts pounding they crouched as if dead for they might well have been, petrified, almost choking from fear. They didn't need to strain their ears to recognise who had boarded. Rapping Hammer flung the ensuite door open then mercifully banged it shut. 'Let's get her underway and round the back of that island before the fuckin` lot notice she's gone.'

'Eh Wayne, you sure you can `ang this thing that far?'

'I friggin` can. You'll see! Fuckin` Fastnet eh, they'll be takin` me once they've got me off the hook with them Italians. Bleedin` statues, who cares? They're crumblin` into the gravy anyway, not worth doin` the bird for eh Rex?'

'You're diggin' at the concrete Wayne `ammer, you'll never get those arse-`oles to agree.'

'Sir Fuckin` Horace'll want his yacht back won't he? We'll sink it if we don't get the PM's friendly ear. There's an election hangin` around, remember, we'll spread the fuckin` dirt on the lot of them, sink them along with this bleedin` tub. If we go down, so will they. I've got it all worked out you'll see we'll get exactly what we want. Now where's that fucker of an ice-lolly gone? That frozen drip, I bet that pisser's fallen in. We need him to pass the message on. Get him Rex and keep him fuckin` tied up. He can go in here with all the dirty washin` until we're ready.'

'At least he'll get a soft landing,' Rex laughed as he shouted the instructions.

Trembling, and hugging as if conjoined, the door flew open, Harriet and Tricia braced for the thud which arrived as the door slammed shut. The limp body slid from their shoulders along with the bedcovers. Jolted, they gasped at the sight of Ross Farquerhart. Harriet immediately put her finger to her lips, pulled him towards them, all of them under the covers, like the laundry pile had just increased. Harriet began untying the rope at his wrists while Tricia felt for the knot at the back of his head. Ross Farquerhart breathed again, overwhelmed with relief as the gag loosened and fell away.

Chapter 86

Joris Sanderson expecting to have been seated next to Harriet, experienced an unprecedented sense of guilt. He'd been so busy ensuring the wellbeing of the PM's guests, he'd assumed Harriet would have been sitting at the front of the ship's ceremonial hall, waiting. Still he'd catch her at the drinks reception in the cocktail lounge. He looked at his watch, very shortly they would all be filing through. For a moment he wondered about the yacht, but yes, it was well tied to the bollard at the berth, and no there wouldn't have been any harm in leaving the gangway in place, save any faff for their sail back. The caterers would be at Lower Tideside now, preparing the evening banquet. He was pleased the weather was in their favour, pleased they hadn't met with any press. No, this was going well, according to plan unlike his relationship with Harriet. Again he wondered why she wouldn't let go of Barry Giordano. Surely if she had any self respect she wouldn't want to have anything to do with the man. Pregnant with *his* child, yet unable to let go of *him*, unable to get herself out of this ludicrous wishing to stay on 'amber' position. His thoughts turned to Amber, to the painting of his little girl. To its disappearance, how uncanny he should first of all lose her, then the painting go missing. Still very suspicious of seeing that black Lamborghini pulling away from the traffic lights the day it disappeared, though he wasn't able to make any sense of any of it. Wondered what the hell Caroline Worsnip was up to, moving back to the area. Loses her job, then gets it back just like that. He knew damned well it was nothing to do with the brief minutes he'd spent with Roger Boxsox. And Belinda Oxfordshire, what was she doing wanting to live next door to the woman? He began to wonder if she'd given up on men, but no, not so. He never missed that look of desire wrapped in anger and sometimes hatred, though he had, somehow, managed to forgive her for accusing him of aborting the baby she was never expecting, trying to influence Harriet against him. Yes he'd forgiven her probably because he was the one who'd broken off their short engagement. He shuddered at the thought of succumbing to parental pressure at his age, besides he'd felt sorry for her when her fiancee walked out. At that time she was playing a key role in getting Starboard Marine North West established, building the property investment portfolio. They were working well together and she wasn't bad in bed either. His parents felt it was time he settled down, thought he should be looking towards having children. At the time he didn't know Belinda was unable to oblige on that count, suffering a congenital abnormality which would have made it impossible. Then Harriet fell into his heart, his mind, his being. She lit his soul in a way he'd never known before. Harriet committed to a long-standing phobic partner with two grown daughters. They'd made love on the Bangles Beach in

Cornwall, a small cove, just the two of them, the water lapping in rhythm to their pulsating bodies. The utter bliss, this spiritual and physical union unprecedented in his life. Just her blue lace briefs eased to the sand, the tiny pearl buttons on her pretty blue dress undone from the neck down to reveal the fullness of her beautiful breasts. In his hand, just the thought, now quickly dismissed as he sensed an impending erection. 'That damned man that fucking Bohemian artist,' he flared his nostrils, took a deep breath, he knew he'd been outwitted. Didn't expect the man to resign his commission, thought he had him all stitched up in Alaska.

' "Best made plans". …and all that,' he said to himself, scratching his head, then in a massive attempt to reduce his cognitive dissonance he thought about her mother. 'Asking for trouble marrying into that family,' he concluded.

He jumped to a tap on his shoulder. 'It's almost finished, we'd best be receiving guests at the drinks' reception Joris, we can slide across and out of that side door just there.'

'Right with you Clive.'

Chapter 87

Barry swivelled his chair round once more to look at his painting of Harriet lying naked on the steps at St. Mark's Square, not quite believing they'd made a double scoop the day they went to Amsterdam. The painting was his and he had all the evidence he needed to prove it, just as long as Harriet and Mark were willing to reaffirm it had been stolen or at least disappeared without trace. Besides it would seem no one had bothered to try to find the owner and it had gone to auction without due process. He was convinced the guy who bought it would wish to lie low since he appeared well caught up in a money laundering scam, no he'd have to forsake his work of art and tempting though it was for Barry to offer to sell it back to him, he dismissed the thought, deciding to go to where the proceeds of the sale rested. He could get them on both counts and felt sure he'd get a fair whack of the million pounds back. What a scoop, investing a fair proportion in the business he and Andy could be made for life, their business could be simply a hobby. Big question? With comparable wealth would he be able to compete with Joris Sanderson for Harriet? After all he had the painting back, he would destroy it for her but he knew that would be so only if he had her. Therein lay the conundrum of the second scoop. He was morally and ethically bound to reveal all, he swivelled once more on his chair deciding he'd tell Harriet the whole story only if she'd commit to him for the rest of her life. Until then she'd only learn half, the half he could deal with. He tossed his long dark hair back over his shoulders, knowing full well that wasn't going to work. He would clutch his secret until the time was right, until he could bear facing up to life without her.

Chapter 88

'Where's he bleedin` gone now?' The three of them quivered with fear as the ensuite door flung open to the sound of the boat's engine revving. 'Rex, Rux, look for friggin` ice-lolly, now. Looks like the bugger's melted into thin air.' In a violent temper Rapping Hammer banged the door shut.

'They've managed to start the engine, we're off,' Harriet whispered.

'I can't fuckin' see him anywhere,' Rex panicked above their screams.

'He's overboard, there's nothing else for it, the bugger's jumped for it, he must have worked out of that rope, Rix I fuckin` told you you hadn't tied it tight enough. He's probably over there raising the bleedin` alarm. Go to full power Rax get this thing's arse out of the gravy, we've got two minutes to get to that island. I'll have to do the talking myself now. Waste of oxy that ice drip fucker, let's hope he went down.'

A quick whisper from under the laundry decided they should stay put. With fingers crossed and Ross flattered at the expletive, though feeling more like one of those Venetian defaced statues, they managed to hold it together for the seven minutes or so it took 'Mare Libertas' to reach the island on the rising tide.

Rapping Hammer dropped anchor, relieved to see Rax speeding the rib round to the side of the boat. 'Get a fucking move on will you, what kept you?'

'Three bleedin` helicopters trailing us that's what. We had to wait for them to get from up our arses before we could land.'

'Go round again while I make this bleedin` call, we might just be needing that helicopter again.'

Rapping Hammer stood on deck watched intently by Rix, Rox, Rex and Rux, never had these Bards been so terrified. 'We're spooked, done for, swim and run, right now.' Rox suddenly screeched, rising to a massive surge of adrenaline.

'Shut it!' demanded Rapping Hammer, 'I'm trying to get this fuckin` thing to work.' Immediately they all stabbed at their phones, poking desperately hard at each key, to no avail.

'These suck these friggin` phones, not a bleedin` signal between us. Come on let's get to hell out of here before we get nicked. Rax where the hell are you?'

At that instant the throb of a small motor approaching, next thing the rib was bobbing precariously alongside.

'Haul the anchor Wayne, let her drift. They'll never know it's us.'

Wayne Hammer took a nervous glance towards the ship, 'Celebration Cruise Stop', deciding there was no time.

'No we're loading now, come on Bards get your bleedin` backsides in, let's get the hell off this baby.'

Ears strained beneath the sheets, duvet and pillows Harriet suddenly twigged as she heard the rib fire to full throttle amidst screaming torrents of filth. As it faded she guessed they were on their way.

'We could be all clear,' she whispered, lifting the covers. They stayed crouched, ears strained but could hear only the lap of the tide against the hull.

'I'll take a look around,' volunteered Ross, looking as much surprised as the girls at the suggestion. 'Better that way, you two get back down.'

Cautiously he opened the door, then with ballerina precision he crept forward on his toes, peering round the bedroom door. Now for the tricky bit. He cautiously ascended each stair peering over the top before finally crawling along the deck, glimpsing under tarpaulins and all else where anyone of them could possibly have hid, gradually moving his way round the cabin and back down the stairs to the ensuite.

'No sign of them at all, I've checked every possible space, they've all buggered off, thank the Virgin Mary. Oh all praise be to Her.'

Tricia glanced at Harriet feeling intense relief coupled with amazement at Ross Farquerhart's sudden conversion. Scrambling out Harriet reached for her phone. We need to get in touch with Mr. Sanderson straight away, he'll be worried sick as soon as he finds out this is missing. He certainly won't want the police on the case right this minute, the next thing the press will be swarming like flies before they even board the motor launch.'

She found it, pressed away at the keys, couldn't get a signal. 'Lets go on top and try and then get off this boat if we can. They could well be back once they've made their call on land. Here Ross you keep hold of this.'

'Oh Harriet let's get off this thing now while we've got the chance.'

'It depends if I can turn her round, the tide's still on its way up. It's going to take too much time to launch the dinghy, too. No, we're just going to have to let go the anchor and sail her back.'

They actioned the winch to bring up the anchor feeling like hours were passing in those few vital minutes.

'Can you motor it Harriet?' questioned a very nervous Tricia.

'No, they wouldn't have had the key, they've messed with the wiring somehow to get it going. No it's an onshore wind we'll hoist the sails and with a bit of luck we'll get on a run straight back to Mr. Sanderson's quay.'

Impressed at their ability to follow her hurriedly issued instructions and grateful the boat had turned, she watched the wind fill both sails to take them back up the river. It was the longest fifteen minutes of her life. Approaching the quay she ordered them back to the winch to drop the mainsail to allow her to turn it into the wind, using only the jib to bring it alongside. Thinking on her feet she couldn't risk either of them leaping off and onto the quay to catch the mooring ropes to secure it.

'We'll need to drop anchor as soon as she's alongside,' she shouted, hoping it would give her the leeway to jump off. 'Quickly, those two big winches,' she commanded, pointing at the handles on the drums either side of the cabin on the port side. 'Get them underway as soon as the anchor drops, take one rope each and whoever's is closest to the quay just throw it at me. We've got to do it or we'll still be on this if the gang come back.'

Nervously Tricia and Ross waited for the call. Almost alongside, Harriet let "Mare Libertas" ride further then pulled out, tacking into the wind urging the bow forward to bring her back to the quay. Relieved the tide had her starboard gunwale as level to the quay as it was ever likely to get, her life flashed before her.

Now, drop anchor,' she called, leaving the wheel, every nerve ending shredded by tension as the target landing spot drifted back and forth. Then she made a split second decision to climb up and go for it just as the boat split away, leaving her with two hands and only one leg ashore struggling to pull the other in before the boat rolled back towards her. Unbalanced she stumbled, her bare feet painfully hitting the hard concrete. In an awkward grab she just caught the tail end of Ross Farquerhart's rope. Trembling, she pulled hard as the boat rolled towards her, looping it round the bollard pulling as tightly as she could, tying it round and round until finally securing it with a half-hitch. Relieved and better prepared for Tricia's throw, she caught it first off to repeat the performance with amazing efficiency.

'Quickly now, both of you, here take my hand and jump, you first Tricia. great, now you Ross.'

For the briefest of moments the three stood on the quay's edge, dazed.

'Quickly up to the house, we need to phone Joris,' panicked Tricia.

'No, not up there,' Harriet decided. 'We can't risk disruption and publicity there today, we've got to find somewhere secluded and quick.'

'Follow me,' instructed Ross, 'It's just a couple of secs from here, I know the exact place.'

With heads down and little choice they followed, scrambling their way through the run of huge brambles lining the river bank to arrive at a well-concealed, small wooden door.

'Now, we'll be OK here, you see,' Ross assured, pulling it open like something out of "Alice in Wonderland". 'It's a bit tight in there but it does open up a bit, we should all be able to get in.'

'Flipping heck Ross you were right!' Tricia moaned as they wriggled through to discover a short tunnel. 'Oh well done Ross, how did you know about this one?' Harriet puffed, sitting, rubbing at her bare feet.

'Never mind that Harriet, here take this back I can tell you now it will work, I'm one hundred per cent certain.'

She pressed redial, jumped when her mobile phone started ringing out.

'Mr. Sanderson, I need to speak to him urgently please, tell him it's Harriet and it's very urgent.' she began.

'I'm afraid he's still seated, the wedding breakfast is not long underway.'

'Please, please, this is urgent.'

'Just a minute, I'll see if I can get hold of him.'

Harriet took a deep breath and waited.

'I'm afraid he's otherwise engaged just now, he'll call back when they've finished eating.'

Harriet couldn't believe what she was hearing.

'He'll call back when they've finished eating. Right, thank you,' Harriet returned, pressing the off key.

'Try phoning him directly,' Ross suddenly triumphed, painting a cross in the sandy soil under his hand. 'His number must be in there, surely?'

Harriet dithered then went for it.

'Harriet where the devil have you two got to, indeed? You've taken me away from the function to answer this, it had better be good, very good, unless of course it's a miscarriage you're having in which case I would have appreciated that information at the outset.'

'No, no, it's not that, not yet at least,' Harriet gabbled concerned her leap from the boat might bring one on.

'Whatever do you mean Harriet, not yet? What on earth have you two been up to now?'

'We haven't much time Mr. Sanderson, I wasn't feeling that well so decided to stay aboard the boat I was going to get the message to you when Tricia and I realised Rapping Hammer and his gang had boarded it. We hid in the ensuite under all the bedlinen so they never saw us but they had Ross Farquerhart tied and gagged. They threw him in thinking he was landing on a laundry pile.'

'Good heavens Harriet please do accept my apologies. Where are you all now? Are you safe?'

'We're just hiding in a side entrance to the tunnel at the far end of your garden Mr. Sanderson, we're OK for the moment but we don't know if they'll come back. Here speak to Ross he'll know what their game plan was.'

'Oh hi Joris, it's a bit of a story but they were using me as their spokesperson. I had to meet them, I thought I could deal with it, ended up fucking tied up, didn't I?'

'Alright young man, that'll do, get on with it.'

'By stealing the boat they wanted you to persuade the PM to get them off the hook with the Italian government for some kind of vandalism I think. They planned on sinking the boat unless you agreed. Yes that's basically it.'

'Good heavens, I had no idea you've been used in this way, pass me back to Harriet will you?'

'Harriet are you sure the three of you are alright?'

'At the moment yes, unless they come back looking for the boat and Ross.'

'Where is the boat, tell me quickly what happened Harriet?'

'They motored her down to the island, dropped anchor, a few minutes later they went off in the rib, I could hear it going past every few minutes, it must have been circling the island waiting to pick them up.'

Suddenly Ross pulled the phone back from Harriet.

'They were supposed to be getting me to do the deal with you but as they couldn't find me I presume they either panicked or were going to have a go themselves. Anyway if they'd tried their phones they wouldn't get a signal. Harriet tried to phone you from the boat but it wouldn't work.'

'Oh, right, pass me back will you Ross and thanks for that. … Harriet where's the boat now and how did you get back there?'

'I managed to sail it back to your quay Mr. Sanderson, we dropped anchor and managed to secure it. It needs sorting though.'

'The bastards, they must have tampered with the engine. Goodness me Harriet what a girl you are! I'll have a word with the PM but the rest of the wedding party need know nothing of this, I'll get one of his security team to fly me back. You stay where you are, leave your phone on and I'll be in touch as soon as I land.'

Harriet put both hands to her mouth, staring at the phone in her lap before repeating what he'd said.

'Well that makes me feel better, Harriet, how about you?' Tricia asked. 'Are you OK Ross, you've gone a bit pale? Anyway how did you know Harriet's phone would work in here?'

'You won't believe this, I know you won't, but I'll tell you the story while we're waiting.'

Harriet and Tricia gasped, both overcome by an immediate and amazing sense of peace.

He looked at Harriet, 'She was a Lady in waiting, too.'

Harriet felt an immediate flutter across her stomach, said nothing, merely smiled across, knowing her baby was going to be alright.

Chapter 89

The two sat wanting to hear Ross's story again, Harriet retelling her own experience on meeting with the beautiful mosaic image of the Madonna and Child on the tunnel wall and yes giving Ross permission to quote her in order to substantiate his experience.

'Thanks Harriet, that's great, now if only I could forge that connection with the lost Roman ninth legion. I'm convinced this place, well that place through there is spooked.'

'So are we, aren't we Harriet? We ran all the way through it don't forget, it was the scariest thing I've ever done in my life.'

Ross listened intently, pondering how his revelation could possibly square with thousands of soldiers meeting their gruesome end in there.

'Yes it is haunted Ross, I definitely heard spooky noises in the night. Mrs. Harris hates even walking past the door. It gives a strange atmosphere to the house, I'm fine during the day but I don't like sleeping there, neither did the cat. I'm sure cats can pick up on that sort of thing.'

'Well I must admit to feeling a bit spooked myself in there. I go potholing so it wasn't being in there that bothered me, I can tell you I was highly relieved to find this route out.' He thought for a while, set his mind on researching every last shred of evidence in order to be able to postulate his way to a satisfactory conclusion. He jumped as Harriet's phone rang on her lap.

'Yes Mr. Sanderson, it's me, we're still here and OK thanks. How about you? That didn't take long.'

'Just across the river in the chopper, fortunately. Look tell me exactly where you are, I've got the PM's security guard with me, we'll escort you all back to the house.' He listened while Harriet explained.

'Right, OK with you in two ticks.'

Relieved to see the light of day stream in as Ross pushed the door open, they stumbled into the fresh air to hear Mr. Sanderson's unmistakeable voice as the two men pushed their way through the last of the brambles.

With conversation reserved for later Mr. Sanderson led the way, the three of them gratefully sandwiched between him and the security guard behind.

'This is Detective Chief Inspector Jones, if you could run the whole of this thing past him, whilst I organise some tea.' Harriet felt Tricia's sharp nudge as they sat themselves down in the library by the French doors. All three glancing the helicopter resting on the pad while Detective Jones stared at the door waiting for Mr. Sanderson's return.

'Right, Harriet Glover and Patricia Harrington,' began Detective Chief Inspector Jones, weighing them up very carefully. 'Umm, there's a certain familiarity about the pair of you. Never mind, no matter, I've made a note somewhere. Now if you would like to begin Harriet and then you Patricia. You'll need to speak clearly into this thing, if you would. You follow on please Ross.'

They were brief, being crouched in the ensuite under a pile of bedding left them with very little to contribute.

'Right girls, thank you, I've got your side of the story, now just run this past me again,' Detective Jones said, turning to Ross. 'You fell off the quay side and into their rib, right?' Ross nodded then changed his mind. 'No I was bloody pushed. I remember being shoved straight in.' Tricia's mouth dropped wide open. Detective Jones made a mental note. 'It must have been one of them, there was no one else around,' Ross continued.

'Oh that's terrible Ross,' Tricia interrupted, feeling a nudge from Harriet. 'Then you were taken against your will and forced to collude with them to get them out of being arrested re. this Venice affair. Now why didn't you take the opportunity to inform the police at that stage?' Ross Farquerhart stuttered, 'I was protecting these two. They threatened they'd have their evil way with them if I didn't do it.'

'Ah, I see,' replied the detective, musing as to whether this obviously academic lad had ever had his evil way with anyone. Yes, of course this was naturally going to ensure this boy's silence.

'I started to tell them something, then he cut in and said they already knew, it was in all the papers about the wedding on the 25th October, er today that is. So I said no it was something else they might be interested to know.'

'Quite, quite, get on with it young man.'

Ross looked across to Mr. Sanderson's stern face suddenly wishing he hadn't just said that.

'Do come along young man we haven't got all day,' the Detective pressed.

'I told them when you were planning to collect the boat from Falmouth.'

Mr. Sanderson raised his eyebrows wondered how he knew.

'I thought if I did that they could do their own dirty work. You know they're losing money not being able to do the gigs. They're desperate to be off the hook and I wanted them off my back, bugger all to do with me.'

'Well thanks a bunch Ross,' retorted Mr. Sanderson, it's a good job we were just about to get underway, we'd have had them scaling the masts, tying us up, indeed taking over the whole kit and caboodle.'

'Well that's exactly what they did to me. It was Harriet and Tricia here that untied me.'

'Apologies Ross,' Mr. Sanderson said, turning to Detective Jones, 'Do please forgive the interruption. I er....' He stopped short to Mrs. Harris rattling the door handle, immediately striding across to assist her with the tea tray.

'Right so I assume you left them on the harbour,' he said turning to Mr. Sanderson.

'We left them climbing out of the water, fortunately we were under way before they had chance to hit the deck. High the lot of them by the sound of it.'

Detective Jones turned back to Ross. 'So by all accounts this double bluff worked for every one except you and them. How did you know the wedding was still to take place today?'

'Well nobody told me any different. They phoned me up wanting to find out what was really going on, so I said it was all in the paper and nothing had changed as far as I knew. He didn't believe me, said he'd read the change of plans in the paper but he thought it was a double bluff. He made me meet them on the road by the field behind the school, threatening me all the way if it didn't happen today. They said they didn't want to have to set it all up again as hiring the helicopter was costing a fortune.' He turned to Tricia. 'They already had to raid your "save Venice" tin they said.'

Tricia fumed, 'Well I want that money back off them, every last penny. You heard that Detective Chief Inspector Jones, didn't you? The flipping cheek of them.'

'Hey hang on here, that had nothing to do with me, I was risking my life to save you two from that gang.'

'Yes, sorry Ross, I know and we really appreciate it don't we Harriet?'

Harriet nodded, 'Yes, very much so, thank you Ross.'

'They're slick these lads, constantly shifting around, going underground, we think they've got plenty of contacts holding cover for them. They're well protected, makes it very difficult for us especially with the nature of the crime. We're trying to co-operate with the polizia in Italy but we've too much else going on, this is something we haven't been able to prioritize,' Detective Jones informed them. He turned to Ross, 'We'll need you to give evidence Ross, their actions have taken a nasty turn, we need to step it up now, get them caught and put away.'

He stood, lifting his cup to finish his tea. 'I'll just have a word with the lads on the boat, I think you need to get some security service in there, at least for a couple of nights. Is there anywhere else you could moor her, a bit more secure?'

'I might possibly get her berthed at the sailing club, I'll have a word with Tarquin, they're bringing the big boats in just now. It would be pretty hard to hi-jack her from that lot.'

'Excellent, do that, must go, get the forensics team onto the boat as soon as poss. I'll see you shortly Ross. He gave him his card, 'Phone this number on

Monday so we can bring you in for questioning. I'd allow the whole morning if I were you.'

Ross Farquerhart pushed his spectacles back up his nose, nodded and thanked him. Harriet and Tricia signalled their relief to see the back of him.

Mr. Sanderson looked at his watch. 'The wedding party will be motoring towards the sea by now. Well done Harriet, not only did you berth her magnificently you left room for the motor launch to tie up alongside. I'll get onto security right away. Thank goodness this event hasn't impinged on the newly-weds, though I'll feel happier when they're up and away. He looked at his watch again, leaving Anglesey around 16:00 hours. A while to go yet.'

Harriet smiled, yet again absorbing the compliment with utmost delight, willing this to be the breakthrough she so desperately needed. She wondered about Barry, whether or not he'd made any progress in his search for Amber, knowing full well Mr. Sanderson's need to have the whole heartbreaking affair resolved would always take priority over her.

Chapter 90

'Right Andy, we're on a mission. We need to get back down to Plymouth but not before I've had another word with the sergeant down at Stetmead, he's going to find it in his best interests to cooperate.'

'Yes, it was some find that but you can hardly threaten him in the hope you'll get hold of the money. It will probably take years to go through the due course of action, you know what these procedural committees can be like.'

Barry tossed his hair back, staring at the shoppers gathering pace in the precinct. 'No, that can wait, though I've every intention of mentioning it. I think I'll give him a bell, see how he's fixed for a trip down there.'

He lifted the phone. 'On secondment,' Barry, exasperated cleared his throat. 'How long for? … Three months you say? Right thanks, if you can get a message to him saying Barry Giordano phoned, get him to give me a call back on this number will you? Thanks.'

'Won't one of the others do?' Andy said, sensing his deep frustration.

'No, it needs to be him, think about it Andy, the money can wait but I'm not letting go of an opportunity to secure it. He was the one dealing with my painting remember?'

Andy nodded, knowing Barry would take as long as it needed in order to get it right.

Chapter 91

Ross Farquerhart piled into the taxi whilst Harriet and Tricia made their excuses deciding they'd prefer a quiet evening at Harriet's place.

'Yes indeed, quite understandable, though I insist on driving you back myself,' Mr. Sanderson said, glancing at their bare feet as he ushered them from the library. I'll get Clive to bring your things back, presumably your shoes and bags etc. are still on the boat? I don't wish to disturb anything until it's undergone the forensics.'

'Oh that's a point, the front door key's in my handbag.'

'Ah not to worry Harriet, Molly has confided in me as to where she leaves the spare keys, I do recall there is a back door key to your house on the ring.'

Safely in, Mr. Sanderson stood in the doorway. 'I must get back but if you two would feel more comfortable I'll pop back tonight, Mac Lyons will totally understand.'

'No, no, we'll be alright, thanks. You've that large dinner party going on, you'll need to be there until late hosting it all. Rapping Hammer doesn't know I live here, I should think they're probably well into hiding by now.'

'Well that's very helpful Harriet but don't forget I'm just a phone call away. Oh and it's been some time since you both have eaten, I'll get Mrs. Harris to put something together for you. Mr. Swift will drop it by.' With a smile he swept away their gratitude.

'Flop out Tricia, oh let's have a glass of wine, what a day! We deserve this.'

Tricia sat on the sofa amazed at the view from the lounge windows. She couldn't get over how the interiors reflected Joris's house. Immediatley understood why Harriet was so happy there.

'Come on Tricia, just a few nibbles while we're waiting, help yourself, golly it's been a day. That taxi guy was certainly a bad omen this morning but gosh we had no idea what was ahead.'

Tricia agreed, making herself comfortable, wondering how Clive was getting on, after all she'd given him free rein with Belinda Oxfordshire today.

'Your baby alright do you think Harriet? You took a massive tumble on his quay.'

Harriet smiled, 'It's fluttering away now Tricia, must be a tough one this.'

Tricia laughed, 'Do you know Harriet, I'm wondering if I might be pregnant after all. Although that test said I wasn't I only had a very short period last time and I was due yesterday but nothing happened. That's why I was going to make Clive think I was, I couldn't explain all that on the boat.'

'Golly Tricia, did you not try testing again?'

'Well no I didn't Harriet, I never got chance what with all that's been goin` on.'

'I've got a couple of spare testing kits Tricia, I was forever testing to see if I was pregnant, I only had to be a day late to use them. It wasn't that long ago so they'll be OK, you're more than welcome if you want to use them.'

Tricia spluttered on her wine. 'Thanks Harrriet, I'll just finish this and give it a try. Isn't this just what I need to get my Clive back? If I was expecting there would be no messing about getting a divorce from Bob.'

Chapter 92

Bob picked up the envelope franked Broadbent, Rudey, Essex & Co. Solicitors & Commissioners for Oaths. In two short months the divorce was through. Tricia wasn't wong about the influence her pregnancy would have in ensuring her availability for marriage.

'Good riddance to that one,' he said out loud, then swallowed hard on the thought she would be taking the kids with her. He thought about Belinda Oxfordshire, my he was going up in the world. Now he could marry her though no one was more surprised than him when she'd accepted his proposal.

They'd been dining out, Belinda having made no headway with Clive whatsoever at the PM's daughter's wedding decided she'd had enough of being on the shelf and would make good with Bob having had her fill of false starts from those less down to earth. She was more than ready!

The waiter lit the candle, instantly flickering seductive light across the pristine white tablecloth. Bob had ordered the wine, barely tasted it before giving his approval, unable to take his eyes away from Belinda who looked particularly ravishing that evening.

She smiled across knowing if he didn't propose first she'd do it herself. She'd entice him with her wealth, reassure him she couldn't have children, speak of Mummy and Daddy and of how they'd always wanted to buy her a luxuriously large house upon the occasion of her marriage. Besides she considered Bob to be a good-looking guy, he wasn't bad in bed either, oh yes she was quite sure her parents would approve.

They left the restaurant beaming, in the event not sure who had proposed to who, though Bob convinced himself he'd got there first. 'New wife comes with seven camels and two horses and wow, a huge house! Oh wouldn't he just show Tricia she wasn't the only one could get in with the Sanderson nobs.

His thoughts broke as the phone rang, he was expecting Mark to call in today. He was pleased he'd found a new partner, considered his mate Mark had had a pretty rough deal regarding Joris Sanderson and Harriet. He was certainly looking forward to meeting this new love in his life.

'Hi Mark, yep come round any time you like. Great, five minutes then, see you. Cheers!'

He grabbed some mugs and filled the kettle, switching it on just as the doorbell rang.

'Come in, it's been a long time. Great to see you mate.'

They punched each other's shoulders. 'On your own?' Bob queried.

'No, it's just that Sasha's gone on to the house. Did you hear via Tricia we already had a buyer waiting in the wings? An Avril Moss and her partner whose name escapes me just at the minute.'

'No but that's great, I hope we get rid of this place as quickly.'

'Getting divorced then you and Tricia?'

'Got divorced, Mark, letter's just come through this morning.'

'Well I hope things work out for you Bob, you've taken some stick, as I have since Sanderson opened that business.'

'Here, sit down, how do you take your coffee these days? I'll tell you the whole tale.

They sat and chatted, Mark hardly able to believe how similar their circumstances were. They could have talked for ever, but he stood, finally looking at his watch. 'I'd better be getting back to the house, Sasha will be wondering where I've got to especially as I'll be leaving her again, I want to pay Harriet a visit this afternoon.'

Chapter 93

Harriet, six months pregnant, had been dreading this visit. She wasn't able to do much with regard to getting the house at The Willows sorted. Two weeks after she'd leapt from the boat to the quay she'd experienced a threatened miscarriage and refusing to go anywhere near the hospital Mr. Sanderson had insisted on complete bed rest. She was recovering now and the baby was gently kicking, letting them know all was well. This was irksome having that Sasha woman cleaning and going through her house. OK there was a rush, Avril's baby was due any time now as her mother had never failed to remind her. 'Violet is most concerned Avril moves in before the baby arrives, Harriet,' she had said. 'Can't you try harder to move it all along?'

'It's all in the hands of the solicitors Mummy,' Harriet had replied, still unable to bring herself to tell her she had another grandchild due in March. It was a couple of months since she'd last seen her and she wanted to know her future was secure with Mr. Sanderson before she said anything. The arrangement was far more complicated than she'd realised; the legal side of Mr. Sanderson footing half the cost of the house to enable Mark to move on. This left Avril and Frazer effectively operating on a shared ownership basis, which they were pleased enough to accept.

Mr. Sanderson had been pleasant enough with Harriet though frustrated Rapping Hammer and his gang were still on the loose. He didn't like that one bit. Harriet had taken maternity leave sooner than anticipated due to the threatened miscarriage, Mr. Sanderson had insisted on it but it had of course left him pretty much running the school single handed, save for Enid Frost. 'If ever there was a reliable woman, she's it,' he'd said time and again. Still, the supply deputy would be starting in January, there was only three weeks to go now to the end of term. His biggest frustration was Harriet, refusing point blank to go for pre-natal care. He was doing his best for her and had resorted to registering her as one of his private patients but naturally he didn't have the facilities to enable the standard checks. He was just hoping and praying all would be well.

Harriet heard the bell chime, nervously crossing the hall to answer it. It had been some time since she and Mark had met.

'Hi Hat, can I come in?'
'Yes of course Mark.' He pecked her cheek.
'Can I get you anything?'

'No thanks, Sasha and I have just had lunch out, but thanks all the same.' He looked around, 'Nice place you have here.'

'Yes, I just love it Mark.'

'Pretty decent of old Joris to bale out Avril Moss and her partner.'

'Well yes, once the takeaway went broke there was no chance of them paying for the place right out. Avril's parents have stumped up the rest.'

'Pretty tough for them that Hat. Still at least they'll have a roof over their heads.'

The initial discomfort between them gradually eased. She looked across at him, glad they were still friends, pleased he'd finally found someone to take him beyond his marriage phobia.

'Have you found your dream home then?' Harriet asked.

'We certainly have, this has all come together really well, couldn't have been better timing.'

'Well tell me all about it. Where is it Mark?'

'Now you won't believe this Harriet, they're moving me back. They've given me my old job back. Well not my old job they're making me CEO down there.'

'Gosh congratulations, you've done well, very well in a relatively short space of time.'

'Thanks Hat, now I promise this hasn't anything to do with me but Sasha loves this place. Oh she can't get enough of the river opening out to the sea.'

'You what Mark?' Harriet declared rapidly trying to prepare for what was coming next.

'Yes you've guessed Harriet, have you been past lately, it's got the "Under Offer" sign on the board?'

'No Mark, oh no Mark, not the house two doors away from Mr. Sanderson?'

'You got it Hat, I was hardly likely to be commuting each day from Basingstoke. What's more Claire and Rachael are moving up, too, you know it's always been on the cards. Got the call late last night, they said they'd been trying to phone you but couldn't get an answer.'

Harriet remembered being instructed by Mr. Sanderson not to even answer the phone, no wonder they'd given up trying. She was pleased they'd tried to tell her first.

'Wow this is good news, such good news, I'll phone them later. So where are they looking to live?'

'Are you ready for this Harriet?'

'No but go on anyway.'

'Just a bit further down the lane from ours, they're buying that large house that was split into two, the one that slopes down to the river. They did try to see you but no one at home.'

Instinctively Harriet hugged him. 'Oh no, I'll get on to them. Oh Mark I'm so pleased they'll be near!'

'And what about me Hat, are you pleased we'll be so close?'

'More to the point Mark what about Sasha, I can't believe she'd want to live this close to me?'

'She doesn't know,' said Mark grinning. 'It's the only house she wants, she's set her heart on it and she wouldn't take any "buts" from me.'

Harriet gasped.

'That's me all over Hat and I'm not going to change now.'

'You're the end Mark, you don't know what trouble you could be storing up for yourself with that one.'

He shrugged his shoulders, dismissing it all with a grin.

'Anyway, you're looking good, baby OK? Fixed a wedding date with old Joris yet?'

'No not yet Mark, but I'm sure it won't be long. Anyway, never mind me have *you* fixed a date yet?'

'Not yet Hat, not yet. You know me, I don't like being rushed.'

'Oh you can say that again Mark, what are you like?'

His grin widened, 'Must be off Hat, give my love to the girls when you phone tonight.'

He gave her a quick hug coupled with his usual peck on the cheek.

'It's almost going to be like old times around here.' He touched the side of his nose. 'Keep it under your hat, Hat for the time being...' He broke off laughing.

'There's nothing much to stop us still being a Hat and a pair of Glovers.'

She waved him off, stunned by his news. Knew he'd never change and deep in her heart she knew she never wanted him to. Deep in her heart she was pleased he'd be living so close. Always the clown, she wondered at his remarkable inability to grasp the reality of the situation. Wondered what her mother would finally make of it all. Smiling she closed the door. At least Mark wasn't her concern any more.

Chapter 94

'It looks like I've got away with it George,' Frances Glover suddenly declared over the breakfast table.

'Got away with what Frances, what are you on about now?'

'You know, me accidentally spilling the beans to the press over the PM's daughter's wedding date. Anyway according to James and Geraldine Harriet and that common girl didn't go. Oh they started out but James didn't have a clue where they finished up.'

'Hang on a minute Frances you haven't mentioned this before, about the press I mean.'

'Well I've been worried about ending up in court, but the whole thing appears to have gone quiet, thank goodness. You know you just can't trust these journalists George. Have your guts for garters as soon as look at you, they would.'

'Your wising up at last Frances, always best to keep quiet until you've considered the consequences of what you're about to say.'

'Well yes George, I'll take note of that in future. Now where was I? I'm sure Harriet's alright. Joris would have told James if she'd suddenly gone missing. No she's alright, little minx deciding not to answer the phone. I phoned a few times last week and the week before. If I can't get her next time I really think we should go down there. I got her new address from James. You know George I think we are going to have to seriously consider moving down there, you know one of those bungalows near that little grocery store they've opened. I've been online and there's a lovely one, you can see the sea from the garden. Oh and before you say we can't afford it we can. It's a good price, just needs a tiny spot of work doing, that's all. I've spoken to that very nice man at Bryce Rae Roberts and he's coming to give us a valuation this afternoon. Harriet's going to get such a surprise when I tell her.'

'Not half as much as me Frances, you do what you like. I'm not moving. Don't go upsetting her with that, she's busy at that school you know being deputy head now. She's got a lot to deal with, not to mention that food bank place she's set up in there.'

'Oh we'll see about that George, she's my daughter, too and I'll tell her just what I like. I'll try again tonight and if she doesn't answer we'll be down there first thing in the morning.'

She paused to sprinkle more salt on the yolk of her softly boiled egg. Thought it better to move the conversation along.

'I can't tell you how pleased Mrs. Moss will be to see Avril move into Harriet's house. That poor girl set her heart on it you know. It was only Sir Joris chipping in with the cost enabled them to go ahead. Of course they're only in it because Violet's given over their life savings for their half but one day they hope to be in a position to buy it.'

'Good Frances, good, now lets hope Harriet gets her head round a wedding date. It's a wonder Joris hasn't given up on her.'

'Oh don't say that George, please don't say that. You know I've an inkling that common girl will beat her to it. Rumour has it she's been getting up to all sorts with that solicitor friend of Joris's. There'll be a divorce there, you mark my words! I just hope they've taken all that pink ribbon from the banister, those two. I'd never be able to look Violet straight in the eye if it gives Avril and her young man ideas. If her husband's got any sense it'll be divorce for that one and if Mr. Engells' got any sense he won't be picking up the pieces.'

Chapter 95

'I don't know how I could ever have thought you'd gone off me Clive,' Tricia mused, basking in the luxury of his new car. He reached to take her hand. 'Oh my sweet petal, the minute I set eyes on you I knew you were the girl for me. Of course I was otherwise engaged then but I had sensed that relationship was about to fall apart. Oh no, my sweetest, I can't believe the way my life has turned round.' Feeling his eyes misting he swallowed hard before continuing. 'After all these years I am to become a father, the father of our sweet child. It was meant to be Patricia, simply meant to be.'

Tricia breathed out a contented sigh. 'Yes I know Clive and I'm now single.'

'Not for long young lady, you're going to look simply beautiful in that delightful white dress laced with pink ribbon and an early marriage will ensure you're going to look as slim as you do now.'

Smiling she twisted the engagement ring round on her finger, wondering what kind of wedding ring she would choose.

'In fact I think we'll call into the vicarage after we've viewed the house. Three weeks I believe is all that's required to call the banns. Let's see if we can't make this a new year wedding.'

'Oh Clive that would be lovely. You know I'm so happy we'll be living near to Harriet. She's such a special friend and we've been through a lot together and with us both expecting we'll have even more to share. We'll push our prams down the lanes and as the babies grow they'll play together. Oh it's like a dream, I never thought I could be as happy as this.'

Clive smiled as the car purred them down the lanes.

'Oh yes, I keep forgetting which lane we turn into. It's the one behind Harriet's, I should remember because we can just see her chimney from the back bedrooms.'

'We did collect all the carpet samples, petal, didn't we?'

'Oh yes Clive I'm sure we did. I like the shades of the sea theme, like Harriet and Mr. Sanderson have both got in theirs.'

'So do I, honey, but if you wanted the whole place carpeted in shocking pink that would be fine, too.'

Tricia giggled, shrugging her shoulders as she drew up her knees to clasp them.

'Do you think they'll get it fitted before Friday Clive? Oh it's moving in day and I can't wait!'

'As long as we get back to them today petal, have no worries.'

'I never do when I'm with you Clive, you know that.'

He changed down as they drove past Molly's place on the corner, preparing to make the next right turn.

'Yes we'll only be with Joris for three days. He's such a decent chap Patricia, nothing's too much trouble for him, ever.'

'A bit like my mum, she's taking the kids for a couple of months to let us settle down. Of course while Bob's still there selling the house they'll be staying there, too so she won't have it all to do.'

'No, quite, Patricia, I shall enjoy having children around the house. Plenty of space there if they want to lose themselves in computers and such like.'

'Oh you are so lovely Clive, they deserve better than they've been getting for a while now. They're very excited about living here.'

Clive smiled, to briefly scratch his head, this was certainly a first for him. At least Harriet's girls were grown up, Joris wouldn't be needing to take them on board.

'Right petal, this is it. My word it looks very grand.'

'Oh it is, it is Clive. I can't wait to show Harriet round.'

Chapter 96

Not long to Christmas. Harriet, six months pregnant, sat writing her cards, pausing every now and then to admire the view. She was happy to be away from school now, planning for the baby, turning the small bedroom into a nursery. Mr Sanderson couldn't have been more caring, seeing him each day, cooking the evening meal for them both. He'd given up suggesting they might eat at his to save her the work and as he'd noticed a remarkable improvement in her cookery skills, which could only be to the good, he'd let the idea lie. Besides he enjoyed being with her, pleased to see her settled and so very excited about their new baby.

With no mention of marriage Harriet let the idea go, there was no way she wanted to walk down the aisle looking as large as this and it wasn't going to get any better until after March 26th when she'd estimated their baby was due. No mention of Amber either, she'd not heard from Barry for a while now. Of course she knew they were busy getting "ab extra" off the ground, though she was hoping he wasn't too busy as to leave the search on hold.

'Time for a coffee,' she said to the cat, 'Oh yes and a nibble for you Pepper since you've been so good staying here not being a nuisance for Mummy. Oh the doorbell Pepper, let's just answer it. Not Mummy and Daddy I hope.'

'Mummy, Daddy, do come in. I was just about to make a coffee. Come in, this is my new place, brilliant isn't it? Look I'm sorry I haven't returned your calls Mummy, I've been so busy trying to ease the load for Mr. Sanderson, especially leaving before Christmas.'

'Leaving Harriet, oh my dear me the size of you, oh let me sit down. Harriet you're expecting a baby and you never said.'

'Look Mummy it's not like that, you wouldn't want to know how things have been, it was just something I needed to keep to myself.'

'When's the wedding Harriet, or is that it? Is that why you've been stalling all this time? Don't tell me it's that good for nothing ex of yours. That mess of a guy who left you standing at the church didn't leave you expecting as well?'

'No Mummy it's not him, it's Mr. Sanderson's baby.'

Harriet watched the mix of hurt, anger, joy twitch through her face to settle in utter perplexity, speechless she turned to George.

'Now Frances, calm down, we know Harriet's had one trauma after another in a quite a short time. By the look of her she's been pregnant all the way through. She deserves a pat on the back for dealing with it all, coming through the way she has.' He turned to Harriet, 'Our congratulations love, your Mother's just a bit shocked, she'll get over it.'

'Oh I am over it George and that board's going up tomorrow. Harriet's going to need a hand with this baby, especially when she goes back to work, there's never been a better time to get moved, they do know we want it you know.' She shifted on her chair.

'Come here love,' she said, elevating herself, unable to speak, her eyes filled with tears. 'Oh don't Mummy you'll have me crying next,' said Harriet dazed, not daring to believe what she'd just heard.

'We're thrilled for you both Harriet, you do know that, don't you?' said Frances, sinking into the sofa by the window.

'Yes of course Mummy, of course I do.'

'You know Harriet, if you have a daughter she's going to be looking just like you, beautiful,' her mother said pointing to the picture on the mantelpiece of Harriet when she was a little girl.

'Do you know what you're having, or do you want to wait for the surprise?'

'No, I don't, just want it to be well with all its fingers and toes.'

'Well Harriet, if it is a girl what will you call her?'

'Amber, Mummy, we'll call her Amber.'

Chapter 97

Harriet showed them out, at least pleased she'd squared things with her mother regarding her pregnancy. The delight at the prospect of grand parenting Sir Joris's child had proved overwhelming and anxious to offload the news to James and Paul she was gone before Harriet had had chance to tell her to keep it under her hat. Gosh she needed to phone them the minute they got home, she didn't want Mr. Sanderson off the planet with rage.

She dialled, no luck. The rest of the morning, lunch time, then finally before tea time her mother answered the phone.

'Oh Harriet but you can't hide your pregnancy.'

'Mr. Sanderson may not want the whole world to know he's the father just yet, Mummy.'

'Surely everyone knows?'

'No, very few know I'm pregnant actually, Mummy, I've been here most of the time. I left school early.'

'Oh dear Harriet, I'd better phone them right now, I'm sorry I never thought about that. I should have realised, he's going to want you married before he tells his family and friends.'

Worried sick she went to check the meal, panicking as to whether or not to say anything to Mr. Sanderson when he came in. Flustered she glanced at the clock, stepping backwards catching the cat's saucer to go skidding into the kitchen table, hitting her head as she crashed to the hard ceramic tiled floor.

Unconscious she didn't hear the key turn in the door. This was unusual for Harriet not to be there. Mr. Sanderson marched straight to the kitchen, turning sick to see Harriet lying there, out cold, Pepper meowing up against her pale face.

A doctor, he knew the routine; she became aware in the ambulance as it screamed through the country to the town. With her stomach cramping violently she feared the onset of a miscarriage.

'No, no, you'll be alright Harriet, the baby's almost six months now just try to calm down.'

'I don't want to stay in there.'

'You won't need to Harriet, they'll check you over, that's all.'

Harriet closed her eyes screwing her face to the spasms of pain hoping he was right.

Chapter 98

'Thanks for the lift home Clive, I'll be staying with Harriet for a couple of days if you wouldn't mind passing the message on to Mrs. Harris,' Mr. Sanderson said as he helped Harriet out of the car.

'Right Joris, just on the end of this if you need me at all,' Clive replied, reaching for his phone. 'You'll be alright Harriet,' he said, winking at her.

'Now just take it easy Harriet, it was a nasty fall but you're OK and the baby's fine, so try not to worry, yes?' She tried to smile banking on Mr. Sanderson being right.

'But I am worried, Mummy called today and she was having to phone James and Paul back not to mention the baby. I knew she'd tell everyone, she couldn't get away quick enough once she'd recovered from the shock.'

He propped up her pillow, gathered her to him, her head on his chest as he stroked her hair away from her face.

'Don't forget you're on maternity leave Harriet, the whole world knows you're expecting.'

'Yes maybe now they've realised, but they don't know whose baby it is.'

He smiled. 'Harriet just as soon as you're ready we'll get married, I'm only waiting for you to name the day, so what difference is it going to make?'

'Hey, now stop it, you've done this to me once before, remember? It's not something to cry about you know.'

'No I'm hap, happy, just so happy Mr. Sand...'

'Pardon me, there's only once condition, you call me by my name, remember?'

She coloured to that pretty shade of pink he loved.

'Joris, yes Joris, just give me time.'

'Crikey Harriet how much time do you need?' He laughed.

She placed her hand across her stomach, that pain again, she smiled deciding it was just the aftermath. Didn't mention it, wasn't going back to the hospital to spend the night there. She managed just a little of what she'd prepared for dinner, insisting Joris went down to eat his. Fidgeting she tried to shake the next contraction away. 'It's just a reaction, it'll settle down,' she told herself, lying in bed as the evening wore on, relieved to hear Mr. Sanderson coming back upstairs.

'Are you alright Harriet?' Intense concern in his voice.

'No Mr. Sanderson no, if feels like my waters have just broken.'

'Oh crikey Harriet, just lie still. Let me get Clive to bring all the kit over.' He lifted the phone by the side of the bed.

'Quick, quickly Mr. Sanderson, then she stopped; panting, creased with pain she cried out.

'Sorry Harriet, I'm afraid these are going to get in the way.' He lifted the covers, slipped away her lace pants. His heart pounding, he set her in delivery position, stroked her forehead, mopped her tears; crying, panting, pushing she felt his strong hands against her. 'One last push Harriet, come on the same strength you found to berth "Mare Libertas". The head's nearly through, deep breath now *push!* He swallowed hard to the misting of his eyes as he eased away the baby's head, the tiny purple body waxed, smudged white with vernix, sliding away into his hands. 'It's a girl Harriet, we have a tiny daughter and she's breathing well, wow what a squawk from such a tiny one.'

'Just the one then?' Harriet smiled in relief.

'Yes indeed, only one, just as well in these circumstances.'

He lay the baby between Harriet's legs then dashed down stairs to answer the door, fighting hard the tears now well and truly blurring his vision.

'She's had it Clive, we've a healthy though very premature little girl.'

He grabbed his case, rushed back to Harriet, leaving Clive dazed, calling the emergency services, standing in the lounge with an assortment of equipment at his feet.

'Alright Harriet, thank God she's holding her own breathing, now just let me clamp and cut the cord.'

All done, Harriet lay against the pillows, tears streaming down her face, now nestling in her arm the tiniest baby she'd ever seen.

'She's so tiny, she's beautiful, she's ours. With all my heart I want to thank you.' Yet again in his throat, that lump, almost threatening his breathing, well that's how it felt.

'My darling Harriet, it's me that needs to be thanking you. I know I'm impossible at times but I love you with such depth I can't describe. My precious amber butterfly, in my hand at last.' He looked down at them both, smiling. 'Amber Harriet Sanderson, and she's beautiful just like you, "the most beautiful woman in the world", he said proudly.

Chapter 99

Friday, the first day of the Christmas holidays, Caroline Worsnip sat on the train annoyed and frustrated her plans with Belinda Oxfordshire had gone right out of the window. She couldn't see how a marriage made out of sheer desperation would work anyway. At least she had her job back, that was something, but wasn't too sure about buying a house on that new development any more, there didn't seem much point having lost her potential to keep close to Joris via Belinda. She'd hoped to get him so hooked on looking for Amber she'd be able to talk him into marriage. After all, in her mind, that's the way it should have been all along for the three of them. No, she'd now need to rethink her plans, deciding they would still need to remain good friends, at least this would be better than nothing. Bob Harrington would always be second best to Joris Sanderson, she knew Joris would never be totally out of her life. She looked at her watch, four minutes past five, she'd be there very soon. She could hardly wait to see Aunty Sharon to tell her the news. She was good Aunty Sharon, she'd be able to help her reformulate her plans.

At four minutes past five, Barry, Andy and the sergeant had a little less than twenty minutes to go.

'I appreciate you hanging on for me Barry with this one, it's been one of those we've been unable to get a real grip of.'

'Favours for favours, that's what keeps the wheels turning, especially in our business,' Barry replied, pushing the new Lamborghini down the last stretches of motorway as fast as it would go.

'As long as you're sure of the facts Barry, there's a big downside to this all going wrong.'

'As sure as I can be in this job, yes, I'm pretty damned sure about this one.'

They veered off the motorway just past Exeter on to the A38 speeding their way to Plymouth and Bramble Court, parking the car in a side-street to walk the short distance to No 1.

'Well you've not been here two minutes Caroline and it's those bloody double glazing people back again. Hang on I'll just give them what for.'

She strode down the narrow hall, swinging the door open in fury, then stopped in her tracks.

'We understand your niece a Miss Caroline Worsnip is part resident with you and is currently here. You are Sharon Hawker, am I correct?'

She nodded her head, having no choice but to let the sergeant and the other two men in.

'Eh I recognise you two, tried to sell me double glazing a few months ago. They can bugger off for a start. Right now!'

Barry pressed his ID at her, turning to Andy. 'We're both from the same unit, so don't even go there.'

Caroline waited nervously in the dining room dreading what was coming next.

'Mummy, mummy, mummy, you've come.'

A blonde haired blue eyed little girl rushed past them, flinging herself at her mummy as she hurried out to meet her. 'Aunty Sharon mummy's here!'

'We need a separate room, can we use this, if you would leave us to the interviewing please.'

Caroline took Amber back upstairs, knowing full well the game was up.

Now Sharon Hawker, if you would take a seat whilst I caution you. You are under arrest and anything you say may be taken down and used in evidence against you, do you understand?

She nodded, inside screaming at herself for going along with Caroline's hair-brained plan.

The interview passed through its initial standard procedure then came the crunch. 'Now let me get this clear, a child went missing from the local nursery Miss Worsnip's child attended by the name of Ember Anderson and the two of you saw it as an opportunity to convince Sir Joris Sanderson it was his daughter.'

Sharon Hawker looked down.

'Now what did you understand Miss Worsnip's motive to be?'

'He never came near, hardly, tried to pay her off when he wouldn't marry her. She's in love with him, desperately in love with him and she'd do anything to get him back, to marry him. That's why she got her old job back at the department store, so she could suss him out, get him helping her to search for Amber.'

The sergeant scratched his head. 'I see, knowing full well the child was here all the time being cared for by you.'

'Yes, but she had no choice, you must know what it's like to be desperately in love,' she said weighing him up, 'But then maybe you don't.'

'Was this supposed disappearance ever reported to the police?'

'No, we're not stupid.'

'I'd call it pretty stupid trying to convince the child's father his daughter was missing when she wasn't.'

'Caroline wanted to frighten him into getting their relationship back on track.'

'And supposing she had achieved this, what plans had you afoot for informing him the child had been found, or was it the intention the child should live permanently here?'

Sharon Hawker hung her head. 'I love children, if it had worked out that way, fine. I never married, never had any of my own. But yes that was the intention at least until they were married. We would have told him a private detective had found her not far away, or something like that, we'd have worked something out when the time came.'

'Incredible, absolutely incredible.'

She hung her head again.

'Mr Giordano would you like to continue with questioning?'

He opened his briefcase to bring out the portrait of Amber Harriet had retrieved from Mr. Sanderson's wardrobe.

'Tell me what you know about this. Where and how did you come by it?'

She shifted on her chair, clearing her throat before speaking.

'Caroline and I had it painted. Caroline sent it to Mr. Sanderson to make him want to be with her, that's all it was.'

'No, that's not so is it Miss Hawker? He reached into his briefcase again, 'Now tell me exactly how you came by it.' She coloured almost to purple, could feel her heart racing.

'We bought it from an antique shop not too far from here. It looked just like Amber that's why we sent it to him.'

Barry slid a further portrait from its wrapping to show her.

'But it's identical, have you photocopied that?' She pointed to the original sat on the table next to him.

'No this is a reproduction, I bought this in an art shop in Amsterdam. You were fortunate enough to buy the original for your scheme not having any idea of the significance it had for Joris Sanderson.'

'Why, what do you mean?'

'How could the remarkable likeness in this painting to her father be merely a coincidence?'

She sat looking perplexed, shaking her head.

'Joris Sanderson's ancestry is Dutch. Historically his mother is of royal extraction and this here is an original portrait of his great grandmother when she was a little girl. It's a popular piece, very famous over there, hence the reproduction.' He picked up the original waving it at her. 'By sheer coincidence you have returned a piece of ancestry to him, no wonder he felt an iffinity with it. Now is there anything else you can add to this sorry tale?'

'No.' He looked across to the sergeant, no more questions, I'm finished.

'Please go through will you and send in Miss Worsnip,' the sergeant requested.

With such identical answers the sergeant had no doubt they were both in it together. A pair of foolish women, headstrong, each with their own motives for carrying it through. For the moment he was racking his brains wondering exactly how to charge them. He turned to Caroline Worsnip again. 'I'll pass you over to Mr. Giordano, I'm sure he'd like to continue the questioning.'

'I understand you were recently accused of shoplifting from the department store in which you worked and lost your job, albeit for a very short time.'

'Yes,' that's true, replied Caroline trying to remain calm. 'It was not my fault, it was all due to Harriet Glover bringing that stupid cat of hers along in a cat basket. I thought there was a baby in it at first, because we had one left in the store a while ago. I insisted on checking inside and this cat jumped out causing chaos, ending up with people colliding. The perfume stand crashed to the floor and this woman with a little boy demanded compensation for getting caught up in it so I gave her a couple of bottles of perfume. That's all it was. Roger Boxsox hit the roof and dismissed me.'

'I see,' Barry waited, let her finish.

'Yes it was Joris Sanderson that got me my job back, used his influence to get me promoted. He must still think something of me to do that. He must want me around otherwise he'd have washed his hands of the whole thing.'

'Now what makes you so sure it was Joris Sanderson? Don't you think it rather strange he would have any influence in the company at all, let alone ensure you ended up with Roger Boxsocks' job?'

'What do you mean?'

'Well let's put it this way, do you recall a certain Mr. Knight, Saville Knight to be precise?'

She paled then blushed hard almost to her fingertips.

'Yes you might well blush Miss Worsnip. Is it correct you were having an affair with this tall, blonde haired blue eyed gentleman, your Chief Executive Officer during your supposed relationship with Joris Sanderson?'

She sat sullen, refusing to answer.

'Come now, I can play back the interview if you prefer.'

'No, no, it was a kind of casual relationship with him.'

'Not too casual for sexual intercourse Miss Worsnip? Now whose baby was it you were carrying at the time? This is something we will establish so the truth now please.'

'Saville is her father, I do know that. Joris was skiing, abroad at the time. I knew it wasn't his.'

'And Saville is patently not aware he has a daughter?'

'No, I never told him, I wanted Joris to think he was the father. It was Joris I was in love with, he'd never have known.'

'Do you not think he's capable of counting to nine Miss Worsnip? Nine months, why do you suppose he couldn't work this out for himself?'

'Because I gave him a false birth date. I'd had her, he wasn't around so I didn't tell him until she was two weeks old. As soon as he came back from skiing we made love. He never thought to question it.

'What a web of lies and deceit you've woven Miss Worsnip, you've been fair to no one least of all the child. I've finished,' Barry Giordano declared. 'I'll pass you back to the sergeant.'

The sergeant stood for a moment wondering what to do. In all his life he'd never come across such a mess. He thought of taking advice, though as far as he knew there was no precedence, there were so many different charges he could make.

'Mummy, Mummy, Mummy,' they could hear Amber crying at the door. 'Let me in Mummy.' He opened it, brought her in along with Sharon, watched the child go straight to her mother's arms clinging to her neck.

'Barry get Saville Knight on the phone will you, I want a word.'

Caroline could feel her legs turn to jelly.

'Right you're in London, how soon can you get here? Good we'll wait.' He turned to Barry and Andy, 'He's flying into Exeter as soon as he can, I need to factor his response into all this. We'll be outside in the car, two at a time mind. One of us will cover until he gets here.' He turned to Barry, 'Find the local takeaway will you, fish and chips for three, no make it five. And what about you, do you like chips?' Amber shook her head, 'Yes please and sosidges.'

* * * * *

In just under three hours Saville Knight rang the doorbell, not knowing what to expect.

'Is this my daddy?' Amber sprang forth. 'Will you be my daddy, pleeese?'

Saville Knight lifted her up, swung her round, looking across to her mummy.

'Is this why I'm here Caroline?'he asked.

Tears flooding her cheeks she shook her head in the affirmative. 'I'm sorry Sav, I couldn't bring myself to tell you.'

'That's it, no more to the story, from my point of view,' the sergeant declared. 'Work out your daughter's welfare with Miss Worsnip here, Mr. Knight. We'll be instructing social services to take the case over. On this occasion we'll be making no charges, what Joris Sanderson chooses to do will be up to him. I'm not doing this for either of you, I'm doing it for Amber as I appreciate there was no mal-intent, serious though it is to deprive a child of her own father and vice versa. The child has been well looked after but she needs her mother to be on hand right here and not behind bars. As long as no one chooses to prosecute the case will be registered without trial but I will advise social services you will both be serving a probationary period of at least two years under their jurisdiction. Now I'm sure Mr. Knight you'll be able to fix Miss Worsnip up with a job closer to home?'

Barry stepped forward, 'Here Amber, have you been looking for this?' He opened his briefcase to pass her a tiny worn teddy bear. She grabbed it hugging it tightly to her chest, then smiling she pressed it against her cheek. 'Thank you,' she beamed, 'I lost him for ever and ever.' He turned to Caroline Worsnip, 'On your front path, it was all the evidence we needed.'

'Well done guys,' the sergeant declared from the back of the Lamborghini. 'Such stupid women, I had to act in the best interest of the little girl though I'll still be able to report and close the case as found. Thanks guys it'll be great to get Sanderson off my back for good.'

Chapter 100

'Christmas eve together, Harriet, this is simply the tops and Amber doing so well. My word it's amazing how well she's chubbing up. She's gaining at least an ounce and a half each day. It won't be too long before she's home with us, here.'

Harriet tucked herself into his chest, warm contented, happy, taking from her finger the plain gold ring he'd very first given her, inscribed with those immortal words "*'our perfect day' ne obliviscaris JS*'" She read them out and he smiled her that most gorgeous of smiles.

'Ah the phone, I'll get it Harriet,' he volunteered.

'It's OK I'll get it. You know we had a Chrtistmas card from Barry this morning, I've got a feeling it might be him.'

Mr. Sanderson turned to his gin and tonic, 'When are we ever going to get this man out of our lives?' he asked himself, waiting what seemed forever for Harriet to return.

'He sends his best, but you're not going to believe this Mr. Sanderson, it's just so unbelievable. He said he'll come round in the New Year as he needs to fill you in.'

'Fill me in Harriet, if he's going to do it let him face me here and now!'

Harriet laughed, 'Look he's got to the bottom of the "Amber" affair, it seems Caroline Worsnip has been deceiving you all along. As it turns out a Mr. Saville Knight is actually Amber's father, she just wanted to marry you that was all.'

'Well I'll be damned, this is preposterous, I'm totally shocked though I always felt there was something not quite right about it. What about the portrait Harriet, how did that fit in?'

'Oh he didn't give any detail, just said he'd explain properly in the New Year. Oh and by the way he's found that horrible painting he did, there's a story behind that, too.'

'Well I never, I'm going to make a call back right now. I can't wait a fortnight to find all this out.' He beamed, topped up his G&T, taking it into the hall, Harriet wondering why he was back so soon.

'Did I hear you dial twice then Mr. Sanderson?'

'You certainly did, just letting Mrs. Harris know there'll be two more for Christmas dinner tomorrow.'

Harriet smiled, snuggled even closer. 'I know it's so very sad Amber was never your child, but I'm hoping for you "one day this will be pleasing to remember". He smiled taking the bangle from her wrist, 'Ah now it's your turn Harriet; "haec olim meminisse iuvabit". In all truth it already is, the tide's certainly turned for me.

My instincts never really took me to that child. It was something I didn't like in myself. Something I never understood.'

Hugging him tightly, she flooded with an overwhelming intensity of love for him, feeling she'd never quite taken on board the terrible position he'd been in these last three years.

'I'm so pleased you've invited them, I know Barry and Andy will love to join us all. Obviously they didn't have much planned for tomorrow.'

'Crikey it's the least I can do for those guys, they damned well deserve it! Besides I'm busting a gut for the whole story - as it happens they were both on their way out. Damned lucky I caught them.'

'Oh I see, I'm so glad you did.'

'Cheers Harriet, life couldn't be better!'

'Cheers Mr. er Joris, there's only one thing though,' she said fidgeting as the cat jumped between them, 'I want to lay Amber down, for myself.'

'You've already done that Harriet, the amber light's finally gone out, out of our lives for good. We've got the only Amber that was ever meant for us and it won't be too long before you can nurse her to sleep and lay her down yourself, if this thing will let you.' He laughed as the cat nuzzled hard into his hand. 'We're on green all the way now Harriet. Here's to Mr. & Mrs. Sanderson and family.'

She smiled, lifting the amber buttercup ring from her finger to read its inscription,

'You were wrong Mr. Sanderson "*'amor caucus est'*" means "love is blind". She turned to the cat.

'We said we'd see about that, didn't we Pepper?'

'OK so you both know better than me.' He laughed. 'I'm not complaining. Indeed a magnificent cause for celebration, now let me see, let me find the right words. Ah yes, "Et rursus aestus". I'll tell you what we'll commission a painting, yes, we'll get Barry to do it, we'll mark this wonderful time with a magnificent painting.'

'What of , what will it be of?'

He drew her closer, 'Ah "Et rursus aestus", Harriet, quite simply, "The Turn of the Tide".

The Turn of the Tide

Smooth dry sand
Resting in bands
Between the ebbing tide.
I cannot reach.
My thoughts stumble, as my feet
On firm ripples etched and left
Between running streams,
Fast flowing their moment away.
Time and sea at one,
Like lovers carving destiny into passion
For them no measure of loss.
Just seen in salt tears,
Falling pain to trickles,
Running their paths
In the sand to the sea.
Washed and tossed away,
Yet remains, at the turn of the tide
This measure of loss,
For me.

Margaret Henderson Smith

www.ingramcontent.com/pod-product-compliance
Lightning Source LLC
Chambersburg PA
CBHW071535260626
47170CB00002B/636